LORD EDGINGTON INVESTIGATES **ABROAD**

BOOK 3

THE ALPINE CHRISTMAS MYSTERY

A 1920s MYSTERY

BENEDICT BROWN

COPYRIGHT

This is a work of fiction. Names, characters, places, and incidents are either the product of the author's imagination or are used fictitiously. Any resemblance to actual persons, living or dead, is entirely coincidental.

Copyright © 2025 by Benedict Brown

All rights reserved. No part of this book may be reproduced or used in any manner without written permission of the copyright owner except for the use of quotations in a book review.

First edition September 2025

Cover design by **info@amapopico.com**

For my father, Kevin,
I hope you would have liked these books an awful lot.

LORD EDGINGTON'S GRAND TOUR

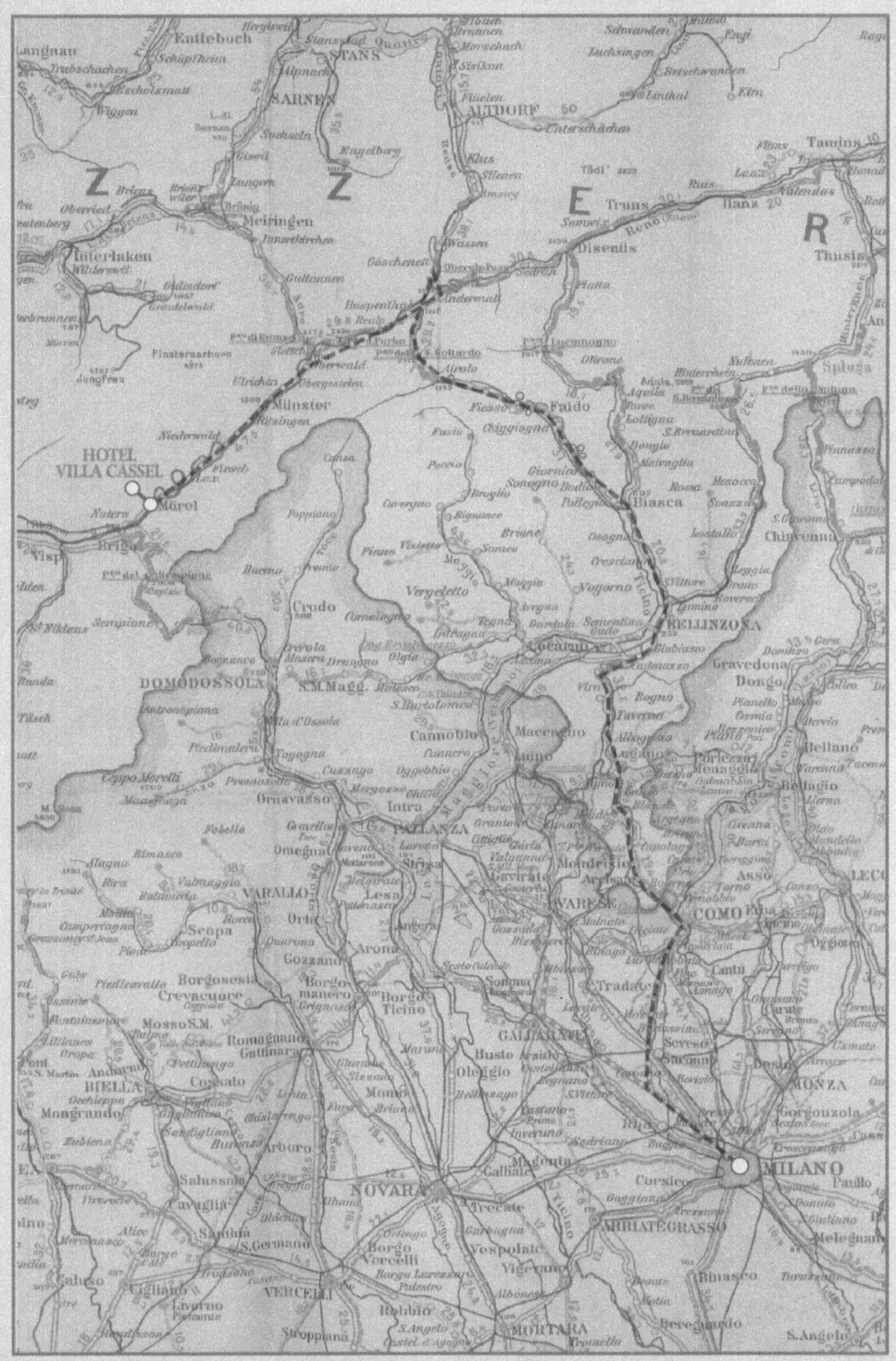

Milan, Italy to Hotel Villa Cassel, Valais, Switzerland

READER'S NOTE

This is the third *Lord Edgington Investigates Abroad* mystery, but all my Christmas releases are free of spoilers, so you don't have to have read any of the other books to enjoy them.

As it features an international cast of characters, there are tiny bits of foreign speech, most of which are unimportant, understandable in context, or they have footnotes to explain them. At the back, you'll find a list of any unusual words I've used. You'll also find a character list and chapters on my historical research and reasons for writing.

I hope the book makes you feel suitably Christmassy, puzzles you right to the last chapter, and that you absolutely love it!

CHAPTER ONE

I wasn't sure how I felt about spending Christmas in a city with very little chance of snow – which is my way of saying that I knew exactly how I felt, and I wasn't happy about it.

Milan obviously wasn't the problem. The city, like so many others we had visited in Italy, was majestic, and I had greatly enjoyed our time there. But after nearly six months away from my homeland, I craved the familiar. Perhaps that was the reason I had given so much importance to finding the perfect Christmas present for my grandfather.

"I think I had better make use of the facilities," we both said at the same time, and then we froze and looked at one another, evidently uncertain of what came next.

We were sitting outside Caffè Biffi, right in the centre of that temple to commerce known as Galleria Vittorio Emanuele II. If there is a more beautiful building on earth dedicated to the humble pastime of shopping, I am yet to hear of it. Above us, a great iron and glass dome rivalled the neighbouring cathedral's. It seemed to be suspended in space, and I had to marvel at the genius of architectural engineering that stopped such a weight from falling down at any moment. On either side of us, two glass-ceilinged arcades offered every kind of item you could desire. There was everything from famous hat shops to the finest *haute couture* (and other merchants who sold more than just clothing).

Of course, it wasn't the architecture or the fine offerings that interested us just then. It wasn't even the Christmas decorations, which had appeared soon after our arrival three weeks earlier, though I did admire the long chains of greenery that hung in boughs between the shops. No, we were busy trying to work out how to extricate ourselves from an awkward situation.

"Please, Christopher." Grandfather bowed his head and slowly wafted his hand. "I am in no hurry. You must go first."

"Yes…" I didn't sound sure of myself. "That's just what I'll do. I will go to the lavatory, and I will see you back here in, let's say… fifteen minutes."

He cocked his head to view me from a more perplexed angle, but he refrained from asking why I would need so long, and I hurried into the café's marble and wood-panelled interior. Once inside, I paused to look out of the window and, as soon as he was talking to the waiter, I nipped round to the far door and back out to the gallery.

The shop I needed was only a short distance away, but I had to cross the large, octagonal plaza at the centre of the building to get there. I once more paused to make certain that Grandfather wouldn't spot me, but he was paying for our drinks, and I knew I would be fine. There was only so long I could pretend to spend on a toilet without his worrying that I was ill, so I ran with all the energy I had to propel myself towards the Libreria Occhio. I had walked past this chamber of wonders any number of times that month, but always with my regular companion at my side, and it simply wouldn't do for him to catch a glimpse of what I wanted to buy.

Of course, what I wanted to buy for my grandfather was as much a mystery to me as it was to him. I pulled the heavy door open and had to wait as several well-dressed gentlemen paraded out of the bookshop, each tipping his top hat to me in turn. But then I was free to explore. It was a truly ramshackle and Carrollese establishment. I half expected to see the Cheshire Cat smiling down at me from one of the high shelves. O, but what shelves they were! You don't need Christmas decorations when you are surrounded by stack after stack of books. They provide their own kind of warmth and joy, and the very sight of them filled me with all the noblest feelings of Christmastide.

But I hadn't forged this clandestine plan to serve my own needs. I was there in search of the perfect gift for renowned detective, supportive grandfather, and all-round know-it-all, Lord Edgington of Cranley Hall. My eyes (and occasionally my fingers) went tripping over the shop's impressive stock, and I was half-tempted to find the very oldest tome on sale to buy for my mentor.

I soon located a shelf that was only accessible by one of the rather rickety wheeled ladders, which could be borrowed from behind the till. All the books there looked as though they had been printed before the invention of the printing press, but I realised that my Italian was so poor that I was just as likely to choose a volume on the importance of efficient sanitary systems in medieval Europe, as I was to find a great work of literature. So I kept looking.

There were piles of old journals, magazines and newspapers here and there on the mosaic floor, but those would never do. There were plenty of works on works of art, too, and each one looked like a work of art in itself, but Grandfather was very picky in his tastes. It was difficult to know whether he would prefer a book on Botticelli or a treatise on Titian.

And that's when I found it. On the wall between the large windows at the front of the shop, there was a selection of paintings. I did not get the impression that any of them were by well-known artists. The majority didn't have frames, for one thing, and they were terribly eclectic in their subject matter. The small portrait that caught my eye, showed a man with the most prodigious moustaches I had ever seen. He wore a grey suit with a black cravat, had a bushy white beard covering his chin, and was the spit and image of Lord Edgington himself – only a touch swarthier and more hirsute.

Yes, the man in the painting was the Latin reproduction of my grandfather, so I walked straight up to the attendant behind the counter and, in my worst (and therefore also my best) Italian, said, "I want that one." I pointed across the room to the present I had selected, just as my grandfather walked through the door.

He stopped to look behind him, saw the painting and frowned before walking over to me.

"Hullo there, Grandfather…" I cringed as I waited for an explanation to enter my brain. "I must have got lost on the way to the lavatory." I didn't actually say this, but I considered it, which shows just what power that man has to unsettle me.

"You appear to have taken a wrong turn," he told me. "The toilet was inside the café, not in a bookshop fifty yards away."

I tried to hide my irritation and failed. "This is so unfair. How am I supposed to buy a Christmas present for the only person I've ever met who lives in a state of permanent suspicion?"

Perhaps understandably, the shop worker was looking at us as though we were quite mad. On the whole, I found Italians accepting of such eccentricity and, sure enough, he shrugged and opened a book of his own.

"I'll tell you how, my boy." Grandfather approached me and, in a confidential whisper, said, "You'll have to try a lot harder than that."

I was about to compliment him on his skills of surveillance when I realised something. "Wait just one moment; you didn't see me enter the shop, did you? You believed I was still in the café, so you came here to buy my present when you thought I was otherwise occupied. If anything, you are the one who's been found out."

A flicker of what I could only think was embarrassment passed over the old man's face. I really thought I had him for a moment, but then he smiled and put one hand on my shoulder to steer me out of the shop. "You can think that if you wish, Christopher, but…" He turned away from me then, and all I heard were mumbles. So I don't know who came out best from this clash of heads, but it was probably him.

I suppose that this was the real reason I had invested such importance in his present. It wasn't because I believed in my ability to obtain the perfect gift for a man who has everything. I wanted to show that I could outfox him for once. I'd been trying to buy something for days and, short of asking a shopkeeper to open at night for me, I couldn't see how I would achieve my aim. Of course, we could have simply agreed to spend an hour or two apart to select something special, but that would have robbed all the fun of the endeavour, so we continued our petty game.

"I wouldn't have wanted the painting anyway," he told me once we were out in the gallery again. "If the truth be told, I have always been jealous of men with the ability to grow truly substantial facial hair." He stroked his own quite substantial beard as he said this. "It would only have made me aware of my shortcomings, though I do appreciate the effort."

Before I could even attempt to formulate a new plan, I spotted our… well, how can I describe him? Our former chauffeur turned indispensable Jack-of-all-trades, Todd, appeared at the end of the gallery with a piece of paper in his hand that he was waving frantically in the air.

"Lord Edgington!" he called over. "Master Christopher!"

It seemed odd that he would make such a fuss considering that we were looking straight at him and he was approaching at a good speed. Our golden retriever Delilah was there too, bounding along at his side.

"Lord Edgington, I've been looking everywhere for you." Much like our dog, he panted as he came closer. "Something strange has happened."

"You must catch your breath, man," Grandfather recommended, and Todd took a moment to do just that.

"I was in the salon of the suite at the hotel. I swear there was no one else with me, but a boy knocked on the door with a bag of laundered clothes. I took it into your room, at which point I found this."

He held out his hand, and I saw that he was holding a sealed envelope. Oddly enough, it had no name written on it. Aside from the fact it had been found in my grandfather's bedroom, there was nothing to say for whom it was intended.

A little tentatively, I removed my calfskin gloves and reached out to take it. Grandfather didn't object, so I extracted the card from inside it and read it aloud.

"Your presence is requested at the Hotel Villa Cassel in the Swiss Alps on the 23rd of December. All expenses will be paid, and you will incur no charges for the entirety of your stay. I sincerely promise that your trip to Switzerland will be worth your while."

"Switzerland?" Todd said in some surprise. "Lord Edgington, do you know anything about this?"

The skin between Grandfather's eyes folded together as he contemplated the note. When I did nothing more, he seized it from me and turned the thick card over. On the back, the only thing written was the address of the hotel in a place called Riederfurka in the canton of Valais.

And then Grandfather uttered something that he rarely admitted. He bit his lip and, looking along the neo-classical arcade in the direction of the La Scala opera house, said, "I don't understand it."

CHAPTER TWO.

The decision was quickly made that we should return to the hotel to investigate further. Delilah evidently thought we were had organised some sort of game for her pleasure, as she threaded in and out of our legs and barked excitedly all the way home.

We were staying in the Grand Hotel et de Milan, or simply "the Milan" as the locals called it. We'd had our own suite of rooms for the last three weeks, which may sound extravagant, but it was nothing compared to the twenty-seven years that the composer Guiseppe Verdi had spent living there. In fact, he'd died in the very same bedroom where I was sleeping, though hopefully they'd changed the bedding since then. Many people would be unnerved by such a fact, but having spent so long with my grandfather, I was used to spending time with the very recently dead, so the long-since deceased didn't bother me.

"Are you certain that the envelope wasn't in the room when we left?" I asked as we entered the hotel and swept up the cantilevered, marble staircase. The Milan was one of those glorious Victorian hotels which are all gaud and ostentation on the surface, but you soon realise when staying there that nothing has changed since it was built sixty years earlier. Not every room has electricity, and the poor staff have to cart vats of water about the place because there are no taps anywhere. This isn't to diminish just how grand the building or fixtures were, but I did find myself dreaming of hot showers on a number of occasions.

"How could the envelope have appeared in the room when we were present, Christopher?" I don't suppose I have to tell you that Grandfather asked this question with some weariness in his voice, and it wasn't because there were no lifts and we were dashing up the stairs.

"Perhaps it was always there, and we didn't notice it," I vainly attempted to answer.

As an exceedingly good retainer, Todd didn't normally show much emotion, but he was clearly insulted by this idea. "I can assure you, Master Christopher, it wasn't there before you went out, but it was when I went to put away your grandfather's clothes."

If we had been characters in one of the adventure novels Todd so enjoys, the solution would have been found in a secret passageway or perhaps a system of tubes that spat out objects into the room when there was no one there. I wouldn't even make this suggestion aloud, though, as I knew what Grandfather thought of such unlikely devices – be they literary or otherwise.

We arrived at our door, and Todd swiftly granted us admittance. I must confess that we entered it much as we would any crime scene. I walked more softly on my feet than normal, as though worried I might wake the dead. For his part, Grandfather's eyes swept the luxurious salon as we approached his bedroom, and Todd stood back beside the door, perhaps thinking that he might have to run off in search of a telephone to call the police. Delilah showed no such caution and ran around the low coffee table to expend some left-over energy.

So great was my feeling that something wasn't right in that elegant location, that I made sure to leave my gloves on as I carefully turned the handle and stepped inside my grandfather's bedroom. There was nothing to find, of course – no one hiding beneath the bed or in the cupboard – and there was certainly no dead body stashed away there. I was being overdramatic, but this still didn't explain how the envelope could have materialised there when he was in the neighbouring room.

"So let us be clear," I said to be clear. "You were in the salon from the moment we left until the porter brought the clean laundry?"

I turned back to Todd. He looked uncomfortable with the question but answered it directly. "That's right, sir."

"Where did you find the envelope?" I tried again, and he reluctantly approached to point towards a small end table at the foot of the bed.

"And the porter didn't enter the room?" Grandfather added, sounding a little tentative. "I mean to say that he didn't cross the threshold; you took the bag from him at the door and then he left?"

"That's exactly it, m'lord. But may I ask what difference it would have made if, for example, he'd brought the bag into the salon and placed it on a table?"

I thought I knew my grandfather's thinking well enough to answer this. "He might have flung the envelope into the room if he'd come inside."

Deep in thought, Grandfather was doing his usual job of stalking about the place, but he now came to a total stop and addressed me. "Does any explanation present itself, Christopher?"

I tried to look as though such a thing was on the tip of my tongue. Sadly, short of ghosts, some sort of mystic guru with the power of transmutation, or the presence of an invisible man (all of which I knew not to mention), nothing entered my mind.

"It does not," I eventually conceded. "Though there is one possibility we are yet to explore."

I didn't wait for his answer. I raced out of the door and cut across the salon towards the far bedroom, where Verdi had composed several of his most famous operas. The door was shut, which should have kept out any invisible men, but when I opened it and wandered inside, there was a second envelope sitting neatly on my pillow.

"But…" Todd had followed me and sounded quite bewildered. "But how is this possible? I swear that no one came past me all morning."

Grandfather entered with trepidation once more and, rather than trying to answer Todd's seemingly unanswerable question, he said, "Come along, Christopher. Find out what it says."

I glanced back at them then, and their expressions were close copies. Both looked quite incredulous.

With all the care that my grandfather would have taken, I extracted the card from its envelope, only to find the same message we had already read. I held it up to show my companions.

"That doesn't help us a great deal," Grandfather said a little precipitously.

"Wait, there's something else." With two fingers, I reached into the envelope and extracted a handwritten note.

I could see just how excited Todd was. "It's rather like a treasure trail. Perhaps this new message will send you racing off across the Continent in search of some stolen gem or clandestine organisation."

The paper was folded, but in a moment it had given up its secrets. I read aloud what I discovered there. "Dear Mr Prentiss," it and thus I began, "I am sorry to summon you in such an unusual manner, but I need your help. I am obliged to travel to the Villa Cassel this Christmas and believe that my life is in danger. I cannot yet reveal any more details or share my name. Even approaching you like this could lead to further risk. Please come to Switzerland with your grandfather. Perhaps I am overreacting and there will be no need to have you there, but your presence will greatly set my mind at ease. I will contact you again when the time is right, X."

"How astonishing." Grandfather was at my side. His eyes flashed back and forth across the page as he reread the simple message.

"Then it sounds as if we'll be going to the Alps," Todd muttered in a serious tone.

I, meanwhile, was torn between considering the danger that this new task presented and the happy thought that we might get snow for Christmas after all.

CHAPTER THREE

We had a week to prepare for our voyage and plenty to do in that time. Todd was quick to call the Hotel Villa Cassel to confirm that an anonymous person had booked a suite for us there and even paid the money for the reservation at their bank in the city of Bern. The manager of the hotel could tell him nothing more, but we were at least reassured that this was no hoax.

"You don't think it is all terribly strange?" I asked as we tried on the designs of a tailor by the name of Miani in his shop on the Via Manzoni a day after we'd found the notes.

"On the contrary," my grandfather replied, and I decided to wait for him to continue before trying to make sense of this response. "I think it *is* terribly strange, but that only heightens my curiosity."

"Yes, yes. That's all very well." I paused to put my arms through the sleeves of a pinstripe jacket. It was far too big for me, but it was only a sample, and whatever we liked would be made to order in time for our trip. "Yet you haven't stopped to consider that this is how every nasty mystery story begins. You know the sort. People are summoned to a party or an abandoned mansion and then picked off by a savage killer. Don't you think that it's a very silly idea to go in the first place?"

"Far from it," he began, and I once more waited before interpreting this comment. There was a rustle of fabric before he spoke again. "I *do* think it is a very silly idea, but that doesn't stop me from wanting to go. Life is all about weighing risk and reward. The risk of our going to the Villa Cassel is that we could be murdered in our beds. The reward is the chance to solve a most intriguing mystery. For me at least, there is no debate to be had."

I believe I swallowed then, as I didn't have the words to express my apprehension at the position he'd taken. Either way, I had donned all the clothes that I planned to put on and could now pull back the curtain of my small dressing room.

"What do you think?" he asked as he admired himself in a wall of mirrors.

I swallowed once more. "If the truth be told, I think we're mad to consider travelling to a place when the only thing we know about it is that someone there fears for his life."

"I was talking about the suit." He glanced at me in the mirror.

The clothes fitted him perfectly, and he was as spruce as could be. The only odd thing about it was that the fabric was brown. He almost exclusively wore grey, and I am quite certain I'd never seen him in such an unostentatious colour before.

For this reason, my only response was, "Brown?"

"That's right, Christopher. You are a most observant young man."

He went back to admiring himself just as a smiley young tailor appeared and got to work without a word. He checked the hems of the new ensemble and pinned them where necessary.

"I thought I would wear something a little different. After all, he who does not evolve is destined to stagnate and die." This attitude greatly contrasted with almost everything I knew about my grandfather, but then he does live to shock.

"And there I was thinking you were a creature of habit like me." Even as I uttered these words, I regarded myself in the mirror and didn't like what I saw there. Not only did I resemble a little boy who had got dressed in his father's Sunday best, there was another obvious comparison, which I left it to Grandfather to make.

"You look like an American gangster. All you're missing is a Thompson machine gun and you could be Al Capone himself."

I turned to stand side on and accepted his point. "Perhaps I should stick to plain black after all."

The tailor, who was himself very dapper, stopped what he was doing to shake his head mournfully.

As was so often Grandfather's way, he took up the topic I wished to discuss long after I had mentioned it. "The point is, my boy, that we mustn't shy from danger. If I had wanted a safe, easy life, I would never have joined the police in the first place. And even if I'd chosen to stay at home and enjoy the fine estate that my parents left me, I very much doubt it would have prevented your aunt's, uncle's or even your grandmother's death."

It was true that people in our family had a worrying tendency to be murdered, and I couldn't blame Grandfather's chosen career for their sticky ends.

The tailor finished with his pins and pencil and stood back to let the old macaroni go free. Grandfather turned to address me in a less enthusiastic tone. "You mustn't worry. We are going to have a wonderful Christmas together. There will be a sprinkling of mystery, a lot of fine food, and I've arranged a surprise for you."

"I hope it's not another suit that makes me look like someone I'm not."

We both laughed, and the tailor approached with a sigh. After he'd given up on fixing my outfit, and I'd selected a more suitable fabric, we left him to his work. Our next stop was a nearby shop that specialised in supplies for alpinism. To my surprise, the owner, staff and the majority of the customers there were all British.

"You know what they say, boy," the cheery attendant told me. "Until we Britons started climbing those Alpine slopes, the locals had barely noticed they were there. Now, what size boots do you take?"

It suddenly frightened me that Grandfather believed I had any wish to scale a rock face or dangle from a rope somewhere. I'm no longer a coward when it comes to heights, but I have my limits. All this talk of danger reminded me why, for the first sixteen years of my life, my primary interests were classic novels, confusing one garden bird for another, and cream cakes.

As Grandfather purchased who knows what, I was led around the impressive emporium by the helpful young man and, by the end of my brief tour, I ended up with a selection of warm unders, walking boots, weatherproof clothing and a pair of poles to prepare me for our journey to the mountains. I begged my grandfather for time and some patience so that I could try the various items in peace. He was so fascinated by all the equipment around him that he didn't give me a second thought, and I darted into the dressing room.

I must say, I looked far more dandy in the thick woollen jumpers and snugly fitting trousers than I had in those expensive suits. An hour later, we walked out of the shop having placed a large order, and our maid Dorie and her young assistant Timothy were on hand to transport our purchases back to the hotel. It was very nearly Christmas, and the smiling faces of the shoppers we passed filled me with a sense of excitement that had been missing until then.

That already incandescent city had been dressed up and illuminated. Candles burned in shop windows, and the air outside every bakery was thick with the smell of roasted chestnuts and honey and hazelnut *torrone*. I was particularly looking forward to trying *panettone:* the local delicacy that is eaten at Christmas in that part of the world. I had it on good authority that the best example of this cylindrical sponge cake, rich with dried fruit and spices, could be obtained from the Motta bakery in the Galleria Carlo Alberto, and I planned to make a pilgrimage there before we left.

I may only be twenty-one but, as already established, I am set in my ways and still longed for a few British Christmas customs, though we were several hundred miles from home. I noticed that Christmas trees were less common in Italy, but whenever I spotted one, it brought such joy to my heart that, had I possessed a camera, I would have captured the moment. The largest one I found belonged to one of the many wealthy families in the city and could only be glimpsed through the gates of a palazzo on the Via dei Cappuccini. It had been decked out in baubles and garlands, and though I couldn't get close to admire it, I appreciated the effort that someone's servant had made.

Unfortunately, none of this could make up for the tornado of emotions which whirled within me. It would be my first Christmas without even a glimpse of my parents or my brother. Travelling with my grandfather was a privilege, and every new place we visited inspired me, but that didn't mean I could forget about my family entirely – especially in winter when we would normally be at home together.

And then there was the added burden of the close-to-breaking heart in my chest. It was in Italy that I had come face-to-face with the most breathtakingly wonderful young woman on the Continent (if not the whole world). The thought of leaving the country where we'd first spoken made my insides burn, even if I still had hope of seeing my sweet Kassara. And now, on top of everything else, there was a dangerous Christmas to anticipate, not to mention my grandfather's apparent interest in daredevil winter sports. I'd made a promise to myself that, if he were to so much as utter the word *bobsleigh*, I would turn and head home to England that very instant.

The days before our departure passed quickly, and I half-wished that I could have stayed to enjoy the various Italian Christmas traditions that were so different from our own – though talk of a great multitude of fish to consume on Christmas Eve wasn't my idea of a perfect meal. When the Sunday three days before Christmas arrived, Grandfather demanded that I pack a bag with only the essentials, as we would be setting off the next morning at first light.

I found it curious that he would be driving the car himself, and we wouldn't have steady old Todd to guide us to our destination, but I remembered our factotum talking about the trip as if he wouldn't be there. Sure enough, when I woke early on the twenty-third, there was no sign of him. I rose, got dressed in my sporty new clothes, and waited down in the hotel foyer, as I had told my grandfather that I would.

Admittedly, I ordered some orange juice, eggs on toast, a variety of pastries and just a little bread, cheese, cured meats and marmalades to kill the time until he appeared. I was enjoying this not insubstantial breakfast when a clean-shaven man with short hair took a seat opposite mine. I thought it rather strange but raised my glass by way of a *chin chin!* Then went back to concentrating on the feast before me. My companion didn't say anything, so I assumed he was a foreigner of some description – as we all are in one way or another.

I didn't like to study him, especially as he was staring straight at me, but after a while, I couldn't resist. Though dressed in casual attire, with a thick, navy blue jumper that might have been worn by a sailor, he looked at home in his refined surroundings. He had an interesting face, and while it was hard to guess his age, there was no way he was younger than sixty. He sat perfectly upright in the saggy leather armchair with his hand half covering his mouth, and I noticed that he had quite the stormiest grey eyes I had ever seen, second only to—

"Grandfather!" The word burst out of me, and I'm sure my own eyes were as large as cannonballs as I sat gawping at him. "Is that really you?"

He didn't reply for a moment. He simply observed my amazed reaction. "Do you doubt it, dear grandson?"

I didn't know how to respond, so I simply said, "Your beard! Your hair! What did you do to them?"

He laughed at me, as he had every right to do. "I decided that it was time for a change. I've spent too long trying to hold on to the past as the world around me shifts. I'm ready for something different." He leaned forward in the chair and dropped his voice. "Are you set for the journey?"

I shook my head then, not in reply to his question, but at what I was hearing. "Do you know, Grandfather? You are a surprise wrapped in a mystery sealed within a puzzle."

"I'll take that as a yes." He rose from his seat, picked up a small canvas bag from the floor at the side of his chair and put his hand out to help me up. "Christopher, what's that?" he asked, pointing to my suitcase.

"My bag with only the essentials."

He took a step back to try to make sense of what I was saying. "And what portion of the contents is made up of books?"

"Ah… now that you mention it, I might have a few in there. But I have no idea how long we'll be away or whether we'll…"

He didn't listen to my answer but turned towards the exit and crossed the foyer at speed. "Come along. I have a canvas bag in the car you can use."

I lugged my suitcase after me and spent the next ten minutes trying to decide how to choose between *Nicholas Nickleby* and Dorothy L. Sayers's *The Unpleasantness at the Bellona Club*.

CHAPTER FOUR

The journey was long, winding, but absolutely extraordinary. When I lived in England, I always thought that the soft rolling hills of Surrey must be the most beautiful countryside on earth, but that was because I had never been to the Alps. Crossing the border from Italy to Switzerland, we caught a glimpse of Lake Como in the lowest reaches of the mountains before winding through narrow lanes up, up and then up some more.

The sights through the steamed-up windows of our sleek black Alfa Romeo 6C Spyder were indescribable. The sun peeking out above the horizon for the first time that day was like an explosion of light, and I felt incredibly fortunate to see it. Even our dog Delilah, who had been happy to doze between us until then, sat up to watch. And the waterfalls, fast running rivers and green mountainsides were so awe-inspiring that the sight of all that snow as we reached the higher ranges was hard to fathom. We'd already witnessed unparalleled beauty, so why did God decide to spoil us by adding a layer of pure white frosting on top?

There were some hairy moments as we squeezed past horse-drawn carts piled high with straw or root vegetables on the narrow, cobbled path through the mountains, and I'd rather not remember the bridges over immense crevices in the rock. They were most definitely designed for one vehicle at a time to pass, and I doubted they could support even that much weight. I did not dare look down at the drop beneath us and tried to ignore the fact that the wall on either side was only two feet tall. Learning that the most frightening of these constructions was known as the Devil's Bridge did nothing to reassure me that we would make it to the hotel alive.

I can't have been the only one who was nervous, as my grandfather, who is well known in my family as a scorcher behind the wheel, chose to drive... *carefully*! He hunched his shoulders and barely spoke a word except to ask me to clear the fog from the window with a rag.

We made it to a high pass between mountains, which marked the highest point of our journey. We surely couldn't have gone much further without scraping the heavens. The ancient route we followed had been a link for hundreds of years between the Italian-speaking southern Alps and the German-speaking northern part of the country. And no, I didn't know that myself. I had a self-narrating encyclopaedia alongside me who, now that we were rolling smoothly back down to lower altitudes, found his voice again. The roads were still characterised by regular hairpin zigzags, and I don't believe that I let go of my seat for a second, but Grandfather was suddenly a real chatterpie.

I'm quite certain that I will remember that journey until my dying day. It was not just the views from the car that made it so special but being alone with my favourite detective as he picked story after story to tell me from the immense collection in his head. All we were missing was a roaring fire, a mug of mulled wine and (as I'm the one imagining this) some kind of cake. Still, I was happy when we arrived at our destination as it meant that we hadn't plunged into an abyss.

"This isn't the hotel," I told him as we parked outside an unspectacular stone building in a small town next to a lake. "Well, I hope it's not. I had something…"

"What?"

"Well, I had something a little more spectacular than this in mind. We didn't drive to the Alps to sit in a dark hovel without a view."

"My goodness, Christopher. I've taken you to so many luxurious hotels over the years that you can't be satisfied with a good honest place like…" He rubbed the window to see more clearly through it. "…the *Bergbahn*."

I couldn't tell whether he was joking or not, as he got out of the car and I could no longer see his face. He opened the back door for Delilah. We'd only stopped briefly on the journey, and she was happy to stretch her legs and enjoy a big yawn.

"*Berg* means mountain in German, doesn't it?" I asked, somehow pulling this information from my usually uncluttered brain. "And I doubt that *bahn* means hotel. This also doesn't look like a villa, and I distinctly remember that the card we received spoke of the Villa—"

"Very well, Christopher," he said. "This is not where we're staying."

I watched as his eyes charted a path up the mountain to the very top before he extended one hand to point at the snowy summit.

"We're going up there. *Bahn* means train!" Throwing his knapsack over his shoulder, he walked towards the nondescript building.

I bustled after him across the clear road and into the building where he had no trouble whatsoever buying train tickets from the German-speaking woman on duty there. I was starting to wonder whether there were any languages he couldn't speak, though this thought was low on my current list of concerns.

At the top of my list was just how strange it was to see him without a beard. The shorter hair was one thing, but for him to lack even a wisp of a moustache was unsettling. I'd always assumed that much of his power came from his well-groomed hair, like a modern-day Samson – which would have explained his choice of name for his dog. Just below this on the list was what would happen to us when we got to the top of the mountain. Then came the question of where – and indeed, whether – we would have lunch, and I believe I might have wondered at some point why our staff weren't with us and what had happened to the rest of our belongings.

The sloping platform where we waited was even colder than the frosty world outside. It felt as if we'd travelled to the Arctic Circle rather than a mere hundred miles from Italy, but the train soon appeared on its spiky-toothed track and a huge group of men holding very long skis over their shoulders stepped off. They were so wrapped up against the cold that they looked like Egyptian mummies, and I wondered why we were the only passengers going back up the mountain at this time of day. Delilah raced to the head of the train to sit looking out of the window. Unlike my grandfather, who reads minds ever so well (be they human or canine) I've never been able to say what goes on in our dog's head, but she certainly seems to appreciate a fine view.

The train juddered up the mountainside in its long underground tunnel, which grew steeper with every passing minute. It stopped twice at different empty stations before emerging into the daylight and a world of blinding white. Although we'd been near the snow for much of the morning, seeing it up close like that was truly mouth-dropping. I pressed my face up to the window just like Delilah and couldn't wait to jump off the train to play. But on we went, higher and higher up the mountain, and I wondered whether we would ever reach our destination.

When we finally did, and Grandfather opened the door to let us off, we found ourselves in another cave-like station built right into the rock.

"There should be supplies waiting for us," he explained with a knowing look before wandering over to a covered wooden box on the platform and extracting a large bag.

When we'd made our plans, I'd vaguely wondered how we might get to the hotel, and one thing is certain: I had not imagined that we would take a rack and pinion mountain railway before strapping tennis rackets to our feet.

"They're not tennis rackets, Christopher," Grandfather said with a tut, though I hadn't uttered a word. "Why do you think such things? These are snow rackets, and you'll be glad of them once we get outside."

I only had one question. "Is it far to walk?"

He shook his head, not in response but lamentation – presumably at the lily-livered attitude of today's young people who can't even endure a trek across a frozen snowscape. I looked down at Delilah who was patiently waiting for me to strap the rackets to my feet. She was such a sympathetic creature, and I appreciated her camaraderie.

Nothing could prepare me for the cold outside, though. The sun was already low above the mountain peaks, and the bitter wind sent flakes shooting at my face as we followed a long path made of compacted snow. When we rounded the bend, I'm happy to say that the sense of being in a windy tunnel ended, and the world felt more accommodating. The view certainly didn't hurt as we looked down the smooth white slope and out to what resembled a valley that someone had filled in with solid ice.

"That's a glacier, isn't it, Grandfather?" I asked, and rather than tut at me for being so ignorant that I would have to ask such a question – or providing me with a list of technical information that I didn't need to know – he put his hand on my shoulder and sighed.

"That's right. And it is simply…" He didn't finish that sentence, but his expression told me all I needed to know.

We were both so taken by the sight that he even let us stop for our picnic already. Thick sandwiches on crusty white bread, with slices of cooked ham and a generous layer of butter inside, were just what I wanted. The inclusion of one of Cook's pork pies made it even better. And while the quince schnapps in his hipflask wouldn't have been my first choice of drink, it sent a pleasant buzz through my body that prepared me nicely for the journey ahead.

Fifteen minutes after we'd finished eating, when we didn't seem to have made more than a few feet of progress, I was less enthused by my task.

"It's not difficult, my boy," Grandfather told me for the tenth time in as patient a manner as he could manage. "Just lift your feet a little higher."

I thought that was what I'd been doing the whole time, but apparently not. Delilah had no trouble as the snow was firm enough to support her small, fluffy feet. I suppose it helped that she could distribute her weight on all fours, but she was so quick that she ran back and forth up the slope just to give herself something to do.

The most worrying thing, as we clung to the side of the mountain on a long path that seemingly led nowhere, was that there were no man-made structures in sight, and it wouldn't be long before the sun ducked out of the sky completely. The adventurous men I met in the shop in Milan spend their holidays engaged in such pursuits, and I believe it's the very concept of endurance that they find so thrilling, but all I could think about was climbing into a warm bed at the hotel and not getting out of it again until the new year arrived.

It took us the best part of an hour to circumnavigate the immense peak that overlooked the glacier until, finally, on exiting a narrow path between two high rocks, we caught a glimpse of a building in the distance. It looked like an overgrown Tudor house. It had the same dark half-timber frame and contrasting whitewashed walls, but this immense construction had approximately thirty windows on the façade, all with their heavy wooden shutters wide open... oh, and turrets. Much of the roof was covered in snow, but I could make out a spire on one side, high above the rest of the building, and it appeared to be made out of shiny brass.

"That has to be the Villa Cassel," I said to myself as much as to Grandfather or our dog, but they both replied.

"I believe you must be right," Grandfather agreed, whereas Delilah barked and sprinted off ahead of us even faster than before.

The last half hour had been hard going, even for her, and I thought she'd used up all her energy, but she'd clearly reserved some for the home straight. She looked pleased with herself as she sat on the porch of the hotel, which was almost completely shrouded in snow. In fact, the lower level of the building, which had surely been designed for such conditions, only just peeked out of the blanket covering and, much like the basement on a London townhouse, the first row of windows could barely be seen.

It was a short hop for the Delilahs of this world, but it would take Grandfather and me some time to catch up with her. This did give me the opportunity to admire the scenery once more. The view plunging down the valley, with a ring of jagged peaks all around us, was perhaps even more majestic than the one we'd seen further down the mountain. Grandfather may have chosen a demanding route to get us there, but it was very much worth the effort.

When we reached the hotel, I had to walk like a man with two plaster casts on his legs to get my racketed feet up the steps to the wooden deck. I don't mind telling you that I was glad to sit down on a bench and untie the blasted things. Walking around after that, the sense of freedom was so great that I felt like a merman who had finally grown a pair of legs.

The inevitable then happened, and I saw a familiar figure pulling a pair of mules on their reins around the building.

"Good afternoon, sir," Todd called to his master, who was not in any way surprised to see his right-hand man there, as they were surely co-conspirators in whatever silly plan they'd hatched.

"Good afternoon, Todd. I trust you had a safe journey."

I believe that it is one of Grandfather's great pleasures in life to keep those around him on their toes. He was forever hiding minor secrets from me, and I was yet to work out exactly why. As he said these words, two more laden beasts appeared, along with our cook Henrietta, and our non-specific assistants Dorie and Timothy (who had few maiding or hall-boying duties to perform whilst on holiday). Grandfather really does like to be well-attended at all times.

"So we could have driven up here and avoided the complicated journey and the ice-cold walk?" I put to the eccentric old duck as the staff approached.

"No, no." He crossed his arms against the cold, perhaps to show that he is human after all. "It would only have avoided part of a complicated journey. We are rather high up in the mountains after all."

"Whatever you say, Grandfather. Perhaps you can give the staff a hand with the provisions you've quite unnecessarily made them cart up here." I turned and walked into the hotel, with a sanctimonious air that I did not mind one bit.

With the snow shaken from her coat, Delilah walked proudly alongside me, and the sight to which we were now treated pleased us both. The foyer of the hotel was all pine, and I mean that almost literally. It was as if someone had taken a log cabin and magnified it. The floor was made of squares of glossy pine, which had been polished in different colours to make a diamond pattern across the spacious room. The walls were panelled (in pine) and the ceiling was… I'll stop there, as you can guess of which material it was made.

Something else I had not been expecting was the number of people present. There was a family with a boy of perhaps seventeen, and I took the woman with them to be his grandmother. As I watched from the entrance, his parents hurried past me to leave, and I got the definite impression they were glad to be shot of him. On the far side of the foyer, two women stood talking most seriously next to the fire – and, yes, the surround and chimneypiece matched the other features of the room. The grandmother hurried off up the stairs, and my eye was drawn to a chubby-cheeked man on a ladder in the middle of the room.

He wore the maroon livery of a hotel receptionist, but he had a long taper in his hand and was lighting the candles on a very large chandelier, which I'm glad to say was not made of wood but metal and sparkling crystals. He had almost completed his task when the phone at the pine (ha ha!) reception desk began to ring, and he somewhat wearily descended the small stepladder to answer it.

As he picked up the mouthpiece and raised the receiver to his ear, one of the two women who had been talking crossed the room in the direction of the stairs. I'd been standing there gawping for long enough and decided to make myself known to the receptionist. I nodded civilly to the lady as we approached one another in the middle of the room. I would say she was around fifty, with long white hair in a complicated plait over her shoulder, and there was something lithe and catlike about her as she moved across that welcoming space.

We'd made it to the chandelier when we heard a strange noise and both looked up. I'm glad to say that I identified the sound of a cord scraping through the hole in the ceiling. My reflexes were just quick enough to push the woman beside me out of the way of the falling chandelier before, somewhat less gracefully, I threw myself to the floor in the opposite direction.

CHAPTER FIVE

I lay looking up into space as voices cried out, my grandfather and his retainer ran into the room, and Delilah came to sniff me.

"Master Christopher?" Todd called from somewhere nearby.

I imagine it was partly tiredness that kept me there for so long. We'd got up before the sun rose. I'd been in a car for most of the day, and then I'd had to trudge across a snowy mountain, so a few moments' rest was very much appreciated. I can't say whether this or my fall on the hard wooden floor had affected me, but I felt for a moment as if everything that was unfolding were a dream or a piece of theatre. I could hear how upset the various onlookers were, but there was nothing I could do about it, so I just lay there.

What snapped me back to reality was my grandfather saying, "His eyes are wide open, so it's probably shock. Will I be the one to slap him out of it, Todd? Or would you rather do it?"

"I don't need anyone to slap me, thank you very much," I told them as I blinked away the haziness and forced myself to stand.

"Sir! My dear sir," the chubby receptionist dashed over to say, "I feel terrible. I don't understand what could have happened."

I brushed off my clothes and turned to look at the ruined remains of the chandelier. There were shards of glass everywhere, as if a large diamond had come crashing to earth to splinter into ninety-nine pieces. Luckily for everyone there, the combination of all those burning candles and a wooden floor hadn't led to a great conflagration. The odd flame still burned, but a well-dressed man, who hadn't been there a minute earlier, now came to stamp them out.

"Are you all right, Chrissy?" Todd asked, apparently so worried that he referred to me by my boyhood name.

"I'm fine. Thank you, everyone. What about—" before I could finish this question, the woman I'd pushed from harm came to speak to me.

"Young man, I'm terribly grateful for what you did. I really can't express my thanks enough." She held her hand to her chest to communicate this. Her blue eyes possessed a rather misty quality, and there was something appealing about her manner.

"It was nothing," I said and meant it. "I'm just glad that you aren't hurt."

The receptionist clapped his hands at this point, and a boy in a similar uniform appeared from a room behind reception to see to the mess.

"Really, boy," the Englishman who'd finished putting out fires came to tell me, "that was quick thinking if ever I saw it. My name is Dunstan Cheshire, and it seems you just saved my wife, Sunday."

I really must have been shaken by my fall, as it took me a moment to realise that Sunday was her name and not an affectionate nickname he'd given me.

"You must have dinner with us tonight, here at the hotel. It's really very—"

Sunday turned those hazy eyes upon him, and he seemed to fall in line without her having to say a word. "Let the boy have a moment to recover, Dunstan." She had a sweet, fragile voice, with a hint of working-class London to it. "If he's feeling anything like I am, he's had quite the shock."

"I'm fine, I assure you," I said to set their minds at ease. "And once we've settled in for the day, I'm sure that we'd like some company for dinner." I turned to the man in charge then. "Wouldn't we, Grandfather?"

"Yes, of course." He bowed his head rather formally, and when he straightened up again, he brought his heels together like the old policeman that he is.

"Settled in!" the receptionist echoed me before taking my arm and leading me over to the desk.

Even without the chandelier, the foyer was bright from the electric lamps on every wall. They had elegant glass shades that glittered like mother-of-pearl shells. What daylight remained bounced off the snow outside too, and the hotel register on the desk in front of me was easy to see. I read the last few names there but, aside from the Cheshires', none of them stood out to me.

"Don't forget why we're here," my grandfather whispered as he drew alongside me, but the receptionist had started speaking again.

"You must be Mr Prentiss, isn't that right?" the jolly fellow with the thin moustache enquired. "I have the royal suite reserved for you and your companion." He had an accent which I managed to identify as Teutonic, but I'm certain a more worldly person could tell the difference between Swiss German and German German.

"That's correct, thank you."

"My name is Victor Ried, and I am the current custodian of Villa Cassel. I am so sorry for the falling chandelier, but I hope everything will go swimmingly from now on!" Despite his strong accent, he spoke in phrases which were so typically British that I wondered whether he'd spent time in my home country. I was about to ask him this very thing when Grandfather took hold of the conversation.

"You mentioned the name of our suite. Have you had royal visitors here in the past?"

The cheery man held his gaze on my companion for a moment or two before answering. "There may well have been before I came to run the hotel. You see, it was built at the turn of the century for a man by the name of... well, Cassel, obviously. He was a wealthy—"

"Banker," Grandfather interrupted. "His name was Ira Cassel, and I knew him well." He put his finger to his chin to stroke his beard before presumably remembering that it no longer existed. "Or rather, I read plenty about him, but our paths never crossed. So you came here after he died?"

The Swiss closed his eyes and bowed his head respectfully as he reeled off his story. "Lord Cassel left Switzerland in 1907, and I was lucky enough to take up the job of caretaker before overseeing the transformation of this wonderful building into a hotel. I have never regretted one moment of my time here."

"I see." Grandfather pursed his lips but seemed to have lost interest in the hotelier and glanced about the room.

"Your signature, please, Mr Prentiss." Herr Ried held out a pen to me. Grandfather was normally in charge of such formalities, but our anonymous inviter had singled me out in his letter, and the reservation was evidently in my name, so I did as requested.

"Thank you kindly, sir. I will now write out a confirmation of the details of your stay. It won't take very long."

I turned to see what my grandfather had noticed only to be distracted by the bustling foyer. A few people had gathered around the porter as he listlessly swept up the mangled metal and shards of glass from the disaster that had just been averted. He wasn't very good at it, though I would probably have made just such a hash of the job. It was almost amusing to see him trying to fit so much into the small dustpan and dropping the same pieces time and time again.

As I was watching him, a woman in a brightly coloured skiing outfit spoke loudly in German into the public telephone. On a bench not far away, the adolescent I'd previously noticed was reading a grubby paperback book with a look of what I can only describe as violent glee on his face. Whatever story he was consuming was evidently to his taste. His grandmother had returned and was replacing her outdoor shoes with soft canvas ballet slippers. The look on her face was quite different from her grandson's, but it did tell me that her feet were sore. The only person who was out of place there was a woman in loose, unflattering clothing that somehow looked both grimy and new at the same time.

The front door opened once more, and a blast of cold air entered, followed by a rather flamboyant woman who marched into the hotel as if she were the owner and we were all trespassing. Above obligatory walking boots, she wore long tweed shorts without tights underneath them. I'll repeat that. Her legs were quite bare, though the hotel was located some six thousand feet above sea level!

Her shorts were complemented by a thick leather belt above which she had a pleated white blouse with large sleeves. As for her hair, it was so perfectly waved that it didn't look as though it had been touched by the wind. She was incredibly stylish and presumably insane to wear such an outfit when the thermometer outside read five degrees below zero in centigrade – which I believe is… Actually, I haven't the faintest idea what that is in Fahrenheit.

A porter placed two bags down beside her as she removed her dark glasses to peer about the place. It surprised me that she paid no attention to the hullaballoo in the middle of the room. Her eyes fell on the reception before she spun on her heel and, with her head tipped back, she released a pained groan.

"Why here?" she bellowed, apparently just as unimpressed with the accommodation as I was charmed by it.

Grandfather had already spotted the sight which now caught her attention. In fact, he'd been looking at it for some time. Just above the door was a large stained-glass window showing St George slaying the dragon. The beast had bright red eyes that seemed to bulge out of the glass in our direction, and the fiery sight made a curious moment all the odder.

"If you are ready, Mr Prentiss, I can take you up to your room." The manager or whatever he might have called himself walked around the desk to lead us upstairs. Todd was lending the porter a hand to clear up the mess, and not even Delilah paid us any attention, so we walked across the foyer without any fuss. The curving, snail-shell staircase (in pine, of course) was an impressive piece of design, and I enjoyed peering up through the hole in the centre to see the floors above.

For a big man, Herr Ried was quick on his feet. He shot ahead of us, all the way to the second floor, where he led us to a door which gave on to the front of the building. With a certain flourish, he took the key from the pocket of his maroon waistcoat and, pausing to look round at us as he placed it in the lock, he opened the door.

He was a blithe-hearted sort, and I had the impression that he viewed his task as akin to that of a man who dresses up as Father Christmas in a village fête and pulls back a curtain to show the assembled children the presents they will receive. He clearly loved his hotel, and I didn't want to disappoint him, so I walked merrily into the room with my eyes wide open to show my appreciation for whatever I would find there.

I briefly worried the room would fail to live up to my aforementioned high standards, but I needn't have. While it is true that, in some ways, this was the simplest space in which we'd stayed in the six months of our European tour, it was no less lovely for it. The pine floorboards weren't buffed and shiny as they were on the ground floor. They were plain and partly covered with animal pelts. In fact, the sitting room we'd entered was really very rustic, and not the sort of place my grandfather would normally have chosen, but this just made it more special. It suited the picture of an Alpine adventure I'd had in my head since I was a child.

And best of all, I believe that it had been prepared with me in mind. There were paper star lanterns hanging from the high ceiling and carved wooden hearts on the walls. Straw figures dangled from silver thread, and red and white felt decorations in the shape of mushrooms, robins and, perhaps less traditionally, goats sat on the windowsill. There were even green wreaths on the doors to the bathroom and two bedrooms. I was concerned that they'd used up all their Christmas decorations in our suite and would have none left for the rest of the hotel. There was admittedly no Christmas tree, which was a little disappointing, but I couldn't complain. It was so festive that I might well have decorated it myself.

I was just about to have a look in the bedrooms – and perhaps claim the better of the two for myself – when Grandfather slammed the door shut behind him and marched up to Herr Ried.

"Tell me this instant: why did you try to kill my grandson with that chandelier?"

CHAPTER SIX

The poor man looked flabbergasted. "Mr... urmmm. I'm afraid I don't know your name."

"Never mind that now," Grandfather continued, jabbing one sharp finger into the manager's chest. "Explain how it came to pass that you were up a ladder dealing with the lamp and, less than a minute later, it plunged to earth, very nearly killing Christopher here."

Herr Ried nervously threaded his hands together before unthreading them and returning his arms to his side. "It was simply an accident. I certainly didn't intend to—"

Grandfather had no interest in excuses and chose a different tack. "Are you he?"

"I beg your pardon." He sounded a little offended by this.

"Are you the man who wrote asking us to come?"

The Swiss looked at me for help, but I couldn't tell what had got into my normally level-headed forebear. "Grandfather, perhaps you should—"

He spoke right over me. "Are you the one who organised all this?" There was an intensity to his gaze and grip that, in anyone else, would have frightened me.

"I can only apologise, but I don't know what you mean." He chose his words carefully, so as not to enrage the clean-shaven, short-haired gent any further. "I am the manager of the hotel. I am generally found at the reception. So in terms of organising all that you see here then, yes, that is my responsibility."

Grandfather looked off through the window and seemed to doubt himself. I was frankly impressed by just how well Ried had kept his nerve. He may have been frightened but, after a few initial stutters, he hadn't let it show. When Grandfather didn't say anything more, the manager tried to think of another explanation.

"I hope it is not the Christmas decorations which have upset you. I thought that, as you were staying in our finest suite for the duration of the holiday, you would appreciate something that enlivens the spirit."

"It's not the decorations," I was quick to tell him, in case he decided to take them away. "We were in Milan until very recently and received a letter from someone asking us to come here. He didn't give his name but said he was in danger. My grandfather wondered whether you were the one who wrote to us."

"Me?" he said, less grammatically than Lord Edgington would have liked. "I'm sorry to disappoint you, but I know nothing of this. The first time I heard your name was when we received the reservation."

This at least piqued Grandfather's curiosity. "How did it come about? My man called to confirm the booking, and we were told that it had been paid in advance. Is that correct?"

Ried had relaxed somewhat now that the focus had shifted elsewhere, but he still took a step back from the madman who was interrogating him. As he did so, there was a sound of scratching, as if someone were listening at the door. I moved to open it, and it swung to with an ominous creak. It may have sent a shiver through all three of us, but it didn't last long. Standing there, peering in at us, was not the person who had lured us to the Alps, but our dog, who looked most disgruntled that we'd left her downstairs.

Her arrival had only distracted Ried for a moment or two, and he answered as if Delilah weren't now lying on her back with her legs in the air, desperate for affection. I knelt to spoil her, so she evidently achieved her aim.

"You are quite correct. The money was paid into our bank account in the city. It did seem strange to me at the time, but I couldn't turn down such a lucrative reservation. We are often deserted at Christmas, but not this year."

Something occurred to me then, but I was too busy stroking Delilah's tummy and saying, "Who's a good girl? Who's a good girl?" in a vaguely doggish voice to be able to make my point. Luckily, Grandfather was there to ask what I couldn't.

"And is it usual for you to have so many Britons here? I would say that at least half of the guests we have overheard since we arrived are our fellow countrymen."

To my surprise, Ried found this question difficult to answer. "It is certainly common to find English-speakers in this part of the world… though sadly we've had fewer American visitors these past months due to the terrible situation since the financial crash. Your compatriots are known for their love of winter sports, but we've never had this number at Christmas before." He'd maintained a cautious tone until now but couldn't help smiling. "I am happy to admit it has done wonders for our coffers."

He must have seen Grandfather's expression and regretted this note of levity, as he frowned, and I felt guilty to have made our rosy-cheeked host turn glum.

"Thank you so much for the kind attention you have granted us," I said in a similarly polite manner to his. "We're very sorry for the misunderstanding earlier. It's all just a jape that a friend planned for us, but my grandfather likes to take these things seriously."

"That's right," Grandfather said to support my story, though his tone was so bleak that it did little good. "It's just a bit of fun, but it's more pleasant if you pretend that it's real. I'm sure we'll unpick the mystery before long."

"I'm glad to hear it." If Ried thought us a pair of mad hatters, he didn't even hint at it. "I will be downstairs at my post should you need anything. Dinner is served from seven."

I nodded my thanks and showed him out as Grandfather fell silent once more. I thought it would be insensitive to run off and gawp at the pretty bedrooms, so I walked to the immense windows at the front of the building instead.

"You know, there's no reason to be down," I assured him. "It's just as you said to Herr Ried; we will solve this mystery in time."

I can't deny that I was distracted by the view. The wide valley before us had a long winding lake at the bottom, and the light was just at that moment between day and night when it seems there is a touch of magic in the air. I turned away so as not to be distracted.

"It isn't the mystery itself that worries me, Christopher." Grandfather stroked Delilah's velveteen ears without looking at her as he spoke. "It is the thought that a person who may be in trouble is unable to reveal himself to us."

"Do you believe it was a man who wrote the letter?"

"I still can't say, but there was an indescribable something in the way it was written that made me think that was the case. There are few certainties in this world. However, I feel a woman would have approached the matter in a different way."

I wondered if that "different way" would have involved sending the main missive to the famous detective rather than to me, but I didn't say anything more. I looked one last time at the sapphire-blue sky and realised how much I wished to explore the world around the hotel. I also wondered for one silly moment if they have reindeer in Switzerland, before remembering that those festive beasts are found a great deal further north.

In case Grandfather had guessed that I would ponder anything quite so stupid, I quickly asked, "Do you think Herr Ried was telling the truth?"

"We have no reason to doubt him." He sat down in one of the burgundy leather armchairs beside the fire, and Delilah followed him, as she was enjoying the attention.

"But what about the chandelier? To be perfectly honest, I didn't question that it was an accident when it first happened, but it is possible that this whole thing is a trap and someone brought us here to…" I didn't like to say the words.

"Kill us?" Grandfather had no such problem. "Well, yes, the thought crossed my mind. However, if I were planning to murder someone, I would use a more reliable method of dispatching the victim." It wasn't the first time he'd made such a frightening statement. He had once admitted that, if he hadn't become a police officer, he would have made an excellent criminal.

I leant against the pine shelf above the mantel and admired the green bough that decorated it. "Besides, it crashed to the floor around a minute after Ried had climbed down from the ladder. I doubt it was intentional, as it would have been very difficult to time it so precisely."

"Perhaps, perhaps, perhaps…" Grandfather muttered, and the word came out as another lamentation. Before he could say anything more, Todd arrived with the possessions I had left at the hotel in Milan. I have come to expect the pair of them to arrange secret schemes wherever we go, and I've stopped saying goodbye to our staff as they always turn up soon after.

"Good evening, m'lord, Master Christopher," he nodded to us both even as he hauled my travelling trunk into the room. I felt sorry for Todd and even worse for the poor mule who had been forced to carry the burden to the hotel like a pregnant woman in Bethlehem. "Well, good afternoon, I suppose, but the light is dying fast."

Our retainer fell into conversation with his master, which gave me the opportunity to look at the bedrooms at last. They did not disappoint. The beds were four-posters (I won't tell you in which material) but they were not nearly so formal and old-fashioned as in most hotels. They had simple shapes carved into the head and footboard, and rounded posts on each side. But it was the overlaid designs on the wood that I found so attractive. They were painted in a chalky turquoise, with flourishes of white and dark green foliage within two rectangular panels.

The room itself had everything I could want, including a window looking out over the snowy mountains and the feeling of being in my own little den – the fireplace and wash basin were of secondary importance, but also greatly appreciated. In short, I had found the room for me – the perfect place to spend Christmas, so long as the mystery that had brought us there didn't intrude.

"Have you chosen your room?" Grandfather asked when I emerged once more. I was surprised that he didn't want to have the first pick. He was being unusually nice to me.

"I have indeed." I did little to hide my suspicious thoughts.

"Wonderful, then we must dress for dinner and look for a library or bar to enjoy a warming mug of hot chocolate. There's nothing like it."

I don't think I'd seen him drink hot chocolate once in his life, so I walked closer, considered sniffing to see whether he'd been drinking, but decided not to push my luck. "I do not intend to disagree."

CHAPTER SEVEN

More than the mystery of the letter, or the man who might be in trouble, I was puzzled by my grandfather's transformation. I don't wish to suggest for one moment that he is not a kind and generous man… but he's also conniving, secretive and forever didactic with it. And it wasn't just his attitude that struck me as strange. I'd seen photographs of him as a comparatively young man, and he'd had his moustache and beard even then.

I would normally have been worried about him making such a drastic change, but I had no specific reason to think that it was spurred on by any great preoccupation or sadness. If anything, he'd been the picture of health and good cheer since we solved our last mystery aboard the night train to Verona. Indeed, as we left our room, he started whistling "Good King Wenceslas". The whistling turned into pom-pa-pa-pom-pom-pom-pomping, and that soon became the song itself.

> **"Good King Wenceslas looked out,**
> **On the Feast of Stephen,**
> **When the snow lay round about,**
> **Deep and crisp and even."**

Delilah decided not to accompany him, but she padded along at my side, just as loyal as ever. However, I felt it would be rude not to join in, so I sang the rest of the verse with him.

> **"Brightly shone the moon that night,**
> **Tho' the frost was cruel,**
> **When a poor man came in sight,**
> **Gath'ring winter fu-oo-el."**

I'm sure I've said it a thousand times, but there is nothing like a Christmas carol to lift the spirits. We both showed our glee as we crossed the now far tidier foyer to reach the areas of the hotel that were reserved for the use of guests. Herr Ried had apparently forgiven us for the harassment upstairs, and I realised that, if he regularly had rich Englishmen staying at the hotel, there was a good chance he was used to such eccentricity.

Just at that moment, he was dealing with an awkward customer.

"I'm truly sorry," he told the glamorously dressed woman who had arrived soon after us. "I wish that the situation weren't so complicated, but I assure you that I am not to blame."

"That's not good enough," she responded in a voice that was close to furious, and I wondered what had upset her. "I've come all this way, and I feel… I suppose I feel tricked somehow. I'd like to know what you're going to do about it?"

Ried was at a loss to know how to deal with the irate woman, and we left the entrance hall before he could deliver a response. We found ourselves in a long corridor with a selection of doors leading off it, each with its own plaque. We walked past something called a *Schwitzbad*, and at the end of the corridor I noticed staff carrying plates and cutlery to what I took to be the dining room. There was a billiards table in another, and I was certain that entering the smoking room would be like diving into the chimney of a tobacco factory.

Just a little way along, we discovered a library on one side of the corridor and a bar on the other. For a moment, I thought that my grandfather would opt to go right, and I would go left to search for some of the books I'd had to leave in the car. I realised that it would make more sense to order my hot chocolate first, and as soon as we stepped into the bar, I knew that we were where my grandfather wanted to be. It wasn't just the collection of bottles behind the pine bar that appealed to him. The room was busy with hotel guests, and there is nothing he likes more than earwigging on other people's conversations.

One advantage of his new appearance was that our entrance drew few glances. Were we at home in England, the arrival of the famous Lord Edgington was likely to draw every eye, and the place would soon be loud with whispers. That wasn't the case now that he'd shorn his famous locks. The only chatter we stirred was from people recalling what had happened with the chandelier. It was the first time in my life I'd received more attention than my illustrious companion.

The boy I'd seen in the foyer was there with his grandmother. She certainly noticed Grandfather, though not for the usual reasons. She seemed quite taken with the tall, dashing gent and watched us the whole time we were at the bar. With our drinks procured, it turned out that there was nowhere for us to sit. Delilah went to lie in front of the fire, and I was about to suggest to my grandfather that we fulfil the second part of my plan when the old lady called us over.

"It seems ridiculous not to share our space, especially as our young gentlemen look like the types who might get along," she told us in an ever so croaky voice, then winked at my grandfather, presumably to suggest that they might get along too. "Won't you join us?"

He showed no sign of hesitation, but I could tell that he would much rather have found a space where he could observe the goings-on without having to contribute to them. "That is very kind of you, madam."

"Please…" She held her hand out for him to kiss. She was that sort of person. "Call me Dolly!"

He took her hand in a rather suspicious manner and then occupied the high armchair beside her as she went into great detail about the origins of her name. From her accent, I would have said she was terribly English, but she claimed ancestry from Spain, Holland and Luxembourg. I soon stopped listening to her and turned my attention to the boy, who kept his eyes on the book in front of him.

"Would you mind my asking what you're reading?" I finally enquired.

"Yes," he snapped back, but he moved the book in such a way that I caught a glimpse of the cover.

"I tried reading that one," I revealed, already wishing that I didn't remember. "I found it gruesome and couldn't get past chapter ten."

He looked up at me with that same rather hungry look that I'd noticed when I first spotted him. "*The Lodger* is by far my favourite book. I've read it six times, and this is my seventh." He had that curious quality of many young men which meant that he divulged more information than necessary but still thought it would be interesting to anyone in earshot. "You know it was inspired by Jack the Ripper himself. I love the scene where the girl almost dies."

"It was all the talk of gory murders that stopped me reading it. I think there are some things which needn't be discussed, and I have no intention of watching the new film they've made of it." I sounded very prim and puritanical, but I'd had nightmares for months thanks to the bloodthirsty killer in that book. His rather improbable and inappropriate name was Mr Sleuth, and I'd pictured him slipping silently through the fog of London like a ghoul.

"I only read books with a bit of violence in them." The boy showed his teeth as he smiled, and his eyebrows flicked up and down suggestively. "My name's Graham, by the way. I didn't want to come on holiday, but my parents made me, and then they swanned off on their own."

"Oh, really?" I tried to sound as if I hadn't already worked this out from the glimpse of their happy faces I'd had in the foyer. "Where have they gone?"

"They're skiing in another valley a couple of hours from here. I have almost as much interest in skiing as I do in algebraic equations or the Corn Laws of the nineteenth century, but I didn't like not being asked to accompany them. They abandoned me here with my boring old grandmother."

"I heard that, you ungrateful little burden!" She turned to glare at him, and there was something very bat-like about her. The fact she was dressed in a black velvet dress with Bohemian glass jewellery certainly did nothing to diminish her vampiric resemblance.

"I'm amazed you can hear anything at your age," Graham snapped back at her, his nose crumpled and his jaw jutting out indignantly.

This made me wonder whether it was one of these two belligerent battlers who had written to me, but when Dolly turned back to my grandfather, she just laughed and said, "Aren't young men funny these days?"

I was very aware by this point that the macabre boy in front of me would have loved to hear about all the dead bodies I'd seen in my short career as a detective, but I found it deeply morbid to extract enjoyment from death, and so I kept my mouth shut and opened a book of my own. *Murder at Pemblewick Manor* wasn't as subtle as our friend Marius Quin's previous novels, but it was jolly good fun.

"Is there a lot of blood in it?" Graham interrupted after I'd read approximately six lines of text.

"People are killed," I replied coldly. "You can work out that much from the title."

"Yes, I know that, but it's not one of those nice stories in which they spend half their time drinking cups of tea and the case is solved by sitting at a fireplace and having a chinwag? I can't stand that kind of book."

As he spoke, the waiter in his smart reddish coat delivered my hot chocolate and Grandfather's... strong, brown drink. I warmed myself on the china mug, but didn't quite know how to respond to Graham, so I simply repeated myself. "People are killed. I'm up to the third victim and I haven't yet read half of it."

"Well, I suppose that might be worth my time then. The bloodier the better as far as I'm concerned." He pushed his glasses up his nose, patted his hair at the side of his head to check that it was neat and awaited my response.

All I could say was, "It's a good book, and I'd like to find out what happens next."

He didn't seem too upset by this, and we both fell quiet. Well, I had a good old slurp of my drink, discovered just how hot it was, and had to wave at the waiter to bring me a glass of water. When I'd largely recovered from my stupidity, I devoured the part of my book where Inspector L'Estrange secretly follows Lord Chigley, thinking that he must be to blame for the murders at Pemblewick Manor. I had just got to the scene where the detective intends to confront the supposed killer when Chigley himself ends up dead. It was classic Marius Quin – ripping a likely suspect out from under the reader's nose when it seems there is no other solution. He'd already done it once in the story, and I'd fallen for it again.

"I used to be a thief," Dolly told my grandfather, and I realised that I'd been aware of their conversation without paying attention to what was said.

Graham evidently heard this proclamation, too, as he looked up contemptuously for a moment before glancing back at his page. I took this to mean that the rather surprising revelation was nothing new to him. Grandfather, on the other hand, was clearly taken aback by her confession, and we both waited to hear what the old lady would say next.

"Oh, don't look so shocked. It was years ago for one thing, but I learnt my lesson and came out a better person as a result." She shuffled in her seat and tipped back her chin rather proudly. "I was known as an exceptionally subtle operator. I was always very well spoken, so if the bobbies ever suspected me, I could tell them a pack of lies and they believed every word of it."

This really made her laugh. She screwed up her eyes and nearly collapsed back against the headrest of her chair. I was worried for a moment that she was having some kind of attack, but she righted herself and returned to the task of scandalising my grandfather.

"I regret it now, of course, but I must say that it made me feel alive." She paused to take a predatory bite of the pink and white fairy cake before her. When she'd finished her mouthful, she leaned towards my grandfather as if to impart a secret. "You might not think it to look at me, but I've had a *wild* existence."

She set her vision squarely on my grandfather and wouldn't let go. I'd rarely seen him get hot under the collar, so perhaps it was the change from his usual form of dress that did it; he looked very close to blushing just then.

"I don't yet know what brought you to the Alps, madam."

She tapped him playfully on the nose before replying. "You cheeky man…" She gave a brief cough before continuing. "I told you to call me by my first…" When she tried to complete this sentence, she found that she couldn't. She held one hand to her throat, and I could see the panic in her eyes.

"Are you quite all right?" Grandfather asked, and I waved to the waiter to bring more water before realising that Dolly's needs trumped mine and offering her my glass.

She drank it down but still couldn't say anything. There was a look of true horror on her face and, in a flash, she must have realised something significant as she pointed to the half-eaten cake on the small pine table before us, even as she clawed at her neck with her spare hand.

"I think she's been poisoned," I said, to jump to the wrong conclusion, and Grandfather was already a mile ahead of me (and on the right road).

"It's not poison. If it's from the cake, it's almost certainly too soon for that." He fired into action, moving the woman's chair around to face him and then leaning forward to open the high lace collar of her black dress. "I believe she has an idiosyncrasy to one of the spices in the cake."

Graham had dropped his book to the floor and looked, if not disturbed, then at least bothered by what was happening. "It's cinnamon. She's always going on about not being able to eat it. I thought she was just being her usual batty self."

The woman's face was swollen. Her breathing was weak, and now she really did need to faint back into her chair as she didn't have the strength to sit up any longer. Luckily the waiter I'd called had arrived, and Grandfather shot up to standing to issue a string of instructions.

"Assuming that you have no adrenaline chloride here at the hotel, bring cocaine or peppermint oil or, if you have nothing else, even coffee to act as a stimulant."

The smart young Swiss fellow nodded and sprinted out of the room, so I hope he understood what his task was.

"*Ich bin Arzt[1],*" another of the guests who was sitting a few tables away from us declared, and I had to hope this meant he was a doctor. "*Was brauchen Sie[2]?*"

"*Adrenalinchlorid*," Grandfather replied. "*Auch bekannt als Epinephrine[3].*" I have no idea what that meant, but the doctor seemed to understand. He nodded his head and threw down his napkin.

It turned out that he spoke excellent English… which was handy for me. "I have a vial in the bag in my room. I'll fetch it."

"The boy," Grandfather replied, turning his attention back to his patient. It took me a moment to realise what he meant. "Christopher, get the bag."

I moved towards the door before I even knew where I was going. "Which room?" I shouted over my shoulder, and the little German or Swiss, or perhaps even Austrian now that I come to— Actually, let's just call him Germanic. The short Germanic doctor tossed his key across the room to me and shouted the number that it said on the fob.

"208! My bag's on the desk. You will not miss it."

Delilah was at my side as I exited the bar and ran back along the corridor we'd previously taken. I was more nervous than I should have been, and I felt that strange sensation which floods your body at such moments.

"Why did it have to be the top floor?" I complained to my dog, but she was having a wonderful time sprinting along beside me.

On the positive side, the fact I was charged with retrieving the

---

1 I'm a doctor.

2 What do you need?

3 Also known as Epinephrine.

medicine meant that the doctor himself could attend to the stricken woman. I also passed the waiter in the foyer, and he had a bottle of something, so I had to hope that would alleviate her symptoms too. In fact, I tried to tell myself there really was no need whatsoever to worry, but I thundered up that spiralling staircase all the same.

Sadly, I went the wrong way when I reached the top landing.

"Why are hotels always so difficult to navigate?" I again asked our dear hound and, again, she ignored me entirely. She and grandfather could have long and really quite complex conversations, even if she never said a word. I wonder how the way I spoke to her was any different.

I got to a dead end and had to turn back, and of course room 208 was just past the stairs in the other direction, but there was no time to curse my luck. I had to save a woman's life. Or at least, I had to enable a pair of far more capable people to save a woman's life. I fumbled with the key in the lock but eventually got the door open and burst through it. I had a terrible image of what I might find inside, but luckily there was no old man coming out of the bath or woman asleep in there, and I didn't have to apologise to anyone. I just ran up to the desk, grabbed the doctor's bag, which really was an unmistakable sight, and sped back out.

My legs were tired by now. The substance that had pumped through my body to propel me up the stairs was running low, but I wouldn't give up. I returned to the foyer and, though my lungs felt as though they would need to be replaced, I made it back along the corridor and across the bar, just in time to see my grandfather and the doctor manhandling Dolly onto the floor.

I was too late. She wasn't moving at all. I knew as soon as I saw Graham's face that I'd failed. The waiter with the bottle was standing over her, and I could tell that whatever he'd brought had done no good. The room was practically silent, and the fact that no one called out to me proved that the medicine in the Gladstone bag I held would not revive her. Dolly was clearly—

Oh, no. My mistake. She sat bolt upright on the floor and looked around as if she couldn't understand what all the fuss was about.

CHAPTER EIGHT

The mood changed after that. Before, the only thing connecting us was that we'd all visited the same hotel at the same time of year. Now, we were united by the shared experience of not just a woman's death, but her unlikely resuscitation.

As Dolly slowly recovered from the attack, Grandfather warmed her hands while the doctor administered a vial of something from his bag. I assume this was the adrenaline that Grandfather had mentioned, but it could have been something else now that she was more alert. A good quarter of an hour passed before the doctor allowed her to get to her feet, and she was terribly unsteady when she did.

"I don't understand it," the chef emerged from the kitchen to explain the situation. "I did not put cinnamon in the cake! It is a simple sponge." His accent was Italian, and he had the stereotypically exaggerated hand gestures to match.

"You mustn't worry, chef," the patient reassured him in a feeble voice. "Even the presence of it in the kitchen has been known to upset me. It is not your fault in the slightest."

"Did you not enquire as to the ingredients?" Grandfather asked, but the already apologetic waiter answered for her.

"Madam certainly did, sir. And I'm sorry to say that I reassured her there wouldn't be a problem." He bowed his head, but it sounded as if it were a genuine accident, and I told him just that.

"There's no harm done, and no need for anyone to shoulder the blame. These things happen."

There was some shrugging, a few sighs, and the waiter apologised once more. After that, the various members of staff returned to their jobs, and the doctor went back to his table. Dolly was far less bold than she had been. Her energy had depleted, but she remained at our table for some time before making her excuses to leave.

It was Graham's behaviour that I found most puzzling. When his grandmother's attack had first begun, he had looked frightened, then terrified and was now back to ignoring her. He certainly wasn't happy when he was called upon to escort the peculiar old lady to her sleeping quarters.

"I do appreciate your care and attention," Dolly purred to my grandfather, and I could see that her usual manner wasn't so far from returning after all.

Graham tutted but took her arm and helped her to the door. Noticing their departure, the doctor came to give her some advice and ended up seeing her upstairs, too.

"You know, she never once asked my name," Grandfather remarked with a soft chuckle.

I had come to believe that he was rather enjoying the situation. Despite always hoping that his reputation had preceded us, now that no one recognised him, he was wallowing in his anonymity like a crocodile in a shallow swamp.

This certainly held true as we entered the dining hall a while later – in case you were worried, yes, my hot chocolate had got cold in the intervening time, but I drank it anyway and it was still delicious. We were not the first to arrive, and everyone turned to us excitedly this time. Normally people regarded my grandfather with quiet awe, a sense of trepidation and in some cases actual fear. Even the innocent often worry that the famous sleuth will uncover a hidden side to them. This was different, though. The murmuring as we cut through the elegant dining hall was pleasant and appreciative. I felt rather like a sports star or some beloved actor.

There's Christopher Prentiss! I hear he scored forty-five goals for Crystal Palace Football Club last season – it was a new record! I imagined them saying, though, in reality, I heard phrases such as "saved a woman's life" and "such a nice old gentleman, and his grandson is just charming".

We sat down at quite possibly the best table in the place, right beside a set of windows with golden and red brocade curtains that gave the room a baroque feel. While there was still a lot of pine on display, it was complemented with marble pillars, golden chandeliers that matched the sadly departed one from the foyer, and blazing Christmas wreaths on every table. The coffered ceiling was particularly eye catching, decorated as it was with egg-and-dart moulding and acanthus leaves.

I should mention that the rings of festive foliage were not, in fact, on fire, but they each held four red candles. It was a perfectly warm and appealing space, and I looked forward to eating our Christmas dinner there. The only thing (still) missing was a Christmas tree. I really couldn't understand it, as I felt certain they originated not far from where we were, and as they'd made it to Britain, they must have reached Switzerland too.

It took me a moment to remember why we were sitting at a table for four, but the previous person I'd saved – I was making a habit of it – now appeared with her husband. We rose to greet them and duly exchanged handshakes, then we all took our places to enjoy the best that Villa Cassel had to offer.

"It's lovely to see you again," Sunday told us in the same sincere voice that she'd used when we'd first met. "I'm so happy that I'm still here to enjoy dinner. I've spent the last few hours in a sort of daze. I feel as if I'm living a life I should never have had."

"I'm afraid that my dear Sunday has a romantic way of expressing herself," Dunstan told us a little apologetically. He was a handsome fellow, with thick black sideburns that ran all the way to his chin but no beard to join them. His eyes were as dark as his whiskers, and he looked a good decade younger than his wife, though I've been wrong with such estimations before.

"There's no need to be sorry," Grandfather quickly responded. "I believe the world needs all the romantics it can get."

"I'm sorry," Dunstan began, then laughed as Grandfather had just told him not to apologise, "but we haven't actually caught your name, Mr...?"

"As it happens, I'm a peer." He looked at me then, and I expected him to launch into his usual grand introduction. *My name,* he would inevitably pronounce with a dramatic pause in order to impose the full importance of the coming five syllables, *is Lord Edgington.* But he didn't say that at all. Instead, he winked at me and, evidently eager to cling on to his inconspicuousness, said, "I go by Lord Ow."

"Lord Ow?" Sunday asked. "What an unusual name." I thought this was a bit rich coming from a woman named after a day of the week.

"Yes, it is rather. It was once spelt with an L, but we dropped that over time." He was saying all this for my sake as, on a previous adventure, he had adopted the identity of... Actually, it's too complicated to explain.

I managed to resist laughing. He was a real ham when the moment took him, and I almost felt sorry for our new friends.

Dunstan looked bewildered, perhaps because he was wondering how the letter L might fit into the name Ow. "Where does it come from?"

"Well, the origins are murky, but it was first heard in Cornwall. On Weston Moor, to be precise."

I liked this frivolous side of his character and was awfully glad of our near misses that day as, were we engaged in investigating some terrible murder, he would have been all scowls and surly looks. Sadly though, his joking did nothing to grease the wheels of conversation.

"How interesting," Sunday looked at her husband as if to say, *This evening might not pass as smoothly as we'd hoped.*

Silence fell between us for a moment, and the sound of the other tables rose to fill it. The German-speaking skier I had noticed in the foyer was speaking just as loudly, even though there was no one at her table.

"Lovely evening we're having!" she bellowed to an English couple some five feet away, as if she were yodelling between mountaintops. "I do so enjoy Christmas here in Switzerland. I was brought up in the area and…" I imagine that she continued like this for some time, but thankfully Grandfather spoke up to heal the fractured atmosphere.

"I must admit that I'm interested in the two of you. What brings you here? Have you been to Switzerland before? What is your story?"

Sunday looked ever so sweet when she smiled, and this brought back dim memories I have of my grandmother. Her cheeks plumped up, and she looked both shy and encouraging at the same time.

"This is my first time in the country," her husband answered. "Sunday came on holiday once. We are supposed to be meeting a friend, but he hasn't appeared yet, and I've had no word from him."

"What is it you do?" I asked, as grandfather had delivered such a list of demands, that I felt they must have forgotten them.

"Me?" Dunstan sounded surprised to be asked. "I own a company in Britain that deals with chemical compounds, though our plantations are in British Ceylon. We are investigating the properties of new materials made from rubber and soybeans, which could be used in everything from homeware to car manufacture."

"How interesting," I replied before remembering that Sunday had recently uttered these very words and hurrying to follow them with,

"Is that how you met?"

This sounded horrendous. It was the kind of question you could ask a suspect but not a new acquaintance over dinner. Luckily, Sunday didn't seem to mind.

"No, no. I have no mind for technical matters. We met…" She blushed again, and I could see that she was even more romantic on the topic of her husband than her continued existence. "Well, my darling Dunstan fished me out of the gutter."

"Oh, please, my dear." He turned away for a moment. "You know I don't like it when you say such things. You may not have come from privilege as I and Lord Ow did, but I believe that there are good people in all walks of life."

"And bad ones," Grandfather almost tripped over his tongue to say, and Dunstan studied him with those dark brooding eyes.

I wouldn't let anyone change the topic. "Consider me intrigued. How did it come to pass that two people from such different backgrounds should fall in love?" I decided not to mention that I had once been in love with our maid.

Dunstan was less reserved now and reached out to touch Sunday's hand. "When I was a very young man – I'd just come down from university, in fact – I worked for an organisation which built houses for the council. You know the sort of thing. An area would be identified as having so many problems that the only solution was to knock it down and clear everyone out. Well, after all the famous crimes that occurred there, it was incredible that it took so long for that to happen to Whitechapel, but by the turn of the century, the hurdles had been cleared and work began."

"So you were a bailiff?" my grandfather asked in a critical tone.

"Not at all," Sunday replied on her husband's behalf, and she looked at him just as lovingly as before. "Dunstan was a wonderful architect; he was trying to make London a better place."

He did not appear to agree with this assessment, but I wouldn't discover his reservations, as the waiter now came to offer us drinks, and Grandfather selected a bottle of Chasselas wine for the table.

"You were telling us about how you met." I really wouldn't let them forget this.

"That's right." Dunstan paused for a moment before continuing.

"I was charged with designing minor elements of the new estate that would take the place of the alleyways, cul-de-sacs and even tunnels that had made up the rookery, but there was one much larger detail which the august London County Council had overlooked: the people."

A certain indignation took hold of his wife then. "I knew from friends in other parts of the city that, when these new houses were built, they were rarely given to those who most needed them. People like me were normally moved on to somewhere even worse, and so I refused to go. I locked myself in my house, and my former neighbours did everything they could to keep me fed."

Dunstan looked quite moved by the story, and I could tell that Sunday wasn't the only one with romantic ideas after all. "It was terrible what happened. Other residents copied her example, and the council wanted to force them from their homes. I reasoned with Sunday, and she promised that everyone would move if there was a provision included for people like them. I spoke to my superiors, and a compromise was reached. I told Sunday in person, and she may not have believed me, but some fifteen years later, when we met again by chance in Piccadilly Circus, she knew that I'd been true to my word."

"I'd never forgotten the kindness he'd shown me." Sunday held her wine glass between two fingers and turned it so that it caught the light of the candle ring.

"And I'd never forgotten that beautiful, headstrong young woman I'd met."

As he told the story, I'd been trying to work out exactly when all this would have happened, but he now made it far clearer. "That was shortly after I returned from the war. My life had been put on hold for four years, and as soon as I saw her, I knew that she was the woman I would marry."

They stared into one another's eyes with all the love that I hope my wife will one day have for me, and I already possessed for her, (even though I'd only spoken to her once and there was a good chance she found me as appealing as a wart on a toad's back). Perhaps describing the beautiful girl I'd met on the train as my wife was precipitous.

"And what had you done in between?" Grandfather asked Sunday, and Dunstan's whole demeanour instantly changed.

"I'm sorry to steer the conversation away to more important

matters, but I really do think we should order our meal." He tried to sound carefree and casual, but the way he clenched his jaw told me this wasn't the case.

Sunday was equally circumspect, and her eyes dropped for the first time. The silence that seized us was mirrored at the neighbouring tables. The Swiss lady, who had introduced herself as Inge to her new friends by the window, had got up from her seat to remonstrate with the chef for some reason. The assorted Britons were busy eating, and the only sound for a short while was the clink and scratch of cutlery on porcelain, but then I heard a noise that I was sure I recognised.

As the others perused the dishes we would be having, I ran to the window.

"Christopher, are you quite all right?" Grandfather asked with evident concern.

"I heard a marmot!" I can't tell you how much this excited me. "I'm sure that's what it was. There was the whistle of a marmot. I mean, I've never heard one before, but I know they live in the Alps. It must have been—"

"They hibernate, boy. You won't hear one on this visit, I'm afraid."

"Ah… You're quite right. I forgot about that." I felt more than a little foolish, but I took my place and hid my blushing cheeks behind the menu. There wasn't actually anything to choose, as the chef had taken that liberty upon himself, but it all sounded delicious.

"And what about you, Lord Ow?" Sunday asked to bring some cheer back to our exchange once we'd confirmed the menu with the waiter.

Wait just a moment. I know that some people are terribly particular about this sort of thing and expect me to blather on lyrically about every mouthful of food I consume. All I will say is that the first course consisted of the unfortunately named "cholera", which turned out to be a hearty pastry filled with potatoes, leeks, cheese from the Swiss valley of Bagnes, and, more surprisingly, apples and pears.

That whet my appetite for what was to come, and I promptly declared myself a lover of Swiss food when the main course revealed itself to be a large quantity of melted cheese. *Raclette* was a dish of cured meats, potatoes, salad and cornichons, but here's the interesting part: one waiter was charged with tending to a half wheel of cheese beside a fire in the far corner of the room. As it melted, he would cut off the gooiest part, and his colleagues would distribute it to whoever had the sense to call him over. The moment I first watched that thick yellow substance flowing over my plate like lava was something of an epiphany for me. I had experienced true genius, and it was cheese-based.

"Is the story of your life an interesting one?" Sunday asked my grandfather, and I promise I'll tell you about dessert before long.

"Mine?" he responded in much the same tone as Dunstan had earlier used. "Oh, no. No, no, no. I would say that I have had quite the least interesting existence one can imagine." He smiled throughout this nonsense. "I was born into a wealthy family. I waited to inherit my title, and then I made full use of my wealth to do as little as possible for several decades until my grandson here convinced me to take him abroad."

"But that must be fascinating to travel to the Continent after so long at home." She sounded hopeful that he would agree (and stop being such hard work).

"I wouldn't use the word fascinating." I really can't say what had got into him. "We have visited a lot of different places and seen many different things. But then Great Britain also has many places and, indeed, things."

Poor Sunday looked at her poor husband, and I felt so sorry for them I decided to chatter away for the rest of the evening to make certain that Lord Ow wouldn't say another word. The only thing I could think was that he'd taken the persona of his dull alter ego to heart and forgotten that he was normally good company.

"So far, I think I've enjoyed Florence best of all." Such was my need to grasp hold of the reins of conversation, I believe I spoke over him. "Verona is a very liveable city, and Rome is inspirational, but Florence was the perfect balance between the two."

They seemed happy to continue this topic whilst my grandfather was busy with his melted cheese. If anything, they were too enthusiastic, and I realised we were all trying too hard to convince ourselves that everything we mentioned was quite thrilling when it wasn't.

It was all very tiring and, when dessert was finally served, I was exhausted.

CHAPTER NINE

We ate our *Rüblitorte* (or carrot cake with pretty little marzipan decorations in the shape of tiny carrots) in near silence, and the only other things that happened of any note were one half of the middle-aged British contingent getting stung by a mosquito, some people complaining about being too hot by the fire – while others complained about being too cold near the open window.

Oh, and a little later, the outlandishly dressed lady from the foyer arrived to a lot of curious looks and the odd muttered comment. The fact she was wearing a striking green gown which had (and it's certainly not my intention to shock by describing it) no sleeves and a hemline that finished just below the knee may have had something to do with this.

"I've seen that woman before somewhere," Dunstan said to himself as soon as she entered, and I had the definite impression that he didn't want to say why he'd recognised her.

"I believe she was married to the Earl of Rotheram," Grandfather helpfully explained. "The marriage caused quite a stir, as she was not the typical bride of a peer. She was a chorus-girl when they met, and he died on their honeymoon."

"Goodness! Did she inherit his every last penny?" I asked – again too eagerly – and Grandfather wore the same uninspired, unflustered and decidedly unimpressed expression he'd had for much of the night. This time, I admit that it was warranted.

"Old families have ways of avoiding such things, but she did do very well in return for her seventeen days of service. Of course, the earl's relatives did everything in their power to limit her inheritance, but she had her day in court in the end."

"There's something a touch frightening about her," Sunday said, wrapping her arms around herself as though she were cold. "I've known women like her before: impulsive, fearless characters who think they own the world."

The new arrival had selected a table on her own, below the main chandelier in the middle of the room, and it gave the sense she was still occupying the spotlight some years after she'd turned her back on her previous occupation. We weren't the only ones staring across at her. The woman who was dressed in decidedly drab and simple clothes had just arrived, and she couldn't take her eyes off…

"Rosetta Mullen," Grandfather finally remembered. "I couldn't recall it at first, but I'm sure that's her name."

We were all occupied by our thoughts, but Dunstan in particular looked troubled. It was hard to say what had upset him, but the previously cheerful man was sullen, and his face turned grey even in the very hot room which, now that the window had been shut, had become quite unbearable.

The evening passed in a mixture of chatter and awkwardness. Grandfather did nothing to help it along, and I felt he wanted me to talk for the both of us.

"Thank you again," Sunday told us when the time came to leave. "I look forward to seeing you at—"

Her husband interrupted and reached out his hand for me to shake. "I'm sure we'll bump into you before long." I didn't blame him for not wanting to be stuck with us for the rest of the holiday. I may have saved his wife from (at the very least) a nasty injury, but that didn't make my grandfather any more bearable. "We will be here until the twenty-ninth, and it is a small hotel."

We nodded and thanked them, then realised we were all going in the same direction and had to repeat the process once more out in the corridor.

"Good night to you both," Lord Ow said in his increasingly grave and gravelly monotone.

We turned to walk in different directions. I wouldn't have been surprised to learn that their room was in the same part of the hotel as ours, but they simply had to get away from us.

"Did you enjoy that?" I asked my grandfather once we were far enough away not to be heard. I could have criticised him outright, but I thought I'd at least give him the chance to express how sorry he was for being a pain.

"Yes, thank you. I had a wonderful evening. I can't tell you how liberating it is to be forgettable for once. There was no need for me to thrill anyone with incredible stories. I could enjoy my meal and appreciate the conversation without feeling as though I had to perform for my audience."

"That's all very well, but did you have to be so insufferable?"

He didn't answer, as he was too busy smiling (insufferably). I was frankly desperate to get upstairs to our suite and dive into bed. I had some extra thick flannel pyjamas that I planned to wear as much as possible over Christmas, and I was greatly looking forward to cuddling up with my book and a hot water bottle. The only thing missing was my mother to tuck me in.

"Mr Prentiss?" We'd almost made our way across the foyer when the manager called to me. "I hope you had a wonderful evening."

I tramped back over to him so as not to appear rude. That was my grandfather's job, not mine.

"The food was exquisite," I told him. "You really do have a lovely hotel here, Herr Ried."

"That is very kind of you to say, and I must thank you for continuing to save the lives of my guests or there would be no one left to enjoy it." He laughed at this and then realised the implications of what he had said and frowned. "I'm sorry, Mr Prentiss. It has been a very long day."

"Don't worry. We've all had them." I tried to reassure him with a smile that was far friendlier than my grandfather's.

"Good night to you both. I hope you'll join us for our Christmas Eve celebrations tomorrow."

"That sounds like just my ticket. Good night." I turned to walk back to my grandfather and somehow knew that the Swiss would have more to say.

"I'm so sorry, I completely forgot why I called to you in the first place."

I turned round to see that he held an envelope in his hand.

"It was on the sun terrace. I found it there this evening when I went outside to…" His voice trailed off, as whatever he would have said was irrelevant. "I thought it rather odd that whoever left it wouldn't simply bring it inside." There was a slight question in this, but as I didn't know any more about the letter than he did, I took it from him and bid him good night for a second time.

"Do you think it might be…?" I asked my grandfather when we were halfway up the stairs, but I didn't dare finish the question. Instead, Delilah and I hurried off ahead of him. I intended to throw myself on my bed and rip open the letter, but when I reached our suite,

I found that it wasn't empty.

"Good evening, young Master Edgington," our kind, though haphazard maid muttered as I entered.

I had explained to Dorie a number of times that my name wasn't Edgington, and that I had my father's surname, but it was yet to sink in. I barely noticed this, however, as she was doing something quite unexpected: her job.

"I'm just unpackin' His Worship's clothes before I go up to bed myself." She spoke in an unusually cautious voice. She was normally so brassy and cheerful that it left me dazed. "I reckon I won't be long."

"Dorie, are you quite all right?" It seemed that none of my usual companions were acting like themselves any more.

"Don't you worry about me, young master. I just had a shock this evening."

I'd come to view Dorie as a constant, unchanging force in a troubling world. She and her sister had once been pickpockets. They'd entered my grandfather's service after abandoning their life of crime, but I knew little else about them. Oh, and Dorie was an excellent arm wrestler, but that wouldn't explain her glum expression.

"I would say that any shock you might have had is a very good reason for me to worry. Are you sure you don't wish to share your burden?"

She had apparently forgotten that she was supposed to be folding the clothes into the wardrobe. Balling up the trousers she had in her hands, she hurled them over her shoulder so that they landed in a heap in the corner. If I hadn't already realised, this proved just how distressed the immense woman really was.

"It was just… Well, I bumped into someone from my past. Someone I thought I would never see again."

A quick assessment of my day turned up an obvious candidate for her description. "Was it Dolly…" I realised that I hadn't learnt the old lady's surname.

"If she's stayin' in a fancy place like this, there's no way she still uses the name I knew 'er by."

I tried to think of a way to narrow it down. "Does she dress like a vampire?"

"How should I know what vampires wear?" She crumpled her face in confusion.

"Was she here with a boy of seventeen?"

I believe she was about to answer when her employer came into the room and, aware that she hadn't completed her task, she took an armful of clothes and forced them onto one of the shelves. I was sure that Todd would be along soon to put them right.

"There you are, Your 'ighness." I wasn't the only one she regularly misnamed. "All done here. I hope you have a lovely evenin'." Although her face was ablaze with her usual smile, I could tell from a crack in her voice that she wasn't at her best.

"Goodnight, Dorie. I hope you're enjoying your time here."

She opened her mouth to reply to him, but all that emerged was an uncertain sound from the back of her throat. Instead, she nodded and trundled from the room.

"Wait, Dorie," I called, but she wouldn't turn back.

I thought that Grandfather might ask after her, but he was just as excited by the new letter as I was. "What have you discovered, boy?"

"Nothing yet. I haven't opened it."

"Hurry up then. Chop chop!"

He clapped his hands and Delilah, who had instantly fallen asleep on the small sofa, jumped up and walked about the room as if to say, *I wasn't sleeping. Who said that I was sleeping?* She returned to her spot as soon as she saw that her master wasn't paying any attention. Grandfather set to work lighting candles around the room to make my task easier, as the electric light on the ceiling was as dim as I'd been at sixteen.

I fished a letter opener from a drawer in the desk where I was confident I would find one. I held it with the uneasiness of a murderer embarking on my first kill and had to force myself to slit open the envelope to extract the guts of— Actually I think I've taken that metaphor far enough.

I held it up to the nearest candle, being careful not to singe the paper. "I believe it's in the same hand as the first letter."

"Well? What does it say, boy? Why have we been called here?" He stood like a statue in the middle of the room, waiting to discover the answers to so many questions that had bounced around our heads that week.

I cleared my throat and began.

"Dear Christopher, thank you so much for heeding my call and making your way here. Although we have never met, I feel as if I know you to some small degree, and I am certain you will help resolve the dilemma I face. Since last I wrote, my suspicions have only grown. I feel quite confident that I have been called here for some form of retribution.

"I will refrain from lying to the man who is trying to help me, and so I must confess that I have not always been the most honest or, indeed, law-abiding citizen. Although I have always tried to do my best by those around me, I have known great hardships in my life and done what was necessary to escape them. But one event in particular has come back to haunt me, and I now know that is why I have been brought here.

"There are people in this hotel who cannot be trusted, and I hope you can identify them before it is too late. More than just my life may depend on it.

"I will write to you again whenever it is safe.

"Sincerely, X."

CHAPTER TEN

I can't say that I slept particularly well that night. If anything, the letter added a number of new questions to my existing list. I had to wonder who the sinister forces in the hotel were. I didn't like the idea that any of the seemingly nice people we had met could be behind the persecution of the mysterious X. Dunstan and Sunday, aside from having slightly unusual names, were genuinely good people; I knew that much. The doctor who had saved Dolly came across as a kind and considerate man. And while her grandson was a little odd, it seemed unlikely that Graham was to blame for my clandestine correspondent's suffering if it were connected to something that happened many years earlier.

To put it in a sentence: we still knew very little, and everything we did know was unfathomably strange.

I woke early the next morning and did my usual check. I've spent so much time with my grandfather over the last few years that, before getting on with my day, I consider it best practice to ensure that no one has been murdered during the night. There were definitely no bodies in my bedroom – that was always a relief. Our small sitting room was similarly corpseless and, once I'd got changed and had a quick look around the common areas of the hotel, I felt reassured that all was well. I know this might sound excessive, but it's better to be safe than sorry, and I can't tell you the number of times we'd started the day with a new body to examine.

In fact, I'm trying to remember the last Christmas Eve that didn't feature an early morning cadaver. Was it 1924 or 25? Or perhaps there was a fallow year in the middle when we got all the corpse discovering out of the way on Christmas Eve Eve. Whatever the case may be, I've come to associate my favourite time of year as much with strychnine and daggers as golden stars and tinsel. Statistically speaking, Christmas really is the deadliest time of year, but that didn't stop me anticipating it just as I did when I was a child.

There's a feeling of warmth and satisfaction that comes at Christmastime that is unlike *almost* anything else – and I only discovered the "almost" very recently. When I think of Kassara – the girl I probably won't marry but like to dream that I will – it feels so very similar to the contented sensation I had as I walked down to breakfast that morning. It is the sense that something wonderful is just around the corner. It is difficult to put your finger on exactly what that thing is, but you know it's coming and you know it's going to be incredible. On that particular morning at the Hotel Villa Cassel, that incredible thing was breakfast.

Oh, peace on earth and mercy mild! Grandfather has taken me to some appetising places for food before, but this took the biscuit – not least because there were any number of mouthwatering biscuits on offer.

"It is a Christmas tradition," the manager told me, as he also doubled as the head waiter in the mornings, and I had a feeling he never slept. "Here in Switzerland, we start baking at the beginning of Advent, and you will not find a home in the country that does not have a good supply of them to last through to the new year. In fact, our chef has been busy this morning preparing a batch of *Grittibänz* with your grandfather's cook."

"How lovely!" I said quite convincingly, looking at the display on the table before me. "Which ones aren't hers?"

"I beg your pardon?" He clearly hadn't tried any of our cook Henrietta's more complex culinary creations, whereas I didn't want to take the risk.

"I was merely wondering which of these biscuits your chef made, as I would like the most authentic examples."

He smiled and motioned to an ornately decorated selection. They certainly didn't look as though they would contain grated mackerel or smoked tongue, so I placed a stack of them on my plate. After that, I helped myself to several varieties of local bread, fried potato pancakes fresh from the pan, cold meats and cheeses, a bowl of cereal with fruits, oats, honey and nuts, and plenty of sausages to keep me going until lunch.

Of course, as soon as my plate was full, I became convinced that my grandfather would arrive at any moment to tell me that there was no time to eat and I was a terrible person for even considering breakfast at a time like this. To my amazement, it didn't happen. I could see that, just for once (perhaps because it was Christmastime) I would be allowed to finish my meal without interruption.

To be on the safe side, I ate as fast as I could and barely took the time to listen to the other guests' conversations. I did notice, however, that Dolly wasn't there. Her grandson was hunched over his plate, devouring his penny dreadful, so I could only assume she was still recovering from the previous evening's brush with cinnamon. The scandalous Rosetta Mullen was hunched over for another reason. I felt quite confident she had drunk too much the night before, as she was holding her head and occasionally groaned in pain. The Cheshires were at a corner table, and we waved politely to one another, but I had no desire to intrude on their time together.

None of the other people I'd noticed the day before had come down yet, but there were a few chatterers whispering about Miss Mullen's exertions the previous evening and the scene she apparently made sitting on top of the upright piano in the bar, singing to whoever would listen. I didn't mind such behaviour as long as it maintained the festive atmosphere, and I was very glad to get all the way through breakfast without further interruption.

"What are you doing here?" my grandfather asked when I had just licked my spoon and pushed my plate away – I was tempted to lick my plate too, but my mother taught me too well for that.

"I would have thought that was obvious." My mother also taught me that if you ask a silly question, you get a silly answer.

"Yes, but we have a lot to do this morning. Your surprise arrives soon, and Todd has prepared an activity for us to enjoy before then." He said all this as if it were the only possible plan, and I should have been able to predict it.

I decided to concentrate on the first of his announcements. "My surprise? It's happening today?"

"Not if you don't hurry upstairs and dress for the cold weather. We're going skiing first!"

Have you ever had the feeling of being overjoyed and then immediately disappointed? Neither had I until this moment. "Skiing?"

"You must have heard of it, Christopher. It's not exactly a new phenomenon."

"Yes, but—"

"Jolly good then." He turned to leave. "I'll see you outside!"

Not wishing to upset his plans, and because I still haven't learnt to say no to him, I did as he'd requested and, approximately fifteen minutes later, I was standing in the snow with long planks of wood strapped to my feet. For a reason I couldn't quite fathom, Todd, a man who, to my knowledge, had never been near a mountain, was to be our instructor.

"I've read a book about it and had a brief run down the pistes this morning, so I think I've grasped the basics," he explained in his always capable and confident manner.

I could already tell that I was going to be terrible. "I suppose it's all in the wrists like everything else you've ever taught me?"

"The wrists?" He looked quite bemused by my comment, and his master corrected my thinking.

"Don't be ridiculous, my boy. It's all in the knees!"

The pair of them slid around me effortlessly with their legs slightly bent to demonstrate the necessary technique. I tried to copy them and immediately fell over.

"That was a good try, Master Christopher," Todd lied as he helped me back up. "Now give it another go without—"

I'd already fallen over again.

"The knees, Christopher," Grandfather told me. "Remember to bend your knees."

"Couldn't I hold someone's hand whilst I do it?" This probably sounded desperate considering we'd only been out there for two minutes.

"I'll tell you what." Todd has such a kind manner that I always feel I can trust whatever he says. "I'll go in front, and you just copy my path and the position of my body."

We were on what had already been described as a "gentle slope", but that didn't prevent me from lurching forward far more quickly than I would have liked. There were not too many people around us, but Inge, the Swiss lady from dinner the night before, had come to spectate. I fell over once more for her pleasure before I could get into line behind Todd.

"Remember to bend your knees!" she told me from a safe distance as I slowly descended behind my teacher.

"That's it, Christopher!" Grandfather encouraged me as he slid gracefully along and even seemed able to move backwards up the hill. New things come naturally to some people, but none of those people is me.

"You're doing much better," Todd promised. "Now, as we're getting to the edge of the piste, we're going to turn back on ourselves with our weight leaning up the slope to make sure that we don't go too fast or fall over."

I was about to try this very thing when I fell over. A couple of workmen were fixing a pipe by the dining room window and found my incompetence most amusing.

"Back on your feet, and we'll try once more." Todd encouraged me like a father teaching his little boy to ride a bike. "It really isn't too difficult, and it's a lot of fun once you master it."

Delilah started barking at me from a bench at the bottom of the hill, presumably to say, *The knees, Chrissy! It's all in the knees!*

I got up, followed Todd for a short while, tried to turn, went too fast, fell over, got up and repeated the process so many times that the law of averages dictated I would manage it at least once.

"That's such an improvement!" Grandfather beamed, having passed me several times on my slow path.

"The hardest step of any journey is the first one," the Swiss skier informed us. She had already descended the highest slope that was just behind the hotel. She certainly made it look easy, though I knew it wasn't.

"No, the hardest steps of any journey are all those in which your feet have planks of wood strapped to them," I said under my breath so as not to upset the lunatics around me who thought that what we were doing was not only easy but also pleasurable.

I had snow in my mouth, my hands were sore from falling over so often, and I was getting very cold. But then the strangest thing happened; I actually started to improve. We side-stepped up the miniature slope – the only other people using it were three eager five-year-olds – but this time when I went down, I was able to follow Todd as if I'd been skiing about the place for years. I turned at just the right moment and, without losing my balance, I maintained a nice steady speed all the way to the bottom. I must admit that, when I came to a gradual stop, I was eager to do it again.

"Was I right, Master Christopher?" everyone's favourite sporty, naturally talented, not to mention dashing polymath told me. I should be clear and say that I'm referring to Todd, not my grandfather, though most of those compliments could apply to him too.

I couldn't help smiling. "You were, Todd. Not that I doubted you for one moment."

"Then you're ready to have a proper go now?"

My heart sank as he pointed up the mountain that looked as if it had been built to terrify me.

"A proper go?" I replied, but he was already pushing himself off with Grandfather alongside him. "What have we been doing until now if I'm yet to have a proper go?"

Because I am a total fool, I didn't say, *No, sorry. I think I'll stick to something I'm capable of achieving.* I followed them up the six-thousand-mile-high piste. The climb was bad enough in itself, and I spent the whole time worrying that I would go tumbling back down again, gathering snow all the way so that, by the bottom, I would be the centre of an avalanche. Which isn't to mention the physical exertion of putting one ski-clad boot above the other, over and over, side-on to the mountain as my deluded companions shouted things like, "Not far to go now, Christopher," and "You're doing so very well."

And the very worst thing of all was that, when we got to a flat shelf at the very top, I couldn't even complain about my ordeal because the view before us was the second most beautiful sight I'd ever witnessed.

CHAPTER ELEVEN

It had evidently snowed in the valley overnight as there was white as far as the eye could see. The hotel was so compact and perfect that it looked like a child's toy. In fact, from such a distance, it made me think of a decoration atop a seamlessly iced wedding cake.

I'd been to the Sistine Chapel and Buckingham Palace. I'd seen Botticelli's *Birth of Venus* and *The Last Supper* of Leonardo da Vinci, but it was hard to imagine that any human hand had made anything so beautiful as a snowy valley with a blue sky above it. It was a different world from any I'd known before, and what I found astonishing was the smoothness of everything before me. It was as if Jack Frost or Old Man Winter had come down in the night with a trowel to make sure that everything was just as it should be.

"Ah, you are lucky," Inge told me, as she made it back up the mountain in a quarter of the time it had taken me. I'd heard of a place in Germany where they had a steam-powered machine for pulling skiers up slopes, but sadly that innovation hadn't reached Riederfurka. "I wish I could see what you are seeing for the first time. The only greater experience is coming up here in the moonlight as I do every Christmas Eve. Night skiing is another sensation altogether." And with that, she shot off back down to the hotel, barely varying from the straightest line possible.

"Are you ready, Christopher?" my nearly eighty-year-old grandfather (who clearly had no fear of breaking his legs) enquired.

"Actually, no," I told him more honestly this time. "I think I'd like to stay up here for a few minutes to appreciate this incredible view."

He and Todd exchanged a knowing glance, then they both pushed off down the mountain before I could say, *Wait! I didn't mean you should leave me up here!* They were already too far away when I found my tongue, and so I collapsed where I stood and, making the best of a bad situation, sat back to enjoy the view. I was fairly confident that I would either die on the way down or never climb another mountain for as long as I lived, so it seemed the right thing to do.

I watched as Grandfather and Todd glided down ever so neatly. My solitude didn't last long, though, as there were two people taking the path up the slope.

"You're not listening to me, Libby!" a voice I recognised complained. "You don't care what I have to say, so there's no reason for me to keep talking."

"It's easy for you, Sunday. It always was. You've had the sorta life that most women dream of. But you forgot all about me. Didn't ya?"

I peeked over the edge of the snowy plateau to catch a glimpse of Sunday Cheshire. She did not have skis on her feet, and I wondered whether she was climbing the mountain out of a desire for privacy as much as any wish to see the view. Next to her was the humbly dressed woman who'd sat alone at dinner. Even her winter clothes were less impressive than her friend's ensemble, which consisted of a thick, yellow and blue checked woollen dress and matching cloche hat.

The woman that Sunday had called Libby had a voice that was tougher and more working class than her companion's. Though we'd learnt that Sunday had been born in a London slum, she had very much gone up in the world, and her soft, gentle tones barely betrayed her roots.

"So what do you want me to do about it?" she called back over her shoulder. "Do you want to live in my home and sleep in my bed? Do you want me to go back to where we came from? I'm not sure you'd be any happier."

"I deserve what's mine." Even though I couldn't see her face, I could feel Libby's anger, and her words echoed around the valley. "I want what I was promised, and you got. For all your husband's well-to-do family, and the lovely little house you wangled yourself, it was that money what kept you afloat."

"Don't you think we should be talking about what brought us here this week?" Sunday responded in a far calmer manner than her belligerent friend could muster.

They were getting closer, and I was sure they'd notice me. I didn't want them to think that I was eavesdropping, and so the time had come for me to descend the mountain. I realised then that standing up with skis on your feet is far more difficult when there is no one to lend a hand. I rolled onto my front, but that meant the pointed ends of my skis dug into the snow, and I looked as though I were attempting some complicated physical exercise. Using the poles that were on loops of fabric around my wrists, I pushed myself back to my original position and pulled the trunk of my body towards my knees.

With my hands behind me, I did my very best to propel myself up to standing, but this did not go as I had intended. Still down on my haunches, I began to slide towards the dramatic incline. There was a clear point of no return a few yards in front of me and, though I tried to slow myself with my gloved hands, I could get no purchase and ended up accelerating towards 99-per-cent guaranteed doom.

And so, as I tipped over the edge of the steep mountainside, I thought, *Total fool was putting it mildly, Chrissy. You really are the king of the dunces!*

The wind whistled in my ears like a choir of marmots, and the wind attacked me so violently that I felt I should be going up the mountain, not down it. I tried to reduce my speed by turning as Todd had taught me, but that was no good as my legs were trapped in place under my bottom. It turned out that Grandfather was right about the knees after all; they really are important when it comes to skiing.

I waved to the two ladies as I passed, but I should probably have screamed for help. Sunday looked particularly surprised to see me sliding down an Alpine valley like a man who'd been taken short before he could reach a lavatory.

I thought I might at least be able to fall over, but I was headed straight down the mountain, and it was almost impossible to veer from the course I was on. All I could do was grab hold of my skiing sticks and push on the ground to force myself up to my full height. And do you know what? It worked! And do you know what else? I was now worse off than I had been before. I still couldn't control my bullet-like descent and was far more likely to end up in hospital than I had been when my centre of gravity was at ground level.

The one good thing I could say was that I was steady on my skis. I kept imagining them splintering out from under me and taking my severed feet with them. Yet somehow, despite that remaining a possibility, it felt a great deal easier than anything I'd tried with Todd. I couldn't understand why we hadn't practised this more direct method of skiing from the beginning. The only drawback was that I was going so fast it would be the teeniest bit difficult to stop.

I cast my eyes further down the mountain to see whether there was anything which might aid me in this endeavour. Ideally, I would have liked a large pile of fluffy snow, positioned somewhere flat so that I could glide straight into it and come to a gentle stop. I imagined it being a refreshing experience, actually. It was certainly a much better idea than flying off the cliff in front of the hotel. There was a raised bank just before the precipitous hundred-foot drop but, at the speed I was travelling, that would merely have functioned as a launch-ramp to make my… what's the opposite of death-defying? …death-incurring final flight all the more dramatic.

Although I couldn't find the snowy safety net that I required, I did catch sight of my dear grandfather. He was standing at the point where I had first learnt to ski all that time ago. I was too far away to see his face very clearly, but I knew the expression on it only too well.

Oh, dear me. What's Christopher up to now? it surely said. *It looks like he's misjudged this whole thing and is about to plunge to his death.*

Todd could only look on as I ducked my head to stop the wind lashing my cheeks and found myself going even faster. He was normally so good at helping me avert disaster, but I had finally used up all my lives. The workmen who had mocked me earlier actually looked sympathetic now, and they'd replaced the pipe in a jiffy, so well done them.

As I approached the bottom of the piste, and prepared myself for oblivion, the only possible solution that presented itself was to bear away from the hotel on the path that we had taken from the mountain railway the day before. It was a very narrow walkway between two jagged, rocky outcrops, and I wasn't sure that I could make it, but it was a better option than a death leap.

"I love you, Grandfather! You've been awfully kind to me these last five years!" I yelled as I passed, but I was going so quickly, it probably sounded like, "…Grandfather! You've been awful!"

I managed to angle my body towards the route I needed and, to my and surely every other person there's disbelief, I started to turn. I wanted to close my eyes and hope for the best, but I knew that would make my unlikely feat even more difficult to achieve, so I focused on my objective and willed myself not to perish. The three young children stood with their mouths agape, pointing and laughing in my direction. And as I glided quite serenely to the very spot I needed, I felt like shouting, *Take that, you bunch of toddlers! Who's the best skier now?*

I felt so alive – which was a major part of my goal accomplished – as I followed that skinny path around the mountain and along the snowy descent that led to the train station. I didn't even question how I would get back to the hotel. The ground was slowly levelling off, and I found that I was no longer shooting along at such a speed. In fact, I came to a natural stop right at the level of the ticket office, which had been unmanned the day before but now had a few tourists waiting for attention and a guard inside. I could see a little way down the mountain that a train would soon arrive, and a minute or so later, Grandfather came to a neat halt with both his skis to one side.

"That was impressive stuff, Christopher," he said without a hint of irony. I nearly swallowed my tongue in consternation. "But how did you know that your surprise would be arriving here at any minute?"

I considered telling him that I'd plotted that daredevil path from the top of the mountain to perfection because I was actually a very good skier and had only been pretending to be useless for the hour or so of the class I'd taken to make my sudden brilliance all the more surprising. I would have liked to say all that, but I was too busy panting and holding my heart.

"Why did…" I began between heavy breaths as I doubled over. "Why did no one…" I tried once more… "Why did no one teach me how to stop?"

He apparently wasn't listening as he pointed towards the station and then, with a quick-spirited clap of the hands, skied away from me. "Never mind that, Christopher. The train is about to arrive."

With every muscle in my body saturated with energy and emotion, I fell back into the snow behind me and considered never moving again. I knew that he would just keep calling if I stayed there, so I untied the ties that went over my boots. In a fit of anger, I seized my loose skis and sent them skidding down the mountain as far as they would go. My feeling of relief only lasted a few seconds, as I knew I'd have to retrieve them before we left.

I got to the platform just in time to see the charming red vehicle come to a stop. It was still early, and there were plenty of skiers arriving. A real flood of people stepped down on to the platform, and

Grandfather urged me forward with a typically sly mien. I didn't trust that beloved old man as far as I could throw him, which, as I'd just shown with the abandoned skis, was not very far at all.

I looked into the first carriage all the same, but nothing in particular stood out to me, so I walked along to the next one. I was about to climb aboard when I noticed a young man further down the tunnel. He had a bag in each hand, a box under either arm, and he was wrapped in a scarf so thick and wide that I could barely see his face, but I would have recognised him anywhere.

"Albert!" I called as I ran towards my brother. "Is that really you?"

"Oh, Chrissy!" I think it's fair to say that he was happy to see me. "I was just saying to my friend here how much I've missed you."

I looked about and saw no one. My brother was giddy brained at the best of times, but I hadn't expected him to hallucinate. He must have realised how I took this comment as he put his down possessions and laughed at himself.

"Oh, how silly. I thought she'd followed me off the train." He leaned back inside the carriage and called, "Aren't you getting off here?"

No one responded, and so I followed him to see who was there.

"I'm sorry, madam, I didn't catch your name, but this is the final stop. If you're alighting from the train, now is the time to do it."

There was a woman sitting squashed into the corner of the final bench, but she just stared back at him.

"I'm sure that…" He evidently didn't know how to finish this sentence, and a look of bewilderment came over him.

She was perhaps fifty years old with curly grey hair and a heavy black cashmere coat. She had a bright smile on her face, and she looked straight at us, but there was something rather vacant in her gaze.

"Albert, I think she must be—" I began, but Grandfather had caught up with us and rushed forward to inspect the unresponsive woman.

He sat on the seat opposite her and, reaching across to pull back her sleeve, he put two fingers to her wrist. He didn't say the words, *She's dead,* because he didn't have to. He just peered at us over his shoulder and shook his head.

CHAPTER TWELVE

I'm sorry to say that my grandfather and I have become desensitised to such moments, but Albert was really quite distressed. He wandered from the train to collapse onto a bench some yards away.

"I was talking to her the whole way up here. She smiled and nodded at everything I said."

I can normally tell how upset he is by the dishevelment of his floppy fringe, and it was a tangled mess by now.

Grandfather was clearly uncertain whether to break the bad news, but he cleared his throat and explained. "I believe that the lady has been dead for some time, Albert. If she nodded her head, it was only because of the movement of the train."

In response, he let out a groan that became a moan and eventually a quiet wail. "Why did I ever think that spending Christmas with the two of you would be a good idea?"

I should probably have taken offence at this, but I looked at Grandfather and shrugged.

That wasn't the only thing Albert found upsetting. "And before we go any further, what in heaven's name has happened to Grandfather's face?"

This was too much to explain just then, so I focused on the here and now. "Don't worry about that, big brother. What matters is that it's no one's fault that you ended up on the same train as a dead woman. It could have happened to anyone."

"Yes, but it didn't, did it? I've travelled nearly seven hundred miles to get here. I've taken four trains, two cars, and in all that time, I didn't see a single corpse. I get within shouting distance of the pair of you and women start dropping dead. I really don't think it's a coincidence."

"That's not very fair!" I thought I should at least offer some kind of defence. "We've been here almost a day and not one person has been murdered… until now."

He turned his ire on me. "You're saying that there were no unusual accidents that might now be reinterpreted?"

I looked at my grandfather in case he fancied answering this question. He did not.

"If you must know, we did have to save a couple of women's lives yesterday, but there's at least a 5 per cent chance that both of the incidents were entirely innocent and we won't now have to identify the killer who is stalking the snowy heights of Riederfurka."

He could do nothing but sneer at this.

"We have a lot of sympathy for you, Albert," Grandfather tried to sound sincere, but my brother hadn't finished.

"From what Mother tells me, this isn't even the first dead body you've found on a train this year."

I opened my mouth to argue before realising he had a point. "Yes, but that was an ordinary train. This is a mountain railway. It's hardly the same thing."

"We have a lot of sympathy," Grandfather repeated, apparently unable to come up with anything better than my feeble response. "So I hope you don't mind if we leave you now to inspect the poor lady more thoroughly."

"Be my guest!" His tone remained frantic, and he gesticulated wildly. "I should have spent Christmas with Father's side of the family. They may be the most boring people in the whole of England, but life expectancy tends to be a lot higher in their neck of the woods."

We waited until he'd stopped nattering before heading back to the carriage where the guard and driver were standing. Grandfather was so used to getting his own way whenever a crime had been committed that the thought of them objecting to our presence can't have entered his mind.

"What do you think you're doing?" the moustachioed guard, with arms like sides of pork and a head the size of a large watermelon, stepped forward to demand. The driver, meanwhile, spoke no English but shouted a long string of angry German at us.

"There is no need to take that tone," the ever calm and cautious Lord Edgington told them. "I was formerly a police officer. My name is—"

"Why should your name interest us?" The guard pulled his immense shoulders back and stood in front of the door to ensure that Grandfather wouldn't pass. "If you are police no more, then you might as well the king of France be."

"France doesn't have a king," I foolishly intervened. "They abolished any form of monarchy in the nineteenth century." I resisted asking whether he'd heard of the French Revolution or the various Napoleons.

"I'll abolish the pair of you if you give me any trouble." I assume this is what he said, though it was delivered in his own language and at a volume for which I did not care.

"I have no wish to cause you problems." Grandfather raised his hands in front of him to show that he meant it. "But that train is the scene of a terrible crime. It must be carefully examined before any evidence goes missing."

The two rather brutish men laughed at this, and the guard explained what they were both thinking in his heavily accented, slightly broken English. "Terrible crime? The old woman died from cold and altitude. These things like this, they happen every day. *Real* police are in the town at the bottom of the mountain. They will be in charge of this."

I'd been willing to stay out of the argument until now, but I couldn't let them get away with outright lies. "You're saying that people die on this train every day?"

He finally looked a little sheepish, even as his friend grinned at the situation. "*Nein. Nicht jeden Tag.*[4]" I thought I understood this much, and then the guard switched back to English. "But yes, it does pass sometimes."

"I'm an experienced detective," Grandfather tried one last time, but the driver had already walked to the front of the train, and the guard wasn't about to change his mind.

"And I am an experienced train guard." He showed his crooked teeth. "Now go you."

The train was already stuttering into life, so the guard hurried to close the final doors and then waved to his colleague. I could tell just how much my grandfather hated to be defeated, but there was nothing he could do now that—

As I formed this conclusion, he sprang into action. The guard had walked away, and Grandfather opened the door of the moving train to dash into the dead woman's compartment.

"Grandfather!" Albert had calmed down just enough to get angry again. "Have you quite literally lost your mind?"

---

4 No, not every day.

I didn't say anything, but I felt extremely happy to see the old devil prevail. When he hurried back out of the train and over to us, he had a wickedly contented look on his face. "Come along, boys. Quickly, quickly. I believe we have a murder to investigate."

CHAPTER THIRTEEN

Todd had planned ahead as he always does and was waiting for us outside the station with Delilah and three pairs of snow racquets. I thanked him, sat on the bench to put them on and then gingerly trekked down the slope through thick snow that I almost disappeared beneath to reclaim the skis that I'd temperamentally discarded there.

"So, brother of mine, what have you been doing since we last saw you?" I asked Albert when I returned, though what I really wanted to know was what Grandfather had discovered on the train.

"Well, Christopher," he began in an oddly feelingful tone, "after the events of the last two years, I decided that the time had come to discover what makes me *me*. And do you know what I realised?"

If I'd had to hazard a guess, the answer would have been falling in love far too easily (though perhaps I could no longer complain on that score), getting carried away with whatever new obsession had struck him that month, and a propensity to be duped by dubious characters. Of course, I couldn't say any of that, so I went with, "Perhaps you have an old man's soul in a young man's body?" I thought this sounded complimentary yet vague enough to suggest I'd had a good think about my answer.

"As it happens, you're not far from the truth." He stopped walking and cast his noble gaze over the landscape as though contemplating the most profound questions that man is yet to ponder. "I have discovered that I am a poet."

Grandfather must have overheard this as he groaned softly to himself. I was not afforded any such luxury.

"A poet? Oh, how marvellous. I can't wait to read what you've written."

He walked on but kept his eyes fixed on the frozen countryside around us. "In a very real sense, my whole life is one long poem. My thoughts are an endless verse which, were I to write it down, would be the longest piece of literature ever committed to paper." He seemed to think this was a sign of quality. "Take this view, for example. My head is full of curious observations which flow so readily from my pen I sometimes have trouble keeping up with them."

He had clearly reached another stage of his existence that he would give up in six months before moving on to the next one. Since leaving home for university, he'd been keen on young women, politics, philosophy, young women, motoring, doubles tennis, young women, marriage, bachelorhood, his job in the City, sitting thinking and now poetry. I'd hoped that his recent period of reflection would lead to a sea change, but I didn't hold out much hope for his literary ambitions, and that was before I heard him trying to rhyme.

"Snow!" he suddenly declared. "Snow: white. So white. *Snow White*. Yet might...?" This was as far as his thoughts would travel on the matter, but at least he admitted as much. "It's a work in progress of course, but I think you can see where it's heading."

"It's certainly... thought provoking," I told him, though I didn't reveal what type of thoughts it had provoked.

He was evidently proud of his work. "Thank you so much."

"Do you intend to make this your career?"

He was still carrying one of his cases, and we both found going up the hill hard work. "Please, Christopher. Must we always place the pursuit of money before the creation of art? If my work is discovered by the masses and I become the leading literary voice of our day, so be it, but I would be just as happy to die in obscurity knowing that I had remained true to my artistic philosophy."

I took this to mean that he had already tried to sell his poems to publishers without any luck.

"You know to whom you simply must talk," I said as I felt that, while I was happy to have my brother there with us, and I looked forward to spending Christmas with him, there was still the small matter of a murderer to address. "Todd is a keen admirer of poetry. I'm certain that he would be overjoyed to hear about your new path."

I did feel guilty for pushing him away like that, especially if Todd had to put up with any impromptu poetry recitals, but I knew they would both understand. Luckily, Grandfather saw what I was trying to do and slowed down to talk to me. Delilah did the same, though presumably she was less interested in the case than whether we were headed back to the hotel for more food.

"Are you pleased with your surprise?" he surprised me once again by asking. "It took some organising to get him here."

"It's fabulous," I said quite sincerely. "The strange thing about brothers is that you are always happy to see them, even when there are other things that seem more important at the time. I just wish Mother and Father could have come."

"Speaking of other things," he said to change the subject, "I have no doubt that the woman on the train was murdered, though I didn't have time to determine how."

"That's just what I wanted to ask," I said with a hint of excitement. "I didn't notice any signs of poisoning, and if she were killed on the train, it would have been hard to force her to swallow something against her will."

I'd ended up carrying everyone's skis over my shoulder. It was preferable to having to help Albert with his heavy bags, but made the exertion required all the harder.

"I agree with your assessment." I could tell he was studying the scene of the murder once more in his mind. "Someone would have noticed if she were short of breath or in great pain. There was no time to inspect her properly, but I believe she was stabbed, perhaps in her back or the rear of the neck. I noticed stains on her clothes, but then the train reached the end of the platform, and it was my last chance to alight."

"And you said she'd been there for some time?"

"Most definitely. From the colour and temperature of her skin, I believe that she has been dead on that train since first thing this morning. It says something about the modern world that a woman could be left like that with no one checking that she was well. Of course, the angle of the train stopped her from falling forward."

I wondered what it said about Albert that he'd conducted a conversation with the woman and not realised she was dead, but that was not our most pressing concern.

"There's something else I discovered." He was surely proud of whatever he was about to reveal. "Her name was written on the luggage tag on the case at her feet. I was tempted to take it, but I trust the police will uncover anything significant and come up to us if their investigation leads them that far."

"So?" I asked, as he seemed to have become distracted. "What was she called?"

"Miss Barbara Nelson!" He swayed happily from one side to the

85

other as he walked, and I could tell this made him happy.

"My goodness! Have you ever heard such an English name?"

He turned more serious then. "Well, the origin of Barbara is Greek. It was formed from the word *barbaros* meaning brutal, cruel or uncivilised. That is where we get the word *barbarian.* Saint Barbara herself was a Greek—"

"Grandfather, is this likely to help us find the woman's killer?"

His brow ruffled, as though what I'd said was quite unreasonable. "You never know, but you must remember—"

I decided to interrupt. "There's a good chance that, no matter the etymology, with a name like Barbara Nelson she was English… or American… or Canadian… or— My point is that we already know that there are a number of English guests at the hotel – far more than have ever been there at Christmas before."

"That is true," he conceded, "especially as her address in Hemel Hempstead was written just below her name."

"Excellent. So the question is, what has brought them all to the Alps and could it be connected to the accidents yesterday and the apparent murder today?"

His face was still quite serious, and he took a few steps before responding. "That is good intuition on your part to connect the various elements of our burgeoning case. Of course, it could all be a coincidence. The accidents might be just that. The manager, Victor Ried, was dealing with the lamp and could have loosened it somehow, and it isn't uncommon for people with some degree of toxic intolerance to consume the very food that is harmful to them without realising. As for all the Britons here, perhaps there was an article in a newspaper about the wonders of Switzerland at Christmastime which sent every last guest off to the travel agent in search of the prettiest hotel with a view of the Matterhorn."

I was about to ask him which of the mountains around us was the Matterhorn, but he was too quick for me. "It's that one over there." We had made it to the break in the high rocks that I had so skilfully navigated on skis a short time earlier, and he pointed out the famous peak. It was the tallest on that side of the valley and had a beautiful pyramid-shaped top. It was easy to see why so many people came to this part of the world to marvel at it.

"Whatever coincidences there may or may not have been," I said to bring us back to the root of our conversation, "Barbara Nelson is dead. Has the time come for you to reveal to our fellow guests who you really are?"

He sniffed at this, and I could see how the suggestion disappointed him. "Do you really think that's necessary? I've been having such a lovely holiday from myself. You might not think it, but I can sympathise with Albert searching for his identity. I've been known as Lord Edgington, the indomitable detective, for so long that I'd forgotten what fun it is to be normal."

He'd finally admitted that he was not normal, but it sadly wasn't the moment for me to point it out. I can't begin to describe how frustrating this was.

"We'll at least have to talk to the manager of the hotel to find out what he knows," I more helpfully contributed. "He should be able to tell us whether Miss Nelson had a reservation here and when she was supposed to arrive."

Various possibilities ran through my head then. I'd expected Grandfather to take my idea and lead it to some interesting conclusion, but he remained oddly quiet. "I believe that what last night's letter told us is very important," I said in the hope it might touch off a response. "Think about all the people we've met at the hotel. Dolly and Sunday and the woman who was married to the earl. Rosetta… What was her surname?"

"Mullen."

"That's right, Rosetta Mullen. Well, we know that they all came from humble backgrounds. Or at least, I assume that was true in Dolly's case as she told us she was formerly a criminal. If you add that to the fact that I overheard Sunday talking to another of the guests – and I got the definite impression that they knew each other from their underprivileged youth – then it seems quite clear to me that there is some kind of reunion occurring here."

Something about the rhythm of his feet, quietly crunching on the compacted snow, told me that he wanted me to continue. I'm aware that must sound quite ridiculous, but if you'd spent as long as I have considering the internal machinations of an unknowable man like my grandfather, you'd completely understand why I would

87

come to this conclusion.

"I know that incredible coincidences happen every day, but this is something more. I'm sure of it."

For the moment, he refrained from passing judgement on my theory but asked for more information. "When you say 'reunion', what exactly do you have in mind?"

"Well, not a formal gathering. I don't mean that they've come here for a party. In fact, there's nothing to say that most of them even know one another. But suppose that someone drew them here. Maybe it was against their will—"

"Are you suggesting it could be blackmail?" He was staring across at the chocolate-box hotel that was still far off in the distance, though we'd been walking for some time.

"Precisely. Maybe someone wrote to the British guests to say that they had to come to Switzerland or a dark secret would be revealed."

I thought he might object to this rather fantastical idea, but instead he dropped his gaze to the path and asked, "Do you know what that secret might be?"

"No, but it would fit with the letters we've received. Think about it. We know that the person who wrote them feels he has been brought here for... what was the word he used? Retribution, wasn't that it? And he spoke of his criminal past." I could see a loose outline of the case beginning to take shape. "So let's imagine that the killer bears a grudge against a number of the guests here. It would make sense that—" I didn't finish this thought because a new possibility had presented itself.

"That was very interesting, Christopher. Why did you stop?"

"Something occurred to me," I told him, as the idea became clearer in my mind. "I hadn't considered before that we might ourselves have been manipulated." I stopped walking and looked straight at him. "How do we know that the killer and our mysterious letter writer aren't the same person?"

CHAPTER FOURTEEN

As the light cut in through the stained-glass window at the front of the building, it cast a red haze on the pine floor of the foyer. Looking back at it, I could see that the dragon's eyes glowed red as if they were on fire. I might have thought that this pretty effect added some colour to the room in time for Christmas, but Herr Ried was already doing that.

"Guten Morgen, gents. It is common in Switzerland to start decorating on Christmas Eve." He was halfway up a ladder again and evidently enjoyed spending time at altitude. He held a long string of silver bells that made a gentle jingling sound as he raised one end and a porter took the other.

I would happily have debated the merits of a last-minute, laissez-faire approach to decorating, but there were more important matters to discuss. "I'm sorry to disturb you, Herr Ried. There's something we'd like to ask."

He remained on the ladder, still tying the garland around the metal base of a wall sconce. "I won't keep you half a mo."

I really did enjoy hearing all his little Britishisms, especially as they were spoken with his soft Germanic accent. It almost sounded as if he were doing an impression of one of us.

"There we are. I'll leave the other side to Christian here." He had a wonderful smile and, as he stepped down from the ladder, he motioned to us to follow him as though we were old friends. "We can speak in my office. I hope there hasn't been any problem with your stay so far."

Grandfather didn't respond, Delilah decided to lie down in the sunshine in the middle of the foyer, and we'd lost Todd again at some point, so it fell to me to answer him as we entered the small room. "No, nothing like that. It's a beautiful hotel, and everything is just as we would wish it to be."

"It warms my cockles to hear you say that, Mr Prentiss. It really does, and I trust Lord Ow feels the same?" He pointed to two free chairs. They were positioned on the far side of a desk that was really too big for the tiny (piney) office. It made me wonder how they'd squeezed it in through the door in the first place.

"Oh, yes, yes," Grandfather blustered as though he hadn't expected to be addressed. "Everything has gone exactly as I'd hoped." I believe he would have winked at me at this point had the manager not been looking straight at us. There really is nothing he enjoys more than searching for a killer.

My brother, meanwhile, who had followed us rather slowly as he was marvelling at the impressive entrance hall, hung in the doorway as if he were surplus to requirements — which I suppose, in almost every way, he was.

"Wonderful, wonderful!" Ried put his hands together on the desk and waited for the conversation to begin in earnest.

"Right, yes..." It was hard to bridge the gap between the nice things we'd just said and what we now had to reveal. As Grandfather was busy being quiet for once, it fell to me to do so. "You see, the thing is..."

"If this is about the room for your brother," he continued before I could get to the point, "there really is no need to worry. Everything is in hand."

"Oh, splendid!" Albert declared. "I must admit that I was worried that Grandfather had forgotten all about me and I'd have to spend the night in a manger somewhere." He had a rather nervous laugh at the best of times, and it now fired up loudly.

"No, that's not what we wished to address," I said to take control again. "You see, we've just come from the mountain railway, and we discovered... well, there's no easy way to say it. We discovered a woman's dead body in the rear carriage. We know very little about her, as the train went back down before we could inspect the scene, but her name was Barbara Nelson."

"Nelson?" The bewilderment on his face belied what I was fairly certain was a note of recognition. "Yes, that name does sound familiar. In fact..."

He walked over to a Welsh (or perhaps Swiss) dresser that was wedged in between the door and the window. On the main shelf, the heavy, leather-bound hotel registry sat open for him to peruse. He ran his finger down one column before coming to a sudden stop.

"Yes, Miss Barbara Nelson. She was due to arrive on Monday, but several guests who were supposed to stay for a whole week turned up a day or two late."

"Is that normal?" Albert asked, as he was apparently now more interested in detective work than our grandfather was. "Don't people tend to pay for the time they actually spend at a hotel?"

"Well, yes, but it is quite common for a traveller to encounter some delay, especially at this time of year."

I sat forward in my chair. "However, it's curious that it would happen to a number of guests in the same week. Much as it is unusual for there to be so many Britons on the property at the same time."

He turned back to me. "Yes, Mr Prentiss, I suppose you're right."

Grandfather finally stirred. I wondered for a moment whether he had got up too early and, what with the skiing and walking and what have you, felt a little tired. "Would you mind if my grandson were to look at the hotel register?"

Being the obliging man that he clearly was, Ried picked up the tome and was about to bring it to the desk when something must have struck him as odd. "I beg your pardon, gentlemen, but may I ask what any of this has to do with you?"

I could see just how exciting this challenge was to my grandfather. His eyelashes fluttered for a moment like a pair of overly enthusiastic butterflies. "We have some experience with this sort of thing."

"With dead bodies?" the Swiss sounded disturbed by this.

"Well, yes, actually." It had been some days since Grandfather had had the chance to clear his throat, adjust his tie (or scarf in this case as he wasn't wearing formal attire) and say, "Perhaps you've heard of me. My real name is… *Lord Edgington*." So much for his holiday from fame. He was clearly overjoyed to be the world-renowned sleuth once more.

"Edgington? But you told me your name was Ow with a silent L." Ried wandered automatically over to us at the desk. "Why did you come here under false pretences?" I bet he was also thinking, *And why did you make up such a stupid name?* but he said no more.

"Grandfather always has a reason for his mad plans," Albert explained, which did little to rehabilitate our lofty forebear in the hotel manager's mind.

I felt it was ultimately my job to defend the old eccentric. "If we trust you with everything we know, you must be certain to keep this information from the other guests."

"You can trust me, sir, but…"

His shocked reaction reminded me of a scene in a fantastical novel that Todd lent me in which we discover that a family of characters we had come to know and love through the course of the book are creatures from another planet, disguised as ordinary humans.

"Lord Edgington..." he repeated, and it was evident that Grandfather's fame had reached the Swiss Alps. "I've read so much about you, but you're nothing like the stories in the books I buy."

He pointed to a high shelf on the dresser, which held a series of books with spines in different colours. I noticed that the first one was called *Die Frühlingsballmorde*[5]. I'd heard on a previous case about the novels that dramatised my adventures with Grandfather, but I'd yet to learn how they came to exist. The German editions would do little to help in that respect.

"As we revealed last night, we were summoned here by another of the guests," I explained to convince him of our cause. "Well, we assume he is a guest. We don't know anything for certain, but the letters he sent us are the reason we came to Switzerland in the first place."

"Wait." Still with an uncomfortable expression on his face, he raised his hand to beg for patience. "Are you telling me that you think the other guests may be in danger?" He was a smart fellow and soon took this idea to its less than obvious conclusion. "You think the woman on the *Bergbahn* was murdered, don't you?"

"We do indeed," Albert was clearly coming around to the prospect of investigating a nice Christmassy murder after all. "Grandfather found blood on her clothes."

As the manager grew accustomed to the idea of who we were and why we were there, a sense of unease had grown within me. "I'm sorry to interrupt, but if you've read all those books about my grandfather, why didn't you recognise me? Our reservation is in my name, isn't it?"

Now he looked apologetic. "Yes, but your surname is never mentioned in the novels. In fact, you're normally referred to *as der pummelige Einfaltspinsel*." Before I could ask him what this meant, he translated with a wince. "In English it would signify something along the lines of *the pudgy little simpleton*."

"Seriously, the pudgy little simpleton?"

"I'm afraid so."

---

[5] Approximately, "Murder at the Spring Ball" (the first Lord Edgington mystery).

Inevitably, my brother and grandfather thought this was the most hilarious thing they'd ever heard. I looked back at the shelf and realised that there were at least fifteen books up there, which surely covered a major part of what I'd previously considered my prestigious career as a detective.

"Doesn't the name change as I grow and become more experienced?" I should probably have concentrated on what we'd gone there to discuss, but I was frankly rather irked.

"Well, yes…" For a moment, I was hopeful that this would improve things, but then he grimaced again, and I could tell there was something more that he didn't wish to reveal. "After the first eight or so books, once you reach the age of eighteen, there are several really very awkward subplots in which you fall in love and have your heart broken by a string of beautiful young ladies."

"What does the author call me?" I demanded through gritted teeth. "Tell me, Ried!"

He looked at my brother, perhaps for permission to insult me further. When no one objected, he revealed, "You're known as *der hoffnungslose Casanova*."

Grandfather couldn't contain his laughter. "The hopeless Casanova? Oh, that's just too rich!"

"And completely inaccurate," I was quick to tell them, as the joy spread to my brother. "It's Albert who's always falling in love and making a fool of himself, not me."

Even Herr Ried couldn't hide his amusement now. "As it happens, your brother doesn't appear in any of the stories. I assume they must have combined your characters into one."

Albert immediately stopped laughing. "How disappointing. I think I'd rather be a plump simpleton Casanova than stop existing altogether." He went to perch on the dresser and looked just as glum as when he'd discovered that he'd made friends with a dead woman.

I don't know what he was so worried about; he wasn't the one that people all over the world found so hilarious. I was already imagining the girl of my dreams laughing her precious French head off at my expense.

I met him once, and he really is that dim! I heard her telling her friends with glee. *He is one of what we French call 'Les Incompétents'.*

"I am truly sorry to break this terrible news to you," Herr Ried said to Albert, and this was the straw that broke the camel's back (and my patience).

"None of that matters. Just give me the register!" I might not have said this quite so harshly, but let me tell you, the tone I used in my head right then was bordering on the rude.

"Yes, of course," the manager said, pushing the weighty volume across the table and turning it around for me to see. "About half of our guests left this morning to return to their homes for Christmas. It will be a small and hopefully intimate gathering we share together this year."

It was curious how he kept changing between the calm, polished persona he had honed as the manager of the Villa Cassel and his more nervous, personal façade. He had looked quite frightened when we'd told him that a team of detectives (and Albert) were on the premises investigating a murder, but talk of Christmas had distracted him from any such emotions.

Grandfather leaned close to read the list of names, dates and (less interestingly) prices. The titles were all in German, but it was easy enough to work out what each signified from the information underneath.

Namen	Aufenthaltsdaten	Preis	Reserviert	Zimmer
D & G Coxon	21-28.12.29	25 CHF	05.12.29	101
D & S Cheshire	21-28.12.29	25 CHF	05.12.29	207
R. Mullen	21-28.12.29	25 CHF	05.12.29	206
Dr Hans Gruber & familie	17-23.12.29	40 CHF	14.08.29	208
Elisabeth Hall	21-28.12.29	25 CHF	05.12.29	105
Barbara Nelson	21-28.12.29	25 CHF	05.12.29	
Blanche & Henry Atkinson	21-28.12.29	25 CHF	05.12.29	108
Inge Weinreich	19-26.12.29	50 CHF	22.09.29	104
C. Prentiss & Großvater	23-30.12.29	60 CHF	05.12.29	204
A. Prentiss	23-30.12.29	25 CHF	05.12.29	203

I found the Cheshires very quickly, and then one R. Mullen. The expert skier's full name was Inge Weinreich, and it appeared that she was the last local staying at the hotel now that the doctor and several Swiss families had left.

Perhaps least importantly for our case, there was a note explaining that our staff were all staying in servant quarters that didn't get a mention in the register. More significantly, I discovered that Dolly and Graham's surname was Coxon. I remembered that the woman with whom Sunday walked up the mountain was called Libby, and based on the list before me, I concluded that her full name was Elisabeth Hall.

There was also a married couple I hadn't heard of before, though I believed they'd been at dinner with us. Judging by the names Blanche and Henry Atkinson, I took them to be as British as I was. What I couldn't say was how any of this would help me shed light on the still tentative mystery we were trying to unearth – though, in this environment, perhaps that should be *un-snow*.

I moved on to the dates and, much as Herr Ried had suggested, all the guests who were staying in the hotel that night had reserved for a whole week. We'd arrived a few days after some of their stays had begun, and Rosetta Mullen had clearly turned up late – as the now *very late* Barbara Nelson also would have. It would take more than a hotel register to explain why she was killed though. But then I saw something unlikely that should have stood out to me from the first moment.

"All the British guests reserved their rooms on the same day," I said, jabbing my finger at the penultimate column on the page where 05.12.29 repeated over and over.

"That's right. I believe I told you when you came yesterday, the money was paid directly into our bank. I assumed it was a group booking by a travel agent."

"So then every British guest's room was reserved at the same time as ours." I positively sung as I voiced this thought. "The person who asked us to come here must have brought the others too."

Ried evidently didn't know all that I was thinking but looked a touch disturbed. Grandfather was still oddly reticent, and Albert was confused by all that was going on and said, "Sorry, I think I must have missed something. Who brought everyone here?"

CHAPTER FIFTEEN

When we came out of the office, Delilah was asleep in her warm spot in the foyer and didn't look as though she had any intention of moving. She could do a very good impression of a rug when she wanted to.

"No, no," my brother assured me as we made our way upstairs to see his room. "I do find what you and Grandfather do remarkably interesting. It might surprise you to know that I've written a poem about you. Would you like to hear it?"

This was a difficult question to answer. On the one hand, I had no interest whatsoever in hearing his poem. On the other... Well, there wasn't really another hand. In this scenario, the man who is weighing up the decision lost an arm in a bizarre cow milking accident.

Of course, Albert was my brother, so I said, "Would I?" though it sounded more like a question than I had intended.

He cleared his throat in the slightly pretentious manner of bad poets the world over.

"I am the grandson of a great detective:
The unwanted reject of a fine family.
I am the boy who keeps trying to grow up but never will.
I am Albert Doris Prentiss,
And I am not what I'm supposed to be."

I didn't know how to respond to this, but I had to say something. "Yes. That's very... Well, it reminds me of a limerick."

"A limerick?" He adopted a slightly different voice when discussing his art. "I just chipped off a tiny fragment of my soul and placed it in the palm of your hand. It is nothing like a limerick."

"That's not true. They both have five lines."

I was most relieved that Inge Weinreich overtook us going up the stairs at this moment. She was fast like that.

"I'm off for my nap," she explained. "It's the only way I can stay up to go skiing late at night. Have a lovely time whatever you young men get up to."

I could see that Albert was about to ask more questions about my appreciation of his work when Dunstan Cheshire appeared on the first-floor landing. He was wearing a thick dressing gown and looked as though he were going for a swim but, as far as I knew, there was no pool at the hotel. If one did exist, the water would have to be very warm for me to go anywhere near it in the mountains in the wintertime.

"I'm off to the *Schwitzbad*," he partially explained when we caught one another's eye. I didn't get the impression he wanted to tell me this, but it was too late, and he clearly felt the need to add, "You can join me if you wish. Sunday is having a lie-down."

"Yes, definitely!" I told him, as anything was better than having to listen to more of Albert's poetry. "This is my brother. He just arrived. Is he welcome along too?" I once again made this question sound far too uncertain, and I think I must have scared poor Dunstan.

"Yes, of course," he answered with almost as much hesitation. "I'll see you downstairs shortly."

"I've always wanted to try a *Schwitzbad*," Albert told me chirpily once we'd waved off our new friend.

"And I've always wanted to know what one is, ever since I saw the word written on a door yesterday!"

We found Albert's room, and I immediately understood why it was less than half the price of mine. It wasn't just that it was smaller. It was a poky octagon with only one window that had been squashed into the turret of the building. The bed wasn't nearly so handsome either, and I felt this made up somewhat for all the times we'd gone away as a family and Albert had ended up with grand quarters, whilst I, the younger brother, had been stuck in a cupboard out of the way. Not that I still think of such injustices now that I am an adult, of course.

"It's lovely," he told me, because he hadn't seen how nice our suite was. "This is real Alpine living, and I'm all for it." He walked to the window to see if he could spot the Matterhorn again, but all we could make was a lot of snow. The weather had changed, and dark clouds now occupied the sky above the valley. "And good old Todd has already unpacked my things," he said, noticing his empty case on a chest at the end of the bed. When he opened the wardrobe, he found jumbled piles of balled up clothes, so it was evidently Dorie who had been put in charge of his possessions.

"There are dressing gowns in the bathroom," I told him as I moved to pop next door. "I'll get changed and come back to pick you up."

This process took no time and, a minute or two later, we were downstairs ready to enjoy whatever a *Schwitzbad* turned out to be.

"I meant what I said before about your detective work," Albert assured me as we walked along the corridor where the bar and dining room were located. "If there's anything I can do to help this weekend, you only need to ask. I can be the Chrissy to your Lord Edgington."

This just made me wonder where the real Lord Edgington was and what he could possibly be doing, but I'm not the world's worst replacement. That job falls to my brother.

"It's good that you should say that," I told him, stopping with my hand on the door to the men's *Schwitzbad*, "as the man we're about to see could know something important about what brought us here. I may have to rake him over the coals, so follow my lead."

He looked genuinely happy at the thought that he could help. The last time he'd been involved in an investigation, he'd ended up with his hands covered in blood and was nearly carted off to a police station, so I hoped we could avoid that fate this time.

I opened the door and found myself in a room full of what I took to be smoke, then questioned whether there was localised fog in the area before the heat hit me and I realised that a *Schwitzbad* was some form of steam bath.

"Come in, boys," Dunstan Cheshire told us from… somewhere. I couldn't see a thing through all that wet-hot mist.

"Is it working properly?" I had to ask as Albert closed the door behind me and my eyes did their best to make out shapes.

"Of course it is, little brother," he replied as though he were far more worldly and debonair than I. "The steam cleans your body. I've heard it's a marvellous experience and does wonders for one's health."

He had already taken off his gown and hung it on a hook on the door, so I did the same. I was glad we had both thought to wear bathing togs underneath, but it was so hot in there, I would quite happily have sacrificed my modesty to be even a fraction cooler.

"Sit down, sit down," Dunstan told us in his ever smooth and persuasive tone. He was the sort of person who frightens me. I was sure that, had he asked me to fetch his hat from the deepest Alpine valley or climb a dangerous mountain – you know, just like my grandfather – I would have said yes without a moment's hesitation.

I knew that this was the perfect opportunity to quiz him on several topics we needed to investigate, but the air was so thick that my breathing had become unusually loud. "I'm glad to have… the chance to… talk to you again," I said between pants. Normally I would have built up to any tough questions, but I wasn't sure how long it would be before I had to run outside again, so I went straight for the throat.

Well, I tried to, but he interrupted.

"Yes, it's nice to be here. I can't imagine doing anything like this back in Blighty, but you know what they say; 'When in Switzerland'."

"No, old boy. The saying is, 'When in Rome'," Albert helpfully corrected him. I couldn't make out his face through the steam, but I am fairly certain that he tipped an imaginary hat, and I could already tell this interview would not go to plan.

"As I was saying," I continued, "it's very kind of you to invite us here …" deep breath because I was sitting in a large, wooden oven. "Especially as, after last night—"

"I'm sorry if neither of us was in high spirits yesterday. The truth is that what happened with the chandelier really shook my Sunday."

I spotted a way to bend the conversation round to what I needed to ask, but then Albert leaned forward and whispered, "No, dear fellow. Yesterday was Monday. Sunday was the day before. I too lose sense of what day it is whenever I'm on holiday."

I pretended he hadn't said anything. "It was clear to me that you didn't want to—"

"I once spent a whole day at the seaside thinking it was Friday and, when I got home that night, I realised it was actually— Ow!"

My brother made this noise because I'd just kicked him, but Dunstan didn't know that.

"Your grandfather was there?"

"No, no," I said to stop Albert from saying anything. "Lord Ow no longer enjoys the seaside. He finds the attractions frightening and doesn't like having sand between his toes. Now, where was I?"

Dunstan didn't answer but took a small towel and started whipping it through the air in an endless circle. This served to push the hot air from the top of the room to the bottom and nearly made me pass out. How could anyone in his right mind need to be hotter than we already were?

"I was about to ask…" My breathing was even shallower than

before. "…I need to know…" I had to stop again as the steam passing through my lungs felt as though my insides had been set alight. It was both sweet and dreadful at the same time. "You must tell me what sort of criminal your wife was before you were married!"

For a moment, there was total silence in the small wooden room. I thought I could make out the fear on Dunstan's face through the swirling mist. His lips parted, and he was just about to answer when Albert fainted and went crumpling to the floor.

CHAPTER SIXTEEN

We took our thick dressing gowns and hurried to get Albert out into the cold air in order to rouse him. There was an exit at the end of the corridor and, as soon as we were through it, my brother yelled out, as though we'd put smelling salts under his nose and he was alarmed by the revival.

"How did we get here?" he asked, as we held him on a step which was the only spot free of snow.

My feet stung from the cold stone, but the smells coming from the kitchen a few rooms away were quite lovely.

"Don't worry about that now," Dunstan insisted. "Just breathe in the fresh air. It's very good for you. In certain Nordic countries, they claim that the sudden change from hot to cold works wonders for fighting off colds and the like."

Albert breathed in and out three times in an exaggerated manner. "That's enough, thank you. I'm perfectly fine now, but I would prefer to be wearing more clothes than I currently am." He turned to open the door, but I couldn't miss the opportunity to probe Dunstan a second time. I stood there – occasionally hopping from foot to foot – resigned to the fact I would most likely lose a toe or two by the time we returned inside.

"I don't mean to sound suspicious, but I would like to hear why you felt it necessary to keep your wife's past from us at dinner last night."

He was bending his knees with his arms outstretched and taking deep breaths. I understood this to be some kind of exercise rather than a sudden mania that had overtaken him.

"There's a good reason that I didn't wish to tell you about the time between my first meeting with Sunday and our later reunion."

"She did something unforgivable that has now come back to haunt you?" I asked, perhaps optimistically, and he stopped his lunging for a moment.

"No, of course not. Where would you get such an idea?" Luckily, this was a rhetorical question, and he kept talking. "I didn't wish to tell you because I am very protective of my kind-hearted wife, and I wouldn't want anyone to take advantage of her. As my attempts to keep her free from suspicion have led you to becoming suspicious of her, I suppose I should just tell you."

He paused to bend his knees once more, and I found myself copying him, if only to do something to distract me from the arctic conditions. People in Nordic countries may enjoy plunging into cold temperatures after a hot bath or what have you, but then there are lunatics wherever you travel.

"After I managed to secure Sunday her house in Whitechapel, I moved away with my job and worked in many different places. Remember, I was little more than a boy and never imagined that such a sophisticated and mature woman would want anything to do with me. During that time, things were hard for her. She didn't have to pay a great deal for the accommodation, but her parents were dead, and she had younger brothers and sisters for whom to provide. And let us not forget that the supposed friends she'd had made in that once less than salubrious area were not your or my kind of people."

I could tell where the story was going, but he clearly needed some help to get us there. "So she was manipulated in some way?"

He bit his lip as he looked out across the landscape to that beautiful row of mountains beyond the peak I'd scaled. The height of the towering Matterhorn made my own achievement look really very paltry, but I could climb it with my eyes at least.

"Perhaps manipulated is too strong a word. Sunday needed money, and an old acquaintance of her father's made a proposition to her." I admittedly thought the worst then, and he hurried to set my mind at ease. "I'm sorry. *Proposition* wasn't the right word either. This old man was something of a Fagin. He had a stable of thieves: not children – he wasn't that bad. He found adults to do jobs that were quite illegal. As Sunday was such a well-turned-out and honest-looking young woman, he thought that she would be able to get into places to which his less… shall we say, presentable employees were denied access."

"So she was a thief?"

He hesitated then. "Not exactly, but when we met for the second time, and I fell quite helplessly in love with her, there was a reason she wouldn't have anything to do with me. I don't mind telling you, Christopher, that when I get a prize in my sights, I am not the kind of person to relinquish it. I pursued Sunday even as she told me that we could not be married. I would not give up, and in the end, she revealed something of her former life to me. She told me there had been desperate moments when she had no other choice but to break the law to provide for her family. She was generally charged with obtaining information rather than outright stealing goods. She has a very guilty conscience over what happened and, while she is normally open about her upbringing, there are some things which she still hasn't told me."

A few small elements that had been niggling away at the back of my mind jumped forward, and I had a new list of questions to put to him. "Sunday eventually accepted you, but did your people accept her?"

It was not just his refined manner that told me he came from money. Grandfather had worked out the very same thing the night before, and he was rarely wrong.

"No, they didn't." He looked away once more, and I took this opportunity to jump on the spot again. "I discovered that plenty of the people I had imagined to be open-minded and generous of spirit were quite the opposite."

"Even in your family?" I dared ask, and his nostrils flared as he released another deep breath.

"Especially in my family. I was practically disowned." He must have realised just how angry he looked, as he smiled to cover it. "But some sacrifices are worth making."

I could tell this was a difficult subject for him, so I moved us back to the present day. "May I ask whether you knew any of the other guests before you arrived here?"

He had started his exercises again but stopped to look up at me. "May I ask why I'm being interrogated?"

I had never before realised how much I make use of Lord Edginton's fame to conduct our investigations. I was eager to tell him who I really was, but knowing Grandfather, he had more reasons than he'd revealed for hiding his identity. However, there was one thing I *could* disclose.

"Because I'm trying to understand what we are all doing here. You see, I received two letters from someone calling himself X. I still don't know who wrote them, but he claimed that his life was in danger and asked us to come to this hotel. Ever since we arrived, strange things have been happening, and I'm determined to get to the bottom of them."

"How curious." He held his hands out flat in front of him, and I was fairly confident by this point that not only my feet, but the entirety of my legs had turned to ice. "I can understand why you would be so inquisitive. I'm amazed you came here in the first place."

"And the other guests?" I reminded him.

"I can't say I know a single one of them." He took a moment to consider his answer. "Well, there is that rather obnoxious character whom everyone has been discussing. Mullens, is it?"

"Rosetta Mullen."

"Yes, that's her. She's the type the society pages are forever mentioning, normally in disparaging terms from what Sunday tells me."

"Does your wife know her personally?"

He straightened up, and the expression on his face told me that he was human after all; the cold was finally getting to him. "No, but they were both born in the same area of London."

"Does she know anyone else here?"

He wrapped his hands around himself, and I thought he might open the door to take us back inside, but he just stood there. "Not that she's told me, but I don't see what that's got to do with your mysterious letter writer."

"Then what about this friend you were supposed to meet? Have you heard from him? Does he have any connection to Sunday's early life?"

"Now, now." He'd said he was protective of her, but that was putting it mildly. "Please don't try to connect the situation in which this X fellow finds himself to my wife. This is the very reason that I don't like anyone to know of her past. It's too easy to blame her for the slightest bad thing that happens."

"That's not what I'm trying to do," I insisted. "But I believe there's a reason we've all been drawn here. There must be something that connects us."

He put his hand on the door handle but remained on the step. I felt he was probably just teasing me now. "Very well then. No, my friend hasn't appeared, and when I sent a telegram to find out whether he would be coming, he was entirely unaware of the arrangement I thought we'd made. So it seems you may be right, young man. Perhaps we've all been brought here under false pretences."

CHAPTER SEVENTEEN

Handsome, debonair and clearly highly accomplished: there was something intimidating about Dunstan Cheshire. I felt I should have extracted more from him, but he wasn't the most accommodating witness. Still, one thing was clear: either his wife hadn't told him of her connection to Libby Hall, or he was lying. The problem was, I couldn't decide which of those options was the more likely.

Dunstan strode back to the steam bath with his usual confidence, and I walked through the hotel thinking over the numerous threads to a still quite intangible case. I was most surprised to find Grandfather in the handsome library, sipping a pink cocktail.

"Christopher! Won't you join us?"

He'd been laughing his head off about something, and Todd was already pouring me a drink as I stepped inside.

"It's called the Rose," he explained, motioning to the pastel concoction. "It has *kirsch*, which is a cherry brandy from this part of the world, mixed with vermouth and raspberry syrup."

He'd made a makeshift bar on a small bookshelf that divided two different seating areas and now slid the glass over to me before slicing open a glacé cherry and placing it on the rim of the glass. As I took my first sip, I looked about the large room. I'd never been in a library with a view of snowy mountains before, but then there aren't any snowy mountains in southern England, where I'd spent every previous winter of my life.

"It tastes like a child's dessert that has gone sour," I said once I'd allowed the mixture to travel around my taste buds.

"I'm sorry, sir," Todd was quick to say. "I can make something that's more to your liking."

"Not at all," I assured him. "That wasn't a criticism. Some of my favourite desserts are largely eaten by children, and the mix of dry, fruity and bitter tastes is exquisite."

Grandfather would most likely have laughed at me then, but he was busy enjoying his own drink.

"I'm glad I've found you," I told him. "I've managed to confirm a few of my theories."

"I didn't realise that we'd reached the stage of sharing theories." Grandfather frowned to show his surprise. "I'm eager to hear what you've discovered."

This once more struck me as strange coming from a man who had done little to help that day. He'd been so notably absent that it had left me feeling quite alone – and then my brother had taken an interest in the case, which had made me feel as if I'd be better on my own after all.

"First, my belief that Sunday Cheshire was previously a criminal turned out to be correct."

"That doesn't make her a killer, Christopher," Grandfather sounded a little haughty then. He evidently felt that I should be upholding his good example even when he wasn't around to set it. "There's nothing to say that a person's indiscretions decades earlier are a sign of a propensity to violence so much time later."

I had another gulp of my red-fruit delight and made him wait for my response. "I wasn't saying that she was a killer, thank you, Grandfather. I'm interested in her because I believe she could be a link between various suspects, and that would help explain what we're all doing here."

"I'm listening," he said as though I had reason to doubt it.

"We know that Dolly and Sunday both have criminal connections of some description. In addition, I overheard Dunstan's wife talking to another guest by the name of Libby Hall. From what they said, I understood that they had known one another many years ago, and Libby feels she is owed something. She said that Sunday received money that was rightfully hers. Perhaps it was a stretch of the imagination on my part to think of this as evidence that they'd done something illegal, but I spoke to Dunstan Cheshire and he confirmed that, before they married, Sunday had been a sort of thief, who ingratiated herself into wealthy houses and perhaps other establishments in order to obtain information."

For the first time that week, Grandfather looked a little impressed by my work. "You said there were various theories you'd formed."

This was not a question, but I treated it as one. "I've also confirmed that Albert is an even bigger softie than I am."

"An important discovery."

"And I realised that I don't understand why you've abandoned the investigation to sip cocktails."

He glowered at me then. My grandfather is a master at glowering.

He can make the most dangerous men quake with little more than a look and, for a long time, he had struck fear in me with that very same technique. Sadly for him, as I was the one doing all the work, it didn't work this time.

"That isn't an explanation, Grandfather. Have you decided that you're on holiday? Have you finally retired for good?"

"No, of course not. Like any reasonable person, I'll retire when I'm dead, or perhaps a short time later if necessary."

"You're still avoiding the question." Something came to me then, and I was half amazed that I hadn't considered it before. "In fact, you've been doing it ever since we left Italy. I thought you were being your usual peculiar self, but there's something more, isn't there?"

"I don't know what you mean."

Even Todd looked a little circumspect as he busied himself with the drinks paraphernalia.

"Yes, you do. You know far more than you've been willing to admit this whole time, don't you?" I didn't wait for a response. New pieces of evidence were slotting into place with every sentence I spoke. I remembered the register in the manager's office, and several things stood out to me that had meant little before. "You have the best room in the hotel!"

"And?" He turned to whisper to his regular co-conspirator. "I believe the boy has lost his mind."

I ignored his aside and continued to lay out the case against him. "And you sound like any one of our suspects who knows he's been found out. My point is that you didn't reserve this hotel yourself, yet you still ended up with the best room here."

"Which shows that my appreciation of the finer things in life is widely known."

"Don't get ahead of yourself, old thing. There's more to come." I was gaining confidence. "Of all the Britons in this hotel, we are the only ones whose booking did not begin on the twenty-first of December, which raises the question of why our anonymous correspondent would have chosen a different day from anyone else for us to arrive. Furthermore, there is the apparently unsolvable mystery of how the letters calling us to come here found their way into our suite in Milan, even though Todd was in the neighbouring room the whole time we were out of the hotel."

Grandfather was bored with the conversation and glanced nonchalantly through the window. "I had hoped that you'd discovered something useful, but I really don't see the relevance of this." He was a decent actor, but not quite decent enough.

"The thing that really gave the game away – the thing that spoilt your little plan – was that, for any of this to make sense, the person who wrote the letters and brought a large collection of people halfway across the Continent to converge on a grand hotel at the top of the highest mountain range in Europe must surely command great resources. Resources which would be well within the grasp of a duke or, let's say, a marquess."

The Marquess of Edgington finally looked back at me. I had walked to the centre of the room to make my point in more dramatic fashion (can you guess where I learnt such a technique?), but I now returned to lay my claims at the feet of the man I had identified as the guilty culprit.

"You arranged all of it, didn't you, Grandfather?" I stopped talking, and the room was so quiet that I could hear the chunks of ice clinking against one another in his glass. My bare feet on the carpet beneath me suddenly sounded loud. "You lured all those other people here, too, presumably as some kind of test for me, and you're about to tell me the whole story."

Silence gripped the pair of us for ten whole seconds as I anticipated his response.

"Very well," he said, still in that same lethargic, slightly superior tone that he'd been using for much of the day. "But first you must tell me why you look as though you've just stepped out of the bath."

CHAPTER EIGHTEEN

When I didn't answer, the tension in the room held for a moment, and then Grandfather broke out laughing. His demeanour changed in an instant, and I could practically feel how proud he was from five paces away.

"Oh, well done, Christopher. I'm genuinely impressed. Todd and I made a bet. He said that you would work it all out by lunch time, and look who's just arrived."

I turned to the doorway to see our cook, Henrietta, pushing in a trolley laden with food. "Has he worked it out yet?" she asked as she reached Todd.

It turned out that she was at the head of a short procession. Following just behind her were our maid Dorie, her assistant Timothy and, now dressed and looking less pale, my brother.

"He must have done after my sensational acting last night," Dorie declared, before her voice fell quieter, and a serious expression graced her broad features. "Oh, dearie! I bumped into someone from my past. Someone I thought I would never see again!" She dropped the act to laugh at me. "My goodness, Little Edgington. You should have seen your face."

Which prompted me to ask, "Did everyone know but me?"

This was an invitation for my brother to join in with the chortling, though I doubt he understood what had inspired it. I considered complaining that it was unfair for the staff to be let in on the secret when I wasn't, but I was feeling peckish after our morning's exercise, and I concentrated on the food that Cook had brought.

It was customary in Grandfather's house for the staff to eat with us on Christmas Eve, and a buffet lunch was quite typical before the heavier fare of the coming meals. However, what brought me the greatest joy was that Henrietta had forgone some of her more *creative* (that is a euphemism, and ruder words are available) dishes in favour of some familiar favourites.

There were a variety of meats available along with plenty of individual steak and kidney pies. I also noticed cheese flans, oatmeal cannelons and fish sausages, and helped myself to a little of each.

There was no standing on ceremony for once, which was good, as Dorie hadn't a clue what ceremony was and piled her plate high. Not-really-so-little-any-more Timothy was far politer and waited his turn. It occurred to me then that I barely ever saw Todd eat, but he did help himself and nibble on a few things. He was too good a factotum to burden himself with a loaded plate, but too friendly a fellow not to partake with the rest of us.

"Wait just one moment," I told my grandfather when we'd ended up in an armchair near the large fireplace which, just to make a change, wasn't made of pine. "Todd bet that I'd work out your little plot by lunch time, but what did you think?"

He must have considered fibbing or avoiding the question altogether but, in the end, he confided in me with a smile. "I told him you'd have the whole thing wrapped up in a bow with tinsel around it by late last night."

I might have blushed at this. "Then I'm sorry to have disappointed you."

His voice somehow dropped lower than its normal bassy tone. "You're never a disappointment to me, Christopher. Your dexterity over the last day has impressed me as it always does."

The noise of our cosy and boisterous group had risen, and he turned to look approvingly at them. In some ways, my grandfather was not a demonstrative person, but I had no doubt that he loved the odd bunch with which he surrounded himself. That he was attracted to unusual characters was shown by the fact he'd chosen a near-hopeless young boy to be his assistant in place of someone competent.

Whatever he was feeling at that moment was soon pushed to the back of his mind as he rose to address everyone. It was not the message of Christmas cheer I'd been expecting.

"Ladies and gentlemen, I am so very happy to have you all here, but the truth is that this may be our last carefree moment together of the holiday. While I planned this excursion as an enjoyable challenge for my grandson, a woman really has been murdered, and I fear that more are in danger." For a team of people who were used to such announcements – and had even come to expect murder to follow us around the Continent just as it did at home – they looked unexpectedly disturbed by this. "Christopher has rightly come to the conclusion that

I invited a group of people here who were all criminals at one point in their lives and some of them may still be."

This caused a stir of excitement as we waited to hear what he would reveal next.

"What he doesn't know, and I suspect that even some of the other guests have failed to realise, is that each of our fellow British visitors was connected to a daring theft some twenty years ago."

Todd was still standing to attention at his bar but straightened a little and pulled his shoulders back, which I took as a sign that he already knew all that his master would convey.

"What theft?" I asked, as Grandfather had fallen quiet. "How could it be important enough to murder someone after all this time?"

He turned to look at me, and his expression was just as stern as he knew how to make it. "I can only answer one of those questions. It is our task to uncover who travelled to meet Barbara Nelson early this morning to murder her on that train."

"So you can tell us what was stolen," Albert rightly surmised.

"Yes, but only because, as a superintendent of the Metropolitan Police, I was assigned to investigate the disappearance of a very valuable item." To be perfectly honest, I felt he was milking the drama by this point, which isn't to say I didn't want to hear what he knew. "A diamond and ruby tiara was stolen from the Princess Royal."

"Princess Louise?" Dorie asked, and she was surprisingly well informed about the royal family considering that she could never get her employer's title right. "The daughter of King Edward and seventh grandchild of Queen Victoria? That Princess Royal?"

"The very same. She was given the piece by her grandmother on her eighteenth birthday in 1885. The stones within it had been presented to the Queen by an Indian rajah, and they featured a pair of fifteen-carat pigeon-blood rubies that were rare for being so very close in shape, size and lustre. The tiara went missing in 1909, at which point I was consulted."

"I never read anything about it in the newspapers." Cook was the second oldest of our party, and the senior figure in the group in many respects. "I would have remembered something like that."

"Well, quite." Grandfather uttered these two words as if he needn't say anything else on the matter, but he eventually continued. "I was invited to investigate the case on the condition that I would not talk to anyone else about it for a period of twenty years. I'm sure you don't need to be told that I was true to my word, but that time has now passed."

"What happened to the tiara?" Albert asked, strolling forward to perch on my armchair with one of Cook's delicious pastries in his hand. "Was the great Lord Edgington defeated?"

"Not at all." He inevitably sounded put out by this suggestion. "Well, not completely, at least. I recovered several smaller diamonds and even the golden frame, but the most substantial jewels were never found."

"Was anyone arrested for the crime?" I asked, as that seemed more important than what happened to some pretty pieces of glass.

"Only one person. A woman by the name of Elisabeth Hall."

I must have gasped at this moment, as everyone turned to look at me. "She's here at the hotel. She's the one I heard talking to Sunday Cheshire on the mountainside. I had the impression that they had worked together when they were younger."

"That's right. She and Sunday Cheshire, or Legyear as she was before marriage, were maids in Fife House, the Princess's home on the Brighton seafront."

Sorry, I have to interrupt my grandfather at this juncture to question what Mr and Mrs Legyear were thinking when they named their daughter Sunday. As if a surname like Legyear wasn't distinctive enough!

"The Princess Royal and her husband, the Duke of Fife, maintained several properties including a hunting lodge in Scotland, a weekend retreat near Richmond Park, and a grand flat in central London. They moved often between these homes, and the princess told me that, though devastating, she first considered the loss to be a consequence of their itinerancy."

"But you discovered something more sinister?" I suggested, and I didn't need one of his slow, dramatic nods to know that I was right.

"I did." I could tell how much he was enjoying taking on his regular role as a detective after so long pretending that he wasn't interested in the case. "I interviewed all the staff in the various locations. I spoke to my criminal connections and other police officers to know whether there was any discussion of such a valuable piece coming up for sale on the black market. I even interviewed distant royals and aristocrats who might have fallen on hard times and helped themselves to a bauble when visiting family. And do you know what I discovered?" He paused to make sure we were paying sufficient attention. "Nothing whatsoever."

"But someone was arrested," young Timothy reminded him. I had rarely spent much time with the boy, but he had a quick mind and an eye for detail. "How could that be?"

"Because the investigation took much longer than I had predicted. I spent that month working on the case. I was taken off all other duties, and yet the thread of evidence I required would not emerge until I could be certain that the jewellery had been stolen from the Brighton residence. For the most part, the staff had been working there for a long time. There were only two who had joined more recently. One was a maid, and the other was the head of household. As far as I could tell, there was no connection between them, other than their both coming from East London, but there was something highly unlikely about their employment in such a fine house."

Everyone was enthralled by the tale. It was fitting for the day, as it is quite common to tell ghost stories on Christmas Eve. The way that Grandfather took us back twenty years made it feel as though he were reviving the dead.

"Both had reliable references from well-established families, though I realised that, in both cases, the people who had vouched for them had fallen in status somewhat over the preceding generation. This is not uncommon, of course. As we all know, even long-standing dynasties, which once commanded the might of the realm, have struggled in this new century, but it was the one thing that caught my attention after a long run of dead ends."

I was keen to know how each of our suspects at the hotel fitted in with the story he was telling, but I couldn't urge him to speak faster, so I waited like everyone else.

"The maid was Elisabeth Hall. She had previously lived in Whitechapel and was born into a very poor family. The chance of her transcending this lowly status and finding work in the home of the King's daughter was almost non-existent. However, when I spoke to her, she convinced me that she'd had nothing to do with the theft of the tiara. She emphasised the fact that, had she taken something so precious, it would have done her little good. She had no criminal record and was unlikely to have the necessary connections to make the most of such a bounty. Perhaps she could have sold it for a small sum to a disreputable pawnbroker, but anyone who saw it would have known it was stolen. If she were to blame, she would not only become a target for the dogged investigator who had been assigned to the case, but also surely lose her job and, over time, more money than she would have gained from the crime."

"So that other woman was Sunday Legyear?" Dorie laughed at this. "Which is a very silly name indeed."

"That's right, but I was just as convinced by her arguments as Elisabeth Hall's. They had both been at the house for months. They had started working there at different times, and the positions they held were stable and paid comparatively well. I struggled to believe that they were involved, though I knew that it made more sense than anything else. Sunday in particular had a good reputation both with her colleagues and back in London, where her integrity and loyalty to her younger siblings was admired by all. I was very close to giving up entirely when I began to hear whispers about an international jewel thief who was believed to have been in Britain at the time that the Princess's tiara was stolen."

"How would you hear of such a thing?" Cook asked. "Do the very best thieves get mentioned in society magazines just as visiting royalty do?"

Grandfather had been deadly serious for some time. Even Sunday Legyear's ridiculous name hadn't made him break a smile, but he always had a special appreciation for Henrietta, and he released a short, breathy laugh before continuing.

"Not quite, Cook. As a good police officer, I had ways of hearing news that wasn't published in newspapers and was certainly never intended for my ears. The thief was known as the Duchess, and she had become something of a legend on the Continent in the preceding years. She was a cat burglar of the highest order and had executed a string of complex and profitable burglaries over the preceding years.

"What was most impressive about her, however, was that no one knew anything of her identity. She had left behind not one fingerprint or thread of clothing at the scenes of her crimes. She was not just feline in her abilities, but ghostlike."

"What could be more frightening than a phantom cat?" Albert

asked a little dreamily, and I wondered whether he would burst into another poetry recital.

Whether she'd come to chase away imaginary animals, or she'd simply smelt our lunch, Delilah wandered calmly into the room at this point and sat looking expectant until, one by one, we all offered her a tasty titbit. She had chunks of kidney, half a pork chop, and several fish sausages – which were admittedly less in demand than many of the other dishes. And when she had finished eating, she went and found a nice warm spot by the fire. She was noticeably less energetic than normal, but I felt this was a sign that she was enjoying the nice relaxing holiday which I would be denied. She certainly seemed happy when she fell asleep on my feet.

Grandfather was barely distracted by the adorable creature and, having provided her with a piece of his steak, he continued his tale. "Of course, the discovery of a spirit, whether criminal or otherwise, wasn't going to help me a great deal, but at least I knew I was on the right track. So I redoubled my efforts to find the tiara – and I must say that was always the goal I had set myself. I cared less about who had taken the treasured item than I did about recovering it for the princess. I called in favours and put pressure on people low down in the echelons of London's criminal underworld in the hope that someone higher up might notice, but none of it did any good."

"I thought you'd never failed to solve a case!" Timothy said with a note of shock in his voice.

"You've been reading those blasted books about me, haven't you, boy?" his master asked him. "How many times have I told you that writers, perhaps more than any other profession, are not to be trusted? They are, to a man, deceitful rogues."

I almost mentioned how highly he had thought of the novelist Marius Quin, but it wasn't the moment to interrupt.

"I've never failed to solve a case since I've had Christopher at my side – that much is true – but over the course of my forty-year career as a police officer, I was far from perfect, and it looked as though the stolen tiara would defeat me until I gave it one last try and contacted an old friend from the *Sûreté de Paris*. My thinking was that, as there was so little evidence to help me make sense of the plot in England, perhaps what we needed was across the Channel. And sure enough, within a few days, the majority of the smaller diamonds had been traced to a jeweller in the French port town of Calais. He said that a young English woman by the name of Hall had come to his shop and sold her grandmother's diamond collection. He didn't speak much English and didn't find it particularly suspicious because so many British people passed through the area, flaunting their wealth as if we still owned the place."

We'd finally got to the part of the story that most intrigued me. "Did you think it was really Libby who went there? Was there any evidence that she'd taken time off work after the theft?"

"No and yes in that order. Although Miss Hall was a rather unrefined, short-tempered individual, she came across as honest. However, a week passed between the Princess Royal realising that her tiara had been stolen from the safe in her boudoir and her calling the police. And in that time, Elisabeth Hall had taken a holiday."

This once more sent a rustle of whispers about the group. I take back what I said before. Grandfather's tale was better than a ghost story. The only problem was that I knew, when it came to its conclusion, we still wouldn't know who was to blame for the crime.

"We interviewed her again, and she told us that she had gone to the seaside to be alone. She said she'd been seeing a young man who had become increasingly demanding of her time, and she needed space away from him, so she went to stay at the cottage of a friend in Dorset. The problem was, though the boyfriend, the friend and even the cottage existed, no one could place her where she claimed to have been. No witnesses in the village where the cottage was located came forward, and she was arrested for the crime."

"I reckon she must have gone to prison for years for such an offence," Dorie concluded, and she should have known as she'd once seen the inside of gaol herself thanks to my grandfather (and her career as a pickpocket).

"But she wasn't arrested for stealing the tiara. I refused to let that happen, as I didn't see how a woman with no previous criminal record could have executed a crime like this one. Instead, she was charged with 'receiving stolen goods' contrary to section 91 of the Larceny Act 1861." I'm not sure we needed this level of detail, though it was reassuring to know that Libby Hall wasn't convicted under a trumped-up charge. "I spoke in her defence at the trial and begged the judge for leniency. If I remember correctly, she served twelve months in Lewes Prison."

"So the real thief walked free?" I muttered, not expecting a response and, for a moment or two, Grandfather didn't offer one.

"The Duchess walked free, but I never gave up on solving the case. I spent years hoping that she would be arrested on the Continent, but there were no more crimes attributed to her, and any whispers of her name soon died away. As soon as the twentieth anniversary of the crime had passed, I set to work once more. A friend of mine at Scotland Yard is one of the best investigators I've ever met. P.C. Simpkin never gets his photograph in the newspaper, and you won't hear his name mentioned among the great detectives, but if there is a piece of information you need and it exists on paper somewhere, he will be able to find it. To tell you the truth, I don't know exactly how he managed it, but he traced the Duchess out of England in 1909 all the way here to Switzerland."

"Do you mean to say—" Albert began, but Grandfather evidently wished to reveal this piece of information himself.

"On the day that they went missing, someone travelled from Brighton to Dover and from Dover to Paris, then all the way to a place called Riederfurka in Switzerland. We can't say for certain, but there is a good chance that the rubies were once here at this hotel."

A quiver travelled across the room. It was just the kind of dramatic moment that my grandfather adored, so I'm sure he was disappointed to be upstaged by the scream which carried down to us from the floor above.

CHAPTER NINETEEN

We heard the thump of heavy footsteps, and Grandfather leapt into action.

"Lord Ow!" the manager yelled along the corridor, but we'd already left the library and were hurrying to the staircase in the foyer.

As we arrived, I heard another voice yelling in anguish. "*Sie ist tot*[6]*!*" a woman called and, as I hadn't noticed any female members of staff, I took this to be Inge Weinreich. "She's dead," she said upon seeing us. "I went to visit my new friend Blanche, and I found her dead in her room."

Victor Ried looked as though he were about to pass out from the stress and was presumably relieved when we swept past him to see what we could do to bring Blanche… I couldn't remember her surname… back to life (or at least inspect her body). Grandfather flew up the stairs with almost as much speed as he'd descended the mountain. He didn't look quite as impressive without his usual billowing coat, and I did now understand the appeal of maintaining one classic outfit. Of course, as I was still in a dressing gown, and feeling pretty silly about it, I couldn't complain about anyone's sartorial choices.

We followed Frau Weinreich to room 108, and she paused in the doorway as if it were too much for her to go in there a second time. Herr Ried approached ever so cautiously, and I felt that, no matter how good a manager he might be, he wasn't cut out for dealing with dead guests.

"Was the door open when you came?" I asked the Swiss lady, but panic had set in, and she wouldn't answer directly.

"Blanche Atkinson and I started talking at dinner last night. In fact, she was at the table near yours. The one beside the window. We arranged to meet for lunch, as her husband Henry was going for a long walk in the mountains. I was in the restaurant at midday as we'd planned, but she didn't appear."

"Was the door open?" Grandfather asked her, and she looked back and forth between us, her hands shaking as she raised them to her lips.

"I can't say now. Everything feels as if it's spinning in my head.

---

6 She is dead.

I do know that…" She paused to remember the sequence of events that had led to that scream. "Yes, I believe I must have opened it. I knocked for some time and, when there wasn't an answer, and I hadn't seen her the whole day, I decided that I would see whether it opened."

I believe that Grandfather must have found this suspicious, but everything I'd seen of Frau Weinreich until now fitted with my picture of her. I was confident that she was a blunt, outspoken woman who, were she to find a door closed, would open it forthwith.

"There's no need to worry," I said in the hope of reassuring her. "You've done nothing wrong. You may accompany us inside or wait here as you see fit."

We left her in the, if not capable, then at least sturdy hands of the hotel manager, and Grandfather pointed the way for me to go ahead of him. I know this will sound like a facetious thing to say, but deathbeds – or I suppose deathrooms might be a more accurate description – tend to be abnormally quiet. Approaching one is like diving under water or filling your ears with paper. The stillness is overwhelming, and each time I catch sight of a dead body, I can't help but think how frightening it would be for the unlucky person suddenly to sit up. It's an undeniably cruel trick, though I would quite like to see my grandfather's face were someone to play such a practical joke on him.

The room was smaller than ours, and aside from a bed, a pine wardrobe and two chairs, there was little in the way of furniture. I stood beside the window while Grandfather examined the body. I don't mind admitting that I was happy to let him take charge again.

I knew exactly why he'd brought us and all the other suspects here. He might have thought it was a Christmas game, but it was really just another stage in my training. He wanted to see how I would unravel a mystery without his help. Of course, neither of us could have predicted that it would get so much more complicated than he'd intended. Actually, hang on a second. Anyone could have predicted that it would get more complicated as that's what happens on all of our cases. My grandfather is a walking complication factory.

Poor Blanche Atkinson was lying on her back, looking up at the ceiling. Or rather, she would have been, but her eyes were closed, and she was quite dead. She was a small woman – petite, you might say – with brown curly hair and a bony chin. Now that I had a chance to look at her carefully, I realised that she looked rather like her husband, and I found myself worrying how we would break the sad news to him.

"What do you think did it?" I made myself ask as grandfather opened her eyelids and turned her head from one side to the other. "I hope it wasn't food poisoning."

He looked at me then as if I'd said something terribly stupid. I considered listing the many newspaper articles I'd read about people going on luxurious holidays only to end up dead because of undercooked prawns or what have you, but he'd only have tutted and returned to his examination.

"It's much harder to say now that she's been dead for some time, though I don't suppose you're too far from the truth."

"You mean praw—"

"No, not prawns, Christopher. I mean poison!"

On the one hand, I was disappointed that I'd said something he considered stupid. On the other, this made me a little nostalgic for a few years earlier when I'd *only* said stupid things. It had been a long time since he'd tutted at me quite so vehemently.

"It's hard to tell exactly what it was." He opened her mouth to look inside it. "With poisoning, it certainly helps to be there before or soon after the victim dies to determine the likely cause. Without removing organs post-mortem, it is a challenge to identify the precise substance that killed her."

I knew he was knowledgeable when it came to medical matters, but this made me wonder whether he'd ever had to resort to cutting open a dead body. Trying not to think such morbid thoughts, I walked to the other side of the bed from him and examined the victim as he would expect me to. I even touched her forehead, but there was a certain clamminess there that made me shiver, so I took her icy hand instead.

"She's very cold; is that how you know she died some time ago?"

"Among several other criteria, yes. The rigidity of her muscles is another. We must assume for the moment that her husband left the room this morning thinking that his wife was in good health. It's quite possible that she was already dead when he rose and departed."

"Do you know anything about the pair of them that you haven't yet told me? I don't really understand why you brought so many people here if it was only Sunday and Libby who were employed at the princess's house in Brighton." I suddenly wondered whether I'd got my facts wrong and every last guest had once worked at Fife House, but that wouldn't have made any sense.

"There's not a great deal to tell. Blanche married shortly after the theft and much like Sunday, and even Libby Hall, she appears to have led a *spotless* life ever since." He released a gentle laugh at this moment, but it didn't last long, and I didn't get the joke anyway. "Blanche!" he repeated, thus ensuring that I really didn't get the joke. "Spotless? Oh, never mind."

"Few poisons kill instantly," I said when neither of us had spoken for some time.

"That's right. Why do you mention it?"

"Well, I was just wondering whether it could have happened at dinner last night."

He didn't look up at me again as he searched the pockets of his flannel pyjamas. "The timing would certainly fit with death occurring sometime this morning. Why do you ask?"

"Oh, I'm sure it's nothing."

He went through a series of checks, some of which I couldn't begin to imagine the importance, before stopping with Blanche's right arm in his two hands and suddenly staring straight at me. "Come along, Christopher. What is it that you won't say?"

"I don't want you to think I'm an imbecile just because I have an idea that doesn't match your expectations."

He sighed and put her arm down. "I promise that I won't make the faintest sound of disapproval even if you suggest she was trampled by an elephant."

"I just wondered…" I began, blustering a little as I spoke. "You see, I was just thinking that perhaps an insect is to blame."

"An insect?" He said, trying his best not to sound disparaging (and failing). "And what insect could kill someone stone cold dead?"

"As it happens, I didn't get his name, but I do know that poor Mrs Atkinson here complained of being bitten by one last night, and there's a large swollen welt on this side of her neck."

CHAPTER TWENTY

I don't think Grandfather knew whether to be grateful that I'd spotted something important or annoyed at himself for failing to do so. To be fair to the old genius, the bite or what have you was low down on the back of the victim's neck.

"I don't think it was administered by an insect," he soon concluded, having circled the bed to get a better look. "I've never seen a reaction like this, and the central puncture wound doesn't look like anything that an animal commonly inflicts. Add that to the fact that the vast majority of insects are dormant at high altitudes and low temperatures, and I think we can rule out an entomological assassin."

"So then how could it have been administered?"

He looked up at me, and I thought he was about to deliver a dramatic revelation that would change the course of the investigation. I was wrong. "I really cannot say. My best guess would be that the killer passed the victim's table at dinner last night with a small syringe, but that would have made detection difficult to avoid."

Before we could discuss this further, I heard Inge talking in the hallway and, a moment later, Henry Atkinson appeared at the door. As I mentioned before, he was small and curly like his wife, but whereas the dead woman in the bed looked oddly beatific in her final repose, a tortured grimace shaped his face.

"Not my Blanche!" he cried out, stopping five feet from the bed when he saw that what he had just been told was evidently true. "It can't be. Please tell me that someone's playing a joke."

He had a nasal, working-class voice, and a perpetually crumpled look about him.

"It is no joke," my grandfather had to explain. "I'm sorry to tell you that your wife has been dead for some hours. I believe she died early this morning. May I ask at what time you left the room?"

The man looked hard at the beardless aristocrat, as if trying to make sense of our presence in his bedroom. I should have realised before why the great Lord Edgington had disguised himself. He'd brought together a gang of former criminals and would surely have run into some of them decades before. Whether Henry Atkinson was involved,

I couldn't say, but he didn't seem to recognise the famous detective.

"I was…" The broken-hearted fellow searched for his words. "I got up before the dawn but took my time over breakfast in the dining room."

"Did any other guests see you?" I asked to be clear with our facts.

He put his hand to his face and looked distraught for a few quiet moments before forcing himself to answer. "There is one other guest whose name I don't know. She is a little…" He searched for a polite term. "She is less well-turned-out than many here. Oh, and Herr Ried will tell you he saw me. He was already hard at work when I got downstairs."

"Yes, I observed you leaving the hotel as I went to breakfast," Grandfather said to confirm his story.

"Did you notice whether your wife was breathing when you left?" I asked Mr Atkinson, though I should have found a better way to phrase such a question. He immediately let out a cry and looked back at the blanched woman in their bed. Sorry! That's poor phrasing again. I don't know what's wrong with me.

Wait! I just got Grandfather's joke.

"Breathing? Oh my good Lord." Henry took a few steps away from us. When he turned back, he still couldn't believe what I was asking. "If you're wondering whether I knew my wife were dead but left her here to go for a walk, then no, obviously not!"

"Did she complain of discomfort before you went to bed last night? Did she suffer any particular symptoms that were uncommon to her?"

Although my grandfather had asked this question with great sympathy in his voice, our witness put one hand to the back of his head and began to cry.

"I can't… I just don't believe this is happening. My Blanche said she weren't feeling her best after dinner, but I thought it were a cold of some sort. Up here in the mountains, I figured she would be more susceptible to that kind of thing. Now you're telling me she's croaked it."

"Did she mention a pain in her neck?"

"The bite, you mean? You think that's what done it?" His eyes were as big as the largest conkers. "She found a stinger or what have you and said it bothered her, but I never thought she would die!"

Grandfather raised one eyebrow, and it was clear that he had realised something that I had not, but he gave the man a minute to let his sorrow out before speaking again. "I don't wish to upset you, Mr

Atkinson, but I must ask about your wife's past. I believe she was a criminal at some stage in her life."

The poor grieving fellow dropped onto the nearside of the bed just a short distance from his dead wife. He looked up at us, unable to form a response for a while, and when he did, it was coated with despair.

"So even in death, her struggles follow her. Yes, Blanche was a counterfeiter in her youth. She did what was needed to escape from poverty, but she had a kind soul, and that can't be faked."

"We're not looking to condemn anyone for their past deeds," I assured him, perhaps untruthfully. "We only need to know who wanted to hurt her."

"Hurt her?" Every new thing he said was more amazed than the last. "Are you saying she was…" He couldn't utter the word, so Grandfather did it for him.

"Yes, I'm afraid there is a good chance your wife was murdered. Another woman was already killed on the rack railway that brings people to the mountain. Her name was Barbara Nelson, and she was—"

"Babs?" he interrupted. "Babs is dead too? How can it be? We were expecting to see her here this week. You see, she won the same competition in the paper that we did, only she was meeting a friend here. I told my Blanche that it were too good to be true. I didn't even remember entering nothing, and it looks like I were right."

I could see that Grandfather took some responsibility for the series of events that had led to two women's deaths. He was always respectful when dealing with the loved ones of our victims, but the fact that they would never have been murdered if he hadn't brought them out here surely weighed heavily upon him.

"You knew Miss Nelson?" I asked so that he didn't have to.

"Of course we did. Babs and Blanche went back years. They'd grown up together. She were one of the few people from back then that my wife still knew. I'd say they were thick as thieves, but I reckon you'd take it wrong."

Grandfather obviously found something interesting in what the man had told us, as the pace of his speech increased. "When was it that you met your wife? You made it sound as if she had already turned her back on her previous occupation. Is that true?"

"June 1911. That's when we met. I remember it well as it were just a week after the coronation. Blanche were the prettiest young lass I'd ever set eyes on." This sentimental trip back through time caused his voice to wobble again, but he persisted with his tale. "We were on the same bus in Dalston, and it took me the whole journey to stump up the courage to talk to her. I was just about to say something when she called to the driver for her stop. I couldn't help myself, so I followed her to the door. She'd nearly stepped off when she turned around, and we bumped straight into one another."

His eyes travelled slowly up the dead woman's blanketed form until they lighted on her expressionless face. "It turned out she'd felt quite the same way that I did and was waiting for me to speak to her. We haven't stopped chatting away together for the eighteen years since... until now of course."

Grandfather was beyond the point of catering to the emotional needs of the man. He'd caught a glimpse of something important and had to pursue it. "You said that Blanche was a counterfeiter. Did she ever tell you what that involved?"

"She weren't making a fortune faking paintings, if that's what you're thinking. Her old man were a rag and bone man with an eye for anything that sparkled. He brought her up with a knowledge of jewellery, though he never had nothing worth owning himself. Even as a young'un, Blanche were a dab hand at putting together bits of glass and metal and making something beautiful. She turned that into a career for herself, selling fakes to unscrupulous jewellers who didn't mind tricking gullible customers out of their money."

A new question occurred to me. "Then why did she stop?"

"Very few people want to be criminals, you know. She'd made enough to open her own shop making costume jewellery that didn't claim to be anything more than what it was."

I was reminded of what Libby Hall had told her former friend on the mountain. She'd said that she didn't get what was rightfully hers. Presumably Blanche Atkinson had been paid for her work to help steal the Princess Royal's jewels. Was Libby the only one who didn't benefit from the crime while also being the only person who was punished for it?

"And what about Barbara Nelson?" I asked to see whether my theory held water.

"What about her? Her story was much the same as my Blanche's. As soon as she could, she stepped back from her pickpocketing."

"And the other guests at the hotel, do you recognise any of them?"

His sadness was mixed with confusion now, as if he couldn't fathom why we'd ask such a thing. "There's that one who married the duke or what have you. You know, the one with the Spanish name. But we didn't know any of the others, if that's what you mean. Until we got here, at least. We had a lovely conversation with that Swiss lady. She and Blanche were supposed to go for lunch today, but that ain't going to happen." His sobs returned, and he spoke more angrily. "Now if you've stopped being a pair of nosy so-and-sos, I'd appreciate you leaving me in peace."

We both looked at the poor man, and I had a real sense that he'd told us all that was likely to be of use. I didn't want to upset him any more than we already had, so I was grateful when Grandfather tapped me on the shoulder and motioned for us to leave.

CHAPTER TWENTY-ONE

Outside in the corridor, the hotel manager, his one remaining Swiss guest and the porter were waiting to see what we would tell them. There was a certain look of expectation on their faces, as though they were hoping that Inge had been misinformed and Blanche was doing fine.

"It's a sorry business," Grandfather said to leave them in no doubt. "We believe she was poisoned, though I can't say for certain what it was or how it was administered. Did you learn anything last night about how she was feeling, Frau Weinreich?"

Inge looked alarmed at being addressed. "Me? We only exchanged pleasantries. She told me nothing of her health."

Grandfather studied the nervous woman's features for a moment before turning to Herr Ried. "You must call the police immediately. Two women have been murdered. They should dispatch plenty of officers here to ensure that no one else will die."

Even before he replied, I could tell that Ried would not run off to the telephone. "That is definitely the right course of action, but I'm afraid it's impossible with the snow that's currently falling." He pointed to the end of the corridor, which gave a view of very little indeed. The storm I'd previously noticed moving closer had now broken, and the air was filled with falling snow. "The railway will be closed in this weather, and the roads up the mountain will be quite unpassable. The only hope we have is for the police to come up on mules, but that would take hours, and I doubt they'll agree to it."

I'd discovered a drawback to living in one of the most beautiful places I'd ever visited.

"What should we do, Grandfather? Should we make an announcement of some sort?"

He put his hand to his chin to stroke the beard that was no longer there. "Not yet. There's someone I wish to interview before we tell everyone what happened."

Ried was already issuing instructions to his porter to return to the foyer to keep an eye on the guests, but it was a large hotel and there were not nearly enough employees to watch over everyone. Grandfather muttered his thanks, and we moved back towards the front of the building.

"My anonymity has been a blessing so far," he said without looking at me. "I see one easy resolution to the case, and I would like to explore it before we reveal who I really am."

"Is it Libby Hall?" I guessed, as my own suspicions had lingered on her since I'd overheard her conversation with Sunday that morning. "Do you imagine her to be the killer?"

"I imagine nothing," he said rather superciliously, before realising how this sounded and softening his tone, "though you seem to have boarded a similar train of thought to my own, and I heartily approve. Let us find her before someone else dies."

"Have you noticed that no one here seems to know everyone, but most of the guests know someone?" I asked as we walked on. "Libby and Sunday grew up together, as did the two dead women. We haven't asked Dolly yet. In fact, we haven't seen her since last night, so I hope she didn't take a turn for the worse after her collapse, but there's every chance she is acquainted with another of our suspects."

"I have indeed noticed. I invited six people to come here this weekend, along with their relevant companions." I thought that the word *invited* was a little disingenuous, but I didn't interrupt him. "We will soon discover whether this connection applies to all of them."

"It's gone on long enough, you know," I told him in as stern a voice as I could muster. "I've worked out plenty of what happened, but I still have questions. Most importantly, how did you find the names of the suspects involved in stealing the tiara if you failed all that time ago?"

"I really did very little," he confessed. "It was old friend P.C. Simpkin at Scotland Yard. I asked him to look at my old case, knowing that he takes great pleasure in picking over my failures and seeing whether he can do better. Half the time, his re-investigation of such cases comes to naught, but he picked up the trail of the Duchess and perhaps the rubies themselves. It's amazing he can discover anything so long after it happened, but he is a master at following metaphorical breadcrumbs."

"And yet you don't know a great deal about the six whom you summoned here. Why is that?"

He stopped in front of room number 105. "You know that I've made mistakes, Christopher. I've never suggested I'm perfect, and this time more than ever, I've allowed my capricious nature to get the better of me. First, I brought a group of criminals here without concern for the consequences. All I considered was the joy of giving you a case to solve. I didn't take the time to worry that something worse could come of it."

"And second?" I asked when he said no more.

"My goodness, boy, you do like to see me suffer, don't you?" He smiled even as he complained. "Second, I decided not to read all of Simpkin's notes on the case but to challenge myself to come to the same conclusions that he had by relying on the information that we alone could obtain."

"So the answer to all this may be sitting in a file in our bedroom?" I must have sounded scandalised as he instantly reassured me.

"No, no. Simpkin explained in his letter that he hadn't narrowed down the pool of suspects, but I could have learnt more about each of them, and I would have done if I'd thought that anyone was in danger. I've already asked Todd to read them and let us know anything he considers essential."

With his position made clear, he knocked on the door before us, but there was no answer. I didn't remember in which room Miss Hall was staying, but I concluded this was it.

"To be perfectly clear," I began, "in response to your much-admired former colleague discovering information on a case that you had been unable to solve, you spent a small fortune to bring six of the suspects halfway across the Continent, shed your famous locks, changed your wardrobe and pretended to be someone you are not in order to observe them here. Am I right?"

It didn't surprise me that he had to qualify my statement. "Not quite, my boy. Most of this was planned as a Christmas present to my favourite assistant." It took me a moment to realise he was talking about me, not Todd or Delilah. "I'm obviously now quite aware that there were better ways to go about it, but my intentions were good."

The door to room 105 was not going to open, and so he turned to leave, whistling as he went. To be honest, I didn't think much of his justification. I could imagine one of our culprits standing before a judge to say that, while he was guilty of theft, betrayal and murder, his intentions were good. More urgent for me at that moment, however, was my need to get changed. I'd carried out far too much of this investigation in a dressing gown, and I was determined to rectify the problem.

"Wait there for just a moment," I told my grandfather and, in a flash, I popped upstairs. I reappeared a minute or two later in one of my new suits. It was Christmas Eve, after all, and I was happy to look my best (and no longer show off my ankles). "Now, is there anything else I should know about Elisabeth Hall before we speak to her?"

We had returned to the elegant staircase that spiralled down to the foyer, and he held his leg in space over the first step before deciding on his answer and continuing our journey. "She is the person here who I thought was most likely to recognise me. I only interviewed Sunday Cheshire once, but after Miss Hall was arrested, I saw her several times. I was never very comfortable with her conviction. She spent a year in gaol, though the worst she did was to transport the jewels of lesser value from Brighton to France and sell them at a pawn shop. There was no way she could have had the knowledge to break into the safe from which the tiara was taken, and the rest of the crime was planned so meticulously that it made me wonder whether Miss Hall was sacrificed for the sake of the others involved."

"You mean the other criminals wanted her to be caught?"

He considered this for a moment as we passed the first-floor landing. "Yes, I believe that was the case. The Duchess, or whoever was in charge of the plan, was surely too clever to make use of a common-or-garden pawnbroker when it could easily lead back to those responsible for the theft. And then you have to consider what advantages there were. If they'd wanted to make a little extra money, they could easily have sold the smaller diamonds in Britain. Taking them abroad like that was a risk with little reward. None of it felt right and, on top of that, Miss Hall wasn't even paid for her trouble. I can honestly say that I wouldn't blame her if, on coming for the apparently free Christmas holiday she'd won in a fictional competition, she saw her old accomplices and sought revenge."

"Yes, but that would only make sense if she knew the dead women. From what we've seen so far, there was some separation between them. For example, Blanche Atkinson must have been employed for her counterfeiting skills and presumably had nothing to do with the maids who worked at the Princess's house. I think it is far more likely that this Duchess person found a way to hire the various criminals she required, and it was simply chance – and the tight-knit nature of East

London society – that meant any of them knew one another."

"Perhaps," Grandfather replied, and I was expecting a rebuttal of my theory, but it never came.

We had reached the foyer, and he stood at the bottom of the stairs looking around thoughtfully. If the case had been a simple one, Elisabeth Hall would have been right there stroking our lazy dog, but we weren't that lucky. The only person I could see was young Graham, and he was engrossed in another no doubt violent book. Libby was in the first room we tried off the guest corridor, so it could have been worse. It was a smoking room, and the smell of twenty years of cigar, pipe and cigarette smoke had altered the composition of the very air we breathed.

It turned out that Delilah *was* in there being stroked rotten. Elisabeth Hall didn't look up from the soppy beast when we first entered, and so Grandfather had to clear his throat ever so delicately to get her attention without startling her.

"Miss Hall," he said, "we were hoping to have a word with you."

CHAPTER TWENTY-TWO

Even though he had tried to make a subtle entrance, Grandfather's deep voice rumbled through the room, and Libby Hall was clearly alarmed to see us there in the doorway.

"Is this about that scream I heard? Is everyone all right?"

There was something permanently grubby about her appearance. It was not that her face was covered in smut and soot, but that I was immediately put in mind of some of Dickens's less fortunate characters when I saw her. She was a match girl, going unnoticed by Scrooge as he strides through the streets, or an impoverished customer of The Old Curiosity Shop, scraping together a meagre pittance to… well, I'm sure you understand my meaning.

"I'm afraid not, madam," Grandfather replied, and I noticed just how readily we had returned to our old roles. A few hours earlier, I'd felt as if I were the only one investigating, but now I was back to standing in the shadows as he conducted an interview.

He motioned to the armchair nearest to where she was sitting on the carpet before the fire, and she nodded before he sat down in it. Delilah craned her neck to look at her master but soon returned to her lazy pose in the hope that her new friend would continue spoiling her.

Grandfather took so long getting comfortable that Miss Hall couldn't take it and had to ask, "Can you tell me what happened? I don't wanna be nosy, but that scream set me on edge."

"A woman is dead." He let these four words hang in the air like the lingering presence of past smoke. "Her name was Blanche Atkinson. Did you know her?"

"Atkinson?" she replied. "I don't think so. If the truth be told, I weren't expecting to know anyone when I came out here. I thought I'd be alone for Christmas, and I didn't mind it one bit."

"But there was someone?" Grandfather kept this question vague on purpose.

"That's right. Someone I knew a long time ago. We were good friends – neighbours even. I had never expected to see Sunday Legyear here with her husband, but I s'pose it's a smaller world than we ever realise."

"Truer words were never spoken."

Once again, Grandfather allowed the conversation to lull. He had a special skill for asking difficult questions without our suspects objecting. I suppose it worked on people with a particular character, but I'd often seen him grilling his subjects before they noticed what was happening. I'm sure he could have continued, but he decided to try a different approach.

"Miss Hall, did you know me once, too?"

His grey eyes glistened, and she held his gaze. I watched as the puzzle of the strange man before her slowly resolved, just as it had for me the previous morning. It was fascinating to watch the various thoughts and emotions reflected on her face. I noticed suspicion, possibility, recognition and then disbelief.

When she spoke again, her voice was weak. "Superintendent Edgington… is it really you?"

It was hard to tell what she thought of him at that moment. In the next instant, she might have reached for a lump of wood from the hearth and swung the flaming log straight at him, or run closer to wrap the old devil in an embrace. I suppose a point approximately halfway between the two was the most likely outcome, and that's what happened.

"You…" she continued, keeping her emotions in check. "You was always fair to me. Unlike most of the rozzers I met, I'm not sorry to see you again."

His fine fingers drummed on the arms of the chair, and he leaned forward just a fraction to reveal another of his secrets. "I don't think you understand, my dear. This isn't a coincidence. I brought you here this week. I brought all of you here."

She stopped stroking our dog and supported her weight on her hands behind her. From where I stood, it seemed that my grandfather's explanation had knocked her backwards, and she was reeling from the force of what he'd revealed.

"I don't see how you…" she began, but that was all she could muster.

"I arranged for your name to appear in *The Daily Chronicle* as evidence of the prize you'd won. I did the same thing for several of the other guests in several other newspapers, and I wrote to each of you to reveal your good fortune. I paid for everything from the taxi that picked you up from your house to the mule that collected your baggage from the mountain railway. When you replied to the letter to arrange your journey here, it was my staff in England who wrote back to you."

"But..." she tried again. "But why?"

Something about the way that Grandfather shuffled in his chair showed that he wanted me to answer this. Perhaps he wished to keep her in suspense or suggest that, whatever I might say, there was a deeper reason which she would be lucky to uncover.

"Because if there is one thing that my grandfather can't tolerate – if there is one thing that inspires him to keep working – it's an unsolved mystery. And your case is rather special, don't you think?"

Her demeanour until now had been one of quiet wonder, but that seemed to wear off in an instant. Perhaps it was the idea that she was in any way out of the ordinary that didn't sit well with her, but she rounded her shoulders and lowered her head before replying.

"No, I reckon it's a pretty common story, actually. They took advantage of a girl with no money or powerful friends so they could get away with a crime and blame it on me." The same bitterness that I'd heard in her voice on the mountain was evident once more.

"We're certainly not here to make you live through that difficult time again." I didn't know this for certain, so I had a quick peek at my grandfather in case I'd misinterpreted his intentions. Based on his amiable expression, I decided I was on safe ground. "If anything, we want to catch the people who really made money from the theft."

This was never going to be enough to convince her to talk. It would take the man she had known all those years earlier to do that. "You couldn't have realised at the time, but I was limited in what I could do to investigate the missing tiara. I wasn't allowed to try anything that might lead to the public at large knowing that a prominent member of the royal family had been robbed of a great treasure. In one sense, Queen Victoria herself was the victim of a crime..." He realised that this needed an addendum and quickly made it. "...even if she had already been dead for eight years."

"I don't know what you want me to do about it." Although Sunday and Libby were approximately the same age and had been born in the same part of London, that was where their similarities ended. Libby had singularly unkempt grey hair that sprang from her head in tangled clumps. Her brown eyes were rather owlish and, in general, she reminded me of a wild creature who would be more at home in the forest above the glacier than the concrete maze of London.

"I'm trying to explain that I need you to tell me all you can about your time working in Brighton. You're not at risk of going to prison this time. All I wish to do is fill in the gaps in the story and prevent anyone else from being hurt."

She wasted no time in threading together the pieces of the tale we'd told her. "Wait... are you saying that the woman upstairs... Atkinson, was it? Are you saying she were killed?" Her voice was shrill but clear, and she didn't cower from this stark possibility.

"I'm afraid so." Grandfather's manner could be so soothing when required that he made this sound less terrifying. "She is the second person to be murdered in the area today, and we believe they were both connected to the theft from Fife House."

Libby glanced down at our dog, apparently unable to look at my grandfather any longer. "I don't understand. If they'd worked in the house with me and Sunday, I would surely have recognised 'em. I mean, I know twenty years have passed since then, but I worked there for months. I'm sure I'd know 'em."

"You may be right, but the involvement of the two women who have been killed wasn't apparent back then. They were not employed by the royal family. From what we can tell, they were lowly criminals with particular skills. One was a pickpocket; the other, a counterfeiter."

"I'm sorry, sir, but how does that fit with the princess's diamonds and whatnot?"

"We can't say for certain, but the knowledge does strengthen the impression I've always had that this was a grand endeavour with many people involved." He waited for this information to settle before expanding the conversation yet again. "Have you heard of a criminal by the name of the Duchess?"

He had built up this question with such proud and precise pronunciation that the answer was always going to disappoint.

"No."

"That's fine. Don't worry in the slightest. The important thing is that I have long believed it was the Duchess who stole the tiara and perhaps even organised the whole complex scheme. We know practically nothing about her except for the fact that she is a highly accomplished thief. She had stolen any number of priceless valuables from all over Europe before the tiara was taken but one particularly interesting thing about her is that there were never any rumours of her striking again after."

Delilah let out a brief, needy moan for attention, and Libby went back to stroking her absentmindedly.

"So you think the other guests here had something to do with what happened?" she concluded. "Could one of them be the Duchess?"

"It's feasible." Grandfather put his hands together and nodded his head a few times before saying anything more. "Yes, I believe that is a real possibility, but before I consider any such hypotheses, I'd like to know your story."

"You already know it. I were born in Whitechapel, moved to Hackney when I were little, and got a job in Brighton working for a princess. Back then, I really thought all my dreams had come true, and I'd have a steady job for as long as I wanted it, but I couldn't of been more wrong."

"You've skipped a part," he was quick to correct her. "How did you get the job in the first place? Who contacted you? Why were you chosen?"

She looked up at me then, as though suddenly aware of the sappy young man eavesdropping on their conversation.

"I applied for it. There was an advert for a maid in the window of a stationer on Duval Street. It said no experience in the job was required. That were perfect for me, as I didn't have none. Well, none that I could tell an employer about."

"So you went for an interview?" I asked her.

"That's right. I met with a very respectable older lady in a grand house on Wimbledon Common. Her surname were Beresford, or something like that. She was a friendly sort and told me that they were looking for a girl without any preconceptions of what a maid should be. They wanted someone they could mould. I had no idea that the job meant I'd be working for a member of the royal family. I think I'd have been too scared to take it otherwise. But a few days later, I got the letter telling me I was expected down in Brighton on the first of the coming month. At the top of the paper, it said something about the Princess Royal, and I just couldn't believe it."

She stopped to take a deep breath, and I felt that the story still moved her even after so much time had passed.

"When I made my way down there, the person who opened the door had been my neighbour for the first eight years of my life. Sunday Legyear was standing there before me, and I couldn't believe my eyes. The most curious episode had just got a lot... well, you know."

She became a little shy then and, rather than giving our dog the attention she so enjoyed, Libby batted at her messy hair as though she were preparing to step into Fife House again. "It were awful good fun, me and Sunday working together like that. She were more senior than me, but she helped me settle in, and I enjoyed every second of it. Well, almost every second. The life of a maid ain't an easy one, but Princess Louise and the Duke weren't there very often, so it weren't too bad."

"Something changed. Isn't that right?" I continued, as I felt that Grandfather would prefer to keep listening.

"Yes. Yes, it did." She bit both her lips for a moment, which may sound impossible, but she managed it by pulling them into her mouth first. "I had another letter. I doubt it was from anyone at the house because it were sent through the post for one thing, but there was something..." She searched for the right word. "There was something seedy about it – something not quite right. It was typewritten on that thin, greasy paper that's almost transparent."

I didn't need to ask her, *What did it say?* but I was definitely thinking it.

"It told me I would find a package hidden under a bench in the waiting room of the Prince of Wales Pier in Dover Harbour. I was to take it to France and sell it in a shop there. I were told that Sunday would make sure I had time off work, and there was money in the wrapping for my travel."

"That must have sounded like a real treat," I said, trying to lift her up a fraction. "A few days away on the Continent is many people's idea of a dream come true." Even as I uttered the words, I knew I'd spoken too soon, and her tone confirmed it.

"The letter said that, if I did as instructed, I could keep the money I got for the package and there'd be a hundred pounds on top for my trouble. But if I failed in any way, they'd kill someone I loved. They didn't even say who, but I only had a mother and a couple of cousins, and I weren't particularly close to either of 'em." She broke off once more and directed her words at my grandfather. "You know, I told you all this back then, and you didn't believe me."

"Yes, I did," he quickly replied. "The problem was that you couldn't prove it. You were the one who bought the tickets to travel across the Channel. You even admitted that you took the jewels and the remains of the tiara to the pawn shop and walked away with the money. From what I remember, you no longer had the letter you'd received, and your story of how you'd come by your position in the house struck me as dubious. I wanted to help you, but there was no escaping the facts as they were presented to the judge."

"Right," she said with a cold laugh. "Thanks for trying, I s'pose."

"Is that the whole story?" I asked, mainly in the hope that there was a significant fact she'd held back that could still explain all that had occurred.

"What do you want me to say?" Her voice was more distressed than it had been. "There was nothing I could do to save myself back then. What do you think I can tell you now that twenty years have passed, and I've forgotten most of what went on?"

"The woman who interviewed you in Wimbledon," Grandfather began. "This Mrs Beresford you mentioned – can you tell us anything more about her?"

Libby rocked back on her hands again. "She was... Well, she was stately. Do you know what I mean?" She didn't wait for an answer. "I wouldn't say she were a toff exactly, but she were well spoken and sort o' haughty. She had a monocle and a squint in her other eye. She sat up very straight and looked down her nose at me – literally, I mean. She was perfectly nice in her manner."

"Would you recognise her if you saw her again?"

"I don't know. It's strange the way that memory changes everything. For a long time, and especially when I were sitting in that gaol for months on end, I could see her face just as clearly as yours right now. But the picture has faded over the years. All that's left is a blank shape where she'd previously been. I can't even tell you how old she was. I was much younger then, and she seemed ancient to me, but perhaps there were only ten years or so between us. Or perhaps it was thirty. I wish I knew for sure."

"What about Rosetta Mullen?" I asked, because a theory had just sprouted in the intermittently fertile soil in my head. "Is there any chance that she was the woman you met?"

"That woman what killed her husband?"

Grandfather hastily intervened. "There was never any evidence that she killed the earl. The fact that he died so soon after they were married, and the discrepancy in their relative ages and backgrounds, were the only things that suggested the circumstances of his death were in any way suspicious." He spoke as if he were afraid that we'd be sued for slander.

"Could it be her?" I tried again, and Libby at least had a good think about it.

"I don't know. I've seen her here at the hotel, and I didn't immediately think, *Oh, we met all those years ago*. I suppose she looks the part, but I can't say anything more than that."

"Perhaps you should talk to her if you get the chance and see if anything about her seems familiar." I thought this was a sensible suggestion, but Grandfather disagreed.

"I'd rather you didn't. If it turns out that she's the killer and we put you in danger, I will feel very guilty about it." He looked at me then to suggest that I would be obliged to feel the same way. "I'm already aware of the part I played in what has happened here. If I'd left sleeping dogs to their slumber, two women would still be alive."

Delilah looked up at him then before returning to her own restful pose.

"I'm sorry that I don't know anything more." From Libby's tone, I could tell that she was sceptical of our chances of solving the case. "But then that's hardly surprising if this Duchess person is as good as you say. It sounds like she organised the whole thing without getting her hands dirty."

"It's also possible that she isn't one of the people whom my old colleague at Scotland Yard identified." Grandfather's voice was suddenly less warm than it had been, and his stare had hardened. "There's nothing to say that the women who were killed today died to protect the Duchess's identity. Perhaps they were murdered by the one person who never benefited from the crime you all committed together."

"Who do you..." Libby began before the implication of what he was saying hit her. "You're talking about me?" Her hand came to a rest on Delilah's glossy coat, and she struggled to produce anything more. "I couldn't… I mean, why would I do anything so evil?"

"As I told you earlier, I believed you when we first met. I knew that you had been treated harshly and that other people who had done far worse than you had gone without punishment. I'm also aware of the effect prison can have on a person. While plenty in society wish to believe that incarceration will reform errant souls and wipe slates clean, I've seen enough evidence to know that isn't always the case. And so I must ask you this simple question: do you hate them, Elisabeth?"

He leaned forward to increase the pressure on her.

"No. I don't hate anyone." Her eyes were clear and fixed straight on him, and her tone was so resolute that I knew she was telling the truth. "I don't even know the names of the other guests for the most part."

"And what about Sunday? You were friends once. Are we to take it that things have since changed between you?" When there was no reply, he offered some evidence. "My grandson overheard you talking on the mountain earlier. He thought that you were angry with Sunday. You said that you wanted what was meant to be yours. What would you do to get it?"

She was breathing more heavily, desperately trying to put things in order in her mind before answering. "No, it's not like that. I was angry. Of course I was. I have been my whole life if you wanna know the truth, but I'm no killer. I told her that I thought it were unfair that, if she had played a part in the theft of the tiara and been paid, I deserved what she'd got. But honestly, I don't blame Sunday for what happened. When we got to the top of the mountain, we looked out at that precious view, and she took my hand. You can ask her if you don't believe me. We grew up like sisters, and I have nothing but love for her."

It was at this point that she started crying, and now I really did feel guilty.

"Oh, please don't." Surprisingly, it was my grandfather who reacted like this. He was upset to have upset her. "I certainly didn't mean… Handkerchief?"

He held out the square of cotton that he kept in his breast pocket, and she accepted it gratefully and blew her nose. "Thank you, Lord Edgington. I do appreciate it, and I'm sorry I'm no help. After taking the blame for something I didn't do once in my life, I can't stand it when people think badly of me."

Her sobs continued, and Grandfather looked very awkward indeed, which made me feel rather competent for once!

CHAPTER TWENTY-THREE

I believe that we were both a little deflated when we left the smoking room with Delilah at our side. I could hear our friends in the library playing festive games and enjoying the last of the food. They sounded perfectly cheerful – despite the dead bodies we'd found. Some people would think this callous on their part, but when you work for Lord Edgington, you get used to reports of murder. If they didn't go on with their lives as normal, they could never enjoy Christmas, or the summer… or holidays, day trips, family parties or even weddings now that I think about it.

"What comes next?" I asked my grandfather in a weary tone. "You said before that Libby Hall being the killer would be the easy solution. So, even if she hadn't burst into tears and made you look silly—"

"I did not look silly, Christopher." He pulled on the front of his waistcoat as though to prove just how upright and serious (and definitely not silly) he was. "I merely showed my compassion for a woman who was suffering."

"Even if the emotion hadn't overwhelmed her, we've found little to suggest she is to blame."

"No, you're quite right (except about me looking silly)." He didn't actually say these last five words, but I was certain he was thinking them. "We placed her at the top of our list simply because she had a good motive, but as we have discovered time and time again, motive and opportunity do not always make a killer."

"So we're back to where we started," I muttered under my breath, but he was having none of it.

"Hardly. We're painting an increasingly clear picture. We started with an outline, then added some colour in the background, and now we have to fill in—"

"Yes, thank you, Grandfather, I have grasped the metaphor."

"My point is, boy, we're coming to understand who did what and when back in 1909. We know why Barbara Nelson and Blanche Atkinson were hired, and that could be vital to solving the case."

"Could it?"

"Really, Christopher, have a little faith!"

We were walking along the corridor back towards the foyer. I didn't know why we were heading that way, but I was willing to let my grandfather take charge. Before he could say anything more, we heard footsteps behind us and my brother calling. "Wait for me. I don't want to miss all the fun."

"Fun?" Grandfather replied disdainfully when Albert caught up with us. "I can assure you there is nothing 'fun' about seeking out killers, interpreting clues and formulating complex theories."

He looked so stern just then that it took me a moment to realise what absolute tommyrot he was talking. "Grandfather, those are quite literally three of your favourite things."

He relaxed his normally straight shoulders, and the air came out of him – not that I would ever describe him as a windbag. "Oh, very well. It is a lot of fun, but you should choose your words more carefully. We can't have our suspects knowing how much we enjoy this job. It would be unseemly."

He continued walking, and my favourite poet had a question for him. "Are you going to tell me what you've been doing? Have you stumbled across any juicy titbits?"

"'Fun' was bad enough, but 'juicy' is quite unforgivable," the old grump retorted, and he was once more disappointed to discover that he no longer had a moustache to ruffle. "I've just spent the last four and a half years training one of my grandsons to think deductively. Please don't tell me I have to start all over again with you."

My brother and I laughed at the cross-grained lord, and I answered his question. "Grandfather was just saying that we have connected the two victims to the theft of the Princess Royal's tiara twenty years ago. We now know that your friend Barbara Nelson was a pickpocket of some sort, and the woman who died upstairs was a counterfeiter who specialised in jewellery."

"Oh, how interesting." Albert rubbed his hands together, just as he had before tucking in to lunch. "And how do we think they were involved in the burglary?"

Grandfather must have forgiven Albert's previous offences, as he was happy to respond. "I very much doubt they were responsible for planning the crime, if that's what you're asking. But it is curious to me that whoever designed this audacious scheme would require the services of such lowly criminals."

"Let us imagine that the tiara Libby took to France was a forgery," I suggested, but I'd already made a mistake.

"No, that's impossible. From what her husband told us, Blanche Atkinson was no master jeweller. She learnt her trade from her father, who was a rag and bone man. Had the thieves genuinely wanted to create a replacement tiara that could not be identified as a fake, they would have required a higher grade of workman." I thought he was being snobbish, but he had some proof to back up his assertion. "It also entered my mind that the item Miss Hall transported abroad could have been the fake, but the diamonds that were recovered were examined by experts and there was no doubt that both the stones and the gold frame were original."

"So then what good did it do anyone to have a fake tiara?" Albert already sounded as if the case was just too complex for his not entirely useless but at the very least restless brain.

"We know that the theft was an embarrassment in some sense to the Princess Royal and her family. Isn't it possible that the reason they didn't contact the police for a whole week after it went missing was because she simply didn't look at her jewellery in that time? It's not as if she needs to wear tiaras every day, and I know for a fact that she has more than one. The Fife Tiara, which her husband gave her on their wedding day, is one of the most beautiful in the world."

We had reached the foyer by now. Delilah returned to her usual spot, and the manager and porter were excitedly chatting away about something in German. Both Grandfather and Albert looked at me as though they were trying to understand how I possessed this knowledge.

"What?" I asked with a hint of indignation. "I read the newspapers. Is it really so astounding that I should know something about our own royal family?"

Neither of them wished to answer this, and so Grandfather just ignored it. "You're saying that the Princess was embarrassed by her own wealth? I suppose that's possible. At a time when some people couldn't afford to feed their families – i.e. any moment in human history – the fact she hadn't noticed a piece worth tens of thousands of pounds going missing might have been looked upon poorly by the common man."

"Precisely. I think there's a real chance that the thieves replaced the real tiara in the princess's safe for a fake one. They were not hoping to trick anyone for any length of time but to slow down detection. To the naked eye, whatever Barbara Nelson produced would probably have done the job. And the next time that the Princess picked it up or moved its container or what have you, she would have realised it wasn't the right weight or the metal wasn't real gold and contacted whichever of your bosses set you on the case."

"Very good, Christopher." Grandfather really had learnt to give credit when it was due. "It would explain why Princess Louise was so vague in her conception of where the tiara had been when it was stolen. Now what do you make of the pickpocket?"

"I think that's an easier case to explain." Albert sounded far surer of himself now. "It goes without saying that, if a professional jewel thief were given the task of stealing the ruby tiara, a certain amount of surveillance would have been required."

"Yes, but that was surely why Sunday was placed in the Princess's house as the head of household."

"Perhaps, but…" He'd lost a little of his confidence. "What's a Sunday?"

"The wife of the man with whom we had the steam bath," I reminded him.

"Do try to keep up, dear boy." It was nice to hear Grandfather spurring on someone other than me for once. "At the same time, if you were implying that a pickpocket was paid to pinch the keys to the Princess's bedroom from one of the footmen at Fife House, then that would make sense if whoever was in charge wished to deflect suspicion away from Sunday Legyear."

"Yes." Albert nodded and looked proud of himself. "That is exactly what I meant. Well done me."

I thought this contradicted the idea that Libby had been placed in Brighton as a scapegoat, but maybe there was no way of protecting Sunday without doing the same to her friend. I don't mind admitting that I found the whole thing thoroughly confusing.

"So that's settled then."

"Is it?" Albert and I both said at the same time, but our grandfather wouldn't explain himself as we'd arrived at our destination.

I hadn't been paying a great deal of attention, but we must have climbed the stairs at some point, and we now stood outside room 102. He knocked first but immediately opened the door, and I realised that he must have known that no one was staying there as we'd looked at the list of reservations in Herr Ried's office, and his memory was a lot better than mine.

"What are you hoping to find?" Albert asked, but I thought I already knew.

Grandfather took five long steps into the spacious bedroom and then two to the left. He glanced down at his feet before banging one of the pine floorboards with his leather brogue. I knew what he was looking for, so I knelt to look at the joins.

"I think one of them has been levered up recently. Or rather, there are marks where a tool has been inserted."

"What on earth are you doing?" This was Albert, obviously.

Grandfather has often said that he liked it when I was naïve and inexperienced. I tended to say all sorts of unhelpful things that would jog his brain into life. With my brother alongside us, I was beginning to understand what he meant.

"When we arrived yesterday, the chandelier in the foyer fell and almost killed Sunday Cheshire," I explained. "We've come here to see whether someone could have loosened it on purpose in an attempt to kill her."

"If he wished to have any hope of succeeding, whoever did so would have had to be up here watching through the hole where the cable runs down to the room below." Grandfather pointed out, and Albert shuddered as he still wasn't used to talking about murder quite so casually – that odd bird!

"I think I can remove the plank if I have something thin enough to—" Before I could finish what I was saying, Albert held out a Swiss soldier's pocketknife with a small white cross on the wooden handle.

"I bought it while I was waiting for the train. I've always wanted one."

"Like all four of my grandchildren," Grandfather began, and I had to correct him as usual.

"Five!"

"Oh, yes. I do always forget about one of you... Like all five of my grandchildren, you never fail to surprise me, Albert." He patted him on the shoulder. Albert beamed as bright as a candle on a Christmas tree, and I managed to resist pointing out that my youngest cousin Francis can surprise our grandfather merely by existing.

I extracted various attachments from the thingummy to find the ideal one. There was a reamer, a corkscrew, a bradawl, a pair of tweezers and a regular knife, but the final one I tried was the most suitable option. The head of the screwdriver was just the right size to fit into the gap between floorboards and, after a few moments of jiggling it from side to side, I'd pushed it in far enough to lever one of them free.

"That's a good start." If we were ever to plan the theft of some great treasure, you can be certain that I would be the one getting my hands dirty while Grandfather stood nearby telling me what to do. "Now look at the contraption that held the lamp in place and check whether it was in good working order."

I did as suggested and peered into the space I'd opened. I could see the hole and the cable that had been pushed back up through it. It was too dark to make out much more than that, so I moved my head out of the light and tried again.

"There are two screws and a bracket that held the cable, and it seems that was all there was to support the chandelier."

"Which is a truly unsafe design considering the size and weight of the thing. What were they thinking?"

I reached back into my trouser pockets, remembering within the acceptable margin of time that I'm supposed to wear gloves when handling anything that a killer might have touched. With my hands suitably covered, I put them back into the hole to feel my way around.

"The screws are tightly secured." I looked back up at the others, and a rather excited grin crossed my face.

"What does that mean?" Albert wasn't the quickest on the uptake. "Does that make it more or less likely that the killer tried to kill that lady with the chandelier?"

"More likely!" I replied just as Grandfather said, "Less likely!"

152

CHAPTER TWENTY-FOUR

"Be reasonable, Christopher," he insisted, as though he were ever any such thing. "The fact that the bracket is tightly fixed means there is no evidence that the killer tampered with it."

"*Au contraire*, my wise mentor," I replied as I got to my feet. "If that were the case, the chandelier wouldn't have fallen in the first place. It fell because the screws were loose. They're tight now because the killer tried to cover her trail."

As usual, Albert focused on the wrong thing. "Have we already decided the killer's a woman then?"

"Yes!" we both said at the same time without bothering to offer any evidence.

"Touché, Christopher Prentiss," Grandfather continued in a gruff, deep and frankly terrifying voice. "You have outdone yourself!"

He held out his hand for me to shake, and I took it most willingly. "Thank you, my wise mentor." I repeated the phrase I'd used before but with a lot less sarcasm this time. Perhaps I spoke too soon, though.

"Unless, of course, the mechanism, which we've already identified as being insufficient to maintain the weight of the chandelier, finally gave up the ghost when the manager of the hotel lit the candles yesterday."

"Either way," I replied so as to avoid saying anything tetchier, "does this get us any closer to identifying who was up here?"

"Let me think." He paused, presumably to do just this. "Who was in the foyer with you when the chandelier fell?"

I cast my mind back one day. It felt like far longer. "Dolly's grandson Graham was there reading his book, but his grandmother had gone upstairs shortly before. I believe that Rosetta Mullen was yet to arrive. Herr Ried was at the desk answering the telephone, and Sunday Cheshire was obviously there when it fell."

"What about her husband or the woman you just interviewed?" Albert sounded almost as enthusiastic as we had, but that was because he hadn't realised the implications of what I'd revealed.

"They weren't there. In fact, none of our main suspects were. We can't even rule out the manager, as he could have set the lamp to fall a short time after he walked away."

Grandfather punched one fist into his open hand. "What a disappointment. Perhaps the other attempted murder will be more helpful."

"There was another one?" It was hard to know whether Albert was impressed or frightened. "You were busy before I arrived."

"Dolly almost died when she ate a cinnamonless cake which had cinnamon in it."

My explanation clearly hadn't gone far enough as Grandfather added, "She has an idiosyncrasy to cinnamon. The chef in the hotel restaurant insisted that there was none in the cake she ordered, but she had an attack of anaphylaxis and would most likely have died if a doctor hadn't been on hand and your brother wasn't quite so fast a runner."

"Then shouldn't we be interviewing the chef? Perhaps he's the one behind all these mysterious goings-on."

Grandfather gave him a stern look. I shot him a hard stare, and between us we communicated our dissatisfaction.

"Just imagine if we went to all that trouble of investigating the case of the missing rubies only to discover that some vindictive chef was to blame for the killings!" I said through gritted teeth. "It would be like cooking Christmas dinner then only serving bread and water."

"So where does all this leave us?" Grandfather asked, much as I had a few minutes earlier.

I couldn't remember a case in which we'd made quite so many important discoveries without settling on a likely suspect.

"The question is: should we concentrate on the theft all those years ago or the killings now? As much as I detest the idea, it is possible that the princess's misfortune is a smokescreen for some other motive."

"So you do think the chef is—"

"No, Albert." Grandfather and I spoke in unison once more. Did this mean I was becoming just like him?

My brother flicked the hair from his eyes and smiled. "It was only a suggestion."

"I was thinking more along the lines of the bitterness between the pairs of old friends," I told him a little more softly. "Or perhaps one of the criminals never gave up her old profession and was afraid of being exposed."

"They are both possibilities." Grandfather was already drifting from the room, so I hurried to put the board back into its space and went after him.

Albert left the room just ahead of me. "More importantly than where this investigation will now take us, we should be addressing the question of what my role is."

Grandfather turned back to us on the landing. "You have a strange understanding of the phrase 'more importantly', but please continue."

"You see, it's fine when it's just me and Chrissy, as I can pretend to be his dim assistant." I decided not to tell him that it would take less pretending than he might think. "But what am I supposed to do when the three of us are together?"

"Well, Delilah is being particularly lazy today," our forebear replied most pithily. "You could take up her post by running along at our heels and occasionally begging for food."

"Don't be so mean, Grandfather," I told him, whilst doing my very best not to laugh. "I think that you've already defined your role, Albert." I put my hand on his shoulder and looked as sincere as I knew how. "You are… *a poet*."

I was nodding by now, and he copied me. "Yes, you're right. I am a poet! I don't need to waste my talents trying to solve a case when there are two experts already in charge of it. I can document these exceptional circumstances for posterity— Nay! For humankind."

It is clear that something has gone wrong if someone starts using words like "nay" and "posterity". I was already afraid of what I had unleashed, but there was no turning back now.

"Come with me, Albert." I walked off without further explanation.

He followed me as I mounted the stairs to the top floor. I believe there was a loft of some variety above that level, but from what I'd seen in the reservation book, it was only servants and staff up there. Taking Albert to our room, I threw the door open and stood looking at him with my arm out.

"What do you think of that?" I asked, still nodding as I awaited his appreciation.

"It's a perfectly nice sitting room." He sounded unimpressed.

"Not the room, brother. The view through those magnificent windows." I turned to look and realised the problem. There was no view there to appreciate. All we could see was unbroken whiteness.

"Ah, I forgot about the storm. My point is that you can sit here and be inspired while we go about identifying the killer."

To my surprise, he was enthused by the idea. "Oh, this is perfect. I will sit here and watch the night fall. I will find my muse in the all-encompassing nature of darkness."

I froze for approximately three seconds, unable to decide how to respond. "Right… Very good, Albert. That sounds like a wonderful plan."

He immediately sat down in a chair facing the window and got to work listing ideas for a poem. "Detective – detection. On an investigation… Does that work as a rhyme?" I don't know where he'd found a pen and a book of paper, but he was scribbling furiously as I stepped from the room. "My brilliant grandfather. The king of the family. We all live in his shadow. He is rather a… Hmmm… what's a word for dictator that rhymes with family?"

By the time I'd gone back down one flight of stairs, Grandfather had already got into an argument.

"If it's nothing of any importance, why won't you show me it?" he demanded of Dolly Coxon's grandson.

"Because it's none of your business," the young man insisted, but I could tell from the way he was holding his hands behind his back, and the expression on his face that he was not telling the truth. It was the same look my unruly friend Marmaduke had adopted at school whenever a teacher suspected that he was up to no good.

"None of my business? You may not know this, boy, but my name is…" He paused for a moment, perhaps trying to remember whether we had dropped that particular charade. "… Lord Ow."

"And? I didn't realise there was a law that said you have to relinquish personal possessions to complete strangers so long as they have stupid names."

"Young man, you're acting suspiciously."

"Old man, you're acting superiorly."

All I'd seen of Graham had given me reason not to like him. He was forever skulking about the hotel, and his sanguinary interest in the grim and grimy books he read made me doubt he had any good in him. Of course, I was willing to overlook all that when I heard him giving as good as he got to my grandfather.

"Now, now. There's no need for rudeness." I believe that the fake

Lord Ow was as amused by the situation as I was. Rather than lose his temper, he gave a low chuckle and tried to reason with him. "I'm sure you'll have heard about the woman who was recently discovered dead on this very floor. Well, we're cut off by the snow and there will be no police coming, so it has fallen to my grandson and me to investigate. If there's really nothing suspicious in your hand, you won't mind if we examine it, will you?"

The fight had drained out of Graham. His always pale cheeks looked even more sallow, and his arms dropped to his side, but he still didn't comply.

"That's..." Grandfather struggled to get his words out as he realised what the boy was holding. "That's mine. You've been in my room and stolen my Montblanc pen."

The boy had a rectangular leather box. It was easy to recognise, as I was the one who'd bought it for Grandfather for his birthday. The pen inside was sterling silver, and I'd had to save up for some time to buy it.

"You don't understand," Graham protested, but his appeal fell on deaf ears.

"I certainly do. You're continuing the family business. It's no wonder that your parents were so desperate to get away from you; you're a thief."

CHAPTER TWENTY-FIVE

"It's not like that. I swear it isn't. I was trying to put it back. You don't understand what I have to—" He gave something of a growl at this moment and abandoned his defence. "Come with me."

As I could see that my grandfather was about to accuse him again, I lifted one hand to bid patience, and the boy beckoned us to follow him. His room was only a short way along the corridor. "Grandma's downstairs. She really was ill last night, and I was terrified when I woke up this morning because I couldn't hear her breathing and I feared the worst. She's been in bed for most of the day."

Before unlocking the door, he looked around to make sure no one else could see us.

"I hope you're not just wasting our time, boy," Grandfather told him, but there was something quite genuine in Graham's attitude. Was he afraid for some reason? Was that why he moved so furtively and the look on his face remained cautious even after we'd crossed the threshold?

The room was a mirrored copy of the one we'd last entered. There were clearly two standards of accommodation at the Hotel Villa Cassel, and I could see that Grandfather had chosen the best for us. There were no decorative patterns on the beds here, or Christmas decorations hanging on the walls. There was nothing but plain pine wherever I looked.

Graham walked directly to a nightstand in the corner of the room and pulled open the cupboard door. He didn't stop there, though. He moved onto the wardrobe and did the same.

"It's my grandmother," he explained. "It's like this wherever we go together, and no one ever accuses her because she's a sweet little old lady."

We moved closer to discover what he meant. Inside the two pieces of furniture, I could see a collection of a sort that a wing-strong and dexterous magpie might make. There were earrings, pipes, stationery, hatpins, a coney stole complete with head, and several items that I recognised as belonging to the hotel.

"Those were Rosetta Mullen's," I said, pointing to a pair of fur-lined leather gloves that I'd seen the one-time chorus girl wearing when she arrived at the hotel.

"Grandma never takes anything too valuable, and she doesn't do it for the money. She's got a whole room at home full of these little treasures. She does it for sport. She says it reminds her of her misspent youth and makes her feel alive."

"It's a strange kind of hobby. Has she considered taking up painting? I find that it relaxes me, and I've improved immeasurably in the last few years," Grandfather claimed… inaccurately.

"I really can't say." Graham looked just as lost as when I'd seen him out in the corridor.

His inquisitor soon returned us to the matter at hand. "This is all very well, young man, but you haven't offered any proof that your grandmother was the one who stole these items and not you. How did she take them without anyone noticing?"

As was common in our interviews with witnesses, suspects and anyone who falls in between, Graham looked to me in the hope I might offer support. I did what I could.

"You're not in any trouble, Graham," I reassured him. "Not if you tell the truth, at least."

He bit his lip so hard that, when he released it, I could see a little white mark there. "My grandmother…" His whole being was limp and defeated. "…she's always been good with locks. That's why people don't think too carefully about the items they lose. She doesn't snatch anything from pockets or bags like most thieves; she picks locks and goes into rooms when she knows their occupants are out of the hotel. I think most people must assume they've mislaid whatever has disappeared or the hotel staff are to blame. As soon as anyone makes a fuss, she stops for a while."

I couldn't hold in my thoughts. "That's terrible. She must have left any number of unemployed maids in her wake. Hotels fire their employees if they suspect stealing, you know. People might even have ended up in prison because of your grandmother's little game."

"I know that!" He balled his fists up in frustration rather than anger. "Why do you think I was walking around with this pen? I was hoping to take it back. I do it wherever we go, and I try to make sure that no one gets in trouble, but it's not always easy because Grandma protects her lock picking tools the way most people guard diamonds and rubies."

This made Grandfather's eyebrows rise. "And what do you know about diamonds and rubies, my boy?"

Graham closed the wardrobe and sat down on the side of the bed looking thoroughly exhausted. I couldn't say I liked him – he still had a tetchy, nervous quality and clearly felt terribly hard done by – but I could sympathise with his predicament.

"I don't know anything about anything except for the stories that Grandma tells everyone. I love her, but she's just about the least discreet person I've ever met. She thinks it's wonderful to boast about her past. She's like an old soldier who never stops talking about long-finished battles."

"She told us she was a thief in the bar yesterday," Grandfather stated disbelievingly. "You're saying that she openly admits to her crimes and then no one suspects her of stealing their valuables?"

"I can't explain it myself." His voice was brittle. "She seems to have a special charm over people. We travel together often because my parents are too busy enjoying themselves to worry about me. I've seen her work her peculiar magic so many times. Everyone thinks she's wonderful, and in all the time I've known what she gets up to, I've never once seen anyone accuse her of a crime."

This reminded me more of my grandfather than I would willingly admit in front of a boy like Graham. I'd known a few people in my life, in fact, who had the seemingly supranatural ability to bend others to their will, including a number of highly competent criminals. The fact that Dolly openly discussed her sordid past apparently wiped the possibility that she could still be a thief from people's minds.

Grandfather decided to concentrate on the key question. "Do you know anything about the theft of a tiara in 1909?"

In response, Graham only looked more confused. "I wasn't even born until three years later."

I should have been contemplating how what we'd learnt about his grandmother could fit together with the rest of the case, but instead I was quietly impressed with myself. I'd guessed he was seventeen, and I was right on the nose!

Luckily, Grandfather's much better at staying on course than I am. He walked to the window to look at the whirling flakes of snow that vainly attempted to cling to the glass before blowing away again. In one dramatic move, he spun back around to us and declared. "I believe you, boy, and we must now speak to your grandmother." He held out one hand. "But first I'd like my pen back."

CHAPTER TWENTY-SIX

Before we could search for Dolly, we had a Christmas duty to undertake.

"Do you know to whom most of the stolen items belong?" Grandfather asked the downhearted boy.

"I think so."

"Good, because you and Christopher will have to return them. You'll soon discover that few people in this hotel will be surprised to hear that there is a thief on the premises."

Graham looked just as frightened now as when Grandfather had been barking at him. "What if they're not in their rooms?"

"That won't be a problem." That intimidating figure turned and headed for the door, leaving the two of us alone to arrange the various items that needed delivering.

"Are you ready, my little helper?" I asked once we each had an armful to transport around the hotel.

"I think so." I doubt that Graham had ever been 100 per cent sure of anything in his life.

"Off we go then." I smiled in the hope it might settle his nerves.

I remembered that Rosetta Mullen's room was on the floor above, and sure enough, the door was locked and no one answered our knocking.

"Now what do we do?"

Before I could have a stab at answering the young man's question, Grandfather appeared from our suite, two doors along the corridor. "Fear not, young ones. Old Father Ow is here."

He'd clearly realised the same thing that I had: our task was a twisted re-enactment of what Father Christmas got up to every twenty-fourth of December. We were distributing desirable items about the place but, instead of presents, we were dealing in stolen goods.

As Graham and I stood on either side of the door to give him space, Grandfather reached into his brown suit jacket and extracted a set of fine tools arranged on a metal ring.

"Since when have you known how to pick locks?" I asked him, unable to disguise just how much this shocked me.

"Since long before your parents thought, *Hmm, it might be nice to have a child or two one day*. There have been odd occasions on which we might have made use of my picks in the past, but it always feels like cheating to me, so I prefer not to." He said all this with his tongue poking out of his mouth as he concentrated on opening the door using just two pieces of metal. "Here we go!"

Graham smiled for perhaps the first time since we'd met. I signalled for him to go ahead of me, and he scurried into the room to place Miss Mullen's gloves at the end of her bed. She would certainly have a pleasant surprise when she got back to her room, and the only disappointment was that I didn't have a clementine orange or perhaps a few chocolates to leave too.

We worked our way around the rooms thanks to Grandfather's excellent memory of the list we'd seen in the manager's office. It was a good thing that everyone was busy elsewhere in the hotel (or dead, in Blanche Atkinson's case) as it avoided having to explain too much.

Soon enough, our task was close to completion.

"Oh, Lord Ow," Sunday Cheshire said when she opened the door at the sound of Grandfather's fiddling with the lock. "How can I help you?"

We'd got so used to the rooms being empty that we'd forgotten to knock.

I'd rarely seen him look so guilty. "Hello, madam. We're sorry to bother you, but this young gentleman has something he wishes to say."

Sunday turned to me expectantly, and I pointed in Graham's direction.

He cleared his throat to speak, then looked a little helpless, and a strange rasping sound emerged before he found his words. "We discovered these and thought they might belong to you."

He held out the single-diamond earrings so that they dangled from his hands. Sunday can't have believed his tale as she glanced back into her room, presumably to the spot where she expected to see them. Her resultant frown spoke volumes.

"Thank you for returning them to me," she said, but her usual warmth was not in evidence. She positively scowled at Graham, and the effect it had on him was immediate.

"I'm sorry. That was a lie," he managed to admit, but he could only stare at the polished pine floor as he did so. "We didn't really find them. I stole them from your room. It's a habit of mine, and I get carried away sometimes, but I didn't mean anything by it. I promise I didn't."

She couldn't stay angry with him for long and was soon smiling again. "Thank you for telling the truth. I think it would be best if we forgot all about it and started afresh, don't you?"

Graham looked uncertain whether the nice lady before us actually meant what she was saying, but he nodded all the same.

"It is Christmas Eve, after all," she said to convince him. "It would be silly to hold grudges on today of all days."

"And tonight of all nights," Grandfather added as he placed his hand on Graham's shoulder. "Thank you for your time, Mrs Legyear."

"You mean Cheshire," she corrected him. "Legyear was my maiden name."

"Oh, of course. I am sorry. I hope to see you downstairs later." He leaned closer to her but spoke in just as loud a voice as before. "Herr Ried told me that he has a surprise for us."

"I'll be coming quite soon." She closed the door, still with the same cheerful expression on her pleasantly round face.

"That was very noble of you to protect your grandmother like that, Graham," Grandfather told the boy once we had walked back to the stairs and could no longer be overheard. "You clearly love her very much."

"I do," he replied with such earnestness that I was a little moved. "She's the maddest person I've ever met, but I'm terribly fond of her."

"I could say the very same thing about my grandfather," I said without thinking, and the glare I received in return was so intense that it almost burnt a hole through me. "Not you, Grandfather. I mean the other one," I tried, before realising he knew full well that my father's father had died before I was born. "And when I say the other one, I mean someone else's entirely."

Graham looked as though *he* felt sorry for *me* then, which I thought was rather rich. "Well, I had better be going. I promised I would play cards with Grandma before dinner."

We waved him off and were both quite cheerful as we descended the stairs once more. And yet, the closer we got to the ground floor, the more the ends of my mouth and my good mood dipped.

"You know, the falling chandelier may have given Graham ideas. He could have added a little cinnamon to his grandmother's cake on purpose. He was there when I saved Sunday's life, but there's nothing to say he isn't our killer."

"Come along, my boy. He has just made it abundantly clear that he loves his grandmother a great deal."

"The grandmother who spoils all their holidays by stealing from the other guests?" I hope my tone adequately put across my doubt on the matter. "I can only imagine that his feelings are mixed at best."

"Are you really saying that he killed the two victims as part of a plot to rid him of the woman who looks after him when his parents are too busy elsewhere?"

"That's exactly what I'm saying…" I had to pause then, as I wasn't sure that *was* exactly what I was saying. "Well, either that or there's a second killer. Who else but Graham would have known that his grandmother would react so strongly to a common spice?"

"Anyone who heard her talking to the waiters presumably." Grandfather regarded me through the side of one eye and looked a touch suspicious. "Really, Christopher. Must you be such a cynic?"

CHAPTER TWENTY-SEVEN

Although Grandfather was unconvinced by my theory, I could not forget the violent glee I'd witnessed when Graham told me of the book he was reading and, now that I have constructed that sentence, I can only imagine how idiotic it sounded. The simple truth is that there are people who like gratuitously nasty books but would never kill a fellow human. And that's because there's no accounting for taste; much as some people love Brussels sprouts, and other people are sane.

As we reached the foyer, Herr Ried rushed out of the office to talk to us.

"Good afternoon, gentlemen." He looked just as nervous as the last time we'd seen him and dabbed at his brow with a handkerchief. To be fair, the hotel was a real furnace, with radiators in every room and fires blazing in all the larger spaces. I felt sorry for whoever was running up and down the servant stairs to tend to them, but they were doing a good job. "I must tell you that I spoke to the police, and it is as I feared. They will do their best to come out to us, but the weather isn't expected to improve for some time."

"We understand, Herr Ried," I replied in a grateful tone. "Hopefully we'll be able to present the killer to them when they do arrive."

If anything, this made him even more nervous. As though he were saying a small prayer, he glanced up at the stained-glass window on the front of the building before attempting a smile. "Oh, I do hope so. Especially as I have planned some seasonal activities for us at six this evening. It is a tradition in Switzerland on Christmas Eve to… Actually, I won't spoil the surprise. All I will say is that I hope to see you all in the ballroom before dinner."

He was a curious character. His emotions kept changing and, in the course of a short conversation, he'd worked his way through regret, fear, excitement and anticipation. The fact he was discussing festive entertainment soon after two of his guests had been murdered was a little odd too, and he must have realised this as he added a brief, "We either continue with our lives or spend them mourning, and it is Christmas after all."

"Oh, I agree entirely," a voice called from behind us, and the

Swiss lady Inge Weinreich came over to share her thoughts on the matter. "When I grew up in a small village just one valley away from here, my mother always told me that we must find the happiness in everything – even the deaths of two innocent women."

She smiled ever so sweetly then. So sweetly that it almost made me think that what she'd said made the slightest bit of sense.

"Well, quite," Grandfather muttered, but he was as puzzled by this as I was.

I thought we'd got to know all the most eccentric inhabitants of the hotel, but there was one we'd barely glimpsed. I had to wonder whether she still intended to go skiing that night despite the storm. It really wouldn't have surprised me.

She sighed happily, and it was hard to match her demeanour to the one we'd seen an hour or so before when she'd discovered her new friend's poisoned corpse. "Switzerland is unlike anywhere else at Christmas. Now, can I tempt either of you to a game of *Jass*?"

She was one of those unusual characters whom Grandfather found indecipherable, and so it fell to me to answer her. "I'm afraid we're a little busy at the moment, but I'm sure we'll have the time before long."

"Yes, this is clear. I promised my new friend Dolly that I will teach her to play *Schmaus*. But I will hold the three of you to a game of *Jass* before you leave here." She had a mischievous look about her, as though she believed she had caught us out somehow.

"I'm very much looking forward to it, madam," Grandfather replied with a magnanimous bow, and Inge hurried off along the corridor towards the library.

"Grandfather?" I asked, still pondering how I would phrase my next question. "What is *Jass*?"

"I haven't the faintest idea. Now let's keep going before someone else dies or we're forced to endure another conversation about some mystifying topic of which we know nothing."

Delilah was still imitating a rug in the middle of the foyer. She looked up at us for a moment before deciding that she really wasn't in the mood to be a detective's dog and staying where she was. As we left her behind, the only problem I saw with our plan was that the person whom we wished to interview was presumably now busy with a game of… some variety.

Grandfather walked quickly along the main corridor and peered through every open door. We saw Dunstan Cheshire writing a letter in a small reading room. Henry Atkinson had found a bottle of something strong and was understandably drowning his sorrows in the otherwise empty bar and, to my astonishment and Grandfather's mild amusement, Dorie and Cook appeared to be grappling together in the library, where Timothy was looking rather worried and Todd was busy reading a file of papers.

Grandfather even opened the door to the men's *Schwitzbad,* though there was no one inside, and I'm glad to say that he left the *Schwitzbad für Damen* [7] well alone. As suspected, Dolly and Inge were sitting down to a game of what turned out to be cards in the billiard room, and Libby Hall looked as though she had been reluctantly roped in to playing with them. I was already bewildered by Inge's explanations of the rules in the short time we were there.

"Grandfather, didn't you want to speak to Dolly?" I asked, but he shook his head and retreated.

We continued along the corridor past the empty dining room to the only area we were yet to enter. The ballroom that the manager had just mentioned was as fine a space as the one next door. The floor was made of… you guessed it: shiny pine! And it was sprung for dancing. I could just imagine groups of young people making their way up to this lovely spot for a ball in the summertime. I could almost see the ladies' long, elegant gowns flowing as they danced about the room with their smartly dressed partners.

For now, the ballroom was empty except for a lone and rather lonely-looking woman who was sitting at the grand piano in the corner. Rosetta Mullen, who had once caused such a scandal in British society by marrying above her class, played ever so well, and she soon started singing sweetly too.

> **"Ain't got no honey,**
> **And not much money.**
> **So I'll sing this Christmas song.**
> **The snow is falling.**
> **I could be bawling.**
> **But that would feel so wrong."**

---

[7] Women's sauna.

She looked up at us as we came to a stop in the middle of the room, and I could tell that she wouldn't finish until she was ready to do so. She played in a bright, music-hall style that reminded me she had once been a chorus girl before the Earl of Rotheram had plucked her from the stage and sent her down the aisle to be married.

> **"The lights are shining,**
> **And I am pining,**
> **Because I always believe.**
> **The lights are dimming,**
> **And I'm still singing**
> **For you this Christmas Eve."**

Her fingers worked their way faster up the keyboard, and the chords she played grew louder as the piece built towards the chorus.

> **"I may not have a rainbow, or a pot of gold.**
> **There may not be a man here for me to love and hold,**
> **But it's Christmas Day tomorrow, the world outside is white,**
> **And as long as I've my memories, then I'll sleep well tonight."**

I thought she would go into a third verse, but instead she brought both hands crashing down on the keys, and the discordant sound echoed about the room.

To drown it out, Grandfather applauded.

"Bravo, madam," he called over to her. "That was delightful. Just delightful. You were born to perform."

"Very droll, I'm sure." She must have thought he was mocking her and closed the wooden fallboard down over the keys. "Could you do better yourself?"

There was a moment's hesitation during which I believe he considered taking her up on the challenge but, in a rather flamboyant gesture for him, he put his hand to his heart instead. "I very much meant what I said. You are a wonderful singer and a fine musician. I see what old Harold saw in you."

This seemed to have done the trick, and her previously squinting eyes widened. "You knew my Hal?"

He walked a little closer, now all charm and confidence. "Only when we were boys. We were at school together at Oakton Academy."

Until this point, I assumed he'd been making up a story to win her over, but this was too precise a detail, and besides, half of the richest aristocrats in England went to Oakton, so it's really no wonder he knew her dead husband.

"Your name is Lord Ow, isn't it?"

"He might have known me by another name back then." He smiled, and I was waiting for him to lie, but he kept telling the truth. "My nickname when I was a boy was Reprobus, or often Reprobate. Few pupils at Oakton went by their real first names."

She looked pensive for a moment, then shook her head. "It's been a long time since he died. Perhaps I've forgotten, or he simply never mentioned you."

"I was very fond of him either way. And I was terribly sad when I read about his death in the newspaper. It is a shame that we lose the acquaintance of people from our youth, but that is what comes of having a full life."

"He was a good man." She had a rather hazy, mysterious tone of voice, as though she were thinking of a secret that she wasn't sure she should share. I found it very appealing. There was something profoundly alluring about her. It wasn't just the style of her elaborate dress or the sheen of her wavy, well-groomed hair. She positively oozed glamour and sparkle, as though she had never left the stage.

I hadn't noticed it when we first came in, but there was a large, towering object entirely covered by a long black sheet in the opposite corner of the room to the piano. There was no time to work out what could be underneath it, but I did notice the Christmas decorations that decked every surface in there.

This was what I wanted to see on Christmas Eve! There were gold and red garlands strung across the glossy wooden ceiling. Green wreaths hung on the pilasters between the large, high windows, and there were intricate lanterns hanging here and there made from what looked suspiciously like turnips. This was certainly a better use of that odious vegetable than eating it, and I looked forward to seeing them illuminated. It was just a shame we still had a couple of murders to solve.

The conversation had fallen flat, but Grandfather was determined to revive it, even if he was required to reveal the reason we had come to see her. "Before I say anything more, you must understand that the past crimes of almost everyone in this hotel are irrelevant to me. My primary concern is to stop anyone else from being murdered."

"What do you mean 'murdered'? I heard a woman had died. I assumed it was simply food poisoning or something of the sort."

I felt like exclaiming, *See, Grandfather! It could have been prawns,* but I doubt it would have looked very professional, and now that I came to think of it, there hadn't been any on the menu. "There have been two murders," I said instead. "Barbara Nelson and Blanche Atkinson are both dead. One was poisoned and the other presumably stabbed."

I waited for her reaction to these two names, but it never came. She remained just as inscrutable as before, so Grandfather pushed further.

"Did you know those women? They were both criminals at the turn of the century. It does not appear that they were in any way violent or particularly well connected, but they were involved in the theft of a valuable item, a large part of which was never recovered."

"Which item?" she sounded more interested all of a sudden.

"It was back in 1909. A tiara which held two extremely rare rubies was stolen from the house of the Princess Royal in Brighton. At the time, the police were unable to identify the people who were responsible, but it seems that several of the women here were involved."

"And you think I must have been too because I was such a scandalous young woman. Is that it?" It was easy to see how such thinking unnerved Rosetta Mullen. It was the kind of narrow-minded attitude that had plagued her for most of her adult life. However, it just so happened that, in this case, it was true.

"No. I think you were involved because, at the time, you were fighting your husband's family to obtain the money that you were owed after his death. You would have needed substantial funds to wage that battle. I also know that, of all the people here, you were the only one who travelled internationally, hobnobbed with people at all levels of society and had the knowledge and contacts to be…" He paused for the count of three before delivering the accusation that would draw a gasp (from me, at least). "…the Duchess."

We both held our breath then, but she wasn't impressed by his conclusion. "What does that mean? I was never a duchess."

"Not *a* duchess, *the* Duchess," he tried again. "She was a highly accomplished jewel thief and safe breaker who, around the time you won your court case against your husband's family, gave up the profession and disappeared."

"And you think I must be her because..." She scoffed then. "Because I was married to an earl? Surely I would have called myself the Countess if anything."

"No, no, that would have been too obvious. You're cleverer than that."

She didn't reply immediately. She leaned back with her bare elbows on the flat of the closed piano lid and considered his case. "Tell me, Lord Edgington..." This was enough to make my grandfather draw a loud breath of his own, but she hadn't finished. "...when exactly was the Duchess committing her string of international burglaries?"

Grandfather blustered for a moment. To be quite honest, I thought it was a bit silly that he had persisted with his pretence for so long. "Well done, madam, you have seen through my flimsy disguise. I am indeed (the great) Lord Edgington." Fine, he didn't actually call himself great, but it was implied in his delivery. "And as for the career of the once famous criminal, I believe it started in 1906, and the tiara was the last thing she was reliably believed to have stolen."

"So you're suggesting that, shortly after the man I loved was taken from me on our honeymoon on the Côte d'Azur, I donned a mask and began to infiltrate banks and country houses, snatching diamonds and emeralds wherever I went?" Unlike the less-informed Graham upstairs, I believe she'd intentionally avoided mentioning rubies. "And between these daring raids I was busy securing legal representation, learning about the arcane laws governing probate and doing everything in my power to stop Hal's family from tarring my name in public. Is that what you think, oh great detective?"

She certainly had his number, but I wasn't about to laugh at the situation or show that she had in any way dented his high opinion of himself. I maintained a serious mien as I ignored her question and delivered a summary of my thinking. "We know that you were involved in the theft of the tiara. You needed the money to do everything that you've just mentioned and so you agreed to provide a certain service.

Perhaps you aren't the Duchess, but that doesn't mean you can't help us work out who is."

"Well, boy, you did a better job than your tired old grandfather, but I'm not the kind to betray my friends."

"I told you. It's not the jewels or the theft that concerns us now," Grandfather insisted, sounding more agitated than he had all day. "It's the murderer I want, and the rest of you can go free."

She sneered rather than scoffed this time. "Why would anyone believe that? After all, you lured us here, didn't you? I assume you're the one who wrote to tell me that a great aunt no one in my family had ever mentioned had died leaving me a holiday to the Swiss Alps? Surely that was so you could catch the thief." She walked over to him slowly and confidently, and I could understand why a man like the Earl of Rotherham could have been enchanted by her. "I'm sorry, Your Lordship, you're not going to get me so easily. Now, if you don't mind, I was happy playing the piano until you interrupted.

CHAPTER TWENTY-EIGHT

Grandfather was flustered by his run-in with this steely character. He normally liked a good challenge, but I believe the pressures of the day had started to affect him.

"It's not quite fitting together as we had hoped, is it?" It was unusual to see him admit anything quite so… what's the word I need? Oh, yes: human.

"Perhaps she really doesn't know anything."

He was walking up and down the corridor outside the ballroom we'd just left. "Oh, she knows something. She practically admitted that her co-conspirators are among us."

"Yes, but that doesn't make her the Duchess, does it? It could just as easily be Dolly or Libby Hall or – though I'd really rather it wasn't, as she's ever so sweet – Sunday Cheshire. The problem is, we've now spoken to all of our suspects at least once, and I don't think that jumping back into another interview will do you any good."

He stopped walking, pulled himself up to his full height, and looked dubious in my direction. "So what do you suggest?"

"That's right, Lord Edgington," Cook told him in the kitchen twenty minutes later. "You're doing a fine job."

In the meantime, we had donned aprons and made the dough for more biscuits, while another batch had cooled for us to start decorating.

Grandfather was holding an icing bag with a small hole cut in the end so that the sugary pink substance came out in a thin line. He had started to decorate his first biscuit with the outlines of tiny stars.

"I'm sorry, Christopher, but I really don't see how this will help us find the killer or understand what happened in 1909."

"Who said we were doing this to help with the case? I just wanted to make some before Christmas." I couldn't keep my face straight for long and finally admitted, "Oh, very well. I think this will be good for you. It will help you clear your head, and who knows what brilliant ideas might emerge from it."

He did not look as though he agreed, though perhaps his grimace at that moment was due to the snowman shape that he was now trying to make on the round butter biscuit. "Oh, bother! His head is all squashed.

This really isn't as easy as it looks, and I do not find it relaxing."

I considered pointing out that I had felt just the same when he had tried to teach me fishing, fly tying, painting, and… well, any number of things.

As we had colonised his kitchen, Icilio, the Italian chef, watched us with as much care as our own cook. "These biscuits they are known here as *Mailänderli*," he explained. "It means *cakes from Milan*, but I've never eaten them quite like this in my homeland." He popped an undecorated one into his mouth and immediately showed how tasty it was by rubbing the ends of his fingers together.

"They look delicious," I told him as I iced my ring shape to resemble a wreath.

Grandfather was still having trouble. "Now his nose has become squashed into his eyes. He looks like a big blob of pink sugar. This is infernally frustrating."

"It's all in the wrist," I told him, a touch vengefully. He was normally the one who excelled at whatever we tried, and I'd finally found my forte. "Perhaps I'll give up this detective lark and become a pastry chef."

As Grandfather scowled, the two professionals looked happy at the idea that I would follow in their footsteps.

"You've certainly always been a great admirer of food," Cook told me, and I did my best not to think she was calling me greedy.

"Yes, but you need a little more on your bones to do our job!" her Italian counterpart commented, tapping his round stomach as he did so. "I trust no chef who is too meagre."

He did not seem to notice that Henrietta was as thin as a stick insect, but she didn't mind. Our cook had a thick skin and a good sense of humour. She was also very gracious in other people's kitchens. All that, added to the fact that she was trying to help her employer ice a biscuit, meant that she made no reaction to her colleague's ill-chosen words.

As I worked my way through the plate of biscuits, and Icilio produced another batch from a tin, I considered the various elements of the case. It felt as if we had spent more time trying to identify the Duchess than we had on the murders themselves. There were certainly several elements in the affair which struck me as unusual. I suppose it was odd to be investigating a group of people who had all previously engaged in criminal activities. But it was also quite surprising that each of them had seen the error of her ways and moved on to better things – well, except Dolly of course, though I put her kleptomania down to eccentricity more than anything else.

I had to wonder whether the fact that, as far as we had seen, none of them now supported themselves through illicit means meant that the theft of the tiara had been so profitable that they had been able to retire or move into other work. It would have made sense for the Duchess to have paid well if she had wished to maintain her anonymity. So far, of course, no one had admitted to having met her, which could suggest that she had found ways of keeping her distance until the day of the theft itself. Well, it was either that or our witnesses were all lying.

The hardest part of any investigation is knowing whom to trust… Wait a moment, that's not true. The hardest part of any investigation is knowing who the murderer is, but determining which of our suspects are manipulating us comes a close second.

Rather than continuing down the same road that we'd been walking all day, I decided to think about the circumstances of the two murders. The first had occurred early in the morning, perhaps just as the first train arrived at the top of the mountain. Did this mean we could rule out Dolly as the killer? She was by far the oldest of our suspects and the least likely to have the ability to dash down to the train station, greet Barbara Nelson with a knife of some variety and then hurry back to the hotel.

There were two problems with this hopeful theory. First, I'd learnt from my grandfather never to underestimate people based on their age or sex. I'd seen him doing things on the mountain that morning which I would never achieve, and there was nothing to say that Dolly hadn't been a champion skier in her youth – aside from the fact she'd grown up at a time when there were few skiing competitions, in a country without many mountains or an abundance of snow. And the second problem was that she had an accomplice to help her should she have needed one.

Just as I had willingly become my grandfather's apprentice, I could imagine Dolly's occasionally ghoulish grandson going along with her violent plans. If she'd known that the soon-to-arrive Barbara Nelson could expose her secrets, she might well have sent Graham to do her dastardly work. As for Blanche Atkinson, there was nothing to say that the mosquito bite of which she had complained had occurred whilst we were in the dining room. Perhaps whatever nasty substance had been injected into her neck had been administered before we went to dinner, and she only noticed it then. Perhaps Dolly used the supposed anaphylaxis to provide herself with an alibi for the time when she expected Blanche to die.

I tried to remember who else had been in the dining room. I knew that both Libby Hall and Rosetta Mullen had come later, but Sunday and her husband, as well as the Swiss lady Inge Weinreich, were all present at the time of the supposed insect attack.

None of this answered the second most significant question of all: we still couldn't be certain why anyone had to die. We'd considered the possibility that Libby Hall had been so angry at going to prison and not getting her fair share of the loot that she'd murdered two of the people involved, but if she held such rage inside her for so long, wouldn't she have found them back in Britain and bumped them off at a time when no one knew of her involvement? It would also make more sense for her to target her supposed friend Sunday before anyone else. It was possible that the falling chandelier was meant for her, but why hadn't Libby tried to finish the job if that were the case?

There was a terrifying moment, just as I attempted to ice one biscuit to look like a crescent moon (and not a banana), when I was afraid that we had ignored the possibility that a member of staff was to blame for everything. It didn't last long, and I soon returned to considering our main suspects.

"You're definitely improving," I heard Cook lying to her master.

While I doubt my grandfather would be petty enough to withhold the special envelopes he gave out to his favourite employees on Christmas Eve, I would have been just as complimentary if I'd been in her place.

I realised then that there was another element of the case to which we hadn't given nearly enough thought. It also occurred to me that I was in the perfect place to do just that.

"Chef," I said to the cheery Italian, "where do you keep your cinnamon?"

"Concentrate on your biscuits, *giovanotto*[8]. You do concentrate on

---

8 Italian for young man or lad.

your job and leave the rest to me. We need these for the celebration of this evening. It is not Christmas Eve without more biscuits than anyone can eat."

I smiled at his passion for sweet treats – and his acceptance of free labour. "You misunderstand me. I'd just like to see where the cinnamon is kept because of what happened to the old lady in the bar yesterday."

His easy demeanour of moments earlier disappeared. "No, no. This has nothing to do with me. I don't put spices in the signora's cake. I tell her three times after and I tell her twice before she eat."

Grandfather looked over at me, but he was still squeezing out icing, and his angel biscuit was instantly uglier than it already had been.

"I'm not accusing you of anything, Icilio," I told the chef. "I just need to know how it could have ended up on the cake."

He was more defensive than necessary, and I had to at least consider the possibility that he had added the cinnamon to Dolly's cake on purpose and used bad prawns to kill Blanche.

"I'm telling you, boy. I didn't use no cinnamon. I know this because this cinnamon it goes missing yesterday morning. I wanted to make the *Brunsli,* but I can't because the last of the cinnamon it disappears and no mules are going to bring me ingredients to the hotel in this weather!"

CHAPTER TWENTY-NINE

Perhaps this wouldn't be the turning point in the case that we needed. Perhaps it would come to nothing, but at least I had an idea of my own, which had not been the case for much of the day. I'd become so used to my grandfather knowing more than me that I'd been guided by him rather than thinking for myself. At the very least, it was time I spoke to Dolly.

I left Grandfather to his task – mainly because the chef would have lost his temper entirely if I'd deprived him of another worker – and went to the billiard room to find her. She was still sitting with Inge, but Graham had joined them and, as soon as I entered, the Swiss woman shouted, "A fourth for *Jass*! A fourth for *Jass*! You must play with us, young man."

I still didn't know exactly what *Jass* was, but I was sure that I'd be bad at it, so I had to turn her down. "I'm truly sorry, madam, but I'm afraid I need to talk to Dolly. Perhaps you can teach Graham how to play mouse. I think you implied that was a game for two players."

"*Schmaus* not mouse!" she replied a little impatiently. "Very well. Come along, Graham. You have a lot to learn."

She may have been single-minded, but she did as I'd suggested. She took her pack of cards – which had festive pictures on them of golden bells, and what looked like holly – and then led Dolly's grandson to the far corner of the room.

The old lady who remained crossed her arms over her chest and looked excited about the prospect of our conversation. "What can I do for you, young Master Christopher?" She was dressed in an even more gothic style than the day before. Her blouse was of black silk, and she wore a blood-red skirt that matched the colour of her lipstick.

"I'd like to talk to you about cinnamon."

She flexed the muscles in her face to show that she was not impressed by my choice of topic. "I can't say it is my favourite thing to discuss, but very well."

"When did you first realise that you were sensitive to it?" I kept my questions short and my tone even.

"I believe it came on when I was still quite young. It was once not so severe, but I've found that, as I've got older, I must avoid it entirely."

"Have you ever had such a strong attack as the one yesterday?"

"No, but that's because I always ask several times to confirm that there is nothing that could hurt me in any meal."

"So it's not just cinnamon then?"

"No, there are a few spices that seem to affect me. I believe nutmeg and cloves have a similar impact." She might just as well have said that she was reactive to Christmas itself. "I have never tested which is the most dangerous, but I avoid anything that contains spices in order to be safe."

"And when did you arrive at the hotel?"

I believe it was at this point that she realised I wasn't simply playing a game or engaging in a Christmas frolic. She might have thought that I was doing some homework from school for all I knew, but I could tell that she wouldn't humour me for much longer.

"I don't see why it's of any interest to you, but we arrived on Saturday. I was determined to make the most of our stay here. I paid for a room for my son and daughter-in-law for the first few nights, and they left yesterday to spend time alone without the boy. They are not patient people, and they find him very queer."

"I can hear you, Grandma!" Graham shouted over to us.

She craned her neck to reply. "That doesn't mean I don't love you, Graham. And I'm not saying anything that you haven't heard a hundred times before." As she looked back at me, she crumpled her nose to suggest that he was the unreasonable one.

It was hard to know how to follow this interruption, but I did my best. "You told us that you were a thief in your youth. What sort of things did you steal?"

"I'm glad you asked." This excited her again, and I remembered how much she had enjoyed talking about herself the previous evening. "Young bucks like you might not look twice at an old thing like me, but I have lived an extremely interesting life." She leaned closer and dropped her voice to a whisper, as if she didn't wish anyone else to know what she was about to say. "I discovered when I was quite a bit younger than you are that I was adept with a hook and pick."

This meant nothing to me, so I was glad that she explained.

"My father was a well-to-do locksmith – that is to say, a lock maker. He was very good at his work – a highly respected man in East London – and he gave me a set of lock picks and would pay me a farthing a time to test the locks that he built. If I could pick them in five minutes, he would make a new one. The problem was that I was soon unlocking the things in seconds, and he had to change his criteria. When I reached adulthood, I didn't like the thought of settling down or going into service, so I put my skills to good use."

"So you were a professional lock picker?" I asked to put a finer point on it.

It was not just her mouth that curled up in a smile but her whole face. "I was one of the best that London ever produced, and there have been many before and since. I didn't like to draw attention to myself, but I did a job or two a month for people who paid well enough, and it was a good existence. Much better than slaving over a stove for an ungrateful husband or being spoken down to by some dreadful baroness."

"Then why did you give it up?"

"Well…" She crossed one hand over the other and looked for her words. "The truth is, I did something rather silly. I fell in love." Her high-pitched laugh sounded, and she cast her gaze up to the ceiling. "Don't worry, it started off quite mercenarily. I was trying to win his confidence so that I could rob him, but he stole my heart instead. He was wealthy enough to afford to keep it, and within a month, we were married. It was on the strict understanding that I would never be his *good little woman*, and we had thirty happy years together before he died."

Although the end of this short tale was a sad one, she maintained her blithe expression, and I still didn't know what to make of her. I did a quick calculation and realised that, based on Graham's seventeen years and the approximate age of his parents, Dolly's husband would have died around the time that the tiara was stolen.

I was about to ask a question to find out how close I'd got, when she spoke again. "That was in 1909. I was only fifty (approximately enough), and to my genuine horror, I discovered that I was awfully lonely without him, so I looked for something to distract me."

"And that something was stealing again?"

She wiggled her body to get more comfortable in the oversized armchair that made her look even smaller than she was. "Aren't you a clever boy? Well, yes. That was my idea. However, I didn't have the same sensitivity with my hands that I'd once had. Picking a lock is a lot like playing a musical instrument."

This sounded like the kind of thing that people say without any evidence, so I asked, "Oh, in what way?"

"First, it takes years of practice, and you must do it every day if you wish to master the art, and second, once you reach a certain level, both in music and thievery, it is no longer a conscious process. Your body takes over, leaving your mind free to soar."

I liked the way she spoke of her criminality as an art form. Grandfather had often talked of the exceptional thieves he had known. He had held some of them in high respect, and I believed that, now I'd met Dolly Coxon, I could understand why. What I didn't understand was how this related to the theft of the Princess Royal's ruby tiara.

"What I'm trying to express is that, when I returned to my previous pastime – I prefer that term to *occupation* – it took me months to get anywhere close to my previous level, but even then, I was one of the best in the city, and people started coming to me with jobs. I am happy to say that I turned down almost all of them. I had no desire to go to prison, and the kind of criminals who contacted me, for the large part, couldn't be trusted."

"But there were exceptions," I told her without a hint of doubt in my voice.

"No, there was one exception. Just one. Until then, I'd been breaking into places which most people thought quite impossible to enter. I didn't do it for the items I could take but for the puzzle they offered. And then one day I received a letter. It was unsigned, but it promised that I could make a great deal of money by unlocking one single door in a house on the south coast."

"So you were recruited without meeting anyone involved in the crime?"

"I didn't even know what the crime was. But something about the way the note was written appealed to me. I believe it was the mystery – the unknowable essence of a clandestine endeavour. I couldn't say whether I was helping the hard-done-by director of an orphanage to steal enough money to keep his wards in gruel or helping a loathsome gangster exact revenge on his foes."

"And that moral ambiguity didn't concern you?"

She looked away at the billiard table then, as though offended by the very idea. "How could I be concerned about something of which I had no knowledge? All I did was unlock a door. I didn't fire a gun through the keyhole or toss a lit match inside."

I wanted to know exactly what had happened that day, and so, when she remained silent for the first time, I put a question to her. "Which door did you have to unlock?"

There was a noticeably wild glint in her eyes, and I could tell once more just how much she enjoyed boasting of her achievements. "It was within one of the bedrooms of a grand abode on the Brighton seafront. I believe it belonged to the lady of the house, but as no one told me any of the details, I never knew for certain."

She sat forward a little in her chair as she got to her favourite part of the tale. "It looked like an ordinary cupboard, but it had an extraordinarily complicated lock. It's called the Chubb detector, and while it is not entirely unpickable, it does present someone like me with a real challenge. It can't just be forced, for one thing, because doing so would alert the owner of the lock that it had been opened. You see, the detector is rather clever because, if you make one wrong move, it jams itself in such a way as to leave a trace."

"Wait a moment, how did you get into the house in the first place?"

"It was all in the letter. I was given the exact time to go to the back door of the property, and it was open. I walked through the kitchen and upstairs without seeing a soul, so someone had clearly studied the place on my behalf. I knew I had ten minutes to unlock the cupboard, though I hadn't a clue what was inside."

"Did you manage it?" I admit that I was absorbed by her story and eager to hear what had happened.

"I had a pocket watch with me to check exactly how long I was taking." She paused again to draw out the suspense. "Nine minutes and fifty-two seconds. I completed the task with eight seconds to spare, and then I had another two minutes to get out of the house. I admit that, as I was leaving, my curiosity got the better of me, and when I heard the sound of a young woman addressing a group of people at the bottom of the servants' stairs, I peered through the window in the door to the staff dining room to see who it was."

"Did you recognise her?"

Dolly pulled her head in as though what I'd said was ridiculous. "No, of course not. I didn't know anyone who lived in the area. I suppose she was the head of the household addressing the maids and footmen. The person who planned the whole thing clearly knew when the staff would have their meeting, but I can't remember what the people I saw looked like. It was twenty years ago after all."

Now that her story had reached its conclusion, I found myself relaxing a touch. "So that was that?"

"That was that. I never did find out what was to be stolen."

"You must have looked through the door you opened?"

She frowned much as my grandfather often does. "Of course I did, but all that was in there was a metal strongbox that was secured to the wall. I had nothing more to do with it. I walked along the seafront to the centre of Brighton, had a cream tea on the prom and then got the 12:25 bus back home to London."

Something still didn't sit right with me. "How did the mastermind behind the plan pay you?"

"I honestly thought that I'd never hear another word about it, but then I received an envelope with two hundred pounds in bank notes a few weeks after it was done. I found it all very exciting. Whoever was responsible could have got away without paying me, but they decided against it. And do you know, after that, I didn't feel the urge to try anything so daring again? I thought, *You've taken enough risks, Dolly bird. It's time to retire in earnest this time.* And from that day to this, I've only ever stolen trinkets for fun."

I bit the inside of my cheek and thought about everything she'd just told me. I believe I clicked my tongue a few times, not to make her wait, but to decide how to phrase what I had to say. "I don't believe you."

"I beg your pardon?" She sounded amused rather than insulted.

"I said that I don't believe the story you've just told me. It's ever so convenient that you avoided meeting a single other person. It gives you good reason not to recognise anyone else here this weekend."

The light coming through the window changed as the storm shifted, and her face turned a shade or two darker. "What are you suggesting?"

"I'm saying that the other British women at this hotel were all involved in the theft of a priceless tiara from the Princess Royal, whose house you admit to entering in 1909. Two of them have been murdered, another was almost crushed by a falling chandelier—"

"And someone tried to poison me with cinnamon," came her retort, her voice rising in volume and anger.

"Or you went into the kitchen one night when no one was in there and used your famous light fingers to take it and put a little on your cake so that it would look as though you were in the same boat as them."

It was at this point that Graham over his hand of cards down and stared across at us. Of course, he was under no illusion as to his grandmother's character, but what I'd said still alarmed him. "Not murder, Granny! Please say you didn't—"

"Be quiet, boy. The grown-ups are talking." I thought this was quite a compliment, as most people still treat me as though I'm seven, but I had to keep the pressure on her.

"I think you were the one who planned the burglary down to the very last detail. You employed Barbara Nelson, whom you killed before she could come here and give the game away, and Blanche Atkinson, whom you managed to poison before she could recognise you. Libby Hall told us that she had been hired as a maid in the house by a glamorous older lady, which I would say fits your description perfectly, and as for Sunday Cheshire who would have been flattened by the chandelier if I hadn't been there to push her to safety, you just admitted seeing her in the house that day."

She glared at me then. If the truth be known, she was quite intimidating. "You've got it all wrong. You've filled your head with nonsense and fashioned a story that wouldn't be out of place in a tawdry novel."

"I don't think so. I think every word I said was true, and more than that, I think you're the one who broke open the safe that was behind the cupboard door. I think that you're the Duchess."

She didn't say, *Who's the Duchess?* or *Why are you talking such rot?* She looked alarmed, and I could tell that she knew just who I meant.

"You made a fortune from stealing the rubies and diamonds from the Princess Royal's tiara. After you obtained them, you left the least valuable stones for Elisabeth Hall to take to the Continent, and you made sure that she was arrested for doing so, and then you continued on your journey all the way here to the Villa Cassel where I can only assume you sold them to the highest bidder – perhaps to Mr Cassel himself, who was apparently a very wealthy man."

From the glazed look in her eyes, I could tell that she was in shock, but then something quite unexpected occurred. She began to laugh at me. "Oh dear, dear, Christopher." Her laugh became a cackle. "You know, I will never grow tired of the exuberance of youth. You have such a wonderful way with nonsense. You thread it together like the finest of seamstresses."

I kept my calm. "Then prove me wrong."

"I'm not the Duchess, you little fool. Picking locks and breaking into safes require a completely different set of capabilities."

Even Inge was looking at us now, and I don't think that Graham had so much as breathed in minutes.

"You can keep on denying it, but—"

"You didn't ask me whether I met anyone else that day."

It was my turn to say, "I beg your pardon?"

"You commented on how convenient it was that I would get in and out of the house in Brighton without anyone seeing me or my noticing the other conspirators, but the truth is that there was another person there. I suppose I had taken too long peering through the window at the staff who were in the meeting as, just as I was leaving, I passed someone in the yard outside the back door."

Now I was the one holding my breath.

"You see, there had to be someone coming to complete the next stage of the plan. I'd granted them access to the cupboard without making a mess of the place, so they clearly didn't want the owners of the house to know that anyone had been in there. But someone had to open the safe to steal whatever was inside. I'd heard of the Duchess. She'd become something of a legend in the circles in which I once moved, and no one could say for certain if she were real. I never imagined it was her though, because, all those years ago, the person entering the property as I was leaving was a man."

CHAPTER THIRTY

"Grandfather!" I yelled as I ran along the corridor and nipped through the dining room to reach the kitchen. "Grandfather, I know what happened."

As I entered, the Italian chef was shaking my floury forebear's hand.

"These are magnificent!" He looked at the plate of biscuits on the sideboard in what I can only describe as wonder. "Truly, these they are remarkable. I have been living in this country for nearly twenty years and making *Mailänderli* all that time, and I have never seen such perfection."

I wasn't the least surprised that, in the twenty minutes I'd been gone, Grandfather had become the world's best biscuit decorator.

"You were right, Chrissy!" he called, ignoring my urgency. "It was all in the wrist! Once I'd mastered a certain way of holding the bag and manipulating the paste inside, everything fell into place."

I approached to take in the celebrated sweets, and I must admit that he'd done a good job. His designs had become more intricate than before, and he'd made us of far more shapes, patterns and textures. There was a nativity scene with Jesus, Joseph, Mary and even the friendly beasts, and you could make out their very expressions. On others, he hadn't just made simple star decorations; he'd created whole galaxies. He was infuriatingly accomplished, and I couldn't help loving him all the more because of it.

"We're very proud of what you've achieved, m'lord," Henrietta told him with no small amount of amazement.

"That's fabulous," I interrupted. "However, there's the little matter of a murderer I believe I've identified. Would you care to come with me?"

"The biscuits were a good idea after all," he told me as though he were the one who'd suggested making them. He had at least taken off his apron and brushed the icing sugar from his clothes. "I have often noticed that, by not looking at a problem head on, we can see it more clearly. And in addition to that, I have picked up a useful new skill."

We were walking back along the corridor towards the room where I hoped to find the killer.

"That's marvellous. Please feel free to make use of it as often as possible so that I always have something sweet to nibble on. If you really want to be useful, you could make Delilah her dog biscuits too."

"Now, let's not get carried away, boy. We'll tie up the last few details of this case, enjoy the Christmas Eve celebrations and, in a spare moment tomorrow between presents and games and what have you, I'll give you some tips so that you can be just as good as I am."

I didn't know what to say to this, so I stayed mum. We'd almost reached the writing room, but the door was closed. We drew up to it, and I decided to warn my companion before we went in.

"Obviously we don't know how he'll react to the truth, but if he denies it, please don't abandon my theory too quickly. I've realised something truly astonishing."

"Oh, very well, but let's not take too long. I'm familiar with Swiss Christmas traditions from several books I've read, and I know you're going to enjoy what Herr Ried has prepared for us." He really was taking our holiday, if not the case, most seriously.

I put my hand on the door handle, took a deep breath and, without even knocking, pushed it open. Dunstan Cheshire was sitting in a chair straight in front of us, and I could tell from his reaction as we flew into the room that he knew he'd been found out.

He attempted to cover his fear with his usual civility. "Lord Ow, Christopher, how nice to see you."

"You can spare your empty words, Cheshire," I told him and, for once, my voice sounded just as I wished it would. It was hard and direct. Gone was the little boy who didn't know how to say anything without an *umm* or an *ahh* or a sudden embarrassing squeal. I was every bit Lord Edgington's grandson. "We know who you are."

"It's funny you should say that," he replied with that pleasant smile of his. "I've spent most of my life wondering, so I'd love to know your opinion on the matter."

"I'm talking about who you were between 1906 and 1909... approximately. I'm not quite sure of the dates." My directness might have gone off the boil just a little, but I was still confident of what I'd gone there to say. "We know you were responsible for directing the gang of women who were hired to steal the Princess Royal's tiara."

He had no reply this time. He leaned back in the leather chair and was so alarmed to be caught that he could give little more than a shake of the head.

"Dolly Coxon was the person chosen to pick the lock of a cupboard where the princess kept her valuable jewellery. As she was leaving, she saw a handsome young man with sharp cheekbones. I asked her whether it could have been you, and she said that it wouldn't have surprised her one bit."

"But Christopher," he replied in a voice so innocent he could have been singing the words in a parish choir, "that's hardly evidence that I was the man in question."

I paid him no attention but kept listing the evidence I'd gathered. "You had already met Sunday once through your work in Whitechapel. You could have met the others in the same way. You knew who to choose for each job, and I can only assume that you picked women so that no one would doubt that the Duchess was one too."

"I appreciate the effort you're making, but this is tenuous at best." He looked at the fire as though nothing I'd said was of any concern. "You'll have to do better than that."

"Did Sunday know that you were the one who organised everything? Did she realise that you were responsible for placing her at the house to learn the habits of the staff and residents? That story about meeting her again after the war and feeling swept away in an instant, was it all a lie?"

His eyes flicked back to me. "No, Christopher. It wasn't a lie. That is genuinely how I fell in love with the only woman in my life who means anything to me."

I felt a little sorry for his mother when he said this, and it did nothing to improve my opinion of him.

Grandfather was beginning to worry. "I'm sorry to hurry you, my dear grandson, but I'm afraid that everything you've said so far is circumstantial."

"Then how about this, *Dunstan Cheshire*?" I didn't take my eyes off our suspect for one second. "I know how you chose your alias. If you put together the first syllables of your names, it sounds just like Duchess!"

CHAPTER THIRTY-ONE

You could have cut the silence with a knife and then used that knife to butter toast. The only sound was the crackling of a smoky log in the fire. Dunstan stared at me in horror, fully aware that his secret identity had been uncovered after— No, my mistake. He started laughing.

"I'm truly sorry, young man. I don't mean to be dismissive, and I swear that I want to find the blighter who killed those poor women just as much as anyone, but—" For the next ten seconds, he fell about in hysterics.

Grandfather at the very least tried to hide his amusement. "If we're being honest, my boy, the first two syllables of his name spell Dunches!" This only made Sunday's husband laugh more.

"It all fits!" I shouted over them. "Dunstan is the connection between every last person here. We were looking for a woman since we found the first body, but if I were a jewel thief who was wanted all over Europe, it would suit me down to the ground to make everyone believe that I was a woman. He could have spread the stories of his exploits to reinforce the idea."

"That may be, Christopher." Dunstan was doing his best to sound reasonable, but when he fought to quieten his snickering, it burst out of him once more. "Do face facts, though: someone's name sounding a bit like another name isn't evidence of a dark criminal core. The name Christopher Prentiss sounds a bit like Christmas presents, but I won't be putting you in a box and giving you to my wife tomorrow."

Grandfather smiled but he still looked sympathetic. "No one is laughing at you, my dear fellow. It's just…"

Dunstan finished this point for him. "It's just the things you said." A further wave of hilarity swept over him. It wasn't actually that funny, but he'd gone past the point of self-control.

"I'm not saying that it's unfeasible that Mr Cheshire here is the man to blame," Grandfather insisted.

"Oh, no, of course not." Dunstan almost sounded worried I would think this. "You must explore every possible avenue."

The capable detective, who did not jump so readily to conclusions, regarded the man in question. "It's actually quite possible, based on the little we know of him, that he's the type to do all that you've just said."

Our perhaps-not-a-culprit-after-all shrugged at this. "I definitely can't deny that I had the ambition, the resources and, if I'm being totally honest, as a hard-headed businessman, the moral flexibility to plot a grand theft. But I'm definitely no killer."

Grandfather walked closer and put his hand on my shoulder as he considered the non-existent case against a man who happened to have an appropriate name. "Was there anything that Dolly said which could prove it was him? Could she even say for certain it wasn't the milkman she saw?"

"He was wearing all black clothes and had a brown leather bag full of clinking tools."

Grandfather wandered off, muttering as he went. "Fine, not the milkman, but perhaps a plumber."

"What about other witnesses?" To give him his due, Dunstan was ever so helpful. "Did anyone else see me there?"

I don't know whether I spoke my reply or just thought it. "No."

"What year did you say it was? 1909?" He put his hand to the back of his head and had a good scratch. "I'm sorry to tell you this, Christopher, but I was living in Ceylon at the time. I can't remember if that was the year I came home for a holiday when my uncle died or… no, I think that was 1910."

Even as they tried to help me prove my case, I knew that everything they said reflected badly on me. I suddenly felt like going to bed. At least that way Christmas Day would come around quicker. Who knows? Thanks to the magic of the season, the killer might have simply given himself up in the meantime.

It was at this moment that the man's wife appeared in the doorway. She was wearing a graceful white frock with satin hems, but she looked concerned by whatever she'd heard of our discussion.

"Ah, there you are, darling," Dunstan said, holding his hand out so that she would come closer. "You're just the person I need. Would you mind telling these gentlemen where I was between 1908 and 1911?"

Her brows knitted together, and I thought she was a mite flustered by the question, but she answered just the same. "You were living in British Ceylon. You'd gone there to explore a potential business concern, which was when you moved away from architecture to work in manufacturing."

"Thank you so much, madam." Grandfather was sincere in tone and manner. "It was very kind of you to clarify that for us. My grandson was exploring the idea that your husband was a killer and an international jewel thief, but there's nothing to worry about after all."

"How reassuring," she said, beginning to smile. "Imagine how I would feel to be married to such a man!"

The guffawing of earlier was now replaced with a polite chortle before Dunstan addressed his wife. "I do think you should tell them anything that you might know, my darling. These gentlemen believe there could be a connection between the deaths here today and what happened with the princess's tiara all those years ago."

She became nervous again but took a few steps closer. "I'm not sure there is a great deal I can tell you. What would you like to know?"

"We have learnt that you spent some time working in Brighton for the Princess Royal in 1909," Grandfather began, giving little away about how we knew this or why it was of any importance.

Sunday was understandably reticent. She looked across at her husband as she answered. "That was a long time ago. I can't say I'm proud of that period in my life, but we learn from our mistakes." This was a perfectly noble answer, but it was clear she had avoided providing any specific details of what her job there had involved.

"I'm sorry, madam, we will need to know more than that."

To my surprise, Dunstan lent his support to the appeal. "It's all right, Sunday. There's no need to be afraid. Tell them whatever you think might be helpful."

If anything, this served to make her more nervous. It didn't help that she was still standing halfway into the room like an uninvited caller, but she attempted to respond, nevertheless. "It's true. I worked at Fife House for most of that year. I was appointed head of household."

"Despite the fact you had never held such a position before?" I decided to check, but she flinched at the question, and so, instead of forcing her to reply, I motioned to the nearest comfortable chair and said, "Perhaps you should sit down, Mrs Cheshire. In order to solve the murders, we wish to know exactly what happened when the tiara went missing."

I don't know if it was the mention of murder or the purloined jewellery that did it, but I noticed her whole body remained tense even as she acquiesced and took a seat.

"Your position at the house, darling," Dunstan reminded her. "Perhaps you could explain how you came to have it."

It would take her another few seconds, but she answered with a gentle sigh. "It's true. I had never worked in service before. The man who secured the position for me—"

"That would be the Fagin character that your husband mentioned to me in the steam room?" I interrupted, and she gave a quick, mouse-like nod... not that mice are known for nodding but... well, I think you know what I mean.

"That's right. His name was Charlie Gammon. Or at least, that's what everyone called him. We grew up just along the street from one another. Like a lot of people, he was forced out when the neighbourhood was rebuilt, but years later, when I could no longer afford to provide for my siblings, I went to him to ask for help. He was a criminal, but he was a gentle sort, and I trusted him as far as I could. I did a few small jobs for him that involved gathering information on significant people. In one case, I befriended the daughter of an influential politician who stepped back from public life soon after I won the young lady's trust."

It wasn't difficult to infer how this had occurred, and she appeared to have no particular compunctions of conscience over the blackmail she had facilitated. Perhaps aware that we would think this, she offered a defence.

"I sought to be moral in my immorality. I considered each job I was offered and tried to understand whether people would be genuinely hurt or merely inconvenienced by my deeds. In the case of the politician, he would still lead a comfortable life. The only thing of which he was deprived was his standing."

"And what about the princess?" Grandfather said as she took a deep breath.

"The princess had other tiaras. From what I understand, the person who entered her bedroom to steal it left the vast majority of her jewels. I'm sure that she has barely thought about it since."

"Well, I have, madam." Grandfather's booming voice seemed to vibrate through the floor. "I have spent the last twenty years imagining what happened to the stolen rubies and diamonds. And you appear to be the very first person to whom we have spoken who has knowledge of the crime itself."

Her expression hardened, and a look of stubbornness flashed in her eyes. "I had nothing to do with the jewels. I was merely given the job of learning about the workings of the house and arranging a time at which the staff would all be occupied so that the lock picker and the safe breaker could reach the bedroom undetected."

"Then I must repeat: you have shown more knowledge of the intricate workings of the plan than anyone else. Why should I believe that you were not the mastermind behind it when you had the most authority of all the criminals involved?"

She released a strangled gasp and had to wait a few seconds before she could muster a reply. I watched her husband to see whether he would intervene, but he regarded her with just as much interest as we had.

"You can think what you like. That doesn't make me any more of a jewel thief than you are." Once she'd delivered this rebuttal, she fell silent for a few moments. "I know a little about what happened afterwards because Charlie Gammon told me."

Of all the ridiculous criminal names that I've heard over the years, Charlie Gammon has to be the worst.

Grandfather was beginning to lose patience. "Yes, but how did he know? How did he hear about the job for you in the first place? How did the person who hired you share out the ill-gotten gains once the rubies had been sold?"

She maintained her composure and attempted to answer his questions at last. "I never found out who organised the job. The only other person I knew was Libby, and I fear that she was chosen as they needed someone to blame for the theft. You see, unlike me, she wasn't required to pass on any information from the house to our employers. I sent Charlie a letter each week to explain what I'd learnt about the princess's movements and my fellow staff."

Grandfather opened his mouth to speak again, but she hadn't finished. "All I knew after the job was complete was that the tiara had been successfully obtained. They had fashioned a replacement, so the princess didn't raise the alarm for some time and, by then, the most valuable stones must have been sold."

Dunstan cleared his throat to share his thoughts on the matter.

"It seems to me that it's Mr Gammon you need to interview, not my wife. He must have had some connection to the person who planned and benefited most from the crime. Sunday admits the part she played, but she didn't have a hand in the crime itself. Her only intervention was to organise the servants' schedule to provide a short period when the house would be otherwise deserted. I'm uncertain whether she could actually be charged with any crime."

Grandfather had no such doubt. "Of course she could be. She was a conspirator and profited from the theft. And now, unless you have something more useful you'd like to share with us, I think this interview is complete."

I believe he brought things to an abrupt close to show them that this wasn't really the end. They hadn't proved beyond doubt that Sunday was truly innocent, and our investigation was not complete.

Mrs Cheshire looked as nervous as at any time during our stay. It was true that, unlike Libby Hall or Dolly Coxon, there was a direct line running between her and the mastermind of the plan. Perhaps the Duchess had hired her through Charlie Gammon, or perhaps this was a ruse, and she had done the whole thing herself, but I couldn't force the issue because Grandfather had already risen from his seat to leave the room.

I followed him to the door as the couple sat waiting to be alone, but just as I was about to step from the room, something occurred to me. I turned around to them in the hope of making my case more effectively. *Just one more thing,* I imagined myself saying, but the disparate thoughts in my head didn't combine to make a solid whole, so I merely told them, "The Christmas Eve celebrations will be starting any time now. I hope to see you there."

CHAPTER THIRTY-TWO

It was almost six o'clock. Normally at this time on Christmas Eve (dead body permitting) I'd be at home with my family getting ready for a feast or heading off to the candle-lit parade in our village. I'd been thinking about my parents a lot that day. I would be lying if I said that I'd missed them terribly since I'd left England, but not seeing them at all at Christmas felt quite wrong.

Perhaps this is why I was so glad to see Albert and Delilah as I stepped out of the reading room.

"Oh, brother of mine," I called to him. "I'm happy you're joining us. Have you a poem or two to share?" Fine, I may have gone overboard. My momentary homesickness had been quite intense, and I was eager to hear his voice again. Delilah wagged her way past me, perhaps to avoid having to hear any bad poetry.

"Not yet, Chrissy." He appeared to have already secured an iced biscuit from somewhere and was chomping on it as he replied. "I've got some very good beginnings, and the view from your bedroom, though obscured by the howling storm, certainly helped lubricate my wits and get the juices of inspiration flowing."

I'd rarely heard such an ugly phrase, so I didn't hold out much hope for his compositions.

"Well, you're here now," Grandfather said in a sombre tone, as though doing his best to find a silver lining. "Actually, why are you here? How did you know that the manager had organised his surprise for this time?"

"That Swiss lady knocked on my door. She brought me a biscuit and told me to be down here at six. She says that there won't be the same festive ambience without a large group to enjoy the celebrations. I think she must have gone around every room in the place to drum up interest." Albert looked awkward for a moment, which is far from rare for him. "She's rather an odd sort."

"The world is full of them," Grandfather replied, and he released an unusual hooting laugh to prove his point.

When we reached the ballroom, it turned out that we were not the first to arrive. A queue had formed at the closed door. Inge was at the

199

front of it, and she had somehow managed to rope in poor grieving Henry Atkinson, whose wife's lifeless body had now been transported to a cool outbuilding.

"It is better you come and enjoy yourself than be moping alone," she told him as though he'd merely lost his favourite book or had some minor injury. "We have fun, yes?"

Henry looked at her despondently but didn't have the energy to complain.

Behind them in the queue were our staff from back home and then Libby Hall and Dolly, who had clearly now recovered from her near death the night before. Graham was there too, but he was reading his book and didn't look up at us. When the Cheshires joined the back of the line, the only person still missing was Rosetta Mullen.

I got the impression that she wasn't a sociable sort. I hadn't seen her speaking to anyone at the hotel except the manager. I'd met people who considered themselves outsiders before, and it was clear from what she had told us of her life that she had suffered the callous treatment of a society which is always quick to condemn those who are different. Still, that didn't mean she couldn't enjoy a Christmas party.

After a minute or two's anticipation, I heard the double doors opening and there was Herr Ried looking genuinely excited about what was to come.

"*Herzlich willkommen, meine Damen und Herren*[9]. Come in, everyone. Please, come in!" His voice was not his own. He projected it like a compere at a variety show, and it had taken on a deeper quality than it usually had. "I'm so happy to see you all here. I know that circumstances today are far from ideal."

This understatement led to a cry from Henry Atkinson, who immediately ran over to a small bar covered in bottles. Unsurprisingly, Todd was there with two waiters, already mixing drinks. I could only think they'd heard of his cocktailian prowess and asked him to lend his magic. There were no new decorations, as far as I could tell, but the carved turnip lanterns hanging around the room had now been lit. They were etched with intricate patterns through which the light shone, lending a warm glow to the proceedings.

---

9 (Literally) A hearty welcome, my ladies and gentlemen.

The manager's message had come to a halt, but he soon found his words again. "It is still Christmas, and we are here together. We must make the most of this special time of year and continue with the traditions that have long been followed in my country. You see, to those who don't know, here in Switzerland, we have a special custom."

He walked across to the spot by the window where the black-cloaked object stood, and Delilah was sitting waiting patiently for someone to give her some food. Whatever was under the sheet was taller than me, and a few thoughts went through my head as to what it might be.

"But first, a song!" Ried clapped his hands and one of the waiters I recognised from the bar the night before hurried over to the piano. He placed his fingers on the keys in preparation, but they were dirty somehow, so he had to wipe them on his uniform before looking over at his employer.

"That's right, everyone. Come closer. Form a little group. I know that there are not many of us, but if we unite, I'm sure we will make ourselves heard. Even as the snow falls, our combined efforts will carry the song across the valley."

We did as instructed, though a little sheepishly as, in my experience, we Britons are far less disposed to communal displays in public than most nationalities.

"Excellent, excellent. Now, I will start the song in German, and you can all join in however you wish." He looked across to the porter who was standing next to the black sheet, presumably ready to reveal the manager's surprise when the right moment came.

Putting his hand to the lapel of his maroon jacket, Herr Ried began in a lovely baritone, and the pianist accompanied him to the tune of "Silent Night".

*"**Stille Nacht, heilige Nacht.**"* The words really did carry around the room (if not the valley), and one by one, his colleagues joined in. *"**Alles schläft; einsam wacht.**"*

Switzerland has several native languages, and I noticed that Icilio the chef and one of his kitchen hands were singing in Italian.

**"Tu che i Vati da lungi sognar,
Tu che angeliche voci nunziar,"**

The bar staff, it turned out, spoke French, and Todd somehow knew the words to sing along with them.

> "C'est l'amour infini
> C'est l'amour infini."

I heard a smattering of a language I couldn't identify from the porter and decided he must be singing in Romansh, which is spoken in... another part of Switzerland, I don't actually know where. As we reached the second verse, the audience joined in, and the English lyrics swelled with the other languages.

> **"Silent night! Holy night!**
> **Shepherds quake at the sight!**
> **Glories stream from heaven afar,**
> **Heavenly hosts sing Alleluia!**
> **Christ the Saviour is born!**
> **Christ the Saviour is born!"**

We didn't get to the third verse because it was at this moment that the porter tugged away the black cloth to reveal an exquisite fir tree, already decked out for Christmas with red velvet ribbons, silver stars, straw goats, golden baubles and snow-white candles waiting to be lit.

We were marvelling at the sight when a cry went up, and Graham pointed to the base of the tree. I noticed what looked like a bundle of rags on the floor. Of course, people don't normally scream when they see rags, and the next thing I spotted was a pair of bare arms coming out of them.

Grandfather rushed forward and, catching hold of the woman's shoulder, he pulled her onto her back. Rosetta Mullen had a spot of blood at the side of her mouth. Her eyes were wide open, and I don't think that a single person there doubted she was quite dead.

CHAPTER THIRTY-THREE

Having inspected the body and found nothing useful but the stab wound in the back of poor Rosetta's neck (which matched the one Grandfather had predicted on Barbara Nelson) we had left Albert to stand guard until a member of staff could replace him. I thought that, if the magic of the Alpine wilds couldn't coax the poet out of him, perhaps the sad reality of death might.

"The arrogance!" Grandfather exclaimed when we had convened in the library together with Todd and the other staff. "That's what strikes me. The killer must possess the most incredible arrogance to think she can get away with murder with so many other people around."

"We must have overlooked something important about Rosetta Mullen. Isn't it possible that this is all connected to the family into which she married? Or perhaps several of the women who were involved in the theft of the tiara knew one another, and whatever is happening here is quite unrelated to anything else."

Grandfather may not have heard me as he was striding about the room at such a pace and didn't respond to my perfectly reasonable suggestions.

"Do you know what I think?"

He didn't wait for anyone to answer, though I heard a brief, "Obviously not!" from Dorie, who had nabbed a plate full of biscuits and was doing her best to obliterate them with Timothy's help.

"I think that this whole thing started before we even arrived. The Duchess knew that, on being called back here, something was afoot. Fearing that she would finally have to pay for her crimes, she killed the people whom she'd met in person." He stopped in front of the fireplace and, with his elbow on the mantelpiece, looked back at us, full of anguish. "Miss Mullen knew more than she was willing to tell us – that's for certain. But the killer got rid of her anyway because she couldn't risk exposure."

He was so angry I thought he might spit. "The same goes for the first two victims. That despicable criminal hurried down to the train station to make sure that Barbara Nelson would never reach the hotel. And the fact that she knew when Miss Nelson was arriving suggests that they had been in recent contact. Yes! This explains things very neatly."

"We know everything but who she is," I replied with forced optimism. "And also whether she's actually a woman. Don't forget that Dolly Coxon claims to have seen a man entering the house after her."

"'Claims', Christopher. That's the key word here. She claims that she saw a man at Fife House. But we know that she's as slippery a customer as any other here. And therein lies our problem. Even the sweetest of this horrible bunch was once a criminal. Sunday Cheshire cuts a fine figure, but that was why people sought her out for a job like the one in Brighton. She is very good at pretending to be respectable. She also had the largest role in the plan. She worked for months in that house, and the Duchess couldn't have stolen the tiara if it weren't for her machinations."

"Is there anything in that file we don't yet know, Todd?" I asked in the hope that a detached discussion of the facts would pacify my grandfather somewhat.

He flicked through the pages as he replied. "It mainly deals with the upbringings of each of the women here and their various skills and convictions. Barbara Nelson was close friends with Blanche Atkinson. They grew up in Whitechapel together, like two of the other four. The same can be said for Sunday Cheshire – née Legyear – and Elisabeth Hall. Dolores Coxon and Rosetta Mullen were born not too far away, but they came from wealthier backgrounds. Dolores's father was a locksmith and—"

"Yes, we know all that, and I doubt going back so far will help us. What about Rosetta? She had a foreign name. Could that link her in some way to this hotel?"

"Actually, she didn't." Todd turned back to the front of the file and ran his finger along the page to find the relevant information. "Her real name was Rosie Miller. She changed it when she became a chorus girl in London at the turn of the century. And while P.C. Simpkin believed that she was connected in some way to the Duchess, he didn't find much evidence of her being a criminal."

I was forever exploring dead ends in our investigations. If there is one thing in which I can legitimately describe myself as an expert, it's theories that lead us absolutely nowhere whatsoever.

My plan seemed to have worked, though. When he spoke again,

Grandfather was a touch quieter. "Is there anything that could be used to identify one of the women here as the Duchess? Perhaps a record of international travel? Arrests for stealing or selling expensive jewellery? Is there anything in the slightest that might help us?" He still sounded desperate, but at least his desperation was expressed at a lower volume.

Todd thought for a second before admitting, "Not that I've noticed, m'lord. And I've read P.C. Simpkin's file three times now."

"That's another problem we must face." I couldn't disguise the gloom in my voice. "There's nothing to say that Simpkin identified all the different players who were involved in the burglary. It's quite possible that our party isn't complete, and the Duchess isn't one of the suspects we've identified."

Perhaps the least likely member of our own party spoke up at this moment to encourage us. "Don't talk like that, Master Christopher, sir," young Timothy insisted. "You're not the type to give in."

The problem whenever this hopeful individual contributed to our investigations was that I and my grandfather felt obliged to kindle his optimism and not let the crushing weight of the world force all the positivity from him. This might sound like a nice idea in theory, but as we were both feeling pretty bleak at that moment, it was easier said than done.

"That's right, Timothy." Grandfather tried to sound buoyed by his intervention (and failed). "I'm sure we're mere moments from solving the case." The weary sigh he then delivered certainly didn't help, so I thought I might have a turn.

"There is no way that the killer is any match for us." I sounded like a presenter on a children's radio programme, in that nothing I had just said was in any way convincing to adults.

Todd stood up from where he was sitting and, for perhaps the first time I could remember, there was a hint of irritation in his voice. "I'm sorry to say this, but we're getting nowhere. May I at least suggest we send Dorie and a few members of staff to make sure that all the remaining guests are gathered in one place so that no one else can be murdered?"

I looked at my grandfather. Grandfather looked at me, and I suppose we both realised that there was no arguing with the man. And yet, such simple measures had rarely occurred to us on previous cases.

It really was the logical thing to do to prevent unnecessary deaths.

"Very well, Todd." Grandfather pointed two fingers at the strongest woman I know to do as his retainer had bidden.

"'Ave a loverlee time," Dorie said, producing a second, larger plate of biscuits to take with her.

Timothy happily waved her away as our attention returned to Todd.

"Thank you." He must have realised that, for a calm, controlled man like him, what he'd just said was tantamount to a tantrum. He pulled down on his waistcoat, checked his neatly parted hair and moved on to his second suggestion. "Now, we haven't yet gone through the different roles of each of the criminals in the original case. Might that not be a good idea?"

"Yes," I replied. "Or rather, no. No, it might be a good idea." I was a little confused as to whether this sentence made any sense, but I persisted. "We've already discussed Sunday and Libby's roles at Fife House. Dolly also went there, but only on the day of the burglary itself. She was a lock picker, and it was her job to open a cupboard door which was almost unpickable."

"Then I have a question for you," Grandfather looked more animated all of a sudden. "Why would they need a lock picker when Sunday and Libby had been in the house for months? Why didn't they simply steal the key and make a copy?"

I was a step ahead of him for once. "I've been thinking about that, and I believe I have the answer. I can only conclude that the key to that cupboard was only held by the mistress of the house and perhaps her husband. It occurred to me that, as Barbara Nelson was a pickpocket, she may have been hired to obtain the key, but it was either impossible to get close to a pair of senior royals, or they never carried it on their persons. That would explain why Dolly was eventually hired and why we haven't heard what role Barbara performed."

"Well done, Christopher!" Grandfather curved his eyebrows at me, and I felt quite proud.

"Thank you. I try my best."

"Of course, there's no way we can confirm your theory, but it is a solid one." He is of the generation that believes every compliment is better when it is qualified by a less effusive adjoinder.

"As for Blanche Atkinson," I continued regardless, "she specialised in making counterfeit jewellery. Sunday confirmed that the Duchess left a replacement tiara in the safe in the Princess's bedroom."

"Which would have been helpful to know twenty years ago." Grandfather had lost a little of his drive and plunged into the nearest armchair to look sulky. "If only Princess Louise had trusted me with all the information at her disposal, there's a good chance I would have been able to find Mrs Atkinson and three people wouldn't have died."

"I've been considering the question of why the princess kept information from you, m'lord," Todd said to offer a rare unsolicited intervention. "It has to be a question of security rather than pride. She must have feared that, if anyone heard her house had been burgled, it would invite others to try the same thing."

"I think you must be right, Todd." Grandfather raised his eyebrows to confirm that he concurred.

"Let's move on to Elisabeth Hall," I said to return us to the main discussion. "She was the only person who didn't get paid and the only one to go to prison for the crime. What did she do after 1909?"

Todd held up one finger. "After Miss Hall was released from prison, she went back home to a small house in Hackney, where she remained ever after her mother died. She didn't get in trouble with the police again, but then she hadn't been before. I guess she tried to keep her nose clean after serving her time. I've known a few people who have been to gaol, and it's not an experience many would want to repeat."

"Who does that leave, Todd?" I asked the man with the file, and he peered down at the pages in front of him as though they were blank.

"No one."

"How can that be?"

"Well, we've gone through all the women who were connected to the burglary. We know to some extent what each of them did, and your understanding of things corresponds quite closely with what's written here."

"Then what about the husbands? Could Henry Atkinson have been involved?" I thought it was worth a try, though I didn't hold out much hope.

"From what we know, the Atkinsons didn't meet and get married until two years later. And as for the Cheshires, almost a decade passed between the tiara being stolen and their marriage."

207

Grandfather had already lost interest in this thread and jumped on to the next one. "Were any of the women connected to any other crimes involving jewels or the royal family? Were there any patterns in their lives or their criminal records which could help to explain what happened?"

"No, and …" Todd paused, looked hopeful for a second, then frowned again. "…no. In actual fact, Simpkin came to the conclusion that, after the jewels were sold, all the women involved went straight."

"I already assumed the same thing," I said, wandering about the place to stretch my legs more than anything. "It seems Dolly is the only one who has continued her criminal enterprise, and that was for fun more than anything else. I believe this reinforces the idea that the Duchess paid her (or his) accomplices extremely well." I was holding on to the belief that Dolly had seen the famous criminal entering Fife House, and he was of a male persuasion… I mean, he was a man.

"Do you know anything about Rosetta Mullen that could tie her to the tiara?" I asked to give it another shot before admitting defeat.

Todd turned to the relevant chapter – and I'm not exaggerating when I say that the file was plump with papers, and each suspect appeared to have her own sizable entry.

"Not really. The only reason P.C. Simpkin put her name forward was that Mullen was in the same city at the same time as some but not all of the Duchess's most significant crimes. Including just after her husband died on their honeymoon in Cannes in 1906."

"And what about here?" Grandfather asked, but something in what our retainer had said stayed with me.

"The hotel you mean?" Todd flicked through the pages once more.

"Yes. We organised our escapade at the top of this mountain because of its connection to the crime. However, our suspects seem quite unflustered to be here, so I wondered whether there was any evidence that the rubies ever crossed the threshold of Villa Cassel."

"Simpkin explains in his notes that it was very difficult to achieve, but he followed the Duchess's path through Europe after…"

I believe it was at this point that I stopped listening. I stayed right where I was for a minute or two longer, but barely a word penetrated my skull. And then, when I'd done all the thinking I planned on doing that day, I wandered from the room.

"Christopher?" I believe my grandfather shouted after me. "What's got into the boy?" I'm not 100 per cent sure he said this, but as he tends to ponder this question at least once a day, it's a fairly safe bet.

I have no recollection of what I saw on my journey, but I do retain the feeling of almost floating along the corridor to that beautifully shiny pine foyer at the front of the hotel. It's a funny thing that we humans can fulfil basic tasks whilst our minds are somewhere else altogether. The next thing I remember for certain was seeing my dog, who was back in her usual spot. I stood next to her, staring up at the window of St George. The dragon's two bright red eyes glared down at me and, when everything finally clicked into place, I spun around to look at the manager.

Victor Ried was slumped over at the reception desk, in a state of apparent dejection. His eyes looked sore. His chubby cheeks were somehow gaunt and sallow, and it would have been easy to conclude that he was depressed to have lost three guests to murder over the last day, but I knew better.

"Are you him?" I muttered far too quietly as I walked closer. "Are you him?"

Ried must have heard the question as he feigned his usual cheery expression and corrected me. "Are you he? I may not be an Englishman, but I know incorrect grammar when I hear it."

"Don't try to distract me, Ried." I decided that posing another question was asking for trouble and so, with the words just about ready to tear out of me, I shouted, "I know you're the Duchess!"

CHAPTER THIRTY-FOUR

Dorie, a porter, a waiter and the chef had gathered the suspects as Todd had suggested, and they all came downstairs just a moment or two after I made this accusation.

After the brief shock of our confrontation, the hotel manager acted as though nothing out of the ordinary had occurred. "I don't understand your question, sir, but I do know that Switzerland no longer has a ducal line. The aristocracy here is very different from yours at home in Britain. Many centuries ago we may have had dukes and duchesses and the like, but those days are long gone."

I wouldn't let him off so easily. "Are you the thief who was known as the Duchess?"

My strange behaviour, and perhaps my raised voice, had caught my grandfather's attention, and he appeared in the doorway with Todd, Cook and even young Timothy.

Ried floundered for a moment or two, looking first at me and then at my grandfather, who had come a little way closer.

"I really am sorry, Mr Prentiss, but I don't know what you mean."

"Answer the boy, Ried," a voice carried across the foyer to support me, and a few seconds later that handsome fellow Dunstan Cheshire was at my side. "If Christopher is asking, then he must have his reasons. Are you the man who conspired to steal those famous rubies or not?"

He hesitated and then, rather than answer my question, he asked one of his own. "Here at the Villa Cassel, we try our utmost to accommodate our guests, and I don't in any way wish to offend, but could one of you explain why you would think it possible?" It was a long, convoluted question, but he got there in the end.

I pointed to Dolly, who was standing on the lower steps of the staircase. She looked pleased to have caught the conversation but was presumably not expecting to feature in the story I had to tell. "First things first: Mrs Coxon over there saw a youngish man entering the house in Brighton from where the Princess Royal's tiara was stolen. I dare say that, twenty years ago, you were a youngish man."

"As were many millions of people across the world." His instincts as a manager ran so deep that he maintained his polite tone even as I accused him of any number of crimes.

"There's more." I would have looked pretty incompetent if there hadn't been. "There was something that never made sense to me. As soon as I knew about the tiara being stolen, I wondered what connection it had to this hotel – or at least, why my grandfather brought us here. Our colleague in London believes that the Duchess travelled across Europe all the way to this mountain. From what I've seen of the place, except for a few small houses scattered about the landscape, the Villa Cassel is the only building of note, so it seems quite likely that the Duchess came here."

"Wait," he tried to speak over me, but I wouldn't let him.

"There had to be a reason for him to choose this location. As you have already mentioned that you're local to the area, it fits that you—"

"There are plenty of young men and, would you believe it? There are even quite a few who come from this part of the world."

"I haven't finished."

There was some excited chatter from the small audience that had formed. Even my brother and a couple of the waiters had come to see what had caused the fuss, but I didn't pay them any attention. I concentrated on my task and tried to explain my thinking.

"It makes sense that you would sell the precious stones and bring your money back home. After all, you were the caretaker of the property at the time. The original owner had died shortly before, and you were waiting for your chance to buy the building and convert it into a hotel. Isn't that right?"

"You're correct on one small point." He was less keen to answer this time, and I knew that my argument held weight. "I was the caretaker, and I did eventually oversee the conversion." He was being very precise with his language, and I realised there was something he had avoided ever since we'd arrived.

"You are the owner of the Villa Cassel, aren't you, Ried?" He wouldn't reply so I continued. "You haven't actually mentioned it, but I assume you bought this place from the estate of the English banker who'd built it. You would have needed a lot of money to fulfil your ambition, of course, which is presumably why you kept stealing different items from across Europe until you had enough money. The tiara was surely the biggest job of the lot. Having sold the rubies, you could afford to renovate and run this place for the rest of your life."

I chuckled then. I hadn't meant to. It sounded slightly mad, and I regretted it immediately, but that's what happened. "It's really quite sweet to think that you were an internationally renowned jewel thief, but what you really wanted was to run your own hotel. It's a shame that my grandfather's associate traced the Duchess to this spot after you'd spent twenty years living your dream."

He clamped his jaws together and pouted, but he said nothing to defend himself.

"Grandfather assembled all your British guests in order to identify the mastermind behind the crime when, in actuality, you were here all along." I turned to the crowd, just as my mentor would have. "Some of you won't have realised this, but the man who has been passing himself off as Lord Ow, is actually the legendary detective…" I paused for effect. "…Lord Edgington of Cranley Hall."

I awaited the gasps of surprise and muttering that I was certain would follow this eye-popping revelation, but the large room remained silent.

"It was obvious," Dolly explained before her grandson offered his thoughts on the matter.

"I can think of far better disguises for a famous English lord who investigates crimes than to pass himself off as a less famous English lord who is investigating a crime. I've read books about the two of you, and it was the first thing I considered."

"Was it that obvious?" I can't say I wasn't disappointed on my grandfather's behalf.

"Sorry, old stick," Dunstan told me, and you know the situation is bad when someone calls you "old stick". "Sunday and I worked it out too. It was all the questions you asked. It rather gave you away."

"You told me this morning," Libby Hall sounded terribly apologetic, which made me feel a bit better.

"I admit that I did consider it," Henry Atkinson confessed.

"*Ja, ich auch*[10]," one of the German waiters concurred.

I glanced at my grandfather, who didn't want to be the centre of attention for once. He looked a touch dejected and was surely now

---

10 Me too.

questioning whether it had been worth chopping off his hair and beard in the first place.

"That doesn't matter," I insisted. "The point is... I'm sorry, I've lost my place."

Libby helped me along. "I think you were explaining why you brought us all here."

"Thank you!" I was losing my audience and my thread. Suddenly my case didn't feel so incontrovertible, and the chubby-cheeked man who had been so kind to us for the last two days didn't look like a killer. If anything, he seemed sorry that I would make such a spectacle of myself. But as the only two options were for me to keep going or confess that I hadn't taken nearly long enough to test my theory, I continued talking.

"Lord Edgington had been hamstrung in the original investigation and failed to identify the culprit. He decided to bring you here in the hope that your reactions to seeing one another again might reveal who was responsible for taking the jewels and organising the burglary of Fife House. We may not have had the instant success for which we were hoping, but there was one person who, upon arriving at the villa, revealed what this building meant to her.

"I thought at first that she was unimpressed with her accommodation, but when Rosetta Mullen entered the hotel, she stopped in the foyer, her eyes fell on the front desk and she turned away to yell, 'Why here?' This was what finally revealed what we needed to know. These two words told me that—"

"*Entschuldigung*[11]! Don't mind me." I was just coming to the good bit when Inge Weinreich stepped into the foyer from the hallway. She glanced at the odd scene, then continued past the gawping spectators and up the stairs.

"It was you she saw, wasn't it, Ried!" I said, swinging round to point my finger at him. This would have been a lot more dramatic had the Swiss lady not interrupted. "Rosetta Mullen recognised you from twenty years earlier. I believe that the two of you met after her husband died – perhaps you even had a hand in that – you crossed paths several times over the following years. We know that Rosetta

---

11 Excuse me / I beg your pardon.

needed money for her battle with her husband's family, so I can only assume she provided some service for you. Just as you needed help to steal the tiara, you recruited Rosetta to aid you with other thefts. Was it her background on the stage that appealed to you? Did she play the parts you required, just as you would later hire Sunday Cheshire and Elisabeth Hall to stand in for maids?"

He wouldn't answer. He was defeated, destroyed. The hotel he had bought with his stolen wealth couldn't have been worth the violence and cruelty it had required to keep. Three women were dead, and he could see that there was no way back.

"You killed the people who could have exposed you. Sunday and Libby were recruited through intermediaries, but Dolly was supposed to die because she caught sight of you at Fife House. She is only still here because the doctor managed to save her." The frame of my theory was beginning to feel more robust, and I pressed on with my accusations. "Is this where you sold the precious stones? Did a buyer come to you? Or did you find a more discreet way to claim your reward?"

I probably sounded a bit pompous – I was my grandfather's grandson after all – but I doubt that's why he collapsed in tears over his desk at this moment.

"You don't understand…" he began, but there was little left to say. He'd brought everything on himself, and it was hard to feel bad for such a corrupt, self-seeking person.

For a moment I was stunned that, after all my mistakes, I'd actually got it right.

Dunstan had been quiet until now. He'd let me lay out the facts uninterrupted, but with the case largely sewn up, he delivered a brief observation of his own. "The one thing I'd like to know is what happened to the rubies."

The crowd had shuffled closer at some point, and I heard Henry and Dolly discussing this question in hushed voices. Perhaps it was this that helped me to my conclusion. Perhaps it was the sense that everyone there wished to identify the final piece of the puzzle which made me, just as Rosetta had the previous day, turn around and glance up at the window of St George.

"There are your rubies," I said without the slightest doubt. "I imagine you sold the more substantial diamonds, using the minor

215

stones to shift suspicion onto poor Libby Hall, but those rubies were too bewitching to lose. I noticed the dragon's eyes almost as soon as I came in yesterday, and every time I walked through the foyer, I marvelled at the way the light would catch them. You set them into the window up there to enjoy them from your desk, didn't you?"

Still with tears on the round cheeks of his perfectly round head, Victor Ried looked up at me. There is a unique kind of tension which fills a room at moments like this. We all wanted to know what he would say, and just before he spoke, a pleasant frisson of anticipation travelled through the air.

"No, of course they're not the rubies." He looked across at the crowd and, to my surprise, he admitted his part in the affair. "For three years, I was the greatest thief in Europe. Why would I go to all the trouble of stealing a tiara that was famous for its rubies only to melt them into a window? And where exactly would I find a glazier I could trust with two stones that could have paid for this hotel twice over?"

Well, I'd got this part wrong, but the rest was spot on.

Ried was still weeping. If anything, his sobs had got louder. "I'm not crying for myself," he insisted. "It was her. It was always her. I met Rosetta for the first time on the day of her husband's heart attack. We happened to be staying in the same hotel in Cannes where, the following week, I would steal a quite breathtaking Fabergé egg from a Spanish count. I don't think I'd ever seen such a lost and lonely soul as Rosetta as she stood weeping in front of the Hotel de la Plage. She told me what had happened as the coroner took the earl's body away, and I felt such sympathy for her. I suppose I was already in love in some small way."

A sharp sound emerged from his throat at this moment, but he pressed on with his story, despite the really quite substantial audience. "You were right. Over the subsequent years, I tried to find her jobs that she could do for me. None of them put her in any great danger of arrest, but it meant I could aid her financially and, in time, we became more than just friends."

He paused to inhale deeply. "I never told her where I came from out of fear that the life I wished to build for myself would fall to pieces. She never visited me here, and the last time we saw one another was in Brighton. Something in the way she spoke that day told me that she already knew it would be our last meeting. She'd been recruited to act as lookout on the day of the theft, and we took the train to the coast almost in silence."

I shook my head then, as it was hard to comprehend his betrayal. "Whatever sympathy you had for her didn't stop you cutting the life from a woman you claim to have loved."

"That wasn't me!" he yelled. "I admit that I took the tiara and left the most valuable jewels in Paris, as instructed, but I didn't plan the theft or hire any of the other people who were involved. Rosetta contacted me about it because someone she knew had formulated a grand scheme that would make us all very rich. I never met any of the others until this week."

"You would say that," I persisted. "I haven't a clue whether the death penalty exists in Switzerland, but the punishment for murdering three defenceless women isn't exactly light wherever you go."

He wouldn't confess so easily. "I was here serving breakfast this morning when the first woman was killed. Do you really think I have time to run a hotel – at Christmastime, to boot – and still trek down to the train station and back at first light?"

The audience was clearly enjoying the Christmas spectacle. Dorie somehow had another plate of biscuits in her hand and was passing them out as refreshments.

"This is ridiculous." I was beginning to lose my temper. "You admit to being a wanted criminal who stole tens of thousands of pounds in your short, illustrious career. Yet you deny the murders, despite being the person who would benefit most from keeping your identity a secret?"

"I would never hurt another person. I stole to achieve my ambitions, and I accept that it was wrong, but there is nothing to connect me to Miss Nelson or Mrs Atkinson. Do you really think I would have allowed any of you to come here if I'd recognised your names in advance?"

I wanted to fire a response straight back at him, but it was no good. My understanding of the case was falling to pieces. "You were there in the restaurant last night when Blanche Atkinson was surely poisoned. She felt a pain on her neck and assumed it was a mosquito bite. You could have easily poked her with something as you oversaw the dinner. You must have passed her table twenty times."

His face was a picture of consternation. "Even if I had it in me to kill the first two women, I would never have touched my Rosetta. You know, when I discovered that she was coming to stay, I thought that fate had brought us back together. The truth was, though, that she wanted to leave that part of her life behind just as much as I did. We spoke in the reception just after she arrived, and it was clear that she had no wish to rekindle our flame."

His voice had a slight quiver in it whenever he talked of her and, after a moment's silence, he said so quietly that I could barely hear him over the wind howling outside the windows, "I hate to disappoint you, Mr Prentiss, but I'm not your man."

"You must be," I mumbled as I felt a hand on my shoulder.

"No, boy." I looked around to see my grandfather, whose soulful grey eyes were filled with such kindness that I instantly accepted my mistake. "I'm sorry to say you're wrong this time, Christopher. Herr Ried is not the killer."

CHAPTER THIRTY-FIVE

"Well that was an anti-climax," Dolly complained through a mouthful of crumbs. "You know, not so long ago, that boy accused me of the same thing. I think he's trying it on with everyone."

I wanted to deny this, but I realised that it wasn't far off the truth. I'd accused three different people of being the killer and been proven wrong each time. I really thought that I'd matured as a detective recently, but I'd fallen into the same traps as when I'd first started out. I hadn't even learnt my lesson after the first two mistakes.

Sunday Cheshire was the closest person to Dolly. She could easily have echoed the old lady's sentiment, but she didn't have the heart. And yet, it was Libby Hall who came to my defence.

"Can you really blame him for tryin'?" she demanded. "Three women are dead, and you're worried about gettin' your feelings hurt? The only thing that matters is preventin' any more bloodshed."

There was a brief burst of mumbled agreement from those around her, but no one had anything very helpful to say, so Libby went over to comfort Mr Ried, and my grandfather did the same for me.

"I made a mess of everything," I told him in as small a voice as I could muster.

"I don't agree. You uncovered an important part of the case that I had failed to see," he said by way of consolation. "I had tried to consider every last suspect – and found the Villa Cassel chef of particular interest – but you revealed some important information that everyone else missed. You deserve my congratulations, not my pity or criticism."

I knew there were a lot of things that he wasn't saying, and so I hurried him along. "Very well, but you might as well tell me where I went wrong."

He looked reluctant to do so for a moment and waited for the crowd to disperse. It was a shame that the festivities Herr Ried had planned so enthusiastically had been suspended, but at least everyone could go to the bar and enjoy their time together. There certainly wasn't a shortage of biscuits either.

"It was not that any of your theories were particularly ill-conceived or outlandish," Grandfather eventually explained, and he put his arm around my shoulders to lead me over to the reception desk which the manager had just vacated to head into his office. "You were merely too rash in forming your conclusion. How many times have we observed that a person's criminal past is not evidence in itself of a murderous nature?"

My head felt heavy, but I tried to explain why I'd ignored so much of what he'd taught me. "We'd barely considered the possibility that someone other than the Duchess had organised the theft. And you were so set on the idea it was a woman that, when I realised Herr Ried was involved, I couldn't hold myself back. I came straight here to put my accusations to him."

He smiled a wry smile and gave a silent laugh. "Which rather proves my point. You were too quick about it. Would it really have been so difficult to talk to the rest of us first? As it happens, if you'd stayed in the library with us for a minute or so longer you would have—" He didn't finish his sentence as Libby Hall put her head out of the office to call to us.

"I'm sorry to interrupt, Lord Edgington, but Victor would like to talk to you."

Grandfather didn't move off immediately. He looked me in the eyes and nodded. I knew what it meant. Deep down inside, the world-famous detective was a dear old fellow and, with this brief gesture, he was saying that he loved me and was proud of all we'd achieved. Well, it was either that or he was thinking, *That idea of the dragon's eyes being priceless rubies was rather silly.* But I prefer to believe the former.

He nodded to Todd, who'd been watching the other suspects as they wandered off along the corridor. We walked around the desk and through the open door to Herr Ried's office. He wasn't behind his desk as he had been when we'd spoken that morning. He had a glass of what I took to be whisky in his hand, and he was staring into the distance, even though the room was only twenty feet by fifteen.

I must say, it was a cosy little space. Ried was sitting in a tatty old armchair next to the fire with a blanket over his knees. There was even a small Christmas tree in the corner, which I felt he had probably selected from the neighbouring grove. It was just the kind of place I'd like to have snuggled down with a book, and I could see why he had gone to such trouble to buy the hotel.

"I will do whatever I can to help you," he said in a small voice without turning to look at us. "I have done bad things in my life, and my chickens have finally come home to roost." I wondered how many of his typically British expressions he'd learnt from his time with Rosetta.

We took the two chairs from the other side of the room and placed them in front of him, whereas Libby stood close by for support.

"Take your time, Victor," Grandfather told him in a gentle voice.

It was easy to see how fragile the poor man was. He clearly felt guilty for the murders, even if he hadn't been the one to commit them.

"I don't actually know where to start." He peered at his hands and rounded his shoulders despondently. "I feel that there must be something I know that can lead you to whoever is responsible."

"But back in 1909, you never met anyone who was involved in the case except Rosetta, did you?" I thought he'd already said as much when denying my claims.

He blinked a few times as he considered my question. "No, I didn't. To tell you the truth, I didn't even realise that I had seen Dolly that day. I was concentrating on the task ahead of me and must have walked straight past her. But there's surely something else."

Grandfather tried a different approach. "Did Rosetta ever give you any hint as to who would benefit most from the theft or mention any names when she talked of its organisation?"

"I really can't say for certain, but I don't think she did. I wish I could look at the list on my desk and point you to the killer. All I can tell you about the person who planned the theft was that Rosetta had known her for a long time, and she trusted her. You see, it was the first and only time that I worked with other criminals to steal something. It was through Rosetta that I was recruited, which must be why she was killed. She knew who was behind everything that happened."

I wanted to beg him to think harder. I wanted to shake him until the truth fell free, but it would have done no good. The women who knew the killer's secret had been snuffed out, just as the candles in the ballroom would be when the night was over. The past was closed to us, and for all his good intentions, even the legendary Duchess couldn't change that.

"I feel like such a fool," he complained with something of a groan. "To think that I could have simply asked her for the name. I was worried that anything I might do would incriminate her."

"I doubt she would have told you." Grandfather still spoke in that same kind, comprehending manner. "We interviewed her ourselves shortly before she was killed, and she refused to give us even the tiniest detail."

"She was loyal, and no one can deny it." Ried leaned back in his chair and looked up at the ceiling.

"She didn't even cough up the name of the person who would kill her." I had no hope or energy left in me, and these words came out at half their intended volume.

"I fear that the truth may now be lost forever."

"No, no, far from it," Grandfather replied in a matter-of-fact tone.

"I beg your pardon?" Ried's pupils grew larger as a deep cleft formed on his brow.

"I mean that I know who the killer is. I worked it out right after Christopher left to confront you."

CHAPTER THIRTY-SIX

There was a moment's inertia as the fact of what he was saying rattled through us.

"You know who the killer is?" A touch of fear had entered Ried's voice once more.

"That's right. You see, the person responsible for organising both the theft of the tiara and the murders today is undoubtedly clever. She sought protection by putting a barrier between the most serious crimes and herself. One way she did so was to hire people at a distance. She used a fence in London called Charlie Gammon to obtain the services of Sunday Cheshire, who could seamlessly pass herself off as the head of household in Fife House when the job became available. I couldn't prove it at the time, but I knew the mastermind of the plan paid or blackmailed some down-on-their-luck though reputable families to offer references for the two women who went to work for the Princess Royal."

He turned to Libby at this point. "Do you know anything about that, Miss Hall?"

She put her hand to her frizzy hair as she answered. "I can't say for certain, but I reckon it was somethin' along those lines."

He nodded and continued with the tale of which I'd only sketched out certain chapters. "From what I learnt today, you were contracted in a similar way. I very much doubt that the person who interviewed you was the mastermind herself. I did wonder for some time whether it was Miss Mullen in disguise. You said she was an older lady, but Rosetta had been on the stage and surely knew how to apply makeup to produce that effect. I believe you mentioned that she was well spoken, which would also fit. The important thing to take from all this, though, is that you were lucky not to meet the person who employed you. Those who did ended up dead."

Libby had nothing more to add on the matter but offered a sad shrug.

"Going back to the organisation of the original crime…" Grandfather continued. "As we've established, the mastermind did all she could to separate herself from her work, but she still had to rely on the people she could trust for certain tasks. We know that most of the criminals came from the same area of London as Sunday Legyear

– as Mrs Cheshire was known at the time. I believe that this, when considered in the light of the large sums that the organiser was willing to pay, suggests one of two things. Either this person was trying to buy the loyalty of her accomplices, or she had a genuine desire to make their lives better."

This almost made me smile to think of an unscrupulous criminal improving her impoverished friends' lives, but then I remembered that she went on to murder three of those same people, so her loyalty was only fleeting.

"However, there was one person who did not benefit from the theft." Grandfather had found a steady rhythm and just the right tone to narrate his story, and we all listened intently. "There was one person who was singled out to take the blame – whose only role, it seems, was to suffer, and I had to question why poor Libby here was chosen as a scapegoat."

"Are you sayin' that the killer tried to help her friends but punish me?" Libby's free arm swung limply at her side as she said this, and I could see what fear the possibility inspired.

"It was only a consideration. I had no real evidence to prove that was the case, but I would now like you to examine who would have wanted to cause you harm back in 1909? Who would have been happy to see you put behind bars?"

She raised her hand to her throat as though it hurt to say the words. "I don't believe… It's really hard to think of anyone. There's definitely no one here I upset so badly."

"I'm aware that Sunday was your neighbour when you were young, but what about the other women? Have you known any of them in any capacity?"

"After you told me that several guests had been involved in the crime, I tried my best to remember Dolly, Blanche and Rosetta. I reckon Blanche lived in the same area as me and Sunday, but I was only eight when I left and can't say for sure. What I do know is that there were never any animosity between us. And anyway, I'm not the type to hold grudges."

Clouds were gathering over Grandfather's fine features, and I could tell that he was frustrated that his theory had borne no fruit. "Very well, but from what I can see, there was no need for you to be at

Fife House other than to have someone to transport the less valuable diamonds to France, sell them in a pawn shop and get arrested while the real criminals escaped with the bulk of the loot."

Ried winced at that moment. It was a common occurrence for him. "I was the one who took apart the tiara in Brighton. I was instructed to remove the rubies and larger diamonds and travel with them to the Hotel Majestic in Paris, where I waited for two days before my payment was delivered to my room by a courier. The golden frame of the tiara, and the tiny diamonds which formed a border at its base, I left in a package under a bench in Dover."

"That's where I was told to collect it," Libby said with some excitement. She was plainly happy to see how the various parts of the plan had fitted together; I knew that sensation from previous cases. "I felt a real idiot crawling about on my knees to look for it. And once I were on the boat, I went into a lavatory to see what it was. They might have been small stones by your people's standards, Lord Edgington, but they were like nothin' I'd ever seen. They sparkled and caught the light just like a magic spell. For a little while, I really thought my luck had changed. For the time it took to cross the Channel, I imagined I'd be able to keep the money, and whoever had made me take the tiara abroad would leave off hurting my mother."

I'd forgotten the threat hanging over her. It must have been a frightening journey, especially for a young woman who had presumably never travelled abroad before.

"That's quite understandable." Grandfather was more patient than normal, and I wondered whether, despite his claims to the contrary, he was still thinking through the sequence of events that had brought us to Ried's office. "I remember when I first interviewed you how sure I was that the story you told me was true. You really had travelled to France and sold the lesser stones to a pawn shop that the police subsequently located with very little trouble. Of course, that doesn't explain why you needed seven whole days away from your job to do so."

The change in him was almost imperceptible. He'd been calmly checking off the facts of the case, and even Libby struggled to know what he wished to imply with this comment.

"Sorry, are you saying I was wrong to take so long? I promise that it were one of the most difficult things I've done in my life. I took all that time because I needed to come to terms with the idea that I were a criminal. I'd grown up among 'em but I'd never stolen so much as a newspaper before. Then all of a sudden, I were a jewel thief."

"Yes, my child." It was Grandfather's turn to grimace. His cheeks puffed out, and his lips stretched wider. "That is one explanation, but I don't believe it. What I believe is that you went to the pawn shop in Calais and then took a private car on to Paris so that no one could trace your route. And after that, you picked up the precious stones from the Hotel Majestic and would have needed some time to arrange the sale with the buyer, pay Herr Ried for his work and return to Britain. Any less than a week could have left you short of time, but I believe your decision to take so long served another purpose."

He didn't say anything for five whole seconds. I know because I timed it on the clock on the mantelpiece. As the fire roared and the snowy maelstrom outside the window continued to rage, Grandfather wouldn't shift his gaze from the apparent culprit's face.

"You wanted to draw attention to your absence. You wanted the police to realise you had gone missing and trace your journey to that really not very grand pawn shop in a small French town because you knew that, when I learnt the facts of your excursion, I wouldn't think for one moment that this was the work of an international jewel thief. I would only think that you had become entangled in someone else's plan and ended up a scapegoat."

If the change in my grandfather had been subtle, what I saw now in Libby Hall was quite the opposite. "You don't know what you're talkin' about, you old fool. I stayed that long in France because I couldn't bear the thought of comin' back home and being arrested. I knew what trouble I was in, and it terrified me. I stayed in the cheapest boardin' house I could find over there, 'cos I didn't dare spend the money from the diamonds. And in all that time, I barely left my room except to buy a bit o' food."

"How very convenient that few people would have seen you." Grandfather had such a… well, a grandfatherly attitude even as he meticulously laid out his case against the treacherous woman before us. "I doubt that you were afraid to return to Britain, seeing as your plan from the very beginning was to serve time for a lesser offence so that no one would think you had anything to do with the burglary.

There was no smart, well-spoken woman who interviewed you for the job as a maid – no advert in the window of a stationer's on Duval Street. I can't imagine how you got yourself and Sunday jobs in the house of a princess, but then you are clearly an enterprising and resourceful woman."

"You're talkin' absolute nonsense. How would I have had the resources to do any of the things you're suggestin'? I didn't have the money to pay all those people."

"Well, if we're only discussing the money, you wouldn't have had to pay anyone until you'd sold the stones, at which point there was plenty to go around. In terms of other resources, I would think that a young lady born in the slums of East London in the 1870s would have had plenty of useful connections to help organise such a scheme. Like your friend Sunday, you grew up on the same road as the fence Charlie Gammon, so perhaps he was your accomplice and backer."

From the slight flaring of her nostrils, I knew that Grandfather had got her, but he wasn't finished yet.

"Unlike Sunday, however, you were never saved from the terrible place by a knight in shining armour. No one gave you a house or risked being disowned by his rich family in order to marry you. You did what was necessary to make a better life for yourself. The only victim was a princess who shied away from the limelight and had so many tiaras that she didn't notice when one was replaced with a cheap imitation. Again, the quality of the replacement you provided was presumably to ensure that you would be caught sooner rather than later."

She didn't answer this time. She looked at Victor Ried, who may have been the manager of the hotel, but he had no power to prevent what was happening as Grandfather strengthened the case against her.

"That is to say, the only victim of the original crime was the princess, but you came here this weekend determined to do whatever was necessary to protect your secret. You must have known when you received the letter announcing your win in a competition you'd never entered that something wasn't right. I had thought it likely that the mastermind behind the theft would simply not come this week, but you couldn't risk that, could you?"

No answer came back to him.

"You decided to travel here and do your very best impression of a put-upon Cinderella, when, in reality, you have presumably spent the last twenty years in the lap of luxury. You may still maintain an address in Hackney, just in case anyone comes looking, but I doubt you spend any time there."

There were several parts of the story that I couldn't fathom, but whenever new questions arose in my mind, he seemed to anticipate them and offer the answers. "You claimed that you didn't know Barbara Nelson, but Henry Atkinson told us that she was due to meet a friend here, which made sense as the killer evidently knew that Barbara was arriving on the mountain train first thing this morning. You would have been even more suspicious after you both won the same competition, and then, when I arrived here yesterday, you finally confirmed the danger in which you found yourself – I have come to understand that my disguise wasn't quite as effective as I had hoped."

Grandfather spoke so smoothly and with such confidence that I felt he could continue indefinitely. This made the sudden halt he now came to all the more grating – the silence that replaced it all the louder.

Victor Ried shifted in his seat. His disbelieving eyes were set on the woman beside him, who had supposedly shown kindness in accompanying him there but really only wanted to find out what he knew.

The last thing I expected was for her to break the silence, but that's what happened. "I tried to help them," she said in a hoarse whisper.

I find it curious how often our culprits give themselves away, not when the case against them is undeniable, but simply because their pride has been wounded by one of Grandfather's carefully honed comments.

She jutted her jaw out, and all the impudence and arrogance that she'd been hiding that day came flooding out of her. "You can say what you like about me, but the plan as it started back then were meant to help the people around me. I heard about the situation Sunday found herself in – unable to feed her brothers and sisters because she had so little. I knew that Barbara, who had been like a sister to me from the time we were eight, had to find a new house because the place where she'd lived were torn down to make a new neighbourhood for people so rich they'd never have set foot there before. I read about Rosetta being blamed for killin' her husband when she'd done nothin' to him, so I looked for a solution."

"And then you murdered them!" My response was so sudden that I almost made myself jump. "You can use all the pretty words you like, Miss Hall, but it won't change the fact that when it came down to it, you put your own comfort ahead of the lives of three people."

"More than three," Grandfather corrected me, and I was worried for a moment that he was about to reveal another string of murders of which I had no knowledge. "She would have killed Sunday and anyone else who got in her way. I believe that was the reason for the conversation you overheard between Libby and her childhood friend on the mountain. She needed to know whether Sunday had ever realised that she was the one who had planned the crime."

Libby fixed her eyes on my grandfather as a flash of incredulity rippled across her features. "I never touched that chandelier what fell in the foyer. Whatever else you think of me, I didn't try and hurt my friend Sunday."

There was no way back for her now, and she must have already known it even if she wasn't ready to give up just yet. "Anyway, you'll never prove any o' this in court. I won't be a good little poor person and roll over. I'll fight, like I have my whole life. I'll fight against people like you who—"

Grandfather's voice soared as he talked over her. "If I were in your situation, I wouldn't finish that sentence. I helped you all those years ago because of the very thing you've just described. While you may be a fighter, I have spent my life trying to make the world in which we live a fairer one. And as for the case against you, I don't think I'll have any trouble collecting the evidence I need to ensure you never set foot outside a gaol again – unless they don't happen to have a gallows on the property, that is."

Herr Ried had sat in silent amazement this whole time. My own success in exposing the jewel thief paled in comparison to what my grandfather had achieved, and I was just as impressed as our Swiss friend was.

When she spoke again, Libby sounded more like the person I thought I'd come to know that day. Her voice was soft and tremulous, but it was difficult to say whether it was an act this time. "I can't go back to prison. Please, Lord Edgington, you must understand that I can't go back. That's the only reason I did what I did. When I heard about the princess's fifth best tiara all those years ago, I was sure I could play the part of a wronged woman and serve twelve months inside, but I had no idea how hard it would be. To be honest, I'd rather die than…"

Before she could finish her sentence, she lunged towards the door and was through it in an instant. I wasn't far behind her, but by the time I escaped the office, she was halfway across the foyer and headed for the stairs. Delilah got to her feet as the woman ran past her, but rather than giving chase, she yawned and walked off in the other direction.

"Don't do anything stupid!" I yelled to the killer, thinking of the windows from which she could jump on the higher floors.

I noticed Todd appearing from the corridor and knew that Grandfather had warned him to be on guard, but he was in the wrong place and couldn't help now. My feet pounded on the solid wooden floor as I tried to gain ground on Libby Hall. And the whole time I was running, I pictured her lying dead in the snow, her mangled body crushed by the force of the fall.

She took the first five steps up the staircase in a flash, and I was impressed by just how fast she was. It probably helped that she was wearing loose-fitting clothes, whereas I was in a suit and damnably slippery leather Oxfords. She curled around the wide spiral staircase, and I lost sight of her for a moment. I was worried that she would hide somewhere on the first floor and manage to get away from me there, but just as the image of her crashing through a plate-glass window formed in my head, she came bouncing back down the staircase towards me.

"Evenin', Christopher, your miniature lordship," our immense maid Dorie sang as Libby sprawled out painfully, her hand clutched to her head where it had made contact with the hard wooden steps. "D'ya reckon there are any more biscuits? I've eaten all mine."

CHAPTER THIRTY-SEVEN

Grandfather was most pleased with Dorie for apprehending the killer, and the other members of staff made a fuss of her. I was unsure whether she had intentionally knocked the fleeing woman off her feet or she just happened to be descending at that moment in search of more food.

Ultimately, it didn't matter in the slightest. We locked the murderess Libby Hall in a windowless room on the ground floor, and the only visitors she had for the next day or so were my grandfather with some food, a maid with a clean bucket and finally the police. I don't like to think about these things too carefully for fear of disillusioning my nine-year-old self, but it turns out that Father Christmas doesn't deliver presents to killers in cupboards.

It was strange to spend Christmas with a cluster of criminals. But then we are all imperfect in different ways, and who am I to judge anyone? That's my grandfather's job!

The relief of the other guests was palpable, and we did all we could to celebrate the season, despite the sad circumstances. For dinner, Icilio the chef made a delicious feast of *Filet am Teig* – or pork fillet with ham, mushrooms and sausage meat in a pastry crust. I find that the key to any dish is to have at least three types of pork on the ingredient list, and the pastry stars on top made an already scrumptious meal even better. It was accompanied by glazed chestnuts, red cabbage and (sadly) Brussels sprouts, not to mention an immense vat of spiced *Glühwein*, which had luckily been prepared before Libby selfishly took the last of the cinnamon. Now that I say those words, I am aware that it was one of her lesser crimes, but it's still upsetting.

I think it's fair to say that the Swiss take dessert seriously and, in addition to all the crumbly round things we'd been eating all afternoon, there was a large pastry stuffed to bursting with dried fruits, nuts, and a lot of pear. I'll spare you the details of the other five or so options, but let me set your mind at ease that I tried a little of everything, and they were all delicious.

We pushed all the tables together in the dining room, and Grandfather insisted that, after the day we'd had, the staff should join us too. So it was quite the party, even if it was a quiet one. And when it was over, we retired to the bar where Inge attempted to teach more people how to play her favourite card games. She was over the moon to have a four for *Jass* at last. Grandfather and I promised that we would play a later game and, in the meantime, we sat beside the fire with Albert and a few glasses of *Kirsch*. Warm, loved and asleep on my feet, Delilah looked happier than she had all week.

"I feel as though I must have missed out on some of the excitement," my brother told me as he sipped his cherry brandy.

"Not really, Albert. You know most of the details," Grandfather reassured him. "It was the usual thing: there were a few murders and, with a lot of help from Christopher, I eventually solved the case." He winked across at me, but I already disagreed with his assessment.

"That's not true. I took us off in the wrong direction on two different occasions. I caught a jewel thief but overlooked a triple murderer."

"No, no. I must disagree with your disagreement. We both had our parts to play. If anything, I owe you an apology." This was a rare thing indeed, so I waited to hear what he had to say. "I broke one of my foremost rules of a detective." This was not nearly so rare a thing as he believed, but I wasn't about to interrupt. "I went into an investigation with a notion that I refused to relinquish. I should have been open to the idea earlier on that Elisabeth Hall was the killer, but that would have meant accepting that she'd already fooled me once."

I looked at my brilliant grandfather and felt quite moved by his confession and sorry that he had found himself in that unenviable position. Albert was perhaps a little less forgiving.

"And don't forget that no one would have died if you hadn't meddled in their lives," he pointed out, which made our grandfather squirm a little.

"I wouldn't put it like that exactly." He looked for a better expression. "I do feel remorseful over what happened. It is a new entry on the long list of mistakes I have made in my life, but I had no reason to believe that anyone involved in the theft of the tiara was a killer. Libby Hall is the one who set off for Switzerland determined to do whatever it took to protect her comfortable existence."

This shut my brother up for a moment at least, and Grandfather continued in a softer tone. "You know, I brought you both here to give you a Christmas challenge, and yet I was the one who ended up learning a lesson."

"Oh, that's so nice." Albert sounded quite emotional. "It almost makes me want to write a poem. Actually..."

He took a small bag that he'd been carrying with him for much of the afternoon and hurried away to another table to get writing. I feared for everyone that we would soon have to hear his composition.

"I accept your apology and admit that it was all thanks to me that we solved the case," I told my grandfather, and I hope he knew that I was joking. "But I do have a question or two."

"Please fire away." Grandfather rubbed his hands together. I can't say if this was in anticipation or he was trying to get rid of some crumbs.

"I don't know how Libby killed Blanche Atkinson. I mean, assuming that she was poisoned when she thought she'd been bitten by an insect, how could Libby be the killer when she wasn't in the room?"

"The marmot, Christopher!" His tone suggested he would have liked to add, *Isn't it obvious?*

"The marmot?" I echoed him. "But when I heard the whistling, you said that they hibernate and it couldn't be one."

"Marmots do hibernate, and so, rather than just superciliously dismissing your comment, I questioned what could have made such a noise. That was actually what pointed me in Libby's direction. At the moment of the apparent insect bite, the only suspects who were out of the room were Libby, Rosetta and Dolly – who could theoretically have faked the attack she suffered but would have been spotted wandering around the hotel."

I still hadn't a clue what any of this meant. "And?"

"And the killer couldn't have been in the room because we would have seen her."

"Seen her do what? Are you still speaking English? Have I lost the capacity to understand basic sentences?"

He grinned and leaned forward to reveal his stroke of genius. "Blanche and her husband were sitting at a table near the window. They were the ones who complained about it being too cold, but I doubt one of the staff would have opened it with the weather as it was."

"So Libby threw something in through the window?"

"Not quite. Do you remember the workmen fixing the pipe on the outside of the building this morning as we were skiing?"

I couldn't honestly say I'd given them a lot of thought, but I nodded and he explained.

"Very good. Well, I believe that Libby Hall—"

"A blow dart!" I interrupted, remembering a rather ridiculous story I'd once read.

"You clever boy. The sound you heard was an object being fired at Blanche through the window. Henry Atkinson mentioned that his wife found the imagined insect's sting embedded in her neck, but it was more likely to have been a thorn or tiny arrow of some kind that Libby had dipped in poison."

I allowed these parts of the picture to fill themselves in before turning my attention to another vaguely sketched area. "But why did she kill Blanche in the first place? She'd shown no sign of recognising her."

"Libby knew that Barbara and Blanche were friends – that was presumably how she hired Blanche to create the fake tiara in the first place. If Blanche had been alive when we found Barbara's body, she might well have pointed us in Libby's direction, so she had to die in advance."

This was all so unusual that I tried to make sense of what he was telling me. "Why wouldn't Libby have chosen to shoot the dart in the dining room. She could probably have got away with it if no one was looking."

He'd been so fair and generous until now, and a disappointed frown was long overdue. "Blowpipes aren't little things you can conceal about your person, Christopher. In the countries where people use them to hunt, they can be six feet in length. Shooting through the window from outside the room was the only possible option." He shook his head now to complement the frown. "When I saw her in the cupboard earlier, I discovered that she would never have had the idea in the first place if mystery novelists didn't insist on using such improbable techniques to dispatch the victims in their books. It's all very silly if you ask me."

I would probably have told him that he was a clever old thing to have worked all this out, but I decided he'd received enough acclaim for one day, and I changed the topic instead. "So that proves Libby came here with the intention to kill. Whatever poison she used isn't the kind of thing you find lying about the place."

"Indeed, though our conclusions on the chandelier appear to have been a little rash. It finally seems that it was poorly maintained, and Herr Ried's efforts caused it to fall accidentally. Of course, that added some excitement to our arrival, so it wasn't all bad."

I smiled at his odd priorities. "What about the rubies?"

"They really aren't in the stained-glass window. I imagine that was installed when the former owner lived here."

"No, I know that. I was wondering if there's any chance that we'll now be able to recover them."

"Do you know what?" He sipped his drink and made me wait. "I think there might be. You see, Libby just admitted to me that she sold the rubies to an unscrupulous Monegasque collector." Before I could ask whether this was a man who collected mongooses, he explained what it meant. "Or rather, a man from Monaco who collects jewels and *objets d'art*."

"How very interesting," I said, happy not to have mentioned mongeese.

"As far as she knows, he still has them in his collection. I doubt she'll give us his name, but I would think that someone with the skills of P.C. Simpkin back in Scotland Yard should have no trouble finding such a person."

"That's fabulous," I told him and, before he could say anything more, Albert had stood up from his work and was clearing his throat to get everyone's attention.

"I'm sorry to bother you all, ladies and gentlemen, but I have something to read to you. I've been trying my hand at poetry recently. It doesn't rhyme or anything, but I wanted to share my thoughts as they were bouncing around my head a few minutes ago, and this is what came to me."

"Hurray for the big little Edgington!" Dorie shouted as though he'd already recited his piece. There was a brief smattering of applause – as Timothy got carried away – but it soon died down again.

"It's called simply 'Christmas', and I hope you like it." Albert cleared his throat a second time for luck, pulled at his shirt collar and began.

"This isn't the Christmas I was expecting.

It isn't the Christmas I would ever have imagined or requested.

Our traditions have gone quite out of the window and, I'm sorry to tell you this, brother, but I haven't even bought you a present.

It isn't the Christmas you read about in books concerning happy families who always get on perfectly.

It isn't the kind of Christmas that would get a mention in a newspaper column or be talked of on the radio.

To be totally honest, I wouldn't inflict this Christmas on my worst enemy.

But it's our Christmas and, now that the danger has passed and the killer has been safely locked up, I wouldn't change it for the world."

The applause that followed was more enthusiastic this time, and I was the one leading it. My dear soppy brother blushed like… well, like an easily embarrassed human, I suppose, and I rose to make sure he felt good about the difficult task he'd just completed.

"Do you know what, Albert?" Grandfather said when my brother returned. "That really wasn't terrible."

"My goodness. I take that as high praise coming from you."

"I have a confession to make," I said as he sat down. "I also haven't got you a present, but if you like, I will listen to whatever you write for the duration of the holiday."

"Marvellous!" He seemed excited by the prospect. "Will you give me your honest opinion of my work?"

"No… Very much, no."

"Wonderful! That's the best present I could imagine. In fact…" So moved was he by my thoughtful gift that he raced back to his previous spot and got to work on his first collection as a poet.

"I fear that the days before New Year's Eve may be the longest we've ever known," Grandfather predicted as Albert scribbled away.

To make him feel better, I asked him to follow me outside. We walked along the corridor and, when we reached the foyer, I bade him wait for me, then ran upstairs to our suite. When I came back down again, he was nowhere to be found.

"I'm out on the terrace, Christopher!" he called when he heard me, and I wished that I'd put on a coat while I was fetching his surprise.

"My goodness," I said as I took in the light of the stars overhead and all around the valley. The storm had cleared away. The world of white before us was as perfect as anything I'd ever seen (bar one very pretty girl I'd recently met), and the sky looked as though it had been decorated for Christmas.

"Yes, it's lovely, isn't it?"

We stood in silent appreciation for a few minutes, and I realised that what I'd bought my grandfather would pale in comparison to the natural beauty all around.

"I miss your mother," he said to break the stillness of that cold, crisp Christmas night. "I didn't think I would suffer her absence so strongly, but she's still my little girl. Not only had a month never gone by without our meeting, ever since she was born, even when I tried very hard not to see anyone after your grandmother died, we never missed a Christmas together."

"I miss her too." This was really no admission, as I wondered aloud what Mother was doing at least once a day. "I miss her and Father, and my school friends and even our creaky old footman at Cranley Hall. And yet…" I didn't know how to finish this sentence without sounding unfeeling. "And yet, it's rather like Albert said in his poem. I wouldn't change what we're doing here for the world."

I reached inside my jacket pocket and withdrew a small black box. "To say thank you, Grandfather, I got you these. I know it's not Christmas Day, but I think the moment is right."

He accepted the small package and turned to look at it in the light. "How did you manage it? I thought I'd kept you busy the whole time we were in Milan."

"Ah ha!" I replied a little too proudly. "When we were both trying clothes on in the alpinism shop, I sneaked out to a jeweller to explain what I wanted. I sent Timothy to collect them the day before we left Milan."

"You cunning fox. I failed in my mission to buy you anything." He winked, and I knew that he was fibbing, and there would be more surprises in store the next day. When he opened the hinged lid of the box, the white gold cufflinks I'd bought him glinted in the moonlight. I could make out the letters CGFC and the outline of our family crest stamped on the smooth, shiny discs. "Oh, they're wonderful. I will wear them and be eternally grateful."

"Happy Christmas, Grandfather."

"Happy Christmas, Christopher." His normally whiskery cheeks turned red in the cold night's air. "Here's to many more."

Neither of us had brought a glass with us, but he raised his cufflinks, and I pretended to be holding a tankard of some variety for a toast. I did consider asking whether the majority of the nice friends we'd made would end up in prison for their past crimes, but I didn't want to spoil our pleasant evening.

Before I could say anything else, the door opened behind us, and it wasn't my brother coming to find out what he was missing, as I had assumed. It wasn't even Delilah, who was wise to stay beside the fire. It was Inge Weinreich, in full skiing attire. She was there to do as she'd told me several times that day and ski down the mountain in the dark.

"You know, you should both join me," she said, and I was tempted to go running back into the house before Grandfather could agree on my behalf.

"I don't think that's on the cards this evening, thank you, madam," he replied instead. "But we will watch you from here and be very impressed indeed."

"You don't know what you're missing!" She walked around the building to put her skis on, and I'm happy to admit that we stayed right where we were.

"I hope it's not rude to say," I whispered when I was sure she wouldn't hear me. "And I know I haven't met many of them, but Swiss people seem like a strange bunch."

"Well, Christopher…" He looked pensive for a moment before coming to a conclusion. "That must be why we fit in so well here."

The End (For Now…)

A very merry Christmas to you, whoever and wherever you are from Osian, Amelie, Marion and Benedict

Get another
LORD EDGINGTON ADVENTURE
absolutely **free**…

Download your free novella at
www.benedictbrown.net

"LORD EDGINGTON INVESTIGATES ABROAD"
absolutely free…

The fourth full-length mystery will be available
Spring 2026.
Follow me on Amazon to find out when it goes on sale.

ABOUT THIS BOOK

Well there we go! Another year has passed, and I have once more had to write like crazy to get a Christmas book out because I was too busy during the summer. I started this book on 1st October and finished on the 18th, with two days off in between. My record is fourteen days, but this is probably the quickest I've written a Lord Edgington novel, which requires a lot more research than any contemporary stories I write.

I should probably point out that I've never used AI to write my books, and I never will. For people keeping track of these things (my mum, maybe?) I did around a third (27,000 words) of the book in the last three days of writing, and my record is 12,000 words in one day. I also have some days when I can only write a thousand words because I get distracted by everything in the universe (i.e. the internet). I knew I had a short time to do this one, so I'm really glad I managed it.

This is my first Christmas book which is set abroad, so that gave me a lot of scope to include traditions that are not just new to Chrissy and his friends, but to me too. I knew in which mountain range I wanted to set the story, and it was handy having the Alps so close to where my characters already were, but I didn't know in which country they'd be spending Christmas until I found the beautiful image on the cover of this book.

It might look as though we took a grand Tudor-Revival house and superimposed it on the top of a snowy mountain, but the Villa Cassel is a real place and, even better, it has an interesting history which made it a perfect place to set a book. I didn't know any of that at the time, though. I just thought, *What a great picture*, and so began the process that led to the creation of this book. I assumed that the chances of this lovely building in the middle of the Alps having anything to do with an Englishman were pretty low, but then I didn't imagine that, as someone rather arrogantly expresses to Chrissy, Brits were at the vanguard of Alpine sports and helped a tourism boom in the nineteenth century.

It turned out that the Villa Cassel was built by one of the richest men in England. Sir Ernest Cassel was a banker who was born in Germany but arrived in Britain aged sixteen with nothing but the shirt on his back. I would really like to have used more of his story in this book, as I often mix history with fiction, but because this story features an old case, it didn't fit in with the timeline, so my plan went awry.

Cassel really was a self-made man. He worked so hard in his early jobs in Liverpool that he soon moved up in the world and found work in a bank in Paris before returning to England, where he established his phenomenal wealth through international trading. Before long, he became friends with the future king, Edward VII, and British prime ministers (more about that in a minute!). He was given various significant titles and roles by the British government, the royal family and countries around the world. He tried to lobby Britain and Germany in the hope of avoiding World War One and was a generous philanthropist, bestowing money to various hospitals and the British Red Cross.

Perhaps this generosity was inspired by his various brushes with ill health, as first his wife and then their daughter died quite young. He himself suffered from cardiovascular and digestive issues for much of his life. In fact, that's what took him to Switzerland in the first place. His (and the Queen's) doctor told him he would no longer treat him unless he took a trip to a place with some of the freshest air in Europe. When Cassel first visited the area, he stayed in the Hotel Riederfurka, of which he angrily wrote home to his doctor to tell him how basic it was. Nonetheless, he seems to have fallen in love with the area as he petitioned the local council for land to build his own home with a view down the magnificent valley from its vantage point at 2,081m above sea level.

It took six years of visiting and many charitable contributions to the area before he was given permission to build, but by 1902 the house was complete. It's impressive because everything but wood and local stone had to be hauled up the mountain by mules. This included the metal for the incredible roof and turrets, and everything inside, including a piano and, oddly, a printing press that made local people believe he was counterfeiting money. The finished building had twenty-five rooms including a wine cellar, workshop, salon and (I think this might be a first in the real houses in which I've set my books) an actual smoking room. Much of the layout I've imagined fits with the real house, as the family's bedrooms were on the first and second floors, servants were up in the loft, and the beautiful (pine) spiral staircase linked it all together.

This gem of the mountains was visited by all sorts of wealthy and important people as the Cassel family hosted grand summer parties there, but by far the most famous visitor was a young man called Winston Churchill. He went four times and spent months at the villa writing his father's biography. He must have liked it to keep going back but was apparently put off his work by the sound of cows' bells in the neighbouring fields. In the end, his friend Sir Ernest had to ask the local farmers to bung straw inside them to keep the noise down – I believe he also bunged the farmers something more for their trouble.

Cassel only got to enjoy his mountain retreat for 12 years as, with the outbreak of war in 1914, he was unable to travel and was subsequently too ill to visit when it was over. The house was inherited by his much-treasured older granddaughter Edwina, who was married to Lord Mountbatten (or our current King's great-uncle). In a six-degrees-of-Kevin-Bacon-way, I can almost claim to have a connection to the couple, as they also inherited their main home at Broadlands in Romsey, Hampshire (where Queen Elizabeth II and Prince Philip spent their honeymoon!). My friend Josh, who was my boss at my last English school before I became a full-time writer, is from Romsey, and he occasionally sees the Mountbatten heirs shopping in the town. Which is honestly the weakest claim to fame I could realistically make.

Edwina sold the Villa Cassel to a local family, who ran it as a hotel for the next forty years before it fell into disrepair and was only saved five years later by a Swiss nature conservation charity, which still runs it today. It was thanks to Pro Natura that I found out a lot about the house and saw some photographs of the interior. As the information they produce on Villa Cassel is not published in English, I ended up reading my first book in French. I probably understood about 90% of it, which was enough to write this silly book and this silly chapter.

I did change the interior somewhat to make it fit my Christmas fantasy. My version is more of an overgrown log cabin, and I've borrowed the look of some beautiful modern Alpine hotels that I found about the place. The real interior when Sir Ernest was there was more genteel and less rustic, but still featured a whole lot of pine, with diamond patterned parquet flooring throughout and even wooden mantelpieces.

I must also admit to taking a few liberties with the geography of the area as the Great Aletsch Glacier is not visible from the house, and there isn't a handy rack railway to get you up there. Having said that, both of those features are fairly close by. The Jungfrau Railway was opened in 1912. It is 9.3km long, rises from 2,061 to 3,454m above sea level, and the final stop, from which you can admire the Jungfrau peak and the more famous Eiger, is the highest railway station in Europe. It took sixteen years to build, as much of the journey takes place in underground tunnels and crews had to bore through solid rock to reach the top. It was built solely to give people the chance to enjoy the view from the top of the mountain, and I think it's rather wonderful.

After writing this chapter, I received the newsletter of a newspaper I get every day and, by chance, it talked of a hotel for the first time since I started reading it. I hadn't heard of the Hotel Bellevue des Alpes, but having read the historical account of life there in the 1920s, it's amazing how close it is to the story I created in this book. It was a hub of activity, visited by ski-mad Brits, mountaineers trying to set records and the odd celebrity. It is at the foot of the Jungfrau Railway and, year-round, is only accessible by the adjoining Wengernalp railway, which takes you a further 20km down the valley. If you would like to re-enact any scenes in this book, the hotel still has authentic 1920s interiors, no televisions, and a stunning bar built in 1929. What surprised me most, though, was that access to the hotel is so similar to Chrissy and Lord Edgington's route, which was a thing of pure fantasy that I made up because I wanted to give my readers that iconic view of the mountains and glacier before reaching the hotel.

As for the glacier, a good viewpoint of which would actually take about twenty minutes to walk to from the Villa Cassel, it is the biggest in Europe and looks just like what it is: a vast frozen river. It's 20km long but has receded by over a tenth in the last seventy-five years. The total volume of glacial ice in Switzerland has almost halved in that time, with the majority of that disappearance occurring since the 1990s. Glaciers are amazing as they are a perfect record of our world's climate history over thousands of years and, just like the rings of a tree, they can tell us so much about changes that have taken place in that time. Its total volume is enough to give everyone on earth a litre of water every day for three and a half years. How refreshing!

As soon as I decided on the Alps, I knew that I had to have a skiing scene, and Chrissy's experience isn't so very far from my own. I had never been anywhere near a snowy mountain until I was twenty-five, but I foolishly married into a family who are crazy about winter sports, and my fate was sealed. My wife Marion trained to be an ice skater for fifteen years, and her family spent time at their cabin in the southernmost French Alps every winter, where they all became excellent skiers. The first time I went with them, I thought I'd done quite well after my morning of lessons, but then her seventy-year-old father came skidding up, before circling me as I ever-so-slowly descended a near-flat piste. Whenever I feel big-headed, I only have to remember how bad I remain at skiing to cut myself down a few notches.

The scene with Chrissy going far too fast down the mountain pretty much happened to me, as it seemed easier than turning or trying to stop. Perhaps the most unrealistic thing in my story is the idea that Todd and Lord Edgington can read a book and instantly start to ski, but I imagine a hundred years ago that was how many people would have done it, as professional ski schools can't have been that common. I know some people will complain about Lord Edgington being too old to try any such thing, but I've met older people who still ski, and there are great videos online of people past one hundred who continue.

My daughter Amelie had her first skiing lesson this year and, while she was busy, and her mother tackled a black slope, I enjoyed a nice medium-difficulty descent. After a couple of hours going up on a lift and skiing back down, I was amazed at how fast I was going and how much I'd obviously improved. My wife came to see me and, while it was true that, in comparison to her, I barely appeared to be moving, I was still confident I would wow my kids with my skills. I saw them coming in the distance and shot across the piste, calling to them as I went. The only problem was that I ended up in an area I hadn't skied on before and, having not fallen over once all day, I found myself on my back in a small hollow in the snow unable to get back up again. Amelie happily declared that she was already better than me, and I was humbled once more.

Despite this, I would still say that one of the best experiences in my life was the day when we went to the very top of the ski resort at Orcières Merlette, just as it was closing. There was hardly anyone left on the slopes, and there was snow for as far as the eye could see. It was simply breathtaking, and then we skied all the way down. The longest route there is about eight kilometres, and I don't know if we did all of it, but we barely saw another person the whole way. So, all in all, I wouldn't say I was born to ski, but it can be a very pleasant experience, and I'm glad that Chrissy got to see the two sides of it.

On the topic of Lord Edgington's age, people regularly e-mail me to say that they've seen the signs that he's slowing down and Chrissy is taking over, but that really isn't my plan. I think they've got to a stage where they complement one another. There'll be cases in which Chrissy excels and others where Lord Edgington comes to the fore. I have realised that I really like writing about older characters. We live in a society where content makers and advertisers seem to prioritise the young beyond all others, to the extent that actors and TV personalities are dispensed with before their time, but I genuinely believe that stories featuring characters with a variety of ages and backgrounds are far more interesting. Just imagine if Gandalf in The Lord of the Rings had been a teenager or Poirot was fresh out of college. Yuck!

This came to the fore with the group of female criminals who are so important to this story. They range in age from about forty to seventy-five and their past lives and experiences all feature in the plot in different ways. I didn't know that would be the case before writing the book, but I'm really pleased with the richness this element adds to the story.

The tiara plot came about because a reader messaged me with a story about a necklace Elizabeth II wore which disappeared from public view for decades before she started wearing it again. I couldn't find any information about that, but I did read a small mystery concerning the jewellery collection of the then Princess Royal. Princess Louise was the daughter of King Edward and was something of a rebel. Despite her mother Queen Alexandra's interference, she refused to make a grand marriage to another European royal and ended up selecting her own husband and going directly to the then queen, her grandmother Victoria, for permission to wed a mere earl, who would become the Duke of Fife.

The couple were apparently extremely happy together, and Louise enjoyed a varied life without embracing the public role expected of most royals. She was very artistic and enjoyed painting, photography and interior design – which was put to good use in all of their many properties – though I don't know if she is responsible for the ballroom at their hunting lodge which, with the 2,435 stag's skulls on display, looks as if it belongs to a serial killer.

Far more appealing is the story in 1911 of the shipwreck her family survived off the coast of Morocco. She and her husband made sure that those more vulnerable were rescued first, and the whole family were swept into the sea at one point but survived. Sadly, her husband the Duke became ill after the affair and died a month later. She also lost a case of jewels, but they weren't the ones that influenced this story.

At the time of her death in 1931, she left a large and exquisite jewellery collection mainly to her two daughters, Alexandra and Maud. There were three well-known tiaras, including the incredible Fife Tiara, which was eventually handed over to the British state to pay a tax bill and can now be viewed by the public at Kensington Palace. In the princess's will, however, some more jewellery was mentioned which had been made with stones from an unnamed tiara that does not appear to have any particular public record. It's something of a mystery what that tiara was and why Louise decided to break it into pieces, so I think I've filled in a few gaps. As she died two years after this story takes places, it's possible that Lord Edgington located the stolen stones from the tiara and returned them to the princess. Job done.

Spoilers incoming! Look away now if you haven't read the book yet! Something else I didn't know when I started writing was who the killer would turn out to be. I did have one idea which, by the time the characters had reached Switzerland, I realised it would be almost impossible to pull off satisfactorily, so I decided to let the story lead the way. I went into this much as you did, and it was only when I got about halfway through that I realised who it had to be and why. I worked out various incriminating plotlines for Herr Ried, Elisabeth Hall, Sunday Cheshire and even Inge Weinreich, and each of them would have revealed a different character as the culprit, but it was only as the pieces fell into place that I could see which was the best resolution.

For me, it's always the *why* that's the key to the pleasure of reading a mystery. The chances of picking the killer from a small group are pretty high, but the hardest part is spotting the reason and the hidden evidence that proves the case. I do think there are certain rules I shouldn't break in a resolution. For one thing, I can't just give someone an alibi which is then pulled away at the last second unless that alibi has been well crafted and cleverly undermined. I also think it's unfair if the killer turns out to be someone who has hardly featured in the book – though I do love the idea of the guilty party being (spoiler alert for a future book, maybe?) mentioned a lot but never seen.

I try to be fair with the solutions to the mysteries and put a lot of pressure on myself to come up with something new, so I enjoy hearing that I've stumped people. There have been studies which suggest that a book can be more entertaining when we already know the ending, though I've never tried that myself. I do know that a lot of people re-read my books, and some who even read the last chapter first, so perhaps the best option is to read once without knowing the twist, and then giving it another go to experience it with the solution in mind. However you read, the important thing is that you enjoy yourself. So if you made it through this much of my blathering, thank you and congratulations!

If you loved the story and have the time, please write a review at Amazon. Most books get one review per thousand readers so I would be infinitely appreciative if you could help me out.

THE MOST INTERESTING THINGS I DISCOVERED WHEN RESEARCHING THIS BOOK...

Right, I think I've shoehorned enough embarrassing stories about myself into this... for a few pages at least. Here is all the curious, funny, quirky and hard-to-believe stuff I discovered whilst researching this book.

Let's start at the beginning (of the book). You've probably heard of Lisztomania, but it seems that, in Milan at least, *Verdimania* was pretty intense too. The composer Giuseppe Verdi was a child prodigy who was already accomplished enough by the age of eight to be paid to play the organ at his local church. By sixteen, he led the Philharmonic Society of the town where he had gone to study, and he had already composed hundreds of pieces of music that he would perform in public. That still wasn't enough to get him a place at the conservatory in Milan, though, which was the cultural capital of Italy and was particularly famous for opera.

He moved there anyway and soon became involved in the world-renowned La Scala opera house. By twenty-one, he'd written his first opera and, three years later, it was performed to some success at La Scala. The death of his wife and two children and the first-night closure of his ill-chosen second work had a great effect on Verdi, but perhaps these tragedies and disappointments poured into his work, as his third opera *Nabucco* was a big hit and spread his fame across the world.

He wrote twenty-nine operas over the course of his career and became a national legend in his lifetime. For twenty-seven years, he took an apartment at the Grand Hotel et de Milan, where Chrissy and co. stay in this book. He was so popular in 1887 that, after a premiere of his new work, *Otelo,* the streets rang with people singing his arias, his fans unhooked his horses and carried his carriage from the opera house, then crowded around the hotel until Verdi and his tenor came out onto the balcony for an encore.

After the success of the opera *Aida*, Verdi wouldn't write another for a decade before *Otelo*, by which time demand for his work had only grown. He wrote it with the young librettist Arrigo Boito, whose *Mefistofele* featured in the first book in this series. The two men collaborated once more on *Falstaf,* which was the only comedy Verdi wrote after the one at the beginning of his career which had been such a flop. For the opening night, tickets were thirty times the normal price (proving that Ticketmaster didn't invent dynamic pricing). The applause from the audience lasted an hour, and riotously enthusiastic crowds formed once more around his hotel. In his final days, after the stroke which would end his life, his admirers placed straw on the streets around "the Milan" to reduce the noise of passing carriages. Finally, at his funeral, a choir of 820 singers and several orchestras combined to create the largest ever rendition of one of his compositions, and an estimated 300,000 people filled the area.

I've only been to Milan once, but its cathedral and (weirdly) its shopping centre are two of the most unforgettable buildings I've ever visited. I still think that Burgos – the city where I live in the north of Spain – has the greatest cathedral in the world, but Milan, Seville and Florence come a close joint second. Sadly, there was no room for a glimpse of the Duomo in this book, but Milan is perhaps even more famous as a shopping city, and so I did include scenes in the Galleria Vittorio Emanuele II. Chrissy does a good enough job of describing this palace to commerce, which was completed in 1877 and has the most incredible glass-work ceilings and an exquisite triumphal arch entrance. It is so wondrous, it was used in the recent Willy Wonka film for scenes of the character's first shop, and I believe it must be the most beautiful shopping centre in the world (especially at Christmas).

Which brings me on to Italian Christmas traditions, many of which I could only hint at before my characters raced off to the Alps. From what I could discover, there was no public Christmas tree in Milan in the twenties, but these days they are lit on 7th December (much earlier than in Switzerland). That isn't to say that trees weren't decorated back then, but Chrissy had to go looking carefully for one, and the place he finds it is the courtyard of a private house which I based on the Palazzo Invernizzi, a building owned by the Invernizzi dairy dynasty, the owners of which bought the place in the 1950s and put flamingos in the courtyard, which you can glimpse today if you look through the gates there. They obviously weren't around in 1929, but I put something bright and pretty in their place.

As in Spain, Christmas in Italy kicks off in the first week of December, in time for the day of the Immaculate Conception, and there is a Christmas market in Milan which dates back five hundred years. It sells bric-a-brac, typical Christmas crafts, and strings of chestnuts for roasting. The name, *Oh Bej! Oh Bej!* apparently comes from the first time it was held in 1510 when Pope Pius VII handed out presents to local children and they cooed these words, which translate as "Oh, so nice!". It starts on 7th December, which is the day of Milan's patron saint, Saint Ambrose. That is also the day when Christmas lights are turned on, and the La Scala starts its opera season with a grand gala. They have public screenings of the event across the city, at which point the music of Verdi echoes around Milan once more.

Most Italian Christmas traditions seem to revolve around food – which both I and Chrissy have no problem with whatsoever. The Feast of the Seven Fishes takes place on Christmas Eve and is famous worldwide. It's common in my wife's French family, too, and on my first year spending time in Picardie at Christmas, I forced myself to eat as much of it as possible. I was not a fish-eater at the time, and I really struggled, then had to spend much of Christmas Day lying down in the back of a car with a stomach ache while the rest of the family visited the Christmassy windows of the department stores in Paris. Happy memories!

Other culinary treats include panettone, and Chrissy seeks out the bakery of one of the most famous makers, Angelo Motta, who helped popularise this fruity sponge cake on a mass scale. He opened his first bakery in 1919, after returning from the war, and reworked the centuries-old recipe to make the dough rise for longer, giving the cake its familiar tall, cylindrical shape and light, fluffy texture. It was so successful that, by 1930, he had opened a factory in Milan to sell panettone across the country. He was not alone in this, however, as rival Milanese baker Gioacchino Alemagna borrowed the new recipe and became just as famous, employing two-thousand workers at his own factory. The two brands were competitors for many years until

Nestlé bought them both. I'm glad to say that an Italian company now owns and produces the famous cakes, which are sold all over the world. Motta also produces pistachio spread to eat with it. I'm intrigued and will try making some with my kids for Christmas.

I've found it interesting as I've read about (and travelled around) different European countries that there are so many distinct legends for the being/person/thing who gives out presents. In Spain we have *los Reyes Magos* or the Three Kings, who come on the eve of Epiphany. They do the bulk of the present giving, with Father Christmas, who is still not as big a deal here, demoted to giving out smaller goodies. In Italy, however, there's la Befana, a friendly, broom-riding old woman whose story may trace its roots back to the Roman era but was adapted in medieval times when she was identified as the guide who led the kings to see Jesus.

In Catalunya there is *Caga Tio,* or the pooing Christmas log, which may sound like something out of an episode of *South Park*, but it's a genuine tradition. Starting from the Feast of the Immaculate Conception, families start leaving the inanimate log bits of food until, on Christmas Eve, they beat the little fellow (often painted with a face and with a red hat on its head) and sing a song asking him to poo out presents. There's a blanket over the back of him and kids reach under it to take one small gift like sweets, small toys or *torró* (a local honey nougat, often made with almonds, similar to what Chrissy eats in Milan). Scatological traditions are common in Catalunya, and they even have a small, pooing figure called *el caganer*. Which is a perfect segue because...

There is one tradition with Italian roots that is now common the world over. St Francis of Assisi is often attributed with coming up with the idea for the *Presepe* or nativity scene but, in the Christmas of 1223, his scene was acted out with real people. By the end of that century, a scene that closely resembles modern nativities was sculpted for a Roman church, and it popularised the tradition which quickly spread around Europe. There are different styles, but one of the most famous is the highly elaborate and baroque Neapolitan scenes that are extremely collectable and reached their artistic peak in the eighteenth century.

They are just as popular in Spain and most towns and even small villages here have very large installations. The biggest I've been to is built by the army in Burgos each year and, when it was on display at the cathedral, it took us about half an hour to walk around, as it didn't just represent the nativity story, but most of the Old Testament too. There was no *caganer* on show, but you will find the small, pooing peasant in Catalan nativity scenes.

Okay, enough about other countries' Christmas traditions. Let's talk about Swiss Christmas traditions. They do not have a Christmas witch or a pooing log, and Father Christmas, or *Samichlaus,* delivers presents on the day of Saint Nicholas on 6th December. He looks a lot like Old Saint Nick but has a Bishop's mitre and crozier, along with classic red and white robes. You leave out a boot or shoe for him and, come the morning, it's full of treats and presents! Result! However, he does not come alone. He has a sooty-faced sidekick called *Schmutzli* who is in charge of punishing naughty children with a broom. Considering that I (honestly) had to stop writing this paragraph to break up an argument between two very tired children, it's a tradition we might have to introduce in this house soon.

The one thing that was clear to me as I read about Christmas in Switzerland is that the Swiss really like Christmas biscuits. There appear to be countless different types, and they span back through the centuries. One particularly popular variety in the weeks leading up to the big event is *Grittibänz,* which are rather ornate baked figures that resemble Saint Nicholas. They are often made holding a pipe, with raisins for eyes and nose. This book also mentions *Mailänderli* (simple butter biscuits with a touch of lemon made in different shapes, whereas the Italian equivalent features candied fruits and almonds) and *Brunsli* (which are made with ground almonds and chocolate).

As a lot of online baking blogs are written by Americans, I had to be careful to avoid using the word cookie instead of biscuit – which is the general word in the UK for crisp, hard-baked treats. However, when I searched for cookies in the twenties in the British Newspaper Archive, the recipes I found were mainly for butter cookies. The word itself came from Scotland and originally referred to a kind of plain bun, but the reason cookie is commonly used in America is that it was the

Anglicised form of the Dutch word *koekje*. As Scotland traded with Holland at the time, it's possible that both independent origins of the word came via the Dutch.

In Britain today, if someone offers you a cookie, you would expect it to have chocolate chips. Chocolate chip cookies (or Toll House cookies, named after the inn in Massachusetts, where they were first made) didn't appear in their current form until 1938. They were popularised when soldiers from that state travelled abroad and shared the cookies they received from back home with other soldiers, who wrote asking their own families to make them. The original chef, Ruth Graves Wakefield, who owned and ran the namesake inn with her husband, received a lifetime supply of baking chocolate from Nestlé in return for the rights to the recipe. I once won a baking competition at Amelie's school for my cookies, and I can't recommend highly enough the Ultimate Chocolate Chip recipe on the baking blog bakerbettie.com. The browned butter makes a huge difference, though I am sometimes lazy and just make the Toll House recipe that my Texan friend taught me.

Much as people in English-speaking countries began to carve pumpkins for Halloween, in Switzerland, they make lanterns out of turnips. It's more common to make them in November on a special day called *Räbechilbi* (or, turnip party). Now, I've made some jokes in these books about turnips before, but I approve of this use of that bland, unpleasant and eternally under or overcooked vegetable.

We've had an Advent wreath in my house in London since I can remember. They are also common in Switzerland, and while I knew that they were from that part of the world, I didn't know the story behind them. They date back to 1839, thus predating advent calendars which have a similar origin, when a Lutheran pastor taught at a mission school in Hamburg. Children asked him every day whether Christmas had arrived, and so he took a wooden ring and attached twenty-four small red and four large white candles to it. The red ones would be lit every day and the white ones every Sunday to mark the weeks of Advent passing. There's a famous kids' programme in Britain called Blue Peter, which regularly features crafts kids can make at home. There was a famous episode in 1964 in which they use coat hangers, bits of tinsel and candles to make an Advent crown to hang from the ceiling. It's a pretty shoddy-looking thing, and I do have to wonder how many carpets (and fingers) were burned in houses around Britain as the candles fell off.

Spas are now very much associated with Alpine leisure, but to be honest, they really weren't in Switzerland in the twenties. Saunas came originally from Finland, and while there were bathing hotels across central Europe and some may have had steam rooms, the main reason I featured one is because I thought it would be funny to make Albert faint in the middle of a tense interview.

Surprisingly, skiing goes back at least five millennia, and some people believe that an approximately ten-thousand-year-old cave painting from the Altai Mountains in China shows people skiing. People have certainly been skiing in the region for a couple of thousand years, and there is disagreement over whether the early form of skiing, made with asymmetrical skis lined with animal skin, originated there or in Sweden. People in that region still use very similar skis for hunting, and though their style is totally different from the modern Alpine variety, they are incredibly capable and have been known to ski about for up to twelve hours at a time.

There are now ski lifts near Villa Cassel, but at the time, such things were rare. The first was built in Germany in 1908, and another steam-powered one was built in America two years later. We live near an abandoned ski station in the Sierra de la Demanda in the north of Spain. Because of a lack of snow, it closed down about twenty years ago, but people head up there at the weekends in winter. You can still see the metal structures that would have held the lift, but I walk up the mountain, normally with a child in my arms or on my shoulders, pulling an old-fashioned sledge behind us. There is a nice sense of achievement when we've gone as far as we're planning to go, but I spend most of the time wishing that the ski-lift were still working. This repeated experience every winter no doubt inspired the scene of Chrissy climbing the mountain.

Night skiing at Christmas isn't actually a Swiss tradition, it's an Italian one, but as the countries share a border, I dare say it happened not too far away from Riederfurka. Also, Inge is a bit of a weirdo, so perhaps it was just an idea that occurred to her. The fashions I mention throughout, however, are accurate, and I used images from newspapers and stock websites to learn about interesting options. Even Rosetta Mullen's daring ensemble was based on a real – though clearly insane – outfit from 1929 which included high socks, short shorts and no tights of any kind. In my searches, I was pleased to find an image of Burberry Christmas jumpers which had been weather-proofed for skiing. They feature an intense pattern of reindeers pulling sleighs, Christmassy houses, gingerbread men, ice skaters and snowmen.

This answers the question I couldn't answer in this year's Marius Quin Christmas book about whether such jumpers existed in the twenties, but it also makes me sad that I don't own such a snazzy item. My Auntie Rose is an incredibly talented knitter. She taught my daughter and wife this summer, and they haven't stopped knitting since – making hairbands, scarves for teddies and jewellery in the process. However, I was promised a Fair Isle sweater for my fortieth birthday, and I'm still waiting. I know you read these books, Rose. How about a late Christmas present?

When Chrissy and his grandfather travel up through the Alps, they drive by a place known as *Teufelsbrücke* or the Devil's Bridge, In reality, it is in the Gotthard Pass, which is an important route connecting the northern and southern Swiss Alps, but they wouldn't really have driven that far to get to the hotel. It got its name because people believed that the terrifying bridge which spans the Schöllenen Gorge could only have been created by the devil. There is a particularly frightening painting of it by William Turner in which the original sixteenth-century bridge looks as though it might collapse at any second.

Around that time, a local legend sprang up which said that the people of the local village tricked the devil into helping them in exchange for the soul of a dog rather than the person he was expecting. As it happens, there are similar myths all over the world, including three in Spain, four in Switzerland (two of which Turner depicted) and nine in Wales. There is a town called Devil's Bridge near where I went to university in Aberystwyth, which it is a rite of passage to visit by steam train if you study there. The legend around it is almost identical to the Swiss one – down to the dog and a tossed crust of bread. I wonder which came first.

From Switzerland to a place far away where birds of prey also soar. Eagle-eyed (pun intended) readers might have realised that the football team Chrissy imagines himself playing for is the team I support. There have been various clues to this over the years, and I've had a few different e-mails to check my allegiance. Crystal Palace F.C. has a pretty interesting history, and now I have an excuse to talk about it. The first team with that name dates all the way back to 1861, when the immense Crystal Palace exhibition centre stood in an area of south London not far from Croydon. The team competed in the first F.A. Cup but disappeared for thirty years before the professional club that still exists formed in 1905.

The club were nicknamed the Glaziers for much of the twentieth century because of their connection to the famous glass palace, which burnt down in 1936. In 1913, suffragettes intended to blow up CPFC's empty stadium on the night before the cup final as part of their campaign demanding voting rights for women, but they were foiled at the last minute. Almost fifty years later, Palace was the first London club to host the Spanish legends Real Madrid, losing by a very respectable three goals to four.

In its history, the club had achieved very little indeed, but they finally won Britain's main football cup this year, having participated at least a hundred times without success. I was a season ticket holder as a kid and went every weekend with my cousin and uncle. The team's success rate at the time was not the best, and they never won a title or cup, but I always loved going. We sat in the family stand, but I definitely remember hearing more swearing there than anywhere else I'd ever been.

Palace (now known as the Eagles) are an admirable team not just because they aren't owned by a petrostate and do well on a comparatively low budget. They do a lot for community outreach in South London. First team players delivered food and supplies during the pandemic, with thousands of meals cooked in the stadium itself. Palace also have their own charitable foundation, which runs a team for young people with Down's Syndrome as well as classes for the visually impaired and disabled. I'm not a football evangelist, and I'm not one of those people who believe that my team can do no wrong on or off the pitch, but it is nice to see what amounts to a multi-million-pound corporation trying to make ordinary people's lives better. So... COYP!

Okay. Here are some weird little facts I discovered. It's bullet point time!

- Mr Fahrenheit, the German scientist who developed the Fahrenheit scale, based his concept of zero degrees on the coldest temperature he could make in his laboratory, and made one hundred degrees the temperature of the human body. Britain in the twenties still used Fahrenheit, but Europe had changed to the easier to understand Celsius (developed by Mr Celsius), which would have been hard for Chrissy to get his head around. Today, only America and five small island nations have stuck with the earlier (frankly baffling) system.

- I needed to check when people started signing off letters with Xs instead of the word kiss, and there is already evidence of it in the 1870s. By 1894, Churchill finished a letter by saying "Please excuse bad writing as I am in an awful hurry. (Many kisses.) xxx WSC." Writing O to mean hugs, however, was not recorded until 1948.

- I was hoping to have a scene in which Chrissy was mocked by a whistling marmot, but alas, as we had both forgotten, they hibernate. I managed to squeeze them into the plot all the same, as I find these funny little creatures charming. In America, they're known as groundhogs, and we often see them when we go to the Alps in the summer. The last time we were there, one kept dashing past us, and he must have used the same paths between burrows all the time, as you could see a clear runway in the grass. Their whistle is really distinctive and sounds like no other mammal that I know of. They are the largest members of the squirrel family and are one of the least genetically diverse wild animals because of habitat loss. There is also no denying that they're cute little fellas, and I'd like to cuddle one!

- Despite Christopher's surprise at this, the goat's connection to Christmas goes back centuries in certain parts of Europe. The Yule Goat in Scandinavia may be linked to the goats that pulled Thor's chariot, and by the eleventh century was associated with gift giving around Christmas. Come the nineteenth century, the benevolent goat had become a Father-Christmas-like figure, and people would dress up as him to give out presents. In Finland, the equivalent to Santa is still known as *joulupukki* or Yule goat!

- 1816 became known as the year without a summer because, thanks to volcanic eruptions in Indonesia and the Philippines, much of Europe and North America was remarkably cold, dark and rainy. Although it only created a total drop of one degree in temperature over the year, this small change led to failed harvests, food shortages, food riots and famine. In fact, because of the reaction of the starving populace, it was the most violent period on the Continent since the French Revolution, despite the fact the Napoleonic wars had taken place just before.

- Sticking with freak phenomena, the Wall Street Crash may have led to a Black Monday (and Tuesday and Thursday), but there was another Black Monday five and a half centuries earlier during the Hundred Years' War between Britain and France. On Easter Monday 1360, a sudden change in the weather, including a drop in temperature and massive, deadly hailstones, killed more English soldiers than any of the battles during the previous two decades of war. Around a thousand men and six thousand horses were killed, as they laid siege to the French city of Chartres. The army had no shelter to escape the icy onslaught, and the English king, Edward III, was so convinced that it was a sign from God that he sued for peace with his enemies.

- Muesli dates back to 1900 and was created by a Swiss doctor to be a filling appetiser rather than a breakfast cereal. He served the mix of oats, nuts and dried fruits to his patients at his sanitorium overlooking Lake Zurich, and the word muesli is a diminutive form of the German word for mush but was previously also known as "Swiss supper".

- The card game *Jass* is so popular in Switzerland that it is shown several times a week on television. There are seventy different varieties (including *Schmaus*, which is a two-player version) and three million people are said to play regularly there.

- The reddest rubies are generally the most valuable and, for centuries, the true pigeon-blood ones came from Burma (a.k.a. Myanmar). However, in the last sixteen years since vast deposits were discovered, Mozambique has become the main producer.

The biggest known ruby was discovered there in 2022. The Estrela de Fura is fifty-five carats and sold for nearly $35 million.

- As you may have guessed from the absence of the word in this book, allergies were not commonly described as such in the 1920s. Although the word allergy was coined in 1906 by Clemens von Pirquet, an Austrian scientist who noticed people's reactions to a particular serum, few of his peers accepted his conclusions and instead the work of his French colleague Charles Richet was celebrated when he investigated anaphylaxis and decided that it was caused by a weak immune system. Richet, a eugenicist and spiritualist who came up with the concept of ectoplasm, won the 1913 Nobel prize for his work, and it was only in the 1960s that scientists re-evaluated von Pirquet's work and began to understand allergic reactions better.

- One of the earliest safes was found in the tomb of the Egyptian pharaoh Ramesses II. The main box was wooden, and the mechanism even included a pin tumbler lock like some that are still used today. Metal safes were made starting in the sixteenth century, and by the nineteenth century, British locksmiths the Chubb brothers had patented a supposedly burglar-safe model.

- It's not only criminals and locksmiths who pick locks. It is also a pastime. Louis XVI enjoyed creating and picking locks, as did one of the leading physicists on the Manhattan project, and it is now a competitive hobby known as locksport. The Chubb detector lock, though designed by Jeremiah Chubb back in 1818, is still one of the most difficult to pick. Soon after its invention, it was presented as a challenge to the best lock pick then in prison, who would be awarded his freedom if he could manage to solve it. After a few months trying, he admitted defeat. It wouldn't be successfully picked until the Great Exhibition of 1851 by a locksmith (coincidentally also from Massachusetts) by the name of Alfred Charles Hobbs, who managed it in twenty-five minutes. Even more impressive is the protector lock of Prussian Theodor Kromer which was designed in 1874 and only picked for the first time (in a fifty-minute YouTube video) in 2022.

- I stumbled across a mystery of my own. I found an article in the paper about a jewel thief who targeted the home of a man named Major Ivor Napier. Napier came home after a party to find a man going through his valuables in his bedroom. The man slashed the major's body and face with an ornamental Japanese bayonet from the wall, but Napier still fought his assailant. Covered in blood and fading fast, he ran after the burglar before collapsing outside. At the end of the first article I read, the culprit had got away with the loot, so I searched on. Three days later, a man had been arrested thanks to the bloody fingerprint on the knife, and the major was recovering in hospital. I know that he served in the Cameron Highlanders, but I hoped to find out more about him, so I searched on once more. Two years after the burglary, there is a story about an ill-fated skiing expedition in the (guess where?) Swiss Alps in which three British majors were trapped by an avalanche. Their guide and one of the soldiers were killed but Majors Napier and Nathan survived. I have no idea if it's the same man, but it would be cool if it was.

- A far more worthy and historically momentous article appears just under the first I read about Napier. It is the story of a little girl's purse (complete with two coins, a button and a postage stamp) which went missing at a school picnic. It turned up over six months later in the stomach of a cow. I wonder if the girl offered a reward for its recovery.

And now all that's left for me to do is tell you about a car, a bit more food, and some songs. Oh, and there's a mountain I've forgotten. Let's start with that.

The Matterhorn, which Chrissy spies from the Villa Cassel, isn't the highest peak in the Alps or even in Switzerland, but it is the most famous. If you've never heard of it, you will definitely have seen it for two very good reasons. First, it is said to be the most photographed mountain in the world, due to its almost cartoonishly perfect, pyramid-shaped summit which is on the border between Switzerland and Italy. The second reason is perhaps even more iconic, as the Matterhorn is the mountain which features on Toblerone packaging. It was already used in advertising the chocolate bar in the 1920s and, since the sixties can be seen beside the trademark red writing. Of course, the shape of the bar itself, with its triangular peaks that you can break off, was said to be inspired by the shape of the mountain – though like many things, even in recent history, that story is debated.

Lord Edgington's snazzy two-seater this time around is an Alfa Romeo. He has had Alfas ever since the first book, but now he's come very close to the place in which they were made. The marque was founded in Milan in 1910, with the initials of the first part of the name standing for *Anonima Lombarda Fabbrica Automobili*. Romeo was added after the company was bought by Nicola Romeo, an engineer and investor in 1915. Their cars found fame for their success in major races, including with a young man named Enzo Ferrari behind the wheel before he went on to found his own racing team and car company.

The sporty number that Chrissy and his grandfather drive up into the mountains in this book is the 1500cc spyder (or roadster, as it would be known in other countries). First introduced in 1927, the 6c would be produced for almost four decades. It won many motoring prizes and was quite simply a sublime motor car in many of its differing incarnations. Even Chrissy enjoyed its smooth handling.

I'm not going to go too deeply into Swiss cuisine, as I'd like to publish this book before Christmas, but there are a few dishes I wish to highlight. The first is the cholera pie that is served in the restaurant on the first night of Chrissy's stay. It really does sound delicious – featuring several of my favourite ingredients in bacon, fruit, cheese and pastry – but I was curious what inspired that name.

It is thought to have come into existence during the cholera epidemic of 1830, when people stayed at home to avoid infection. This meant that they couldn't be choosy with what they ate so chucked a load of ingredients in a pie dish and covered it in pastry. Of course, nothing's that simple, and the name could also have come from the coals on which it was cooked, or the room in a bakery where the coals were kept. Whatever the case, I am going to make this dish soon, and I am going to enjoy it.

A dish I have already eaten a lot of (and I mean *a lot of!*) is raclette. As I'm married to an Alpine princess (who would very much not like to be referred to as such) we have a raclette grill, which we use a couple of times every winter, and I complain we don't use it more. Traditionally, it would be prepared using a half wheel of cheese, melted beside the fire and scraped over meat, potatoes and vegetables. With a modern grill, you take chunks or slices of cheese, put them on individual trays and stick them under a heating element. When reading Swiss food forums online, I found people saying that raclette isn't traditional, but the dish actually goes back to a time when cow herders would keep a chunk of cheese with them which they would then melt over a campfire to spread on bread. There is written evidence of the practice going back to 1574, the gastronome Brillat-Savarin described it as "fondue Valaisanne" in 1834, and by 1909 it was promoted as a national dish of the Valais region where this book takes place.

Chrissy doesn't eat normal fondue in this book, which is another classic Swiss melted cheese dish with white wine mixed in. It is absent because a lot of the culture and cuisine in this book is focused on the German-speaking, mountainous regions of Switzerland, and fondue came from the lower-lying French-speaking region of Romandy. During the nineteenth century, it would only have been eaten by the wealthy, as Gruyère cheese would have been too expensive for peasanty mountain-dwellers. Another problem with fondue for my purposes is that its fame didn't spread until the 1930s, after this book was set, when the Swiss authorities promoted it in order to sell more cheese. Those wily geniuses.

As mentioned in the book, there are four different official languages in Switzerland (sorry to Romansch-speakers, as you didn't get a look-in) and there is a particular divide between the Germanic vs Latin languages in everything from culture, lifestyle and, of course, cuisine. This separation is best exemplified by the consumption of one dish. Rösti are the potato pancakes that Chrissy has for breakfast, but they are so much more to Swiss people. I ate them when I was still a teenager, as my first girlfriend was German and she made a lot of nice hearty dishes like this one. It's not a complicated dish as the traditional recipe calls for nothing but grated potato, fried in a pan, but the division between non-rösti and rösti eaters, is said to follow the language division so clearly that the border valley between the two regions is often referred to as *Röstigraben*, or the Rösti Ditch (whereas the line around the Italian-speaking region is known as *Polentagraben* for similar reasons).

Every Christmas spectacular should finish with a song, and I've got three to mention. The absolute masterpiece of a downbeat Christmas song that Rosetta Mullen sings was written by a frustrated lyricist whose career in a rock band had concluded, uncelebrated, by the time he was eighteen. Admittedly, I was only the drummer in that band, and, yes, my songwriting has always been pretty dreadful, but I rather like this one, and I look forward to hearing my friend Alison record it for the audiobook. Alison was at university with my brother and performs 1920s-50s music at weddings and events under the name Rose Devine. She is very good indeed.

I thought that "Silent Night" was a perfect choice for the book seeing as it was originally written in German, is internationally known, and it gave me a chance to pay tribute to the different languages spoken in the hotel (I honestly did look for a Romansh version but couldn't find it). It was first performed in a small (possibly snowy?) church on Christmas Eve 1818 near Salzburg in Austria. The lyrics were written in 1816 by Father Joseph Mohr, a Catholic priest who asked the local organist, Franz Xaver Gruber, to compose music to accompany it for that night's mass. Its authorship was unknown for many years until the original manuscript was rediscovered in 1995, and Mohr's name was restored. The church was destroyed by flooding, but since 1937 there has been a pretty replacement in its place known as the Silent Night Chapel.

What's particularly interesting is how the song went from a single performance to a small congregation to becoming one of the most recognisable pieces of Christmas music we have. Apparently, the man who maintained the organ at the church liked the piece so much that he took it away with him and it was soon heard by two groups of travelling singers who spread it far and wide. It was translated into English in 1859 by an Episcopal priest in New York, and we still use his version today. It is such a perfect piece that, just as I would never say the Beatles are my favourite band though it's hard to argue they're not the best, I would never describe "Silent Night" as my favourite carol, but it certainly takes some beating. I can think of several exceptional versions (I have over seventy in my Christmas music library), but I'll pick the Joan Baez, Johnny Cash and Low versions as three of my favourites. The definitive vocal performance (prove me wrong!) of "Silent Night" is by the Irish singer Lisa Hannegan, but she changed the lyrics, so it doesn't count.

And last but not least, "Good King Wenceslas". The eponymous monarch was actually a duke, but he was venerated and indeed crowned after his death (at the hands of his wicked brother, Boleslaus the Cruel) due to his piety and his fair treatment of his people. It sounds like he had a difficult life – seeing as his mother had his grandmother assassinated and he only lived to (at most) 28 – with much of his decade-long reign spent defending his land from scheming neighbouring forces. How good he really was as a leader is largely based on the hagiographies that were written about him, but there was a legend which said that he would travel barefoot with just one assistant, giving out alms to the poor. On one of these excursions, a legend claims that his feet melted the snow for his page to follow, and this is the story which inspired the song we know today.

The famous tune dates all the way back to the thirteenth century, with the first extant printed record coming in 1582 in a Finnish hymn collection. It found its connection to the tenth century Bohemian duke in 1853 when the English lyricist John Mason Neale was given a copy of the publication from three hundred years earlier by the British envoy to Sweden. Neale had already written the story of Wenceslas in a children's book and adapted the story for the song. Over the centuries, many critics have taken exception to its adaptation of a piece of music which was previously associated with spring and to its whimsical, historically unlikely influences. They have even hoped it would fall out of use, but the carol lives on. It is one of those which it is hard not to whistle, hum or sing along to when you hear it.

I was planning to tell you some interesting facts about watermelons, Whitechapel slums, the Italian tailor Guglielmo Miani, and Dickens' inspiration for Fagin, but I think we can all agree that this chapter has gone on for long enough. If you're interested in any of those things, please look them up. I have a Lego Christmas village to build!

ACKNOWLEDGEMENTS

I must thank the organisation that owns the real Villa Cassel, who gave me permission to set a book in the building which is now their wildlife and visitors' centre in the Alps. Pro Natura is an NGO which was founded in 1909 and looks after hundreds of nature reserves in Switzerland and helps keep the country the natural gem that it is.

Thank you, as always, to my kind and generous early readers, Bridget Hogg and the Martins. To Lisa Bjornstad, and Jayne Kirk for arduous close editing. Jim Woodworth for his help poisoning people, and to my fellow writers who are always there for me, especially Karen, Suzanne and Lucy.

And, of course, a massive thank you must go to my ARC team... Rebecca Brooks, Ferne Miller, Melinda Kimlinger, Emma James, Mindy Denkin, Namoi Lamont, Katharine Reibig, Linsey Neale, Terri Roller, Margaret Liddle, Lori Willis, Anja Peerdeman, Marion Davis, Sarah Turner, Sandra Hoff, Mary Nickell, Vanessa Rivington, Helena George, Anne Kavcic, Nancy Roberts, Pat Hathaway, Peggy Craddock, Cathleen Brickhouse, Susan Reddington, Sonya Elizabeth Richards, John Presler, Mary Harmon, Karen Quinn, Karen Alexander, Mindy Wygonik, Jacquie Erwin, Janet Rutherford, Ila Patlogan, Randy Hartselle, Carol Vani, June Techtow, M.P. Smith, Michele Kapugi, Helen K, Ed Enstrom and Keryn De Maria.

READ MORE LORD EDGINGTON MYSTERIES TODAY_

- **Murder at the Spring Ball**
- **Death From High Places** (free e-novella available exclusively at benedictbrown.net. Paperback and audiobook are available at Amazon)
- **A Body at a Boarding School**
- **Death on a Summer's Day**
- **The Mystery of Mistletoe Hall**
- **The Tangled Treasure Trail**
- **The Curious Case of the Templeton-Swifts**
- **The Crimes of Clearwell Castle**
- **A Novel Way to Kill** (novella available at Amazon)
- **The Snows of Weston Moor**
- **What the Vicar Saw**
- **Blood on the Banister**
- **A Killer in the Wings**
- **The Christmas Bell Mystery**
- **The Puzzle of Parham House**
- **Death at Silent Pool**
- **Murder in an Italian Castle**
- **Death on the Night Train to Verona**
- **The Alpine Chritmas Mystery**
- **The Case of the Burgundy Vineyard** (Spring 2026)

Check out the complete Lord Edgington Collection at Amazon

The first seventeen Lord Edgington audiobooks, narrated by the actor George Blagden, are available now on all major audiobook platforms. There will be more coming soon.

THE "MURDER IN AN ITALIAN CASTLE" COCKTAIL

David Wondrich, one of the world's foremost experts on cocktails, ponders whether the Rose, which dates back to 1919, might be considered the Signature cocktail of the Lost Generation, and it was certainly popular enough in the twenties and thirties to warrant the title. Contemporary sources attribute it to a barman called Johnny Milta at the Chatham Bar in Paris. The first time it appears in a book is in Harry MacElhone's *Harry's ABC of Mixing Cocktails* from 1922.

It was drunk widely in Paris at the time and soon spread around the globe, not least because of its rather ethereal pink glow and light taste. I had never had a Rose but made a trip to Madrid the week before this book came out to hunt one down. I looked at the cocktail lists online of about twenty bars before asking my cocktail expert friend Francois where to go. The 1862 Dry Bar (who claim to be able to make most classic cocktails in addition to whatever appears on their fancy menu) used to serve it, but they were out of Kirsch, so I had to order the ingredients online instead. I'm going to update this page (and possibly Chrissy's impression of it) when I've made the drink at home. Despite what these pages might suggest, I only have about four cocktails a year, depending on how many Lord Edgington books I publish, and I look forward to trying this one next week.

Of course, I mainly chose it because of the Swiss connection thanks to its key ingredient of kirsch (or *kirschwasser* as it's known in Germany). Here's the original recipe from just over a century ago…

> **2 parts dry vermouth (the Frencher the better, apparently)**
>
> **To 1 part Kirsch - or any dry cherry brandy: perhaps not the easiest ingredient to get, but I found it without much trouble online.**
>
> **1 teaspoon raspberry syrup.**

Older recipes just tell you to shake well and strain; modern ones include cracked ice. To be honest, you can find recipes that tell you to reverse the above proportions, so to me this sounds like a drink that you need to find your own balance for. So experiment a little and see what you like. Cheers.

You can get our official cocktail expert François Monti's brilliant book "101 Cocktails to Try Before you Die" at Amazon.

WORDS AND REFERENCES YOU MIGHT NOT KNOW

Caffè Biffi / Libreria Occhio – The first is a café that is still in the magnificent Milanese shopping arcade, and the second is similar in name to a bookshop (Libreria Bocca) which has been there for a long time, but not quite long enough. In fact, try as I might, I couldn't find a bookshop that was in the shopping centre in the 20s, so I made one up which is similar in appearance to the current one.

Carrollese – reminiscent of Lewis Carroll (who wrote *Alice's Adventures in Wonderland*)

Macaroni – another word for a dandy or fop originating in the 18th century when wealthy young men who went travelling in Europe returned to Britain and imitated Continental tastes (such as eating macaroni, growing courtly curls and using spying-glasses in daily life).

Chatterpie – a chatterbox, it was also originally another name for a magpie.

Mouth-dropping – amazing.

Britons – I didn't realise until this book that the word "Brits" was rarely used until the second half of the twentieth century, especially by Brits.

Earwigging – eavesdropping.

Schwitzbad – as he will later find out, this is a sauna. It literally means sweat bath.

Ich bin Arzt… Was brauchen Sie? – I'm a doctor… What do you need?

"Auch bekannt als Epinephrine." – Also known as Epinephrine.

Chasselas – a white wine varietal which comes from Switzerland.

Rookery – a word for the slums in England (and especially London) in the nineteenth and early twentieth century.

Taken short – today we'd more commonly say "caught short" or needing to go to the toilet before getting to one!

Weeniest – smallest – interestingly, this word appears to have British roots in the eighteenth century, whereas teeny is more American and slightly later. Understandably, teeny weeny came later still.

Nein. Nicht jeden Tag. – No, not every day.

Saint Barbara – she really was Greek. Thought to have been born in the third century, though the reality of her existence is doubted even by some authorities in the Catholic church, she was kept locked in a tower by her horrible father and was eventually tortured and sentenced to death for her Christianity, with her beheading carried out by her wicked old man himself, who was then killed by lightning.

Some degree of toxic intolerance / an idiosyncrasy to one of the spices – the term allergic wasn't common at the time, and so Dolly's reaction would have been referred to in similar terms to these.

Die Frühlingsballmorde – this is the name of the first Lord Edgington book *Murder at the Spring Ball* which my friend Lioba has just translated into German. We discussed the translation of the title for some time, and this was the one we liked best.

Sûreté de Paris – the Paris police force which is often mentioned in Agatha Christie. It was previously significant in my Marius Quin novel, *The Castleton Affair*.

Sie ist tot – she's dead. This was the only German expression I somehow already knew and didn't need to look up.

Common-or-garden – this is a British expression to mean something very ordinary. Several of my early readers from America highlighted this as a typo, so I thought I should explain it here. It comes from describing unspectacular plant species, i.e. the common or garden cabbage.

Rozzers – slang for the police.

Duval Street – the site of one of the Ripper killings, known as Dorset Street until 1904. It was knocked down and built over in 1928.

Prince of Wales Pier in Dover Harbour – this was an important pier which catered for cross-channel ferries on one side and transatlantic liners on the other in the Edwardian era. I checked, and there was definitely a waiting room on it.

Catamaran – an antiquated insult for a grumpy or argumentative person. I had to remove this word in the end as so many people were confused by it.

Swiss soldier's pocketknife – the term Swiss Army knife didn't exist until 1935, but the knife itself was first offered to Swiss soldiers in 1891, and it already had a selection of attachments.

Jass – a phenomenally popular Swiss card game for four players.

Schmaus – a game for two people which is a derivative of *Jass*.

Schwitzbad für Damen – women's sauna.

Safe breaker – safe cracker, which seems to be the American version of the term and was hardly used at the time in Britain.

Brunsli – one of the many types of Swiss Christmas biscuit.

Herzlich willkommen, meine Damen und Herren – A hearty welcome, my ladies and gentlemen.

Entschuldigung! – excuse me.

Glühwein – mulled wine.

ABOUT ME

Writing has always been my passion. It was my favourite half-an-hour a week at primary school, and I started on my first, truly abysmal book as a teenager. So it wasn't a difficult decision to study literature at university which led to a master's in creative writing.

I'm a Welsh-Irish-Englishman originally from **South London** but now living with my French/Spanish wife and our two presumably quite confused young children in **Burgos**, a beautiful mediaeval city in the north of Spain. I write overlooking the Castilian countryside, trying not to be distracted by the vultures, eagles and red kites that fly past my window each day.

When Covid-19 hit in 2020, the language school where I worked as an English teacher closed down, and I became a full-time writer. I have three murder mystery series. My first was **"The Izzy Palmer Mysteries"** which is a more modern, zany take on the genre, and my newest is the 1920s set **"Marius Quin Mysteries"** which features a mystery writer as the main character – I wonder where I got that idea from.

I previously spent years focusing on kids' books and wrote everything from fairy tales to environmental dystopian fantasies, right through to issue-based teen fiction. My book **"The Princess and The Peach"** was long-listed for the Chicken House prize in The Times and an American producer even talked about adapting it into a film.

"The Alpine Christmas Mystery" is the third novel in the "Lord Edgington Investigates Abroad" series. The next book will be out in Spring 2025. There's a novella from the previous series available free if you sign up to my **readers' club**. Should you wish to tell me what you think about Chrissy and his grandfather, my writing or the world at large, I'd love to hear from you, so feel free to get in touch via…

www.benedictbrown.net

THE IZZY PALMER MYSTERIES

If you're looking for a modern murder mystery series with just as many off-the-wall characters, try **"The Izzy Palmer Mysteries"** for your next whodunit fix.

Check out the complete Izzy Palmer Collection in ebook, paperback and Kindle Unlimited at Amazon.

THE MARIUS QUIN MYSTERIES

There's a new detective in town. Marius first appeared in the Lord Edgington novel **"A Killer in the Wings"**, and now he has his own series...

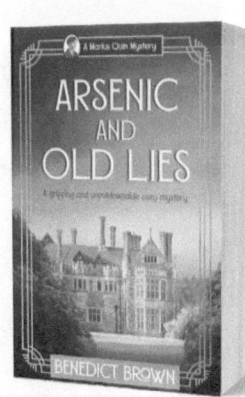

Check out the complete Marius Quin Collection in ebook, paperback and Kindle Unlimited at Amazon.

CHARACTER LIST

At the Hotel

Victor Ried – the Swiss German receptionist, breakfast attendant and hotel manager.

Sunday Cheshire (née Legyear) – a wealthy British woman who was born into poverty in Whitechapel.

Dunstan Cheshire – her comparatively high-born husband

Dolly Coxon – an elderly woman who takes a shine to Lord Edgington and does nothing to hide her scandalous past.

Elisabeth (Libby) Hall – childhood friend of Sunday who also grew up in the slums of East London.

Blanche and Henry Atkinson / Barbara Nelson – more of the East London contingent.

Inge Weinreich – a local Swiss German woman who loves skiing and card games.

Rosetta Mullen – a one-time chorus girl who was married to an earl until he died on their honeymoon.

The Travelling Party

Lord Edgington – former superintendent for the Metropolitan Police, and the Marquess of Edgington.

Christopher Prentiss – his no longer quite so naïve and chubby grandson, whose detective skills have come on a great deal since he left school.

Albert Prentiss – Chrissy's well-meaning, foppish and unlucky brother who is always searching for his role in life.

Todd – chauffeur, cocktail mixer, factotum and general nice guy, Lord Edgington and Christopher both rely on him for different reasons.

Henrietta (Cook) – Lord Edgington's favourite person, who is known for her often-unusual meals.

Dorie – formerly a skilful pickpocket whom Lord Edgington arrested, she has gone straight and now faithfully serves the old marquess.

Timothy – the hall boy back home at Cranley Hall. He has become Dorie's acolyte and assistant.